1-11-08

FAN   c.1
Shinn
Reader and Raelynx

READER AND RAELYNX

READER AND RAELYNX

SHARON SHINN

ACE BOOKS, NEW YORK

THE BERKLEY PUBLISHING GROUP
Published by the Penguin Group
Penguin Group (USA) Inc.
375 Hudson Street, New York, New York 10014, USA
Penguin Group (Canada), 90 Eglinton Avenue East, Suite 700, Toronto, Ontario M4P 2Y3, Canada
(a division of Pearson Penguin Canada Inc.)
Penguin Books Ltd., 80 Strand, London WC2R 0RL, England
Penguin Group Ireland, 25 St. Stephen's Green, Dublin 2, Ireland (a division of Penguin Books Ltd.)
Penguin Group (Australia), 250 Camberwell Road, Camberwell, Victoria 3124, Australia
(a division of Pearson Australia Group Pty. Ltd.)
Penguin Books India Pvt. Ltd., 11 Community Centre, Panchsheel Park, New Delhi—110 017, India
Penguin Group (NZ), 67 Apollo Drive, Rosedale, North Shore 0632, New Zealand
(a division of Pearson New Zealand Ltd.)
Penguin Books (South Africa) (Pty.) Ltd., 24 Sturdee Avenue, Rosebank, Johannesburg 2196,
South Africa

Penguin Books Ltd., Registered Offices: 80 Strand, London WC2R 0RL, England

This is an original publication of The Berkley Publishing Group.

This is a work of fiction. Names, characters, places, and incidents either are the product of the author's imagination or are used fictitiously, and any resemblance to actual persons, living or dead, business establishments, events, or locales is entirely coincidental. The publisher does not have any control over and does not assume any responsibility for author or third-party websites or their content.

Copyright © 2007 by Sharon Shinn.
Map by Kathryn Tongay-Carr.
Text design by Kristin del Rosario.

First edition: November 2007

Library of Congress Cataloging-in-Publication Data

Shinn, Sharon.
Reader and raelynx / Sharon Shinn—1st ed.
    p. cm
ISBN 978-0-441-01469-9
1. Mystics—Fiction.   I. Title.
PS3569.H499R43 2007
813'.54—dc22

                                        2007027389

PRINTED IN THE UNITED STATES OF AMERICA

10   9   8   7   6   5   4   3   2   1

For Kay Kenyon and Louise Marley,
with whom I have shared
the joys and terrors of writing a series—
terrific writers, faithful convention buddies,
and true friends.

⋙ GILLENGARIA ⋘

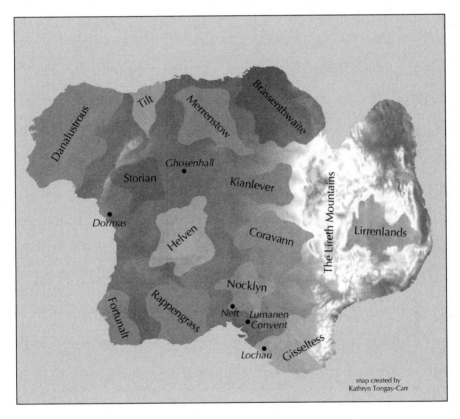

map created by
Kathryn Tongay-Carr

CHAPTER

I

DALCEY rode into Ghosenhall late on a bright, cold midwinter morning. He noted with approval the sentries posted at the outer gates, the royal soldiers roaming the city in their formal black-and-gold uniforms. Before seeking out an inn for the night, he guided his horse past the massive grounds of the king's palace, gawking like any other visitor at the gardens and fountains and architecture visible just behind the walls. The gates to the palace grounds were not watched by ordinary soldiers, but by a handful of King's Riders, elite and ruthless fighters ready to engage in deadly battle at the slightest provocation.

Dalcey nodded and rode on. King Baryn was well defended; that was good to know. A ruler whose throne was under siege by malcontents could afford to take no chances. He had to make it plain to even the most casual visitor that his streets were patrolled, his doorways watched. There was no way to do him harm.

Ghosenhall was a good-sized city, mostly pretty. Dalcey stuck to the wide avenues and well-tended districts where the wealthy lived and the traders did business. He knew there were dirtier, more dangerous streets a mile or so from the palace, but he did not need to recruit a thief or a murderer for this particular venture. He required no help at all.

Rayson had recommended an inn about a half mile from the palace; it was small and discreet and expensive, and Dalcey found it exactly to his liking. The proprietor was a sharp-eyed middle-aged man who had instantly assessed Dalcey's attire—the coat was from Arberharst and very fine; the hat was set with a diamond pin. Most people, Dalcey knew, would guess him to be a trader from foreign lands peddling high-quality merchandise.

"A room for the night, then, sir, or would you be staying with us a few days?" the innkeeper asked respectfully.

"I plan on staying two nights at least, but my business may take longer than I anticipate," Dalcey replied, signing a fictitious name to the register. "Does that cause you any problems?"

"None at all, sir, though I do require payment for the first night's lodgings up front. And it's extra for us to stable your horse."

"Certainly. I already gave the reins to the boy outside. Now, let me ask, do you serve food here or can you direct me to a place where I might buy a decent meal?"

"Daffledon's next door serves an excellent meal, though it comes with an excellent price tag, as well. One street over, there's Blackdoor Pub, where the food's hearty and more reasonably priced."

"That sounds good."

The innkeeper handed him a key and a fresh towel, and Dalcey made his way up the wide stairs to the second floor. The room was not particularly spacious, but it was clean, and the furnishings were good—lace for the curtains, down for the bed, marble for the washstand. Good enough to justify the nightly price of the room.

Dalcey was pleased to see his window overlooked the street, and he stood there a long time, watching the patterns of traffic. Carriages, carts, horsemen, pedestrians, all of them hurrying along as if busy on urgent matters. Impossible that everyone in the city could be good-humored and intelligent and tidy, but it seemed that the majority of the people who passed by for Dalcey's review met those standards. Ghosenhall was an affluent, well-run place, and it showed. In Dalcey's experience, the personality of an overlord was always reflected in the attitudes of those who served him. A bad master bred vicious men; a weak ruler spawned anxious and opportunistic subjects. A good king, by contrast, created an environment of prosperity, and his people were successful, content, satisfied, and inclined to peace.

Too bad, then, that Baryn had to die.

Dalcey removed his hat and coat, storing them carefully in the rich wood armoire, then set his valise on the bed and began pulling out the more essential contents. The black trousers and silk burgundy waistcoat he would wear for his audience tomorrow. No doubt the proprietor kept someone on hand who could press these items for him, since they had grown sadly wrinkled in transit. His black boots had picked up a little dirt on the road, but these he could polish himself once he returned from dinner.

Next, Dalcey pulled out the heavy square of parchment addressed in a flowing hand. His invitation to visit the palace tomorrow and confer with the king. Beside the invitation, he laid all sorts of official-looking documents—a map of Karyndein, a trade agreement from high-ranking Arberharst officials, lists of Arberharst merchants who were eager to begin commercial ventures with merchants from Gillengaria, a discussion of what a fair rate of exchange might be between the gold coins of Gillengaria and the silver disks minted in Arberharst. King Baryn was very interested in improving trade relations with Arberharst, and many in Arberharst were eager to increase their rate of trade with Gillengaria.

However, the Arberharst envoy who had been selected to present the state plan to King Baryn even now was floating dead somewhere in the waters off Fortunalt. Betrayed by factions in his own government who were more interested in war than commerce.

Betrayed by Rayson Fortunalt, who was far more interested in insurrection than business.

Dalcey had traveled the world a bit—enough to mimic an Arberharst accent that would fool a king who'd rarely sailed outside his own country. Enough to be able to wear foreign clothes with a haughty self-assurance. Enough to convey that faint exotic sense of *otherness* that would trick or charm Baryn into believing Dalcey was truly a traveler from lands far away, and not a homegrown villain who had committed more than one foul act for Rayson Fortunalt.

Dalcey did not expect to have to sustain the conversation for very long. There would be a moment when his opportunity would come. Then no more conversation. No more pretense at all.

The challenge would not be to kill Baryn. The challenge would be to get out of Ghosenhall alive. From the valise, Dalcey extracted yet another item—a detailed diagram of the royal palace, from the throne room to the kitchens and all the corridors in between. He had studied this so often during the past three weeks that he was fairly certain he could draw the entire schematic from memory. He would run *here* if soldiers came from *there*; he would go through the kitchen gardens if there was no clear passage to the main door. The advantage would be his because no one would know exactly what had happened. There would be a commotion in the throne room, perhaps, but the cooks wouldn't realize that the king was dead. They wouldn't know why an unfamiliar man was strolling through the pantry, claiming to be lost, looking for an exit. He would have removed his bright waistcoat by then, he would have discarded his accent. He would simply be an unfortunate tradesman who had made a delivery and gotten turned around. He might even flirt with one of the kitchen girls, if she looked friendly. He certainly wouldn't act like a man running from an act of murder.

How to kill the king—that was something Dalcey would decide as the moment dictated. Quietest, of course, was poison. Dalcey took a small silver box out of his bag and flicked it open to reveal an assortment of colorful fruit-flavored candies, a specialty from Arberharst. *Wouldn't Your Majesty like to try one? My favorite is the lemon-flavored drop, yes, the yellow one, though the red ones taste like raspberries and are very popular.* Who wouldn't take one, if only to be polite? Dalcey would eat one, too, or pretend to—sleight of hand would let him fake putting a confection in his mouth. The poison was fast and extremely effective. Dalcey could leave the room while the king was still breathing, nod to the guards at the front door while the king was gasping pitifully for help, slip out through the massive gates as the king fell to the floor dead. Poison would be his choice, if he had a choice—but Baryn might be too canny to take food from the hand of a stranger.

Dalcey pulled a wrapped bundle from the bag and slowly, lovingly unrolled it. Here was a nice weapon to take with you on a chancy venture! Here was the best of the Arberharst exports, if only the king of Gillengaria knew to trade for it! A small device, essentially a handheld crossbow with a single arrow. The trigger responded to the pull of a finger to launch the metal-tipped dart—very fast, but not very far. Dalcey had practiced and practiced with it; he knew his range, and he knew his accuracy. Using this weapon, he had killed a pig at ten paces. He was fairly certain that even a cautious king would allow a visitor to get that close during the course of a conversation.

Dalcey was not stupid, of course. He knew he would not be allowed to carry visible weapons with him into an audience with the king. He had a fancy dress knife he would wear belted over his waistcoat, and he would hand that over willingly the very first time someone announced in an apologetic voice that he would have to be searched before he could meet with Baryn. He would even go so far as to take off his boots, and to laughingly point at the sheath hidden inside the right one, and remark that he normally carried a spare blade there but he hadn't wanted to seem to offer any menace to the king.

They would still search him, of course, but they would find only oddments. Dalcey would have disassembled the miniature crossbow. The deadly arrow would look like a child's toy, and Dalcey was prepared to explain it away as a magnetized compass point that the king could float on a bowl of water. *A gift for the king, something small, but he may enjoy it.* The other parts of the weapon would be scattered through the rest of Dalcey's things—the frame would be in with the shipping contracts, as if weighting them down; the trigger mechanism would be bundled up with a few quill pens that Dalcey had brought along. This was something else he had practiced and practiced: putting the pieces back together, locking them in place, and nocking the arrow. He could do it in under two minutes, even when the components were scattered.

He could not imagine he would not have two minutes to cool his heels between the time he was ushered to some waiting room and the time he was summoned to join the king.

If by some chance the crossbow was taken away from him—if the king expressed no interest in poisoned candy—then Dalcey was prepared to commit the murder with his bare hands. It wouldn't be the first time he'd snapped a man's neck, though he didn't much relish the idea, and he considered it the option that gave him the least chance to escape. He had told Rayson that quite frankly.

"I'll kill him any way I have to do it, but if I'm going to die, then you're going to have to pay me before I go."

Rayson had laughed. He was an overweight, red-faced, arrogant nobleman who had been driven blindly by one ambition for the past ten years: toppling Baryn from the throne. "Well, I will, but I don't know how many dead men have ever had much use for gold."

"Don't you worry about that."

And Rayson had paid him in advance, and Dalcey had hidden the money in his manor house—what passed for a manor house, at any rate, for semi-impoverished Thirteenth House lords who were dependent on their distant relatives for any true wealth or elegance. If he died, his brother and sisters would come swarming over it, fighting over who was to inherit. One of them would search through Dalcey's closets and find the gold.

It didn't really matter to Dalcey which sibling was enriched by his death. He just wanted to make sure that Rayson was forced to pay for Dalcey's final act of loyalty, if indeed it turned out to be his final one. Regicide should not be done for free, not even by a zealot, and Dalcey was by no means one of those. Rayson was, and Halchon Gisseltess, and between them they had fomented this plot to overthrow the king, and they could talk of nothing else, *nothing*, to the point that a man would go mad if he spent more than an hour with either of them. Dalcey didn't care if Baryn was on the throne, or his daughter was, or if Halchon Gisseltess seized it after a long and bloody war. He didn't care if there *was* a war, he didn't care if the Twelve Houses were turned upside down by civil conflict. He just wanted to earn his fortune—and this particular deed had been worth a fortune to Rayson—and forever after be seen by the marlords as a man who could be relied on and raised to high estate.

Rewrapping his clever little weapon, Dalcey put away everything except his court clothes. Draping those over his arm, he left the room and locked the door. As he'd expected, the proprietor was happy to promise that the waistcoat and trousers would be pressed for him and returned that evening; and, most certainly, he could order bathwater to be brought to his room first thing in the morning.

"An important appointment, I suppose, sir?" the innkeeper asked.

Yes, I will be going off to kill your king. "Oh, when a man's in business, every appointment is important," Dalcey said.

The innkeeper grinned. "And every customer is important, that's what I say. We certainly appreciate your business, sir."

Dalcey nodded and went out. Time to walk the city, to determine the best route back from the palace—as well as two alternate courses in case soldiers blocked his way. The walking made him hungry, so he stopped at an anonymous tavern, ate a hearty meal, left an insignificant tip, and headed back toward his room. It was even colder than before, and Dalcey cursed the wind. The weather never got this severe down south in Fortunalt. Dalcey was still shivering as he unlocked his room, and he built up the fire even before he took off his coat. Then he lit a half dozen candles and once again spread the contents of the valise upon his bed.

This was the ritual he always went through: focusing his mind on the great task before him, reviewing all the details of the heist or the assassination. For the hundredth time, he studied his diagram of the palace; for the thousandth, his map of the city. He unwrapped the tiny crossbow again, took it apart, put it together again, aimed it across the room, and imagined that the washstand pitcher was King Baryn's face. His finger tightened on the firing mechanism, but he did not launch the arrow. He wanted its metal tip perfectly smooth, unmarred by dents and nicks.

He had disassembled the weapon again and laid the parts precisely across the bed when there was a knock at the door. "Your clothes, sir," said a woman's voice.

Dalcey tossed his spare shirt over the parts of the weapon and turned the palace diagram facedown before unlocking the door. "Very efficient," he said as he opened it. "You can tell your master I said so."

He was confused at the sight of the woman who stepped through, his coat and trousers folded neatly over her arm. She was quite tall, with messy pale hair, and she looked nothing like any serving woman Dalcey had ever seen. "Shall I just lay these on the bed?" she asked, crossing the room before he could answer.

Dalcey stared after her, his hand still on the latch. She was wearing men's trousers. And a knife at her belt. His own knives were on the other side of the room, closed in the armoire. "Who are you?" he asked stupidly.

She turned and smiled at him, but before she could speak a second figure shouldered into the room. It was a man, huge, dark-haired, dressed all in black, and he had his hands around Dalcey's throat before Dalcey could think to scream. Dalcey fought, or attempted to; he flailed in the man's grip, tried to land punches, tried to land kicks, tried to stomp on the floor to draw the attention of the proprietor or his staff. *Outlaws! Robbing people here in your very inn!* But he couldn't swing hard enough to make an impression on the big man's ribs. He couldn't get a knee near the other man's groin, couldn't shout, couldn't breathe. He felt himself starting to black out. Panic began to replace his first spurt of anger as he realized he was about to die. He clawed at the hard hands clenched around his neck, scratching desperately. No use, no use—

"Don't kill him, Tayse," he heard the woman say, and the stranglehold loosened enough to allow him to suck in air.

Dalcey only had a second to consider mounting a counterattack before the big man spun him around and grabbed him from behind, pinning his arms and bruising his ribs and throat. Gasping for air, he tried to assess the situation. The woman was bending over the bed, tossing through his clothes, his maps, and his disassembled weapon. A third person was standing beside her—someone who must have entered behind the man called Tayse—a slightly built young man with a ragged shock of light brown hair.

"What do you want?" Dalcey wheezed, trying to draw in enough breath to shout for help. It was impossible that brigands could slip so boldly into such a respectable inn! Had they murdered the innkeeper and all of his staff downstairs? "My money is in my coat, on the back of the chair."

The woman turned to look at him. She was actually laughing. In her hands she held the frame of the crossbow, the arrow, and the detached trigger mechanism. "Money?" she repeated. "I imagine you got paid so much money for this act of treason that you couldn't possibly have brought it all with you."

He was astonished. "Act of—act of *treason?*" What could she possibly know? *How* could she possibly know?

She held up the parts of the weapon for him to see and then deftly locked them together with a couple of quick twists. Now he was both stupefied and very, very frightened. "Met a man from Arberharst once who carried one of these," she said. "I would have paid him any amount of money for it, but he wouldn't sell it. Nastiest thing I've ever seen for killing a man at short range."

They had the weapon, they knew what it was, but they could have no idea what he meant to do with it. "Kill a man," he blustered. "Why, I wouldn't—how could you think—who are you people? How dare you come into my room?"

The young man had picked up the various papers littering the bed. "The castle, the city," he recited. "Oh, and look. Here it is. His card of admittance to see the king tomorrow."

"Tomorrow," said Tayse, and his grip tightened so dramatically that Dalcey felt his ribs splinter inward. The woman watched him coolly as he contorted in Tayse's arms, seeming to judge exactly how long he could survive without breathing.

"Tayse," she said at last, and again the big man's hold loosened.

"What do you want from me?" Dalcey panted.

She seemed to think about it. "Well, first, I want you to not succeed at killing the king," she said in a mild voice.

"I—wouldn't! How could you think—"

"And then I want you to tell us who sent you here to try," she continued. "And then I want you to be thrown into a cell for the rest of your life, although I think Tayse would rather strangle you outright."

They had no proof. The weapon, the maps, those could all be explained away. He tried for outrage, though he was too afraid to make it really successful. "How could you come here tonight—and accuse me of such heinous intentions! Who are you? Who do you think I am? I am a simple merchant from Arberharst who has been granted the favor of an interview with your monarch—"

The slight young man spoke up again. "You're a Fortunalt man who has come to Ghosenhall to kill the king," he said. "I could feel you the minute you started thinking about it. There's so much violence in you. It came rolling out of you and almost knocked me over."

Dalcey stared at him in disbelief. The boy was speaking gibberish. "You—what? You felt me—what? Who are you?"

The woman clapped the young man on the shoulder. "He's Cammon. He's a mystic. He can read minds."

"And your mind is a cesspool," Tayse interjected from over Dalcey's shoulder.

"I can't actually read minds," Cammon said.

Dalcey started struggling again in Tayse's hold, feeling a sort of relief wash over him. Still no proof, just the crazy made-up ramblings of an idiot mystic boy! "You can't possibly believe—just because this lunatic says—let me go! I demand to see a magistrate! I demand to see the *king*! He will be incensed to learn how grievously I have been treated, an envoy from a foreign sovereign nation!"

The woman was laughing. "Cammon is never wrong," she said cheerfully. "So Tayse and I believe you have come here to murder the king. And Tayse will find a way to make you tell him who sent you. And you may scream your head off, if you like," she added, as Dalcey drew breath to do just that, "but no one in this inn will interfere with us."

"With brigands? With outlaws?" Dalcey sputtered. "What kind of city is this where such atrocities are allowed?"

It was as if he had not spoken. "Tayse is a King's Rider, you see," she continued. "And his word is law in Ghosenhall."

Now, finally, Dalcey believed he was truly caught. A King's Rider! Fifty of them served the crown, fifty of the fiercest fighters of the realm, all of them fanatically devoted to their king. No one would gainsay a Rider—no one would believe a nameless man caught in questionable circumstances no matter how hard he argued his innocence.

He could not be tortured. He could not betray Rayson. It was a point of pride on Dalcey's part never to leave clues that pointed to the men who had employed him. He would not buy his own skin by sacrificing someone else's.

The candy. The poison. One piece of that and he would thwart the torturer. Time for meekness. "Where—where are you taking me?" he asked in a quavering voice, pretending that all the fight had gone out of him. "Will you allow me to bring my things? Will you allow me to contact my family?"

"Your family in Arberharst?" she asked with mock politeness. "I'm sure you'd like to get a message off to them."

"Grab his clothes and let's go," Tayse said. "Cammon, check the dresser, see if anything's there."

Dalcey stood limp in Tayse's arms, trying to appear utterly defeated, but he watched closely out of the corner of his eyes as the woman and the young man gathered and repacked his personal items. The maps and the crossbow, of course, were laid aside to be kept as evidence, but they seemed perfectly willing to turn over everything else to him. His gloves were tucked into the pockets of his coat, the newly pressed clothes were crammed back into the bag, and the silver box of candies was dropped in on top of them. Dalcey closed his eyes in unutterable relief. The woman glanced around as if to make sure nothing had been overlooked.

"Wait a minute, Senneth," Cammon said, and pulled the silver box back out of the valise.

Dalcey felt the chill hands of fear close over his throat more tightly than Tayse's fingers ever had.

"What's that?" asked the woman called Senneth, taking the box from him. She flicked it open and sniffed at one of the sugary bits.

"I don't know, but he wants it."

Senneth snapped the lid shut and gave Cammon a warm smile. "Then we want it more." She glanced at Tayse. "What do you think? Poison?"

Tayse grunted and squeezed harder. Again, for a moment, Dalcey couldn't breathe. "Likely enough."

"We'll have it tested." She turned back to Cammon. "Anything else we should be wary of?"

"That seems to be the thing he's focused on most."

Rage suddenly enflamed Dalcey, and he made a furious, insane effort to wrench away from the Rider. "*Give it back! Give it back! Give it back!*" he started shrieking, meaning the weapon, or the poison, or his freedom, or his life, he couldn't even have specified. Through the open door, he could hear footsteps approaching and voices muttering, but he was in a berserker fury. "Let go of me! *Give it back!*"

A hard clout to the head from behind, and Dalcey was on his knees, with his senses spinning and his vision blurring. Tayse kept one hand on Dalcey's wrists and used the other to yank Dalcey's head back by the hair. "Be quiet," the big man said in a threatening voice. His black eyes bored into Dalcey's; they looked fierce enough to pierce a man's skull.

Dalcey whimpered and tore his gaze away. He found himself staring straight at the young man, Cammon, the mystic. He wasn't frightening, not in the rough physical way that Tayse was, but there was something otherworldly about him. His eyes were huge and strangely colored; his face was preternaturally calm. He was watching Dalcey as if the stranger was a wild animal brought over from a foreign shore, a creature both fascinating and repugnant.

"May the Pale Mother strike you dead," Dalcey whispered, not that he believed in the goddess, not that he believed in curses, but he wanted to express his venom, and everybody knew that mystics feared the Silver Lady.

Cammon didn't blink or look away or appear frightened in the least, just continued watching him. For a moment, Dalcey had the strangest feeling, as if this boy really could read his mind, scan his heart and retrieve all of his long-held memories, chart the tangled and vicious course of Dalcey's life. Everything he was, everything he had felt, said, offered, refused, stolen, coveted, or destroyed—all of it—the boy comprehended each piece of Dalcey's life in a single glance.

And looked away, unimpressed. "Are we done here?" Cammon asked. "Let's go."

CHAPTER

2

J ERRIL was trying to prove to Cammon that he was stronger than snow, and Cammon wasn't having any of it.

"It's too *cold* out here," he protested for the seventh or eighth time. "I can't even feel my toes."

"You're allowing your body to control your mind," Jerril said in his usual, imperturbable fashion. "You must teach your mind to control your body."

"I can do that when I haven't frozen to death," Cammon said.

Jerril merely smiled and waited. Jerril was the most patient man Cammon had ever met. Tall, bony, bald, and dreamy-eyed, Jerril always gave the impression that he had just been struck by some new and fascinating thought and needed a moment to merely stand and consider it. Cammon had seen Jerril happy, had seen him enthusiastic, had seen him tired, but he had never seen Jerril irritable or anxious or in a hurry.

"All right, I'll try again," Cammon grumbled. He was sitting right in the middle of a snowbank, wearing no coat, and his bare toes were buried beneath an inch of ice. They had been out in the tiny, winter-brown garden behind Jerril's house for twenty minutes now, and Cammon was starting to shiver. "And then I'm going in."

"That's fair," Jerril said. "Close your eyes."

Cammon did, but it scarcely mattered. It was all still visible to him—or, no, that wasn't the right word—*tangible*, perhaps. Jerril sitting before him, perfectly comfortable in the cold snow on the hard ground, Lynnette humming in the kitchen as she began organizing the evening meal, Areel upstairs hunched over some obscure textbook and muttering in his daft way. The busy streets of Ghosenhall, crowded with thousands of residents and hundreds of visitors, some sad, some weary, some angry, some excited, most just concentrating on their particular task of the moment, calculating how quickly it could be accomplished and what their chances of success would be. Fainter, farther, but still, if he strained, discernible, a blurred oceanic mass of thoughts and feelings and desires from all the souls of Gillengaria collected on the continent from northeastern Brassenthwaite to southwestern Fortunalt.

Scattered across that map, five bright, urgent spots of color. Tayse and Senneth closest to hand, only a mile or so away at the royal palace. Kirra and Donnal in restless motion, somewhere to the west and hundreds of miles distant. Justin to the east, so far away he was difficult to detect—still across the Lireth Mountains, then—and followed by a persistent shadow. Ellynor. Cammon still could not sense Ellynor's existence independent of Justin, but he could feel her insistent pull on Justin's attention and by that alone gauge where she was and if she was well.

"Close your eyes and *concentrate*," Jerril said, his voice mildly reproving. "Shut out the thoughts of everything else."

"I can't," Cammon said.

"It's not easy," Jerril corrected, "but you can. You know how to close your mind to the world around you. You can block out the existence of strangers. Shut those doors. Close them off."

It took a tremendous effort but Cammon did it, envisioning, as Jerril said, doors slamming shut between his line of sight and everybody else in the world. First he lost the sense of the great expanse of Gillengaria, then he walled off his perceptions of the city of Ghosenhall. It was harder to overlook Jerril and Lynnette and Areel, and he didn't think he'd ever be able to choke off the other five. It would be like smothering his thoughts completely; it might happen when he was dead.

"Now. Imagine me turning invisible. Remove me from your consciousness. Put yourself in a small shelter, a tiny place made of stone and sunlight. You are there all alone. The heat is beating down. There is only you and air and sunshine."

A snug shelter against weather and intrusions; Cammon could build that in his mind. But what took shape was not a small stone cottage on a bright day. What he saw, as clearly as if he were sitting there now, was a dilapidated temple, half open to the elements, snow sifting in through the fractured rafters. A fire made merry in the middle of the floor. Senneth's magic turned the whole place so warm that they were peeling off coats and boots, turning to each other with appreciative smiles. Justin was settling the horses, while Kirra and Donnal prowled around, examining something painted on the walls. Tayse had a hand on his dagger, still not convinced that danger did not lurk somewhere in the shadows, but all of the rest of them knew that they were safe. Safe, warm, together, unafraid. Finally at rest.

"Cammon. *Cammon.*" The voice seemed to come from a long way off and sounded as if it had been speaking for quite some time. For a moment, Cammon couldn't place it—who had found them in this forgotten temple in the middle of a blizzard, who had been able to track them so far?—and then a hand shook his shoulder. He started and his eyes flew open, and briefly he was confused to find himself sitting outside in daylight face-to-face with an utter stranger.

Jerril.

Jerril's house. Jerril's lesson. The world snapped back into focus.

"I think I might have gotten it that time," Cammon said cautiously. He was no longer shivering, though as soon as the illusion vanished, so did his sense of warmth and well-being. He would be cold again in about half a minute. He checked his toes. Pink and toasty.

Jerril was smiling. "Where did you go? In your mind?"

"To a night and a place when I was traveling with Senneth and the others."

"Well, you succeeded at shutting me out completely—me and the surrounding environment. Which was exactly what I wanted you to do, except perhaps not so completely."

"I don't see how I can shut it out *and* be aware of it." Cammon knew that he sounded sulky, but that was how he felt. Everything Jerril asked him to do was always impossible; except it wasn't impossible because Cammon always learned to do it. But the learning could be extraordinarily draining.

"No, it's most contradictory," Jerril agreed. "But you must find a way to not lose yourself so completely in your mind that it is hard to find your way back. You are very vulnerable if your mind is nowhere near your body—and you cannot call it back instantly."

Cammon's toes were starting to remember that they were tucked into a snowbank, and the rest of his body was beginning to shiver. He was suddenly ravenous and almost too weak to stand, as if he hadn't eaten in days.

"I think I have to go in now," he said. "I'm afraid I'm going to fall asleep out here and then freeze to death."

Jerril smiled again and stood up with easy grace. He was probably in his midforties, a good twenty-five years older than Cammon, but he had more energy than Cammon could claim on his best day, and Cammon was usually inexhaustible. "Yes, you'll sleep well tonight, I think," he said.

"This was a very good day's work, you know. It took me a year to master that particular trick. It took you a week."

Jerril often praised Cammon, to encourage him to try harder, but that was a slip. The older mystic almost never let on how phenomenal he thought Cammon's talents were. Such news always made Cammon uncomfortable and a little afraid, as if he was too strange to be with ordinary folks, too odd to have friends, set apart, lonely. He had been alone long enough, and terrifyingly enough, to never want to experience the state again.

"Maybe I have a better teacher," Cammon said, making the words light.

Jerril touched him on the arm, guiding him toward the back door and the scent of Lynnette's cooking. Jerril, of course, had instantly sensed Cammon's moment of panic. He was a reader; everyone's emotions were as plain to him as hair coloring and skin. "You have the *best* teacher," he said loftily. "You should have learned it in three days."

That made Cammon laugh as he stepped through the door. Lynnette smiled at the sound, looking up from the stove with her face all flushed with heat. She was plain-featured, good-natured, and nearly as patient as Jerril, though not nearly as powerful. "It went well, then?" she asked.

"Very well," Jerril said. "So now he's hungry and then he'll fall asleep before we can even get him to bed."

"I was going to ask him to fetch Areel. Dinner's ready."

In this household, you didn't fetch someone to the supper table by running up to his room and knocking on the door. You sent a thought tendril in the other person's direction—*Dinner*, you might be thinking, or *Come here now*—and he would start, and realize he was hungry, and lay down his pen or close his book and hurry to the kitchen. But Cammon didn't have the energy for even such simple magic, not tonight. He could scarcely keep his eyes open.

"Don't worry about it," Jerril said, pushing Cammon to one of the chairs pulled up to the kitchen table. "I've summoned him. Cammon, you'd better eat while you still have the strength to lift a fork to your mouth."

Cammon was halfway through his meal before Areel had even wandered downstairs. Areel was a strange old man, bent and thin and fierce-looking, with bushy white eyebrows, an unkempt white beard, and a mad look in his eyes. Tonight he carried a book with him to the dinner table and continued reading throughout the meal, not deigning to make any but the most cursory conversation. Cammon, of course, was so tired he could only offer monosyllabic comments, which left Jerril and Lynnette to carry on a discussion by themselves. They didn't mind; they had been married twenty years and still managed to find plenty to talk about. Though Cammon paid little attention to what it was. He finished his meal, stumbled to his room, and fell asleep before he had even managed to get himself undressed.

It went better the next day, if only a little. Cammon was able to build his mental retreat without totally losing track of where he was—to shut Jerril out without falling into some kind of waking dream. But that was when Jerril was just sitting there, gazing off into the distance. When Jerril began a determined assault on Cammon's shielded mind, Jerril was able to stroll right into that firelit, snow-kissed temple.

"That's amazing," Jerril said, the first time it happened.

"What?" Cammon asked. He was feeling grumpy again. He had not realized Jerril was going to try so hard to break through his defenses. Jerril had taught Cammon virtually every trick Cammon knew. How could he keep the other man out?

"I could almost see it, for a moment—that place you've constructed in your mind. Your mental image is so vivid I can almost step inside."

Projecting thoughts *at* Jerril had always been easier than protecting them *from* the older mystic. "Can you see the graphics on the wall?" Cammon said, imagining the lines and circles that were barely discernible in the crumbling paint and then imagining the memory inside Jerril's head.

Jerril paused a moment, eyes only half focused, as if staring at an internal vision. "Very unusual," he said at last. "Do you know what they are?"

Cammon shook his head and the vision faded. "Senneth thought they might be depictions of the sun goddess. The Bright Mother."

"Ah. And this place is a temple?"

"Maybe. It was hard to tell. It was all falling down."

"Call it up again, but this time try to keep me out."

By day's end, Jerril could still break through to the images in Cammon's head, though each try took him longer. And it was becoming easier, if only slightly, for Cammon to keep his mind shut but his senses alert.

"Better," Jerril said when lessons were over. "Time for dinner. How do you feel?"

"Just as hungry as yesterday, but not as tired."

Jerril nodded his bald head. "That's progress."

Tonight, Areel had left his book behind and lectured instead on what he had been reading. *Boring stuff*, Cammon thought, scarcely paying attention. The first day he had arrived, Cammon had been able to tell that Areel was rife with magic, but it had been hard to define exactly what that magic was. Eventually he decided it had to do with *things*. Understanding them, finding them, fixing them, knowing how to put them to good use. If you lost your shoe or broke your spectacles, Areel was the man to see. If you wanted to buy a bolt of lace in a peculiar shade of pink, he could tell you exactly where such a thing might be found. He wasn't especially good with people, except Jerril and Lynnette. Cammon liked him, but he wasn't surprised when many others didn't.

"The sword was broken then, and shipped back to Karyndein, both of the jewels still in the hilt," Areel was saying, finishing up some tale about a king who'd lived two hundred years ago, as far as Cammon could tell. "Never to be seen in Gillengaria again!"

"Perhaps that's just as well, all the trouble it's caused," Lynnette said. "Cam, would you like more potatoes? More meat?"

He never refused, no matter how often she offered. "Yes, please."

"Lots of commotion today at the western gate of the city," Jerril observed, handing Cammon the bread, too. "Did anyone get an idea of what was going on?"

None of them had left the house this day, but all of them had ways of sensing the world around them. "I didn't catch much," Lynnette said. "Lots of horses, but I couldn't tell you about their riders. The guards at the gate seemed impressed—that much I could tell."

"Five carriages," said Areel. "And one of them had this glow to it—this weight—I think it was carrying some kind of treasure. Nothing I recognized, though."

Jerril nodded. "Foreigners, I think. From over the ocean. Largely impervious to us."

It was a regrettable fact that the magic of Gillengaria mystics only operated in Gillengaria. None of them could pick up much information about people or objects that were not native to the country.

"Well, there were thirty horses, so if twenty of them were pulling carriages, ten were probably carrying riders," Cammon said. He was surprised when the others all looked at him. "What?"

"You sensed that much even while you were so busy fencing with me?" Jerril asked softly. "I wouldn't have thought you'd have the energy."

Cammon grinned. "Well, it was hard to miss. There was a lot of excitement."

Areel returned to his food, but Jerril was still watching Cammon. "We might work on that next," he said thoughtfully.

"Work on what?"

"Seeing if you can somehow begin to sense the presence and emotions of foreigners. That would be a valuable skill indeed."

"Can *you?*"

"No. But I might be able to teach you how to figure it out."

Cammon shook his head and helped himself to more vegetables. "I've always thought it was impossible. I saw Kirra try to change an object once—something that came from Sovenfeld. She couldn't do it. And I bet Senneth can't set something on fire if it comes from outside Gillengaria."

Now Jerril was amused. "We'll have to ask her that sometime."

"Tomorrow, I suppose." They all looked at him again. "What?"

"Senneth's coming by tomorrow, is she?" Lynnette asked.

Cammon nodded. "Yes, but Tayse will stay behind."

Areel was staring at him from under his wild white brows. "You can hear them having that conversation?" he demanded in his fierce voice. "Clear as if they're standing here in the room? Or are you just—" He waved a crooked hand. "Prognosticating?"

"No . . ." How to explain it? Cammon glanced at Jerril, but even the other mystic looked baffled. "I can feel her intention. She thought of me. She was making plans." He was a little nervous. Truly, this was a skill neither Jerril nor Lynnette possessed? "I can't do that with everybody. Mostly Senneth. Sometimes Justin. It's impossible to guess what Kirra will do next, because even if she's thinking about one thing, she's just as likely to do something else with no warning at all."

"A most excellent ability to have," Jerril said gravely, but Cammon had the feeling he was hiding laughter or astonishment or both. "Will she be here for dinner? We can have something special ready for the table."

In fact, the next night Senneth arrived a few minutes before the evening meal, complaining about the winter. "A fire mystic should not have to care about weather," Jerril said, taking her in an embrace. She was as tall as he was and her white-blond hair rested for a moment against the smooth skin of his skull.

She laughed. "The cold doesn't bother me, but the snow! The wet! The misery! My boots are covered with mud and my trousers are damp, and I feel most ill-tempered."

"Areel and Jerril cooked for you all day, so that should cheer you up," Lynnette said, offering her own hug. "Areel chased me out of the kitchen, in fact, so I don't know what he's fixing now."

Senneth came close enough to cuff Cammon on the shoulder. "I suppose you're the one who told them I was on the way," she said. "Someday I'd like to take you by surprise. Is that ever going to happen?"

He grinned. "Somebody might surprise me someday, but I don't think it will be you."

"I'm coming back for lessons," she said to Jerril. "You'll have to teach me how to keep this boy out of my thoughts. I know you can do it."

"*I* can keep him out of *my* thoughts, but I don't know if you're strong enough to shield from him," Jerril said. "You have many gifts, of course, but I don't believe you're that good."

Everybody laughed, because Senneth could do anything. "That's why I need the lessons!"

Areel called them in for the meal and, after he kissed Senneth on the cheek, they all settled around the table. The food was good, the conversation was lively, and Cammon felt that particular glow of contentment he always felt when surrounded by people he liked. The more friends gathered in one room, the happier he was. It was as if his own well-being was magnified by everybody else's, as if he added their joy to his own. Some of this, he knew, came from his magic; he absorbed emotions as others absorbed sunlight.

Some of it came from spending so much time divorced from anyone who loved him that he craved that time now like others craved air.

When the meal was finished, Lynnette was the first to stand up. "Senneth, you and Cammon go talk in Areel's study," she said. "The men and I will clean up, and we'll have dessert when you're done."

Senneth was grinning. "And here I was thinking, 'How shall I tell them I want a private audience with Cam?' I suppose you never have to explain things to a reader."

"Don't touch either of the books open on my desk," Areel ordered.

Senneth and Cammon headed for the door. "Now you'll have to set them both on fire," he said, and they laughed as they escaped up the stairs.

Areel's study was a cramped, crowded, mysterious place. Small-scale models of houses, carriages, ships, contraptions, and impossible inventions littered the floor, hung from the ceiling, were sketched on diagrams pinned to the wall. Senneth and Cammon gingerly picked their way through the mess, found two chairs that could be cleared of debris relatively easily, and settled in. Senneth glanced at the bare grate and a fire sprang up, full of yellow, excitable flames. The room instantly warmed by ten degrees.

"So why have I come here tonight?" she asked, leaning back against the tattered fabric. "Since you seem to know everything."

He grinned. "I don't. Just that you were coming." He thought a moment. "Because the king asked you to?"

"Why do I even bother?" she demanded. "Why don't I just let you figure it all out for yourself?"

"It goes faster if you tell me," he laughed. "But did King Baryn really ask about me?"

She relaxed more deeply into the chair. She seemed tired. "Not about you so much as . . . Here's the story: He's decided he should find a husband for Princess Amalie."

Cammon spared a moment to think of that thin, calm, curious girl with the amazing red-gold hair. "Does Amalie want to be married?"

Senneth smiled. "I'm not sure that's the point."

"It might be to Amalie."

"Hush. Listen. Amalie's nineteen now, and all anyone in Gillengaria can think of is what kind of queen she will make and whether she will be fertile and bear heirs. So Baryn thinks that if he weds her off now, perhaps this will stop some of the plotting among the marlords of the Twelve Houses. Pick the right man, one who pleases all the marlords, have her produce a son or a daughter while Baryn is still alive—this might keep peace among the Houses."

Cammon was still thinking of Amalie. "Yes, but if she doesn't want to be married—"

"Princesses don't marry for love," Senneth said. "They marry for political alliances. They marry coastlines and trade routes and standing armies. Amalie knows this."

"*You* got to marry for love," he argued. "And serramarra are supposed to marry coastlines and all that, too. But you're a serramarra and you married a King's Rider—"

Senneth was laughing again. True, she was a serramarra—the daughter of a marlord—but she was hardly the most respectable example of the aristocracy. "Well, I'm different," she said. "I'm a mystic, and the fate of Gillengaria does not depend upon my bloodlines. But Amalie will be queen—if we can keep her alive—and a great deal depends on her heirs. Therefore—"

"That's who arrived yesterday, isn't it?" Cammon said as the pieces suddenly came together. "Some prince from Sovenfeld, I suppose. Is the king going to marry her off to a foreign lord?"

Now Senneth was watching him from her wide gray eyes, keeping her face neutral. It did her no good to try to mask her expression, of course; he could read the astonishment behind the impassive look. "How did you pick up on that, I wonder?" she said. "Or did you see them ride in?"

He shrugged impatiently. "We talked about it last night. All of us had sensed *someone* coming into the city, but we couldn't get the details."

"That was an envoy from Karyndein, not Sovenfeld," she said. "And not the prince himself, but a representative of the prince. I don't think Baryn is seriously considering a groom from outside Gillengaria, though. He believes that a judicious marriage between Amalie and a local noble might be more likely to restore peace to the realm. Myself, I'm not sure that's it. Baryn has never been one to look too far beyond his own borders, and I don't think he wants to bestow Amalie's hand on anyone who seems so strange."

"I think he should ask Amalie who she wants to marry."

Senneth grinned briefly. "The problem is not so much who Amalie would like to marry as who would like to marry Amalie," she said. "Who can be trusted? Which serramar from which House does not have a secret agenda? The thought was that you could help us decide who is sincere and who is scheming."

"I can help you? How could I do that?"

"The king would like you to serve as an advisor to Amalie as she picks her husband."

Cammon just stared at her mutely, and Senneth went off into peals of laughter.

"I'm sorry, but the look on your face—! I did manage to surprise you after all!"

"That's not the kind of surprise I meant," he defended himself. And then, "But *what* did you say? What do you mean?"

She sobered, mostly, but she was still smiling. "Your name came up as the king and I were discussing how best to conduct this—this—courtship of Amalie's. And Baryn said, 'How can we know which of these suitors can be trusted?' And I thought of you. You will at least know who is lying and who is telling the truth when they kneel before her to offer their devotion."

"So—what?—you want me to stand beside the princess when these serramar come calling? Won't they think that's strange?"

"The logistics aren't all worked out yet," Senneth admitted. "But the king wants you to come to the palace tomorrow. There's to be a luncheon for our guest from Karyndein."

Cammon raised his eyebrows. "I won't be able to tell much about *him*."

She nodded. "I know. I told Baryn that. But since he's here . . ." She shrugged. "Can you be at the palace tomorrow by ten in the morning?"

"It will be nice to see Amalie again," he remarked.

Senneth just looked at him a moment, and this time she was more successful at hiding her thoughts. "I don't know how much time you will actually spend with the princess," she said at last. "And you know it was different last summer, when we all traveled together. She was quite open with you then, but now— Cammon, I know you think every person was put in this land just to be your friend, but Amalie's different. You're a nameless mystic and she's going to be queen. You'll have to show her a little reserve—if you're actually capable of that."

Her expression was kind, if rueful, and he didn't take offense. Indeed, he knew she was right. It was hard for him to understand distinctions of rank and class, especially when, as far as he could tell by the emotions that bubbled up from them, all people were pretty much the same. "All right. I won't speak to her unless she speaks to me, and then I'll just be civil and distant."

"That would be best. So we'll see you tomorrow? Come find me, and I'll take you to the king."

That ended their private conference, and they returned to the kitchen for dessert and more conversation. Senneth left shortly afterward, and Cammon informed Jerril he would not be available for lessons the following day—and perhaps for many days to come. He had been invited to the palace to serve the princess, to whom he would not speak.

But later that night, as he lay awake thinking over the day's events, Cammon found himself hoping that Amalie did remember him and did offer him at least a remote and formal friendship. He had been one of her favorites last summer, as her whole retinue crisscrossed Gillengaria making stops on the social circuit. It wasn't like they had ever had a private conversation, for Queen Valri was always two steps away, and they were attended by the regent, four Riders, twenty royal soldiers, and a handful of other mystics. And yet Cammon had liked the princess. She was only a year younger than he was, pretty, with wide brown eyes and that shining hair, and a serious, thoughtful expression that could turn in a moment to an almost childlike delight.

Her life, he knew, had been circumscribed and strange. Until last year, she had almost never been seen outside the palace, for the king feared attempts on her life and had kept her closely sheltered. It was hard, even for Cammon, to tell how she felt about that—she was oddly hard to read, almost as if she were a visitor from overseas and impenetrable to his particular magic. Like everyone else, he had to judge her interior emotions by the expressions she chose to show outwardly, and he had concluded that she was interested in everything, afraid of very little, pleased at small attentions, and wary about the world in general. And lonely.

It was the loneliness that called to him most. More than once he had seen a look on her face that reminded him of one he had seen in his own mirror. She had enjoyed herself last summer, surrounded by attendants, fawned over by titled lords and ladies, moving from breakfast to formal dinner to dress ball to breakfast with no apparent weariness. She had seemed to love all the activity, all the commotion.

She had seemed wistful anytime she thought the season might end.

He had wondered, now and then, how she amused herself once she was back at the palace. He had not seen her since their return about six months ago. Senneth was wrong—he *did* realize he could not just presume on a casual acquaintance with royalty—he had made no effort to continue that careless friendship of the road. But he had thought about her. He had wondered if she was lonely again. He had wondered where she might have made friends within the palace, and with whom. He hated to think of her feeling lost and abandoned and solitary and sad.

CHAPTER

3

Iᴛ took Cammon about an hour to walk from Jerril's house to the palace. It was cold, of course, but sunny, for a wonder, and he enjoyed the brisk exercise.

"Don't dawdle on your way, now," Lynnette had told him as she fixed his breakfast and fussed over him a little. He loved it when Lynnette fussed. Her fluttering attention could drive Areel mad, but Cammon couldn't get enough of the quick pats on the arm, the additional offerings of food, the questions, the worrying. "Keep in mind that you have a *destination*, and don't let yourself get sidetracked."

Cammon grinned. Lynnette had been with him often enough when a quick walk to the marketplace had resulted in five detours because Cammon sensed someone needing assistance. Once they had come upon a man brutalizing a girl in the alley, his hand across her mouth to keep her from screaming. Lynnette had screeched for help and hit the attacker in the head with a rock, and other passersby had taken him down when he tried to run. Another time, Cammon had insisted they go inside a tumbledown, uninhabited building, and they'd found a baby whimpering there, half dead from neglect.

"Not even if it's something important?" he teased.

"I think the princess is even more important," she said in a firm voice.

So he'd bundled up some spare clothes and headed out for the palace, his mind half shielded to keep out the incessant rumble of other people's thoughts. Mostly he managed to ignore the stray spikes of strong emotion that intruded anyway—a shrill scream that modulated into a laugh, a spasm of grief, a flare of anger—none of them seemed urgent or desperate. He did stop twice to give directions to individuals who stood on street corners looking confused and feeling helpless, but those moments of kindness took very little time, and anyone else would have done the same thing.

The gate to the palace grounds was guarded by four Riders, all of them familiar to him. "Hey, coming by to visit for a day?" one of them greeted Cammon. "Tired of playing at being a mystic, so now you want to play at being a swordsman?"

Cammon grinned. "I'll never be as good at fighting as I will be at magic."

"Is Justin coming back?" asked another. Her name was Wen and she was one of only five or six women good enough to be a Rider. She wasn't very tall, but she was stocky and strong; Cammon had practiced against her often enough to know she was an excellent swordswoman. "Is that why you're here?"

"He's still in the Lirrens, from what I can tell," Cammon replied.

"First Tayse married, and now Justin," said one of the other Riders. "Makes you think anything can happen. The whole world can turn up-side down."

Wen laughed along with the others, but Cammon caught her buried pulse of regret. She had been half in love with Justin, not that Justin would ever have realized it. *And now he's gone and married himself some strange little creature from the Lirrens. Never even thought about me.* Cammon hastily shut his mind, not wanting to eavesdrop on her thoughts, but he felt sorry for her all the same. He liked Wen a great deal, and he knew Justin considered her an excellent comrade. Clearly, that wasn't enough for Wen.

"I'm here to see Senneth," he said.

"At the palace," Wen replied. "Go on in."

It was still another twenty minutes before he tracked down Senneth. First he had to traverse the wide lawn from the gates to the palace doors, pass another checkpoint there, and then be escorted through the large, sumptuous building. The footman took him to a sunny room decorated in yellow and blue, where Senneth was writing someone a letter. Her brother, Cammon guessed, since she didn't seem to feel especially warm toward the recipient.

She laid aside her pen with alacrity, and greeted him with a smile that turned quickly to a frown. "Is that the best you have to wear?" she asked. She was most unusually dressed—for her—in a long-sleeved blue gown with bits of lace at the throat and cuffs. Her white-blond hair was almost styled, pinned in place with a clip that sported a row of Brassenthwaite sapphires.

He glanced down at his clothes. "This is the sort of thing I always wear," he said. "What's wrong?"

"You look like a street urchin, that's what's wrong."

"I always look like a street urchin, according to you and Kirra."

"And when's the last time someone actually trimmed your *hair*?"

"Maybe you should have cut it yourself last night."

She sighed. "Come on. Let's see if I can find any clothes that make you look more respectable."

They both knew it was a hopeless task—no matter what he was wearing, Cammon always managed to look like he'd just come back from the ragpicker's shop. He just didn't care enough about *things* to figure out how to wear clothing. He was too focused on people.

But they hunted up Milo, the king's steward, who took them to a huge and starchy-smelling room filled with hundreds of uniforms hanging from two levels of rods. Cammon wandered between the rows of jackets and trousers, fingering the woven cloth and elegant braid, and wondered what Areel would make of all these discards from previous fashions for royal servants. Between them, Milo and Senneth quickly culled out a half dozen outfits that they thought would be suitable, and then insisted that Cammon try them all on, one right after the other. He didn't mind the part about getting half naked, but he was just a little annoyed about all the bother over outward appearances. As if that were what mattered.

They picked one, black with gold trim, and handed it back to Cammon. "We've set aside a room for Cammon's use," Milo said in his stately fashion. He was a staid and portly man who behaved with far more formality than King Baryn himself usually displayed. "Perhaps he would like to get himself cleaned and dressed."

Now Cammon was surprised. "I'm to live here? I didn't realize that."

"No, but you might need to stay overnight when there are visitors for several days," Senneth said. "We're still working out some of the details."

"If you'd come with me," the steward said, and Cammon and Senneth followed him down the halls and up to a room on the third floor. It proved to be somewhat smaller than the ones reserved for Senneth and Kirra and other visiting serramara, but spotless.

"Quickly, now," Senneth said as Milo departed. "We want you stationed in the dining hall before all the guests come in."

So he changed into the black uniform, submitted to Senneth's ruthless combing of his hair, washed his face again although he didn't really think it was necessary, saw her roll her eyes and shrug at the scuff marks on his shoes, and finally she was willing to call him ready. Back down the stairs and through the hallways, past marble archways and rooms decorated with both gold and silver leaf, past statuary, past guards, past every variant of opulence.

She led him to the grand dining hall, very formal, the walls covered with murals interspersed with gilt-edged mirrors. Servants were busy laying the table, lighting candles, and checking the silver for invisible spots of tarnish.

"The king will sit here—Amalie here—the Karyndein envoy here," Senneth said, pointing. "You could stand either there or there. What would work best for you?"

"It doesn't really matter. If I could read him, I'd be able to read him from anywhere in the room, but Senneth—"

"I know. Just do what you can. I'll be sitting on the other side of him, if that helps you any."

He grinned. "Probably the opposite. You're so clear in my head that you'll probably just cover up anything he might be thinking."

She looked annoyed, then she laughed. "I'll try to keep my mind quiet. *You* try to stand there and do nothing to draw attention to yourself."

"Just wait and see how invisible I can be."

She disappeared, and there was a long, boring wait before anything happened. Cammon perched on the edge of one of the chairs and talked idly to the footmen who would be stationed at other posts around the room. When they heard a rumble of conversation in the adjoining room, they all took their places and assumed solemn expressions, folding their hands behind their backs.

Finally, finally, the door swung back and King Baryn entered, followed by about twenty guests. The king was tall and thin, with wispy gray hair and a mischievous expression. Queen Valri, who entered at his side, could not have looked more different. She was small-boned and delicate, with a porcelain-white face set off by very short, very lustrous black hair and eyes of an incredible shade of green. She was also at least forty years younger than her husband—twenty-five or so to his sixty-five. In no way did they appear to be well suited. Yet, as always, Cammon picked up from Baryn a strong sense of affection and trust for his young queen, underlying all the complicated intellectual exercises that the king was engaged in as he prepared to entertain a foreign dignitary over a meal.

From Valri herself, Cammon received no impressions whatsoever. So it had been last summer, no matter how much time they spent together. It was as if she had built herself that walled stone structure that Jerril had described, and set herself within it, and refused to let anyone else inside. If she loved her husband, if she hated him, Cammon could not tell from magic. But she stationed herself at the foot of the table, facing him; she watched him closely; she seemed to pick up his unspoken signals with the ease of long companionship. Cammon's guess was that she was devoted to him, but he had nothing he would consider to be proof.

Behind them came Amalie on the arm of the Karyndein ambassador. Cammon allowed himself a moment to be pleased at the picture she made—gold hair, gold dress, gold jewelry, smiling face—before turning his attention to the man at her side. The Karyndein man was not particularly tall but solidly built, with thick dark hair, swarthy skin, and a pronounced mustache. A certain coarseness to his look was counteracted by his smile, which was wide and seemed genuine. Cammon guessed him to be in his midthirties. Young, for an ambassador. Maybe he was the same age as the prince they wanted to force poor Amalie to marry. Even so, thought Cammon somewhat darkly, thirty-five made a bad match for nineteen.

Cammon couldn't get a true read of either Amalie or the ambassador, and he was starting to feel aggrieved. From Amalie, he picked up a froth of excitement and happiness—she loved being in company, she loved all the attention and the scripted flattery—but the information was faint, little more than he could have gleaned from merely watching her face. Someone, sometime, had taught her how to shield. He had not expected to be able to scan the ambassador's thoughts, but he tried anyway, circling the other man's mind like a hawk quartering a meadow, seeking elusive prey. But the quarry was all burrowed in, safe underground, not to be flushed out.

Senneth was right behind Amalie, escorted by the regent, and both of them were so easy to read that Cammon relaxed again. Senneth's mind, as always, was full of glancing observations, quick assessments, and equal parts worry, humor, and readiness. Romar Brendyn, on the other hand, was all business. He was here to support his king, protect his niece, make alliances with foreign nations, and stop trouble from coming to the realm. Very little pretense or subterfuge about Romar Brendyn.

The others filed in and Cammon scanned them all, but everyone seemed to be just as they presented: aristocrats eager to serve their liege, thinking of little more than prestige, honor, and reputation. No one posing a danger.

"Thank you all for coming," Baryn said, and nodded at his wife. "My dear, shall we be seated?"

The meal seemed to go on forever, and Cammon was soon wishing he'd eaten something before taking up his position, because it was torture to stand so close to such delicious food and know he couldn't even snatch a morsel. He couldn't resist, just once, sending Senneth a quick, pitiful wail of *I'm hungry!*—not as plain as that, of course, because she wasn't sensitive enough to pick up actual words, but clear enough for her to get the idea. She started, gave him one narrowed, reproving look, and then turned her attention back to the ambassador. She tried to keep her face serious, but he could tell she was having trouble holding back a smile.

Cammon had been so intent on listening to the interior monologues that he hadn't paid much attention to the audible conversation, but that changed when the Karyndein ambassador abruptly came to his feet.

"Esteemed king, gracious queen, noble guests, most beautiful princess," he said, bowing in the appropriate directions as he spoke. His voice was heavily accented, but his pronunciation was perfect. "I have so much enjoyed my brief stay here and am looking forward to another week in your excellent company. I would like to express my appreciation—indeed, the appreciation of all Karyndein—with a humble gift. May I have my servants bring it in now?"

Cammon doubted there was anything humble about the offering. It was no doubt the item that Areel had sensed "glowing" in the foreigner's carriage when it arrived at the gates of the city. He straightened a little (it seemed he had started to slump), but so did everyone else in the room. What might a man from Karyndein consider rich enough to serve as a gift to a king? It would have to be quite special.

"Most certainly you may send for it," Baryn said, and one of the footmen disappeared out the door. "But my dear Khoshku, how unexpected! You did not have to buy our favor with lavish attentions." This was a lie, as Cammon could plainly tell. Everyone expected an exchange of expensive gifts. Baryn had a pile of them ready to give Khoshku before he sailed for home.

"Just a trifle, a small sample, something that is very common in Karyndein and we thought perhaps would be unusual and welcome in Gillengaria."

Talk continued in the same vein while they awaited the arrival of Khoshku's servants. Footmen circled the table, refilling glasses and removing plates. Some of the guests whispered to each other, speculating about the nature of the gift.

It took two men to carry in the long, slim casket that held Karyndein's treasure. The box was made of a bright metal that looked more

yellow than gold, and it was randomly studded with an array of jewels.
The servants carried it by handles welded to either end, and they wore
gloves on their hands to keep from leaving fingerprints.

One of the men was from Karyndein and impervious to Cammon's
quick scrutiny, but the other was from Gillengaria. *That's odd*, Cammon
thought. The Gillengaria man wore Karyndein livery and kept his head
ducked down as if overwhelmed by such unfamiliar surroundings. Cammon wondered if one of Khoshku's own servants had fallen ill on the
road, and this man had been pressed into service, hired at a roadside inn,
perhaps, or even supplied by Baryn when Khoshku arrived shorthanded.

Cammon pressed a little harder, poking at the other man's mind as he
might poke at an anthill, waiting for something to spill out. There was a
furtive excitement there, belying the stoic attitude, and it was starting to
expand to almost uncontainable proportions with every slow step the two
men took toward Baryn's chair. Then an image flashed into the man's
mind—brief and clear—a vision of himself dropping his end of the casket, pulling free a hidden knife, leaping for the king—

"*Senneth!*" Cammon cried, and then the whole room went mad.

Chairs crashed to the floor as people jumped to their feet; the air was
full of shouting. A column of fire suddenly danced around Amalie, and
several women were shrieking. Through the kinetic swarm of bodies, it
was hard to sort out exactly what was happening, but the actions of two
people were absolutely clear: Senneth had vaulted across the table to
stand beside Amalie, safe within the circle of fire, and the regent had
drawn his sword and hacked his way to the king. Both Senneth and
Romar Brendyn looked absolutely murderous.

"My liege! What is happening? What is this outrage?" the ambassador
was shouting. Those were the last words he had a chance to say, because
doors blew back from two ends of the room, and King's Riders poured in.
Within seconds, the ambassador had Tayse's sword at his throat, and
every other guest had been shoved away from the table and against the
wall. The Riders were taking no chances. They didn't know why the
alarm had been raised and who might be guilty of what crime. They were
ready to destroy anyone in the room.

"Cammon," Senneth said over her shoulder. "What is it?"

"That man—the one kneeling on the floor in front of the regent,"
Cammon said in a shaky voice. "He's got a knife and he was going to attack the king."

An incredible outcry at that. Wen spun away from the well-dressed
couple who were cowering in front of her sword, and dropped to her

knees beside the disguised Gillengaria man. He yelped and tried to scrab-
ble away, but she caught him by the collar, jerked him back, and planted
her knee on his spine. It wasn't long before she'd uncovered the blade—
a long, sharp kitchen knife, wicked and finely made.

"Messy, but will get the job done," she said, sliding it through her
belt. "We searched everyone before they came through the gates. He
picked it up here."

Khoshku found his voice. "Your Majesty! Most excellent king! I did
not—this is not— I cannot express my horror! This was not my king's intention—I swear, neither he nor I had any knowledge—"

The wall of flame around Amalie abruptly disappeared as Senneth
decided the princess wasn't in danger. Queen Valri instantly came around
the table and hurried to Amalie's side, putting her arms around the
princess. The Riders lowered but did not sheathe their swords, and the
shaken guests began to collapse in their chairs. Baryn was staring fixedly
at the ambassador, who still had Tayse's blade about three inches from his
throat.

"You will be returned immediately to your own country and be very
glad I do not have you executed on the spot," Baryn said in an icy voice.
"I see now why there has been such a long history of distrust between our
nations."

"Majesty, you must believe I had no inkling such a hideous crime
would be attempted," the ambassador begged. "For a man of Karyndein to
behave in such a way—I cannot believe—I cannot understand—"

"He's not a man of Karyndein," Cammon interrupted, and then
everybody was staring at him. He blushed and fell silent.

"Who is he, then?" Senneth said.

Cammon shook his head. "He's from Gillengaria. I don't know how
he ended up in the ambassador's train."

Khoshku looked bewildered. "But—everyone who attends me is from
my own country. Why would I need more servants when I have plenty of
my own? How did he come to join my company?"

"Let's ask him," Wen said in a pleased voice. She twisted her hand
through her captive's hair and yanked back hard. He cried out in pain but
didn't speak.

Suddenly the Karyndein servant broke into low sobs and began confessing in a choked, rapid voice, saying something only the ambassador
could understand. Khoshku looked, if possible, even more appalled. "He
says that shortly after we sailed into Forten City, a few of my men got
into a drunken brawl. There was a dreadful fight, and my servants were

overmatched until a few strangers came to their aid. One of my men disappeared—they believed he had run away—but they were too embarrassed to tell me. And this other man, this impostor, he agreed to come with us so I would not realize anyone was missing." Khoshku looked with horror at the king. "He has been with us all this time. More than a week."

As clearly as if Tayse had spoken, Cammon could feel the big Rider's contempt. *You are so ill-acquainted with the men who serve you that you can spend a week with a stranger and not realize it?* Such a fate would never befall Baryn, who prided himself on a close relationship with each of his Riders.

Though he might not, perhaps, recognize each of his cooks and scullery maids and lower footmen, Cammon thought. How many great lords would? Cammon could catch the same ideas cycling through the minds of all the nobles in the room. *I would know my own men . . . most of them . . . well, one or two might slip by me.* The thought made all of them uncomfortable, Cammon could tell.

"This is a very distressing tale," Baryn said, but his voice was a degree or two warmer. "We must have time to review your story, interrogate this—this—person, and decide if we believe you are telling the truth."

"What's significant is that this brawl occurred in Forten City," Senneth said. "We have long suspected that Rayson Fortunalt is in league with Halchon Gisseltess in plans to unsettle the throne."

Now Khoshku was starting to look angry. Cammon could scarcely imagine how the ambassador could have had a worse day, and he did not look like the sort of man who could always keep his ire in check. "No one told us not to sail to Forten City," he said stiffly. "No one told us outlaws would be lying in wait for us, trying to turn our mission of peace into a bloody debacle."

Tayse glanced from Senneth to Cammon to the king. "They're targeting envoys," he said in a quiet voice. "This is the second one."

Cammon could feel the bewilderment that swept over everyone else in the room, but the three of them nodded back. Of course. The assassin who had crept into Ghosenhall a couple of weeks ago had been dressed in Arberharst colors, but he had been a Gillengaria man with murder to his credit.

"And we have to believe they'll keep trying," Senneth said.

Finally, Tayse slipped his sword back in its scabbard. "And they won't always come in disguise."

"I demand to know what is happening in Gillengaria and why *I* have been chosen to appear as a villain," said Khoshku, truly beginning to work up some righteous indignation. "It seems there is trouble in the realm and I have stumbled into the middle of it! Explain this to me! All of it!"

Baryn merely turned his gentle smile on Khoshku and waved everyone else to their seats. "In good time, my dear ambassador. Let us now finish our meal, so rudely interrupted. I believe there is some excellent wine waiting to be served, and it will make all of us feel very much better."

NATURALLY, the rest of the luncheon was an awkward, rushed affair, strange and uncomfortable even after the Riders had carried off the impostor. Cammon could tell that all the marlords and marladies were relieved when it was over, and Valri hurried Amalie out of the room as quickly as she could. Riders reappeared to escort Khoshku into a private conference with the king, and Cammon was off duty.

He was still in the kitchen, stuffing himself with leftover food, when Senneth came looking for him.

"Well done," she said, ruffling his hair. "The king has directed Milo to give you all sorts of rewards—bags of gold or some such thing. I told him to have it delivered to Jerril's."

Cammon was pleased, more by the praise than the money, because what use did he have for gold? He didn't own anything, and didn't want anything, either. "It seems he would be better off hiring me to protect *him* than Amalie."

"He considers Amalie more valuable."

"So is this going to happen again and again? Murderers sneaking into the city to try to kill the king?"

Senneth sighed, glanced around, and pulled up a chair. He was sitting at the massive table in the middle of the enormous kitchen, and probably twenty cooks and scullery maids were scurrying around them, cleaning up the remains of the meal. Not the most private place to have a conversation. Still, by now everyone in the palace compound, down to the youngest groom in the stables, knew there had been an attempt on the life of the king.

"I wouldn't be surprised," she said. "We have heard talk of war for a year now. If I were to guess, I would say Halchon Gisseltess and his allies are waiting for good weather before making an assault on the throne. They plan to take us into battle—but if they can kill Baryn first, they will be that much closer to their goal."

"Then—like I said—"

She smiled. "He has the Riders to protect him. You need to watch over Amalie." She glanced around the kitchen again. "Actually, I thought you could watch over both of them. If you're living at the palace, you'll be able to sense anyone who comes in and out of the gates."

"Living at the palace? I thought—"

"I know. I've sent to Jerril for your things." She took in his borrowed costume, and her smile widened. "Though I don't know why I bothered. My guess is Milo will provide you with an entirely new wardrobe, since your own is so atrocious."

Cammon felt a certain excitement—What an honor! Commanded to serve at the will of the king!—and a certain disquiet. What if he failed, what if no one liked him, what if he embarrassed himself and the royalty he was set to serve? And what would Jerril and Lynnette do—and Areel—without him there? For he completed many of the harder physical chores, and his sunny disposition cheered their bleaker days—he didn't have to be a reader to know that, they had each told him so. They viewed him as a sort of favored nephew or grandson. "Can I go back some days?" he said. "Just to visit?"

Senneth's face showed a good deal of comprehension. "Of course. You won't be a prisoner here in the palace. And Jerril and the others will get along just fine without you. Why, you were gone for months last year, traveling around the country with *me*. How do you think they managed then?"

He grinned and ducked his head. "I just wanted—it seemed—"

She ruffled his hair again. "You've been abandoned so many times yourself that you hate to abandon anyone else," she said, though he had never told her that, not in so many words. "I know. But this time, trust me, Cam, it's all right. Now, come on. I'm supposed to take you to say hello to the princess."

CHAPTER

4

CAMMON saw the princess and straightaway stopped worrying about anybody else.

Senneth ushered him into a room he had never seen before, much smaller than most of the grand salons that made up the palace. It was on the second floor, tucked behind a stairwell and overlooking the back part of the compound, the walled gardens and lightly wooded acres. There was a feminine feel to it, for all the hangings were in soft pinks and deep creams, and cold sunlight poured in through the tall windows.

Valri was sitting in a striped chair, her hands folded in her lap and her expression grave. It wasn't just her black hair and midnight-blue gown that gave her an impression of darkness; she seemed pooled with tension and gloom. By contrast, Amalie, standing and smiling down at the queen, radiated light. She was still wearing her gold dress and her red-gold hair was unbound. She stood in the sunshine and seemed to be made of some burnished and beautiful element.

"Majesties," Senneth said, and curtseyed. Cammon echoed her with a clumsy bow.

Amalie flew across the room, put her hands on Cammon's shoulders, and kissed him on the cheek.

He forgot everything else.

"Cammon!" the princess exclaimed, stepping back a little but keeping one hand on his sleeve. "Thank you for saving my father's life! What would have happened if you hadn't been there? I can't bear to think about it."

"Well, I was there," was all he could think to say, and it sounded idiotic. He beamed down at her.

"And thank all the gods for that," she replied warmly.

Senneth moved between them with apparent carelessness, but Cammon knew she did it on purpose. Amalie dropped her hand. "What would have happened is that the assassin would have pulled his knife and leapt for the king, and your uncle Romar would have interfered, and probably killed the man, and the commotion would have brought the Riders in, and your father might have been wounded but he would not have died."

"You can't *know* that," Amalie said.

"No," said Senneth, "but that is truly what I believe. Come, shall we sit down?"

They pulled chairs up next to Valri, all of them wanting to bask in the sunlight. The dark queen said, "I admit, I was surprised to see the regent pull a sword. I thought only Riders were allowed weapons inside the palace walls."

Senneth smiled. "Yes, but Lord Romar is a swordsman, and a good one, too, and *his* loyalty is beyond question. So, he is allowed to bear arms."

"I wish we could simply close up the palace and never speak to another soul," Valri said. "Keep everybody safe within its walls."

"Hardly an effective way to govern," Senneth said gently.

"And now we are to have a parade of suitors vying for Amalie's hand, and every last one of them will be lying about something, and we shall have to be on our guard every single hour of every single day," the queen said bitterly. "I spent all of last summer afraid for her life, and now I shall have to be afraid all over again."

Cammon was interested to see that it was Amalie who leaned forward to offer comfort. Amalie was only six or seven years younger than her stepmother, and the bond between them appeared to be very tight. Sometimes last summer Cammon had been unsure who was the stronger, though. Amalie was so fresh and unspoiled, and Valri so intense.

"Don't be afraid, Valri," Amalie said in her soft voice. "We have friends around us night and day. We are as safe as anybody can be."

THEY conferred for maybe an hour, Cammon and the three women who were now, apparently, going to direct his life. Truth to tell, he didn't add much to the conversation, just sat there feeling a peculiar sense of satisfaction. It was as if the strength of their personalities warmed him as much as the sunshine did, filled him with a similar kind of glow. Senneth and Valri discussed what Cammon should wear, what he might expect to hear when serramar came calling, how often they should meet to strategize. And then, as if they could not help themselves, they began speculating on which heirs from which Houses might make the best match for the princess.

"If only your brother Will wasn't set to marry Casserah Danalustrous!" the queen exclaimed. "Think what a good match Brassenthwaite would be for the throne!"

Senneth shook her head. "I can think of nothing, at this moment, more likely to cause discord in the realm. Already Halchon and Rayson believe Brassenthwaite is too powerful, and such a marriage would probably convince a few other Houses to join their cause. No, we need to wed her someplace where the alliance will do us most good."

"Coravann, perhaps," Valri said. "Heffel Coravann has a son who is about Amalie's age."

Senneth nodded. "I have been thinking a good deal about Ryne Coravann. Heffel wants to remain neutral in this war—if there is a war— but a wedding with royalty would most definitely swing him to our side. And Coravann is a strategic ally. So close to the Lirrenlands, on good terms with both Gisseltess and Nocklyn, and yet not such a powerful House that the marlords would rise up in protest."

"But marlord Heffel is a friend to Coralinda Gisseltess," Cammon protested. It was his first contribution to the conversation in at least twenty minutes. "Don't you remember? He invited her to his ball last summer. He worships the Pale Mother. Aren't you afraid that his son might be a fanatic?"

That caused them all to fall quiet for a moment and think. Coralinda Gisseltess led the order known as the Daughters of the Pale Mother, and she and all her followers feared and hated mystics. Like her brother, Halchon, she wanted to remake Gillengaria—but her main goal was to see mystics burned at the stake and every scrap of magic eradicated from the land.

"It's true that Heffel reveres the Pale Mother," Senneth said slowly. "But I would not hold that against him—you can be a good man and still love the moon goddess. What concerns me more is that he does not seem to realize how dangerous Coralinda is. Yet, Heffel is not a fool. I do not believe he could be tricked into battle by either Coralinda or her brother. I do not believe he will ever take up arms against the king."

"I danced with Ryne a few times when we were at Coravann Keep," Amalie said.

"What did you think of him?" Valri asked.

Amalie shrugged. "Well, he was drunk both times, and he knew that made his sister angry, and that made him laugh," she said. "I thought he was charming but not very—very—" She shrugged.

"Not very princely," Valri said in a severe voice.

"He's only seventeen or eighteen, I believe," Senneth said.

Valri gestured. "Cammon's only twenty, isn't he, and he's far more responsible than Ryne! Or so it appears."

"Well, then, let us look at our other options," Senneth said.

Cammon couldn't help himself; he rolled his eyes. He had heard Senneth and Kirra keep up such talk for hours, discussing bloodlines and alliances with an obsessive interest. Amalie caught his expression and grinned.

"It's very boring, isn't it?" she said, leaning over to whisper in his ear. The others could still hear her, of course, and Valri flicked her a look of some annoyance, but the older women continued their discussion anyway. "This very topic forms the chief subject of conversation whenever I'm in the room, and I can't bear it."

"I would think it would interest you, if only a little," he replied. "After all, they're talking of the man you're going to *marry*. I'd be interested if people were trying to figure out who should be my wife."

Amalie glanced at Valri, glanced at Senneth, and stood up, pulling Cammon to his feet. "Let's go talk of something else," she said.

Valri briefly broke off her sentence. "Don't leave the room," she said.

"We won't. Over here, Cammon, let me show you some of my treasures."

They crossed the room to where a tall, cream-colored bookshelf held an array of boxes and bowls. Amalie pulled a box from a middle shelf. It was made of some dark and highly polished wood, and it opened when a hidden door slid out. Inside was a collection of smooth stones in a variety of muted colors, mostly blues and greens.

"Marlady Ariane Rappengrass sent these to me—aren't they pretty?" Amalie said. "Sea glass. I was admiring a few stones that she had had made into jewelry, and she said she would send me some. I don't think they're very expensive, and that's one reason I like them so much. Ariane wasn't trying to impress me, she was just trying to please me. She was just being kind."

"I met her last year," he said. "I liked her."

Amalie picked up a handful of the stones and let them trickle between her fingers, back into the box. "Many people find her terrifying. But I like her, too." She scooped up another handful of stones and let them slowly fall. "She has a son that some people would like me to marry."

"Darryn Rappengrass." The handsome young marlord had crossed Cammon's path several times when he was in company with Kirra and

Senneth. Kirra was particularly fond of him. "He seems like a nice enough man, I suppose."

Amalie dropped the last of the sea glass through her fingers, pushed the lid shut, and replaced the box on the shelf. "This little statue, it's from Mayva Nocklyn," Amalie said, pointing to a moping child carved in white stone. "I don't like it much, but Milo told me it was by a famous sculptor and very expensive. If Mayva comes to visit, I'll make sure to have it on display."

He couldn't tell if she wanted to change the subject or if she didn't know how to talk about it. "It must seem very strange," Cammon said. "To have other people making every important decision in your life. Telling you what man to marry. How to behave. What to do. All the time."

She met his gaze. Her eyes were velvety brown, thoughtful and guileless. He wished again that he could read what went on behind them.

"They might be making plans, but that doesn't mean I will agree to them," she said. As always, her voice was quite soft, her words almost idle. There was no threat in them, no iron. Yet for the first time, Cammon had a flash of intuition about this girl. She could be as stubborn and unyielding as stone; she could be equally hard to wear away. "I will meet whomever they wish me to meet. I will be gracious to everyone. But if they ask me to marry someone I do not wish to marry, I will simply say no. And that means if Senneth asks me, or Valri, or my father. I will not do it."

He felt a sudden keen admiration for this young woman who was both so important and so vulnerable. "They seem to think that both you and the realm are in danger if you do not have the right husband by your side."

She smiled. "But I have many people I trust all around me. My uncle. The Riders. Senneth and Kirra. You, for as long as you are willing to serve. I do not feel particularly afraid."

He wished he knew how to copy a courtier's bow. Tayse and Justin could both give stiff little bends from the waist that looked like respect, but Cammon wanted to offer something with a bit more flourish. "Majesty, I am yours to command for as long as you need my service."

She had turned back to the shelves and was poking around for other treasures, pushing aside vases and bowls as if seeking something hidden behind them. "And yet, you have not been to see me since we returned from Rappengrass so many months ago," she said. "We had been such good friends, as we traveled. I was disappointed when you disappeared so completely."

He was silent a moment, taken wholly by surprise. "I didn't know—it seemed—you're the princess," he said, floundering badly. "And Senneth told me—she said I couldn't make too much of friendships struck on the road. It wasn't my place to come seek you out."

She turned to look at him, her expression a little severe. "It was my place to send for you, you mean?"

"I didn't say that," he answered swiftly. "I didn't want—I'm not very good at realizing where I do and don't belong. People are always telling me that. I have a hard time keeping straight who is so important that I shouldn't speak in front of him, and who is just a regular fellow. But even I know that a princess is not just an ordinary girl."

She shrugged and turned her attention back to the shelves, pulling things out, looking at them, and putting them back. "I don't know what ordinary girls are like," she said. "I don't think I've ever known one. Last year—at the balls—that was really the only time I got to know people my own age."

"The queen isn't much older than you are," Cammon said, wondering what information he might glean in response to this observation. "And you seem to spend a great deal of time with her."

Her face was in profile to him, but he could see Amalie's slight smile. "Nothing very girlish about Valri," she said. "I love her dearly, but she is hardly lighthearted."

"She seems to feel that it's important to stick close to you."

"She does," Amalie said, pulling down a book, studying the cover, and replacing it. "It is."

"Why?" he asked bluntly.

She turned to face him again, smiling, but the smile was a mask. "So many reasons," she said. "So have we settled that?"

"Settled what?"

"We are friends now? You will come to see me, and you will not wait for an invitation, and you will not give me any of these excuses about not knowing how to behave around royalty?"

He felt bewildered but exhilarated, and it was rare that Cammon was bewildered by anyone. "You might find that I am around *too* much—that I don't know when I'm supposed to go away," he replied. "You might find that I don't know when to stop talking or when you need to be left alone."

"I don't mind telling you to be quiet or go away."

He grinned. "*That* doesn't sound very friendly."

She laughed. "I will try not to be too rude, then," she said. "At least at first. If you will promise not to stay away."

"I can't stay away, or haven't they told you?" he said. "Senneth wants me to sit in on all your wooing. So I can tell who's sincerely full of admiration for you and who has smuggled a knife in and wants to slit your throat."

Her eyes widened and she clapped her hands to her mouth as if to push back a laugh. "No, really? I imagine *that* will make it even easier to get to know all the serramar who come calling. You on one side of me, Valri on the other."

He was grinning again. "Why not have Tayse and Justin in the room while you're at it? The whole entourage."

She dropped her hands but she was still laughing. "Well, I suppose any man who's willing to run that gauntlet will at least have proved he has courage. That would be something in his favor, at any rate. So are you planning to come here every day, or just on the days I'm expecting to be courted?"

"Senneth thinks I should live at the palace, at least for a while," he said. "After what happened today—on top of what happened two weeks ago—she thought both you and your father might be safer if I was on the premises." He thought that sounded boastful and added quickly, "Because sometimes I can sense things. Bad things. I can tell when people have violence in their hearts."

All the laughter had left her face. "What happened two weeks ago?" she asked.

By the Bright Mother's burning eye. "Something I wasn't supposed to mention, evidently," he said.

"Tell me," she said.

She was the princess; she could command him. Besides, Cammon had never seen the value of withholding information. "A man had come to Ghosenhall and was planning to kill your father," he said. "He'd stolen the clothes and the papers of a merchant from Arberharst who had been granted an audience with the king. I could—I could feel his thoughts and his plans—I don't know how to explain. So I alerted Tayse and Senneth, and we stopped him."

"What happened to him?"

Cammon grimaced. "I don't know. The Riders took him for questioning. I don't know what else they've learned from him."

Her face was thoughtful. "And they don't ask you to sit in when they—question—someone? I would think you would be particularly useful in situations like that."

He looked away. "No. When there's too much pain or fear, that's all I can feel. I can't block it out. I can't hear underlying truths."

She was silent a moment. Then, "That's good to know. I would hate to think of you being called in to assist a torturer."

He glanced back at her. "I think maybe it's a weakness on my part. Why should I care if someone who's cruel or villainous experiences a little pain in turn? But, really, I can't stand it."

"I don't think it's a weakness at all," she said. "I think it's a strength. But then, my own strengths are peculiar."

That certainly invited the next obvious question—*What do you consider your strengths?*—but he didn't get a chance to ask. "Amalie, come listen to this," Valri called, and Senneth waved them over. They joined the other women, and talk about bloodlines and marriages recommenced, and Cammon was once again very bored.

Or would have been, if he hadn't spent the entire time reviewing his conversation with the princess. Who wanted him to be her friend. And who considered herself peculiar. And whom he would have the honor of defending by magic at least for the foreseeable future.

Life looked to be very interesting for the next few weeks.

In fact, life was fairly dull for the next few days, but that was mostly because Amalie was nowhere in it.

Milo, now, Milo had quickly become a fixture of Cammon's existence. The steward, no doubt alerted by Senneth, came to Cammon's room that first evening and assessed the clothing that Jerril had boxed up and sent over.

"No," he said, and pointed, and a team of footmen carried off every last stitch. They did leave behind one pair of boots, but even those did not impress Milo. "You may wear those, but not inside the palace," he said. A tailor had accompanied the steward, and he now took comprehensive measurements of Cammon's body, swore that he could produce a new wardrobe in two days, and hurried off.

"What will I wear tomorrow, then?" Cammon said.

"I am having the laundresses wash and iron some uniforms that belonged to men who served here previously," Milo said majestically. "They will be brought to you. I believe I have gauged your size with at least as much accuracy as you have managed to do when you commissioned your own clothing in the past."

Cammon couldn't help but laugh at that. He could tell Milo was genuinely scandalized, and over *clothes!* Something that didn't even *matter!* "Mostly I just put on whatever happens to be around," he said.

"Yes," Milo said, "so I surmised."

It became clear that Milo also planned to control Cammon's access to Amalie. "Every morning you will present yourself to me—suitably attired—and I will inform you if the princess will have need of you that day, and when," said Milo. "If she does not, you may consider yourself free until the early afternoon, then check with me again, in case plans have changed. The king would like you to be in attendance at all dinners that feature any guests, which means all dinners for at least the next two weeks. You may eat with the footmen in the kitchen before meals. Someone will bring you bathing water every morning. Make sure you use it. Someone will bring wood for your fire, but you will be expected to make it yourself."

And so on. Cammon felt himself quickly growing out of charity with Milo, though he knew Kirra and Senneth both were fond of the royal steward. Then again, the steward had probably never treated them like servants. Well, anybody who treated Kirra or Senneth like a servant would very quickly be sorry.

The thought made Cammon grin and instantly restored his usual good humor.

Amalie—or, at least, Milo—had no need of Cammon the morning following his first night in the palace, so he headed down to the section of the palace grounds where the Riders lived and worked out. Despite the frigid temperature, a dozen Riders were in the training yard, practicing swordplay and other skills. Wen was engaged in a furious battle with Tayse's father, Tir, a dark, burly man still impressively strong although he was nearly as old as the king. Wen had youth and energy in her favor, but Tir was wily. Even without staying to watch the outcome of the match, Cammon knew who would win. There were only a handful of Riders good enough to defeat Tir, and Wen wasn't one of them.

"Hey, you want to come hack at me next?" she called out as Cammon slipped between the rails of the fence surrounding the training yard. "I'll be in ribbons by then, so you ought to find it easy to bring me down."

He grinned. He wasn't much of a fighter—excellent defense, because he had no trouble guessing where his opponent planned to land the next blow, but almost no offensive skills. He had never actually defeated Wen—but then, she had never actually defeated him, either.

"Too cold," he called back. "I'm looking for Senneth."

"In the cottage."

He nodded. "I know."

In fact, both Senneth and Tayse were at home, though it was still odd to think of them sharing a house just like any ordinary couple. Most

Riders lived in the barracks. The few who chose to marry—and were able to stay married—took up residence in one of the small cottages that fanned out behind the large communal building. Not until Senneth and Tayse had eloped last fall was Tayse willing to set up a household with Senneth. He had preferred her to keep a bedroom at the palace, in luxurious quarters more suitable for a serramarra. But married couples lived together; even Tayse, with his strict notions of class boundaries, recognized that fact. And so they had moved into the cottage, and Senneth had made a few stabs at decorating it, but she wasn't exactly the most domesticated creature in Gillengaria. Kirra had not been able to stand it. The last time she was here, she had spent a small fortune with Ghosenhall merchants, buying curtains and rugs and sets of china, and so the small house actually had a rather homey feel.

Cammon wasn't sure Senneth or Tayse had ever cooked in the kitchen, however. They took their meals in the barracks when they both were present, and Tayse ate with the other Riders when Senneth was needed at the palace.

Tayse greeted him at the door. "I was just going out to practice," said the big man. "You want to come along? I'll give you a workout."

"Too cold," Cammon repeated.

Senneth joined them. "I could ring the whole yard with flame," she offered. "Make it nice and comfortable."

Tayse shook his head. "Riders need to know how to fight in all kinds of weather," he said. "Don't want to make them soft."

"I can't think a few degrees of extra warmth will turn any of that lot soft," she observed.

Tayse was still waiting, eyebrows lifted. *Are you sure you won't join me? You can never work too hard or be too good.* Tayse was not the sort of man who believed in taking advantage of a quiet moment to let his bones go completely idle. A quiet moment was when you cleaned your sword or practiced a new way of throwing your knife. Cammon said, "Maybe later."

Tayse nodded and ducked out the door. Whoever had designed these cottages had not allowed for a Rider as big as Tayse. Then he ducked back in. "Any news of Justin?" he asked.

Cammon nodded vigorously. "They're on the move. Heading home."

That pleased Tayse so much he came all the way back inside. "Where are they, can you tell? How soon will they be back?"

Cammon scrunched up his face and concentrated. He wasn't good with actual physical locations, just general directions. He had the advantage of knowing where Justin had started out, though, and that made it a little easier. "They're traveling pretty fast and going—north, I think. But they're still in the Lirrens. He still feels sort of fuzzy to me. I'll have a much better idea once they cross the mountains."

Tayse glanced at Senneth, a faint smile on his face. "We should find a way to welcome them home."

She laughed. "What, you missed having the Riders throw you a charivari on your own wedding night?"

"Charivari?" Cammon repeated. "What's that?"

Tayse's smile deepened. "When Riders marry. It is traditional to celebrate the event—"

"Since it is so rare," Senneth interjected.

"With a party that sometimes becomes quite boisterous and continues through the night."

"A drunken rout is what it is, and I don't think Ellynor would enjoy it," Senneth said. "Though I do think it would be nice to plan some kind of celebration for the day they arrive. If Cammon could tell us when that is going to be."

"When they get closer, I will," he said.

"Justin will suspect something," Tayse said. "He'll sneak them in during the middle of the night."

"Easy enough for Riders to stay up and wait for them," Senneth said, trying not to laugh. "Riders never need to sleep."

"Well, we ought to mark the occasion in some fashion."

"Kirra and Donnal ought to be here," Senneth said. "We should send them word. Are they still in Danalustrous?"

Cammon nodded. "I'll let them know," he said.

"That will be nice," Senneth said. "The six of us back together again. For a little while, anyway."

"Seven now," Cammon said.

"Seven," Senneth repeated. "I wonder how well I'll like Ellynor once I get to know her."

Tayse shrugged. "She makes Justin happy. That's all I need to know."

Senneth looked at Cammon with a question on her face. *Does she indeed make Justin happy?* He grinned and nodded. "Almost as happy as you make Tayse," he said. That made her laugh and shove him out the door. So, after all, despite the cold, pretty soon he was out on the training field with a weapon in his hand.

Nothing else to do if he was not going to have a chance to see Amalie.

CHAPTER

5

THE princess didn't need him the following morning, either, but Cammon was not going to make the mistake of seeking out the Riders again. He was still sore from yesterday's workout. Instead he bundled himself up in a heavy new coat—provided by Milo—and went in search of the raelynx.

The six of them had come across the wild cat a year ago when they were traveling through Gillengaria on a mission for King Baryn. Most raelynxes could only be found across the Lireth Mountains in the Lirren-lands, and they possessed their own kind of feral magic. They could not be caught—they could not be killed—they eluded every hunter's trap, every householder's poison. With their red fur, spiky ears, and great tufted toes, they were beautiful and lawless and terrifying.

The folk of the Lirrens had learned to control them, or at least keep the great cats from ravaging their communities. Senneth said it was because the Lirrenfolk were protected by the Dark Watcher, and the night goddess had claimed the raelynx as her own. During the long years when Senneth was estranged from her own family, she had lived among the Lirrenfolk and learned some of their customs, and she too had ac-quired the trick of controlling a raelynx's appetite and rage.

Or at least, she had figured out how to keep this particular beast in check, but she admitted it was only because they had found it when it was just a few months old. A full-grown cat would have been more than even Senneth could handle. She had meant to return it to the Lirrens once they were safely done with their travels—and yet their adventures had never delivered them back to the Lireth Mountains. Strangely, once they returned to Ghosenhall, Queen Valri had been quite taken with the no-tion of keeping a raelynx on the property, and she had begged the king to allow her to keep it.

Madness. Even Cammon knew that. But he loved the raelynx, and he had been secretly glad to learn it would be staying in Ghosenhall, where he could visit it whenever he wished.

It was quite a trek through the palace grounds to the walled garden where the raelynx was kept. Several hundred acres surrounded the palace proper, and they were divided into a broad diversity of terrain with a handful of attractions—wooded areas, streams, gardens, living quarters, stables, gazebos, and follies. The garden holding the wild creature was about as far distant from the palace and the barracks as it could be. It was surrounded by a high stone wall and closed with a wrought-iron gate. Winter-bare trees poked their heads above the fencing; dead vines clung to the stone and mortar. Through the open grillwork of the gate, Cammon could see more of the same inside—brown grasses, nude shrubs, the bent and colorless stalks of tall flowers patiently enduring the indignities of winter.

He stepped close enough to set his hands on the rods and peered inside. It should be easy to spot the cat's red fur in such a bleak environment, but at first he could see no sign of the raelynx at all. He could sense it, though, a great vortex of curiosity and hunger and violence. And awareness. The big cat knew Cammon was there just as surely as Cammon could tell the raelynx was near.

Suddenly, as if materializing from empty space, the raelynx stood before the gate, watching Cammon with its huge dark eyes. Its tufted tail twitched slowly back and forth; the peaks of fur along its spine stood taut with interest. Some of its readiness to fight faded; in its place came something Cammon could not identify. Recognition, maybe. *This is someone I have seen before. He is human but he means me no harm.* Nowhere near as clear as that, of course.

"So. You're starting to know me, are you?" Cammon murmured. He was tempted to thrust his hands through the bars and stroke that watchful face, offer a friendly pat on top of the russet head. He knew better, naturally. This was not an animal that could be tamed. Oh, he had seen Senneth actually put her hand out and caress the bright fur, but only once, and the raelynx had been much younger then. Now, more than a year old and almost up to its full weight and strength, the big cat was too fearsome to tempt. "Are you lonely? Do you miss visiting with your wild friends—having your raelynx neighbors over for tea?"

He couldn't help but smile at his own nonsense, but the creature seemed to enjoy the sound of his voice. Its mood mellowed even more. It dropped to its haunches and watched Cammon with sleepy eyes. Cammon could pick up no urgent sense of hunger, so he guessed the animal had fed earlier in the day. Raelynxes were notorious for their ravenous appetites. Shortly after this one had been penned up in the garden—which was much too small to accommodate it—the queen had had a run built for it, accessed through the back wall. She also made sure live game was introduced to the garden every few weeks. Now and then, a watcher with a quick eye could catch a flash of red as the raelynx bounded down the run in pursuit of an unlucky rabbit.

"But maybe you're not a pack animal," Cammon said. Moving slowly, he dropped to the ground on his side of the gate. The raelynx yawned and stretched out on the other side. "Maybe you roam your territory in utter solitude. Maybe you like Ghosenhall, because there's not another raelynx for hundreds of miles."

The big cat snorted and settled its massive head on its enormous paws. Its eyelids drooped, but it didn't quite allow itself to sleep.

"You seem so reasonable right now," Cammon continued in a soft voice. "Almost gentle. What would happen if this gate swung open, I wonder? Where would you run first? And would I be able to control you? That's what I really want to know. Would Senneth? I think I could hold you still long enough for hunters to get in place—but even so, could a hunter really bring you down? What would we do if you ever got free?"

"We would vacate the city and run for our lives," said a voice behind him.

Cammon nearly yelped as he spun around on his knees to see who had possibly been able to come upon him unaware. The raelynx sensed his mood and came hissing to his feet, but both of them calmed down immediately.

It was Queen Valri. Someone to respect, perhaps—Cammon, at least, scrambled up and attempted to give her a formal bow—but not someone to fear.

"Majesty," he said, a little breathlessly. "I didn't hear you coming."

She seemed amused. "That must be a rare experience for you."

Her smile invited his own. "Very rare! You can see I don't know how to behave when I'm surprised."

"I find it so gratifying that I'm still able to surprise someone that I don't care how you behave," she said.

This was, for the dark-humored queen, an almost playful observation. "Well, I'll try not to be too ridiculous, anyway."

Once she was close enough to the gate, she bent down and spread her fingers so that her palm lay exposed between two of the rods. Cammon held his breath as the raelynx sniffed at her hand. The big cat felt recognition for this human, too, that was obvious. Recognition and something else—affection? Was that possible?

"He likes you," Cammon said, speaking in that soft voice again.

Valri nodded, as if that wasn't an absurd thing to say. "I come here once or twice a week, if I can. To check that he is well. He is so far from home and surrounded by people who distrust him. I feel that the least I can do is make sure he is not utterly alone."

Well, and wasn't that an interesting speech? Even someone who couldn't read emotions would have been able to guess that the queen was describing herself and her own situation. "Someday maybe he'll have a chance to go back home," Cammon said.

She nodded again. Her hand was still pressed against the bars, but the raelynx had lost interest and dropped back to the ground. "If he hasn't been ruined by captivity. If it hasn't changed the very essence of his nature."

Cammon was at a loss. Was he supposed to respond to that or pretend she was still talking about the cat? "And do you think that will be case?"

She was silent for a long moment and he figured she wouldn't answer. Then she turned her head and gave him a sad smile. Her green eyes were bright with some emotion—regret, resignation, uncertainty, he could not tell. "At least I chose to come here," she said. "This creature did not."

Neither of them said anything for a long moment, but they watched each other steadily. Most of Cammon's uneasiness had disappeared. He was used to people telling him their secrets; as long as they meant to do it, he was not afraid of what he might hear. "And why did you?"

She looked back at the raelynx. "The king asked me to. How could I refuse?"

"It does not seem," he said cautiously, "like a very hard life."

She shook her head. "It could not possibly be harder."

He thought that over. He knew so little about Valri—only what Senneth and Kirra had told him, and they were as puzzled by the strange young queen as everyone else was. She and Baryn had married six years ago, shortly after Amalie's mother died. No one knew what House she was from, or where the king had met her, and, of course, there was a certain amount of scandal over their significant age difference. In the southern Houses, the whispers had started a few years ago: *The queen is a mystic. She has bespelled the king.* But Baryn showed no hallmarks of a man enchanted, as far as Cammon could tell, and he was pretty sure he'd be able to read the signs. Anyway, Valri seemed to spend far more time with her stepdaughter than she did with her husband. . . .

"Are you protecting Amalie?" he said, before it occurred to him not to voice the speculation. "Is that it?" Then he shook his head. "I'm sorry. I have no right to ask such questions."

But she was nodding again, her gaze still fixed before her. "Every day. With all my strength. Keeping Amalie safe."

"You *are* a mystic," he said.

She shrugged. "Some people might say so."

"What's your power?" But he had figured that out for himself. "Concealment. You can hide your thoughts—you can hide Amalie's. That's why I find both of you impossible to read."

"I can hide her," Valri said quite softly. "So no one can find her."

"But she can't hide anymore," Cammon said, his voice just as quiet.

"I know. And I am absolutely terrified."

She said it with no particular emphasis, but for a moment she let her guard down—just a little—and he could sense a profound and soul-deep fear coiled at her heart. He inhaled sharply. Immediately, the impression was gone.

"But, Majesty, you are not the only one on hand to protect her," he said. "Fifty Riders guard the gates, and royal soldiers can be found on every street corner of Ghosenhall. If any man gets past the soldiers, Senneth can call down fire and burn him where he stands."

Valri turned her head again, just enough to give him a fierce look from those remarkable eyes. "*You* have to be the one to watch out for her," she said. "*You're* the one who can sense danger. You have to make sure no one gets close enough to hurt her."

Now he knew. Why the queen had confided in him. To make sure he was firmly committed to her cause. "That's why I've been brought to the palace," he said, his voice gentle. "I will do my job. I will keep her safe. You were with us last summer—you know I can be trusted."

"Even if war comes," she said, continuing as if he hadn't spoken. "Even if the king and I are both disposed of, and all the Riders chased off, and Halchon Gisseltess installed on the throne. You must watch over her."

"Of course I will," he said, though if all those eventualities occurred, he would most likely be dead as well. Amalie, too. "But once she marries—"

Valri made a small sound and rested her head against the bars of the gate. The raelynx glanced up, decided her nose was too far away to make a leap for, and settled its chin back on its paws. "How will we ever find the right man for her?" she said in something like despair.

Cammon was in agreement with the sentiment. "Perhaps the king shouldn't be rushing her into a wedding."

Valri straightened up. "And perhaps a wedding is the very thing that is needed," she said. "I don't know. I can't tell. I just know that Amalie will require a very special bridegroom. And I don't know if one exists in all of Gillengaria."

Stranger and stranger. "I suppose you will have to make the search to find out."

Now she groaned and almost smiled. "I suppose we will. A parade of serramar coming through the palace to woo her! Could anything be more disastrous? There are days, Cammon, when I do not believe I am up to the task before me."

"Well, on those days maybe you should let other people do some of the work. The Riders. Senneth. Me."

Now she smiled outright. "You will have your own work cut out for you, just you wait and see. I think there is a young lord coming by tomorrow—or the day after—you will get your chance to eavesdrop on a suitor's conversation soon enough."

The tone of her voice made him think she was about to bring the dialogue to a close. He would not put it past her to pretend it had never happened. "I don't entirely understand what you're afraid of—or what you're protecting Amalie from—or what you want from me," he said bluntly. "But anytime you want my help, just say so. I will do whatever I can." That sounded too casual, almost lighthearted. He tried for more formality. "I am yours to command, Majesty."

She turned away from the gate, back in the direction of the palace. "You may escort me to the door, if you would," she said. "It is almost din-nertime, and we both should be back. I must change my clothes, and you—" She gave him a sideways glance.

He laughed. "I must change, too, or Milo will throw me over the wall and feed me to the raelynx," he said.

"Well, then," she said. "Let us go make ourselves presentable."

THERE was no chance to find Senneth immediately and repeat the gist of the conversation with Valri. While Cammon scrubbed his face and changed into a freshly pressed uniform, he had leisure to consider whether, in fact, he *should* tell Senneth about the encounter. Valri was a mystic; surely that was something Senneth needed to know. Yet perhaps

Valri had been confiding a secret to him, and Cammon knew all about protecting secrets. A reader, as Jerril had told him more than once, had a sacred obligation to respect the privacy of others.

For now, Cammon decided, he would keep the information to himself.

He stood before his mirror and fastened the last three buttons of his coat. He almost looked neat, in the severe black jacket and highly polished boots. He had used water to slick down his reprehensible hair, and, for the next five minutes anyway, it would stay in place. But he doubted he would look anything near this tidy by the time the dinner was over.

With the other footmen, he ate a hasty meal in the kitchen and then took up a post in the dining hall. Tonight, the guests were all from Gillengaria, and most of them exuded goodwill. Cammon's attention lingered awhile on a sullen young woman who came with her parents and sat only a few places removed from Amalie. But fairly soon he was convinced that her dark mood sprang from resentment and a quarrel among family members and had nothing to do with Amalie or the king. Everyone else made every effort to be cordial, and the collective mood was amiable.

About halfway through the meal, Amalie beckoned him over. For a moment, he didn't realize he was being summoned. The king would often call over one of the footmen and murmur a private command in his ear, but Cammon had never been singled out, and Amalie had never motioned anyone to her side. Uncertainty kept him in place until she frowned and signaled him again.

He tried to imitate the noiseless tread of the other footmen—who all looked quite amused—and crept to her side. "Majesty?" he whispered.

"Why have you not been to see me in two days?" she asked in a low voice.

Surprise almost sent him crashing into the table. "Majesty?"

Her expression remained serene, her attention still appeared to be fixed on the table before her, but her low voice was furious. "You promised you would be my friend. But for two days you stay away and I only see you when you're standing in the dining hall, watching all of us eat our food."

"Majesty—but—Milo told me you didn't need me," he said, very quickly and very quietly. "He said he would tell me when you did."

She compressed her lips for a moment, then smiled and nodded at something a plump older woman had said. "You'll have to leave now," she said under her breath. "Go from the room, stand outside for five minutes, then come back in and whisper in my ear."

Now he was completely confused. "Majesty?"

"Go! Because otherwise everyone will wonder why I called you over. Then come back and pretend to tell me something. Oh, marlord Martin," she added, speaking suddenly in an ordinary voice, though with a happy lilt to it, "I wish I had been there to see that!"

Cammon gave her a slight bow and exited the room. He was aware of Valri watching him—no doubt wondering why, two hours after promising to guard Amalie with his life, he was deserting his post. Feeling like a fool, he lurked in the hallway for a few moments, still concentrating his attention on the diners in the other room, just in case someone decided to reveal a violent intention. No one did. After the requisite time had passed, Cammon arranged his face into a grave expression, reentered, and headed straight to Amalie.

"Milo told me to check with him every morning, and that's what I've done," Cammon whispered without preamble. He was feeling a certain righteous indignation, and he didn't care if she realized it. "I thought *you* didn't want to see *me*. I can't just come barging into your study anytime I feel like it. You wouldn't want that, even if I *am* your friend."

"Tomorrow morning, then," she said, not looking at him. "I will make sure Milo realizes that's my command."

"It's not my *fault*," he added, even though he realized she had just dismissed him. "I didn't abandon you."

"I didn't say you had," she hissed. "Lady Belinda, what did you say? I'm sorry, I couldn't hear you."

That dismissal he could hardly overlook, so he offered another stiff bow and returned to his station against the wall. He couldn't tell if he was more angry at being berated or elated at being missed, but he *was* beginning to think this particular situation was almost unbearably funny. In fact, it was all he could do to keep from bursting into laughter right there in the middle of the dinner, and he thanked the various mysterious gods for choosing to keep Senneth away from tonight's meal.

But soon enough he became aware of Valri watching him again, her expression unreadable. To Cammon it seemed she was turning a new idea over in her mind and finding it so momentous that she hardly knew whether to be pleased or horrified. What that idea might be he absolutely could not guess.

CHAPTER

6

In the morning, Milo brought an entire new wardrobe for Cammon, cut and stitched to fit him, and the news that the princess had need of him.

"She is in the rose study," the steward said. "Do not stray far from the palace today, for you will be wanted in the afternoon, too. A noble suitor will be making his bow to Amalie, and your presence is required."

Practically a whole day with Amalie. Cammon was so pleased that he managed not to be rude to Milo. He dressed with a little additional care in one of the new uniforms and was forced to admit that quality tailoring might make even him look natty. Certainly the black uniform, with its discreet gold braid and small gold buttons, fitted him perfectly, with no tendency to bunch or bag. It was possible the crisp white shirt would stay tucked in for an entire day. He might actually look presentable for more than fifteen minutes—certainly long enough to stride through the corridors and arrive at Amalie's study.

She and Valri were seated in the deep chairs set before the window, sipping from teacups. A third chair was pulled up beside theirs; a third cup sat on a table next to the queen. Cammon entered, bowed, and hesitated, but Amalie waved him over.

"Come, sit down! Your feet must be tired after standing for hours watching over our dinners every night."

He grinned and took a chair, trying to sit straight enough to keep the new jacket from wrinkling. "I don't mind. The hard part is watching everyone else eat. It's not so bad when I remember to have my dinner beforehand, but I'm still starving by the end of the night. So then I eat dinner again, and pretty soon I'll probably grow quite fat."

"Sooner if you drink this stuff," Valri said, pouring dark liquid into the remaining cup and handing it over. It smelled sweet and steamy and wonderful.

"What is that?"

"Hot chocolate. Imported from Arberharst." Valri sipped from her own cup. "It must be what the gods get drunk on."

Cammon had to agree, it was the most delicious thing he'd ever tasted. But. "Different gods in Arberharst," he said. "No one ever mentioned the Pale Mother or the Bright Mother or the Dark Watcher while I was there. They worship a redheaded warrior god, and he's very violent."

"Did I know you lived in Arberharst?" Amalie asked, holding the cup of hot chocolate suspended before her mouth. The liquid was just a shade or two darker than her eyes. "When were you there?"

"Oh, we lived there for a few years when I was pretty young. Then we moved to Sovenfeld, and back to Arberharst a year or so before I ended up in Gillengaria."

Amalie glanced at Valri, and they both smiled. "Usually you're much more forthcoming than that," the princess said. "Ask you a question, and you'll answer it for ten minutes."

He grinned. "Senneth reminds me from time to time that I talk too much. And I don't know that the story of my life is very interesting."

"I'm sure you're wrong there," Valri said. "It seems as if it's been very adventurous."

"I wouldn't really call Arberharst an adventure."

"You don't have to talk about it if you don't want to," Amalie said.

"I don't mind. Stop me if you get bored." So he launched into some of the tales about Arberharst and Sovenfeld that, in the past year, he had found entertained almost anybody—Senneth's brother Kiernan, the Riders, Jerril. He and his parents had been on the move for most of his life, never spending more than a month in any one place, so he had seen plenty of foreign sites—Sovenfeld's muddy villages and sophisticated cities, Arberharst's bright red fields of honey spice.

"It truly does sound fascinating," Amalie said at last. "What took your parents to Arberharst?"

He smiled. "Some kind of business deal. My father was always looking for the next scheme, the next opportunity. He was always going to make a fortune. It never happened."

"Did he want you to go into business with him?"

"My father—" He hesitated. How much to say? "My father wasn't all that interested in me. I don't think he was that interested in my mother, either. I think he would have left her behind except that she was determined to stay with him and bring me along. Maybe it was because she thought he should take care of us, and she wanted to force him to be responsible for the people he'd accumulated—or maybe she just loved him and wanted to be with him. I was never sure."

There was a shadow across Amalie's eyes. "Was your mother interested in you?" she asked.

He shrugged. "Well, most of her energy went into trying to hold together a household, trying to feed us on what little money came in, and trying to keep track of my father. I was on my own a lot."

"In strange countries, with no friends and no family, moving every week or two," Valri observed. "You must have been very solitary."

"Oh, I got by. I made friends. There was always an innkeeper's wife who was kind to me, or a blacksmith who hired me to run errands, or a boy my age who would help me get into trouble."

"So where are they now?" Amalie said. "Your parents?"

"My father died in Arberharst, my mother on the journey back."

He said it casually, but he saw Amalie flinch, and even Valri's cold face looked sympathetic. "So, then you were completely alone in the world," the princess said.

"Well," he answered, "they hadn't been much company to begin with."

He said it to make them smile, but neither of them did. "So, here you were, an orphan, sailing back to Gillengaria all by yourself," Amalie said. "How dreadful."

"A nineteen-year-old orphan," he corrected. "Not so young and helpless as all that."

"Did you look for your family once you arrived? Aunts and uncles?"

He shook his head. "I'm pretty sure my father's family cast him off. My mother's parents died when I was small, and she didn't have any brothers or sisters. There must be aunts or cousins somewhere, but I've never sought them out."

"I'm finding this to be one of the most depressing stories I've heard in quite some time," Valri remarked.

An excellent opening for a change of subject. "Do you have a big family, then?" he asked the queen. "Are you close to them?"

"Yes to both questions, though I have not been to see them in a few years," Valri answered. "But they are most protective of me. One of the reasons I wanted to leave—to try what my life would be like without their close attention."

"Wait—I want to finish with Cammon's story before we get to yours," Amalie said.

Valri looked amused. "Well, that's enough of my story for now, anyway."

"And enough of mine, don't you think?" Cammon asked.

"No," the princess answered. "So what happened when you arrived in Gillengaria? What did you do?"

He gazed at her for a moment, debating how much of the truth to tell. It had been horrible, really, the worst six weeks of his life. He had wondered how he would stand it—had seen no way out.

And then Senneth came along . . .

He had hesitated too long. "Tell me," she commanded. "All of it. I am your princess, and you must do as I say."

He gave a tiny shrug. "I didn't have the money to pay for the rest of the trip. My mother had apparently struck a deal with the ship captain—she worked in the galley as part of the price of our passage. So now that coin was gone. When we arrived at Dormas port, the captain had me indentured to a tavernkeeper there. I wasn't clear on the terms. I don't know how long I was supposed to work off my debt. The tavernkeeper didn't care much for mystics and something made him think that's what I was. I'd never heard the word before—I didn't know what it meant. But he put a metal shackle around my throat and set it with a moonstone as big as my thumb. It pretty much made me useless to do anything except stumble around the kitchen helping the cooks and shuffle around the tavern serving customers."

He put a hand to the base of his throat, where he still bore a faint scar. Moonstones were deadly poison to mystics; Senneth was the only mystic Cammon knew who could bear their contact. The Daughters of the Pale Mother wore the gems as a way to mark their dedication to the goddess—and a way to expose mystics by watching who shied away from the jewel's fiery touch.

"The moonstone burned my skin," he said. "I didn't know why. It made it hard for me to think, and I didn't understand that, either. But I started having strange visions—strange thoughts—from outside myself. I don't know how to explain. I was able to sense the moods of the people around me. It was so disorienting. But useful! I could tell when Kardon—the tavernmaster—was furious enough to want to beat me, so I would hide until his rage died down. I think once or twice he would have killed me with his bare hands, and magic was the only thing that saved my life."

Now Amalie looked absolutely horrified, and Valri looked both angry and sad. "The crimes that have been committed against mystics by ignorant and stupid people," the queen spit out. "Someday there will be a reckoning for all that."

Amalie seemed to swallow with some difficulty. "So, what happened? How did you get free?"

He smiled, because he still liked this part of the story. It almost made it worth enduring all the wretchedness that had come before. "Senneth, of course. Actually, Senneth and Tayse and Kirra and Justin. And Donnal, but he was outside the tavern with the horses. They were passing through on their way somewhere else and Senneth realized I was a mystic. So, she rescued me and brought me with her and—and that's how I've ended up in Ghosenhall today."

"Oh, no, I want more details of the rescue!" Amalie exclaimed, finally able to smile again. "I knew that you had met them somewhere on the road, but I didn't realize it had been such a dramatic encounter."

So he told the tale, which made Amalie offer up a small cheer, and then obligingly recounted a few of their adventures on the road. These were much happier stories, although there had been some desperate moments last fall when Justin was falling in love with Ellynor.

"I know Justin, of course, but who's Ellynor?" Amalie asked.

"She was a novice at the Lumanen Convent. He met her when he was spying on Coralinda Gisseltess."

"She's a Daughter of the Pale Mother?" Amalie demanded. "And a Rider fell in love with her? Oh, that sounds very risky! Is he sure she can be trusted?"

"It's even more complicated than that," Cammon said. "She was sent to the convent by her family—she didn't join because she had any particular devotion to the Pale Mother. In fact, Ellynor worships the Dark Watcher. So it became very dangerous for her when—"

But that had caught Valri's attention. "She worships the Dark Watcher? Is she from the Lirrens? That's their goddess there."

Cammon nodded vigorously. "And she's a mystic! So, here she is, surrounded by the fanatical Daughters, slowly realizing that she has magic in her blood and that if Coralinda finds out, she'll be put to death. And then she's got Justin showing up at the convent every other day, because he's in love with her and he's too stubborn to be turned away—she had a very tricky time of it."

"If she's a Lirren girl, she'll never be allowed to marry a Rider," Valri remarked. "Outsiders are murdered before they're allowed to make off with Lirren women."

"Yes, but she *has* married him. They're on their way back from the Lirrens now," Cammon said. "Ellynor became—became—she declared herself something special. *Bahta-lo*, that's it. That means she's free of the interference of her family. Apparently Lirren women can only become completely independent if they take this sort of vow, but if they do, they can run their own lives. I didn't really understand it, to tell you the truth," he ended up.

"That's quite an incredible tale," Valri said, and it was hard to tell if she was serious or if she was mocking him. But something about the story had struck an emotional chord in her, for her green eyes were bright with interest. "And you say the Rider and his Lirren bride are on their way back to Ghosenhall even now?"

"Yes. I think they'll be here in a few days."

"Let us know when they've safely returned," Valri said. "I would like to meet the *bahta-lo* who has eluded Coralinda Gisseltess and tamed a Rider."

Amalie sighed theatrically. "Yes, I'm very interested in love stories these days, since I'm supposed to be making a match of my own. Mine won't be nearly so romantic, though."

"You might fall in love with your husband," Valri said. "Just because you choose him primarily for rank and politics doesn't mean you can't choose him for character and looks as well."

"Milo says one of them will be arriving this afternoon," Cammon said.

Amalie nodded. "Delt Helven. You're supposed to listen in to our conversation."

Cammon glanced around the room. "In here? Where shall I stand?"

Valri was shaking her head. "No. There is a more formal receiving room on the first floor where Amalie will entertain her suitors. This room is too comfortable. We don't want them to be at ease just at first."

Amalie giggled and Cammon grinned. "I can't imagine that *any* of my suitors will be at ease *ever*," the princess said. "How intimidating! To come to the palace to seek your bride! And I'm sure their fathers and mothers have been lecturing them for days on how to behave, and how important it is that they impress me, and how prestigious it will be for their House if one of their heirs one day becomes king."

"I hope they are also explaining to their sons that if they marry you, they may well be gambling their lives," Valri said in a dry voice. "For if Halchon Gisseltess has his way, you will never sit on the throne, and neither will any man you take as your husband."

That seemed a harsh thing to say, Cammon thought, but Amalie was nodding wisely. "And even if their parents haven't made it clear, you can be sure I will before wedding vows are ever spoken," she said. "They may find they are not willing to risk so much for the chance to wear a crown."

Just then the sunlight strengthened through the window, turning Amalie's red-blond hair to gold. The effect was so dazzling that it didn't even occur to Cammon to say the words aloud. *Maybe not, but they might be willing to risk everything for the chance to marry you.*

It turned out the royal receiving room was not just formal and uncomfortable. It was set up specifically to allow a courting couple the appearance of privacy without leaving them alone for a second. The central portion of the room consisted of a half dozen stiff-backed and heavily upholstered green chairs surrounded by thick-legged tables in some dark, forbidding wood. The walls were covered with decorative paper in a distinctive green-and-gold pattern—but the walls were fake, barely more than reinforced parchment. Behind them, around three sides of the room, ran a narrow corridor just wide enough to accommodate the body of a man. Here the various spies and guardians of the household would be set up to audit any visitor's conversation.

Cammon, Valri, Wen, and Tayse were all in place a good half hour before Amalie's suitor came calling. Tayse, of course, had prowled through every corner of the main room, checking for potential danger, before concealing himself behind the false wall. They had debated where each of them could best be deployed, and they had ultimately decided that Valri and one Rider would stand together on one side, Cammon and the second Rider on the other.

Cammon and Tayse were leaning against the true wall, waiting, when Cammon sensed Milo leading a procession up the hallway. He straightened and jerked his head, and Tayse came smoothly to an upright position. Cammon didn't even have to look to know Tayse's hand would be on his sword hilt. If it was humanly possible to protect Amalie from physical danger, Tayse would be the one to keep her safe.

The door opened and five people entered. Cammon closed his eyes and envisioned the scene on the other side of the barrier. Milo led the way, Amalie and the young lord followed, servants came behind them bearing trays of refreshments. No one seemed bent on malice. From the young Helven lord, Cammon picked up only nervousness and hope. There were the sounds of chairs being moved, trays being laid on tables, drinks being poured.

"If you have any need of me, Majesty, I will be within call," Milo said, his voice heavy with significance. *And so will four others, waiting to leap to your aid.*

"Thank you, Milo. I will let you know."

Footsteps, rustling, the sound of a door closing, then Amalie's light laugh. As always, Cammon found it annoyingly impossible to tell what she might be thinking. Was she, too, nervous at meeting a prospective husband? Was she intrigued? Indifferent? Contrary? He didn't know.

"So tell me a little about yourself," Amalie invited in a voice that was much softer than the hard chairs and grim furnishings. "I met you last summer, I think, but only briefly."

"Yes—I was in Nocklyn and Rappengrass," Delt Helven said in an eager voice. "You favored me with two dances."

"No one can talk in a ballroom!" she said gaily. "So you must start at the beginning, as if we were strangers. You are marlord Martin's nephew, are you not?"

"My mother is his sister. I spend a great deal of time at Helvenhall and my uncle trusts me absolutely."

"I've never been to Helvenhall. Is it pretty?"

"It is the richest of the middle Houses, and everywhere you look you see fields of grain. My uncle has an interest in many of the brewing houses. Have you ever had a glass of Helven beer?"

"I'm not sure."

"You will have to journey to Helven sometime soon and try all the varieties that are made there."

He continued on in this way for quite some time, listing Helven's advantages as if he were trying to make a sale of the House to a somewhat reluctant buyer. A couple of times, Amalie tried to turn the conversation back to more personal topics, but it was clear Delt Helven had been well coached about what information to convey, and he was not easy to divert from his script. After a while, Amalie stopped trying, although she remained gracious. "That is most interesting," she said a number of times. Or, "Really? I had no idea."

The tedious conversation dragged on for at least an hour before the tone of Amalie's voice changed. "Goodness! It's almost time to dress for dinner! How long will we have the honor of your company?"

"I will be here another day, perhaps two. I was hoping to take you riding tomorrow? Or escort you through the city? I would love to buy you a gift from one of the fine merchants of Ghosenhall. Anything you pick out. Anything at all."

"What a most generous offer. I'm afraid I don't get many chances to shop in the local markets, but we might certainly ride for a while tomorrow. There are a few trails on the palace grounds that are very lovely, though you cannot canter, of course."

"Majesty, I would do no more than hold your horse's bridle for you if that would please you."

"Oh, no, think how dull. We shall ride. Or even walk. It will be most delightful."

In fact, it would probably be even more awkward than this little encounter, since obviously Amalie's retinue would have to be visible for such an outing. Unless—Cammon smiled—the Riders could perhaps hide behind various trees and follies along the route that Amalie planned to take, ready to leap out at any moment and rescue her from danger. But he saw no way he and Valri would be excused from such an expedition, and he imagined the queen standing on the other side of the room and mildly cursing.

Delt Helven said, "I live for the hour."

CHAPTER
7

THAT evening's entirely uneventful meal was followed, the next morning, by a chilly parade through the palace grounds. It was sunny but cold, and Amalie had elected to stroll instead of ride. She was prettily bundled up with a fur hat and a long wool coat, and Delt Helven actually looked a little more impressive wearing several layers of clothing to bulk up his body. Riders walked before and behind them; Cammon and Queen Valri were a few steps behind the trailing soldiers.

"They're too far ahead of us. I can't hear what they're saying," Valri said.

"I can't, either. We could get closer."

"No! It's a relief not to have to sit through that dreadful chatter. Poor Amalie, I don't know how she'll bear it. There must be twenty-five young lords who want to come calling. Scheduling them so they don't overlap has become Milo's primary responsibility."

"I hope they won't all want to go hiking around outside when it's twenty degrees out," Cammon grumbled.

Valri gave him a smile as cold as the sunlight. "Really? I like winter."

Without thinking about it, he held his bare hand out and she laid her own briefly on top of his. Her fingers were like ice. She dropped her hand and tucked it back into her pocket. "You like freezing half to death?" he said.

"I like—" She turned it over in her mind. "Everything shut down. Held in place. Still and quiet. There is so much less going on in winter that it is easier to keep track of it all. Keep track of it and control it."

He made no effort to disguise his reaction. "That's a very peculiar thing to say."

She smiled again. "I suppose so."

"What are you trying to control, besides Amalie's safety?"

"At the moment, that's all. That's enough, don't you think?"

They were passing by some ornamental bushes, stripped and shivering. Cammon snapped off a thin, brittle branch and began switching it methodically against his thigh. "I've been meaning to ask you," he said. "You say you must stay near Amalie to protect her. But yesterday you wouldn't even leave her alone with me. Do you really think *I* will harm her in some fashion? Do you really think *I* can't be trusted?"

She focused her intense green eyes on him for a long moment, not watching where she placed her booted feet. "I don't know," she said. "Can you be trusted?"

"Not to harm the princess? I should think so!" he replied. "Or you've taken a very grave risk to bring me into the palace to watch over her night and day."

Another one of those strange smiles, this one seeming sad rather than cold. "I do not believe you would offer her any kind of physical harm," the queen said. "Fair enough? There might be other ways you could hurt her."

"Well, I don't know how. And I wouldn't, even if I learned a way."

Valri nodded and finally turned her attention back to the path before her. "Maybe. We'll see. For now I believe Amalie needs me beside her no matter who else is in the room." She made a sound that was halfway between a sigh and a snort. "Which means that you and I have many more torturous days ahead of us, listening to the inept wooing of aristocratic swains. At least you have a new wardrobe out of it. I think I shall ask Baryn for a bracelet or a ring. Something tangible to prove he is grateful for how much I have devoted myself to his daughter."

AFTER dinner that night—during which Amalie kindly agreed to Delt Helven's request to stay for another day—Cammon slipped down past the barracks to look for Senneth and Tayse. They were ensconced in their cottage, radiating a comfortable domesticity. Well, not entirely. Tayse knelt before the fire, an assortment of blades laid out before him as he methodically cleaned and oiled each one. Senneth sat on a sofa nearby, lost in thought. Her hands lay cupped in her lap as if she held a delicate bowl. Instead, flame wriggled between her fingertips as she idly watched it, sparking higher and dying down in a complicated dance.

The warrior and the sorceress enjoying a cozy night at home.

"I don't care much for the Helven candidate, do you?" Cammon asked as he stepped into the room. "It's hard to imagine him as a *king*."

Senneth looked up with a smile and let the fire in her hands go out. "Just what Tayse was saying."

Cammon dropped beside the Rider, disposing himself easily on the floor. "He's *boring*," Cammon said. "All he wanted to talk about was crops and taxes."

"He's right about Helven beer, though," Tayse said, picking up a knife and examining it by the fire that still burned in the grate. "I've had it many a time."

"I think Amalie needs to marry someone who has more assets than a few exceptional brew houses," Senneth said.

"He's too young," Tayse said.

"I thought so, too!" Cammon exclaimed.

Senneth looked unsure. "Maybe. But an older man might feel he could influence or intimidate Amalie, whereas a younger man—" She shrugged. "He might be overawed enough to hang back. Let her develop her own style and her own strength."

Tayse grunted. "Some truth to that. But if she takes the throne at a young age, a more seasoned husband could guide her through."

"She's got the regent," Senneth pointed out. "He can advise her as long as she needs guidance."

"Then why make her get married at all?" Cammon said.

"The succession," Senneth said. "The marlords are worried about stability in the realm. If Amalie marries and produces heirs right away, there's the stability they crave. It will perhaps provide a disincentive to war."

"Unless she marries the wrong man," Tayse said, holding up another blade to the firelight. "Then the rebels find it even more imperative to push her off the throne."

"Yes," said Senneth. "There is that."

"So she's not safe no matter what she does?" Cammon demanded.

Tayse glanced at him. "No king, no queen, no prince, no princess is ever entirely safe. That's why there are Riders."

Cammon groaned. Senneth laughed and changed the subject. "So, how close is Justin now?" she asked. "Can you tell?"

"They're over the mountains," Cammon said. "I think they're in Kianlever. I'm guessing they'll be here in about a week."

"I need Kirra!" Senneth exclaimed. "We have work to do!"

Cammon felt surprise. "Oh, she'll be right here. I thought you knew that."

Tayse glanced up, trying to hide a smile; Senneth looked irate. "What do you mean, 'right here'?" she demanded. "Give me a time frame."

"She's at the door."

He barely had time to take in Senneth's expression before there was a knock and the door was pushed wide. Kirra entered in a swirl of hair and laughter, Donnal a shadow behind her. "Hello? Are you home? Oh, look, it's the newlyweds. Don't you appear fat and contented. What a picture of domestic bliss!"

Serramarra Kirra Danalustrous tossed back her golden curls and dropped a few bundles on the floor. She was blue-eyed, beautiful, and utterly impossible to contain; even the stone walls of the cottage seemed to bow out and quiver at her entrance. By contrast, Donnal was a dark pool of silence, a well of deep stillness. Sometimes, when Cammon would visualize the two of them in his head, he pictured them as fuel and flame, or a meteor shower over black water.

Kirra came dancing in, pulled Senneth into a hug, and dropped a kiss on Tayse's head because he did not bother to rise and greet her. Tayse always treated Kirra like an impulsive and reckless younger sister whom he had long ago given up any hope of controlling. Donnal followed in her wake, kissed Senneth on the cheek, and settled smoothly on the hearth next to Cammon and the Rider.

"Good trip?" Tayse asked.

Donnal nodded. "Easy."

"*Cammon!*" Kirra exclaimed and bounced over to give him a hug, too. "Look at you, someone's dressed you up a bit. I like the look, but you need to cut your hair."

"I just had it cut," he said, grinning.

"Not by anyone with any fashion sense. Is there anything to eat? We're starving."

"Didn't you pick up dinner on the road?" Senneth said. By *dinner*, she meant *wild game*, since Kirra and Donnal were shape-shifters who almost always traveled in animal form and hunted for all their meals.

"Tired of raw meat and stringy rabbits," Kirra said. "If there's nothing here, we'll run up to the palace. One of the cooks will feed us."

"You don't have to go so far. Plenty of food at the barracks," Tayse said.

"What? But—but—your new wife doesn't make sumptuous dinners every night to please you?" Kirra demanded, affecting shock. "Doesn't cook and bake and wait on you at the table just to prove she loves you?"

"She pleases me, and proves she loves me, in a sufficient variety of other ways," Tayse said in the dryest voice.

Kirra burst out laughing, though Cammon could see the faintest blush on Senneth's face. "See, if I needle him long enough, he'll always break down," Kirra said, a note of satisfaction in her voice. "I don't know how he got a reputation as the most stoic of the Riders."

"That title would belong to his father," Senneth said. "Will you sit down? You're fluttering around so much! You're setting my nerves on edge."

"I'm too hungry to sit."

Donnal was on his feet. "I'll go fetch food from next door," he said, and disappeared.

Kirra bent over the bundles she'd dropped at the door. "I brought you a present," she said, and pulled out what looked like a thick, flat square of cloth. "Do you like it? I had it commissioned by one of the weavers up by Danan Hall."

Senneth took it with some foreboding, and then laughed and tossed it to Tayse. Cammon craned his neck to see. It was a finely worked tapestry designed to fit over a small pillow. The busy background of twining vines and flowers was overlaid with the initials "S" and "T" done in Brassenthwaite blue. "Very pretty," Senneth said. "I'll sleep with it always under my head."

"No, no, you display it, you don't ruin it by sleeping on it," Kirra said. "I had one made for Justin and Ellynor, too, would you like to see it? I wasn't sure what colors Ellynor might like, so I used the king's black and gold. It turned out very nice, I thought."

"I like that one even better," Cammon said.

Senneth gave him a look of derision. "As if Justin would ever want a thing like that! That's why she bought it, of course."

"Well, of course he'll make fun of it," Cammon said. "But it will please him that she did it."

And since they all knew that to be true, they laughed.

"He's not back yet, is he?" Kirra said. "We're not too late?" She appealed to Cammon. "I could tell you wanted us to return, and I could tell that it was because Justin was on his way, but I couldn't actually sort out dates and times. You have a very strange way of communicating. It's just this—odd feeling—this belief that something needs to be done. Right away. And it's very clear what that thing *is*, but the rest of the details are murky."

"They're not here yet," Cammon said. "But they're over the mountains."

Kirra clapped her hands together. "So they'll be here in a few days! The king has granted them a cottage, of course. Have you done any work on it yet?"

Senneth shook her head and resettled herself on the sofa. "I was waiting for you."

Something about Senneth's movements had caught Kirra's attention.
"Oh, but what's this?" she said, stepping closer to Senneth and bending
down to inspect her throat. "You're wearing a new necklace, aren't you?
Hold it up and let me see. You've got such a nice figure—I don't know
why you insist on walking around in high-necked shirts and *trousers*.
When you could look so pretty!"

"You sound like my sister-in-law," Senneth said, tugging at the gold
chain just visible under the collar of her shirt. For years she had worn a
necklace hung with a simple gold sun charm, but she had given that to
Justin when he was wooing Ellynor and needed a gift with some history
to it. "Tayse bought this for me. Had it made especially. I can't tell you
how much I love it."

It was a small sphere made of many fine gold wires; inside the mesh
cage was a tumble of jewels. Brassenthwaite sapphires, Danalustrous ru-
bies, Fortunalt pearls—all the great Houses were represented. "Oh, yes,
indeed, that is quite a marvelous piece," Kirra said, examining it closely.
"He must have spent a whole Rider paycheck on such a bauble! Clearly
the man loves you."

"It's not like you needed proof," Cammon said, and was a little annoyed when both women burst out laughing. "What?"

"Never mind," Kirra said, reaching over to ruffle his hair. "And how
are *you*? Why are you at the palace tonight? Merely to tell Senneth I was
coming and ruin my surprise?"

"No, indeed, he gave us barely a second's warning," Senneth said. "I
think he thought that because *he* knew you were on the way, we all did.
Cammon is living at the palace now."

"Really? In training to become a Rider?" Kirra said in a mocking
voice.

"Much more specialized than that," Senneth said. "Mystic's work."

Kirra's eyes widened, but before she could ask another question,
Donnal came back carrying a tray of food. "Wild Mother kiss you," Kirra
said fervently. "I have to eat before I say another word."

Tayse stayed by the fire, but Senneth, Donnal, and Cammon joined
her at the small table in the corner of the room. Dinner in the royal
kitchen had been a long time ago, so Cammon helped himself to a bit of
meat and a thick slice of bread.

"Where were you?" Senneth asked. "Danalustrous?"

Kirra nodded and talked around a mouthful of food. "Helping to plan my sister's wedding. Scarcely two months away now. Impossible to believe."

"You weren't in Danalustrous the whole time," Cammon said.

She glanced at him and tried not to laugh. "No, you're right, of course. By all the sweet gods, Cammon, are you going to track my slightest detour?"

He shrugged. "Well, not on purpose. It's just that I always know where you are." He flicked a look around the room. "All of you. It's not like I'm trying. You're just there."

Donnal was laughing silently, but Kirra looked a little unnerved. "But what if I want to run away? Disappear?"

Senneth put a hand to her heart and tried to look soulful. "Why would you ever want to run away from Cammon?"

"But if I did?"

"Leave Gillengaria," Donnal said. "Am I right?"

Cammon nodded. "I think so. Although I could still feel Justin when he was in the Lirrens."

"The Lirrenlands are part of Gillengaria," Kirra objected. "Well, sort of. So that doesn't really count."

"Let's commission a boat and sail for Sovenfeld," Senneth said. "We'll see how far we have to go before Cammon loses sight of us completely."

He smiled. "I won't lose sight of you at all," he said. "If you sail away, I'm coming with you."

"So tell us, then," Kirra invited. "Where was I when I wasn't in Danalustrous?"

He waved a hand, indicating a generally southern direction. "Somewhere else. Down near Fortunalt, I think. Donnal was with you."

She nodded, trying not to look impressed. "We were at Carrebos for a few days."

Senneth licked her fingers. She had just had another small sliver of pie. "Never heard of it."

"I think it's a place you need to explore," Kirra said. At Senneth's inquiring look, she went on. "It's a coastal town that's a little north of Fortunalt. Not very big, but it's been settled mostly by mystics. They've developed this whole community there. It's like a haven. Some of them are readers, so they're posted as guards to make sure soldiers and Coralinda's men don't come calling in the night. Some of them can cast fire, like you—some have powers I don't even know how to describe."

Senneth's eyebrows were still raised. "Oh, yes, indeed," she said softly. "I would very much like to go meet a town full of mystics."

"Carrebos," Cammon repeated, pleased. "Is that what it's called?" They were all staring at him with varying degrees of wrath. "What?"

"You knew about this place?" Senneth demanded.

He spread his hands. "Well, I could tell there was this concentration of magic somewhere over in that direction—I couldn't tell exactly what it was."

"Why didn't you ever mention it? You know I've been looking for ways to recruit mystics to the king's army."

"I didn't know you didn't know about it! You never said so."

"Well, I could hardly *say* I didn't know about—oh, forget it," Senneth snapped, and then they were all laughing again. "Sometimes, Cammon, you are far more irritation than you're worth."

Kirra laid a quick hand on his arm. She was still laughing. "Oh, no, he's not," she said. "Cammon is always worth any amount of trouble he causes. You just never know when he's going to bother to justify his existence."

THEY talked so late into the night that Kirra decided she shouldn't go strolling up to the palace to demand a room. She stayed in Ghosenhall so often and she was such a favorite of the king that rooms were usually kept ready for her; still, common courtesy required that she give Milo a little notice.

"We'll sleep here," she said, glancing around. "Except I can see there's no spare bed."

Donnal slipped from his chair and melted into a furry black dog. Well. Cammon could tell that Donnal had changed shapes, he could tell what that shape was supposed to be, but the creature now nosing around beneath the table still held the unmistakable essence of Donnal. The pointed face was not quite Donnal's face, and yet it was; the dark eyes were exactly Donnal's eyes.

Kirra sighed. "Yes, I suppose we'll sleep on the hearth like a couple of hounds. Easiest all around."

"I'll bring you an old blanket," Senneth said, straight-faced. "Put out a bowl of water. Would you like a bone?"

Donnal barked and wagged his tail. Kirra sighed again. "Tomorrow I'm sleeping at the palace, as befits my station in life," she said. "And I will *never* sleep on the ground or the floor again."

Cammon yawned and climbed to his feet. "I'll see you tomorrow, then," he said. "When I'm done with the princess." That evoked a storm of hoots and derision, and he felt himself flushing. "I meant—in the morning—we're supposed to accompany her on an outing. I'll see you when that's finished."

"Don't neglect your duties just for us," Kirra said.

He grinned and went out into the bitter cold air. He was shaking his head, but smiling at the same time. Kirra and Donnal back, Justin on the way. Cammon was almost completely happy.

CHAPTER
8

KIRRA spent the next day with Senneth—Cammon could feel their merriment all afternoon as they browsed the shops of Ghosenhall—but before nightfall she presented herself at the palace and claimed her usual room. Naturally, as a high-ranking serramarra, she was invited to join the formal dinner that night, and she sat next to Delt Helven and spent the entire meal charming him.

She also, Cammon could tell, spent the whole meal trying hard not to look at Romar Brendyn.

She had fallen in love with Romar Brendyn last summer as the regent joined them on their tour of the prominent Houses. He was married, of course; his wife, Belinda, even now sat a few chairs over from him, round with her first pregnancy. Kirra had used magic to make the regent forget that he had cared for her in return, but she had not had recourse to any such spells to heal her own heart. Donnal had always adored her, and she had finally allowed herself to love him back, serf's son though he was; but there was still a great ache inside her when she was anywhere near Romar Brendyn. Cammon could feel it through the entire meal, her clenched core of sadness, alleviated not at all by her light flirtations with the Helven lord and the Brassenthwaite man who sat on her other side.

Romar Brendyn was deep in conversations of his own, but from time to time the sound of Kirra's laugh could catch his attention so hard that his head would turn and he would pause to look at her a moment before completing whatever sentence he had been uttering. A mixed, inchoate mess of emotions seized the regent every time he glanced at the golden serramarra. Cammon could sort them out much more easily than the regent could himself. Basic male appreciation for a lovely woman—admiration for her quick intelligence—an inexplicable wistfulness—a sudden surge of confusion—and an abrupt realization that he had a wife, he loved his wife, his wife was carrying their child. Romar's eyes invariably would go from Kirra's face to Belinda's, and he would smile, and some of his bewilderment would fade.

This sequence of blocked memories and remembered responsibilities occurred perhaps ten times during the course of the meal. By the end of it, Cammon was not surprised that Kirra was feeling a little grim underneath her bright exterior.

No one else at the table was having to work so hard to have an enjoyable time. Delt Helven was still nervous, Amalie still gracious, the other visitors happy just to be in the room with royalty. By most standards, a successful meal.

"Let's withdraw to the salon, shall we?" Baryn said as the dinner came to a close. "Perhaps another glass of wine and a little conversation before we end the evening."

Chairs scraped on the floor as people stood, talking quietly to their neighbors. Belinda exited on the king's arm, Amalie accompanied by Delt Helven. Kirra had been detained when a young Merrenstow woman asked her a question, and so she wasn't able to escape when the regent approached her.

"Serra Kirra," Romar greeted her. He was almost as fair as Kirra, with dark gold hair tied back from his strongly modeled face. "It has been some time since you have last graced us with your presence."

The Merrenstow woman curtseyed and left; Kirra was left face-to-face with her former lover. Cammon knew he was supposed to follow the others into the adjoining salon, but he lingered in the hallway just outside the dining room, listening. He could feel Kirra's sudden panic.

It didn't show. "Lord Romar!" she exclaimed. "I wondered if you might be here. Have you abandoned your estates entirely so that you might stay close to Amalie?"

"I'm afraid I have," he said. "I travel back once a month or so, but I am much in demand here. In the past I had left my wife to care for the land while I was absent, but, as you see, she is in a delicate state, and I do not like to have her there without me."

"Yes, I had heard you were expecting a child. You must be so pleased."

"Excited and afraid," he amended.

"I think all new fathers feel the same," she said.

"There is news from Danalustrous, I hear," he said. "Your sister is to marry Senneth's brother Will. An excellent match by any measure."

"Yes, and I am delighted for her, but oh!—the wedding preparations! I think I shall be driven mad. You will know how frantic we have been when I tell you that I came to Ghosenhall for a little peace, for it is never quiet in Ghosenhall."

As she spoke, Cammon could pick up a small spiral of actual pain rising through her bones. She was digging her fingernails into her palms, perhaps, or holding her hands behind her back and pinching her flesh. Yet her voice retained its easy lilt, and her face no doubt still showed its warm smile.

"How long do you plan to stay?" Romar asked. "Will you be joining us every night?"

She laughed. "I don't know how long I'll be here, but I cannot commit to endless dinners! I am very restless, you know, and *not* very proper. I am sure I will be pursuing much more entertaining activities that do not revolve around the social life in the palace."

Cammon could hear the clink of plates and silver being piled together as servants started to clear the table. Kirra, he thought, might be edging for the door, but Romar Brendyn was not yet inclined to leave. Cammon could sense the regent's puzzlement—*Why am I standing here exchanging inanities with this woman? Yet I cannot bring myself to walk out the door*—and his complete focus on Kirra.

"And how have *you* been, serra?" the regent asked in a low voice. "Safe, I hope? I remember some of our adventures from last summer, when it seemed you endangered yourself every other day."

It was as if Kirra had been knifed in the heart. Cammon felt her pain that clearly. Yet her voice was steady still. "I believe *you* were the one who was endangered, lord. I happened to be nearby once or twice when you needed rescuing."

Romar sounded amused. "Perhaps. Although I think our recollections differ."

"Oh," she said, "I believe that is often the case."

Cammon could stand it no longer. He reentered the room and bowed to them both, then turned his attention to Kirra. "Serra," he said. "Serra Senneth has sent me to fetch you. Are you free?"

"Senneth is as bad as you are," the regent remarked. "She tries to avoid meals in the king's dining room as often as she can."

Cammon offered Kirra his arm, and her hand closed spasmodically over it. Yet she managed to respond lightly to Romar Brendyn. "Still, I had better go see what she wants," she said. "I'm so glad we had a chance to catch up tonight."

Again, a moment's confusion passed over the regent's face, and then he bowed. "Yes. Very glad. I hope to see you again while you are in residence at the palace." And he bowed again and finally left the room.

Kirra gasped and doubled over, her unbound hair falling over her shoulders and trailing on the floor. The serving girls gaped at her, then hurriedly gathered up more plates and left the room.

"Kirra," Cammon said, grabbing her shoulders, pulling her upright, and taking her in a rough embrace. He sent out a frantic call for Senneth, careful not to alert Donnal that there was any trouble. "Kirra. *Kirra*. Sit down a minute. You're trembling. Do you want some wine?"

She shook her head. "No—I'm—I'll be fine. I've seen him a half dozen times since last summer, it shouldn't still be so hard. But when he looks at me—and he doesn't remember—and yet he almost remembers . . . Cammon, it is like I can't breathe."

"I know," he said, tightening his arms around her. For a long moment, they stood in silence, Kirra trembling in Cammon's embrace. He could feel the despair inside her chest, like a silver bubble the size of a clenched fist. He stroked one hand over her curly hair and imagined that silver turning to white, iridescing, and slowly shimmering away into nothing.

She jerked upright in his arms and pulled away, staring at him in wonder. "What did you do?" she asked suspiciously. She was trying to frown but Cammon could pick up her sense of overwhelming relief.

He opened his eyes wide, to indicate innocence. "What? Nothing."

"Yes, you did—you—I don't feel so bad. All of a sudden. You did something."

"Well—"

But he didn't have to answer. Senneth came skidding in from the kitchen door, Tayse a pace behind her. She looked apprehensive and he savage. Tayse had a knife already loose in his hand.

"What's wrong?" the Rider demanded. He glanced around. "Where's Amalie?"

"Amalie's fine," Cammon said. He should have realized Senneth would bring Tayse along to any nonspecific emergency. "I was worried about Kirra."

Now Tayse's gaze locked on Kirra, but since she wasn't bleeding, he instantly dismissed any concerns about her immediate danger. "What's wrong with her?"

Kirra had freed herself completely from Cammon's hold and was smoothing down her hair and gown. "Nothing. I'm fine. Everyone is alive and healthy."

"Then why did Cammon call for us?"

But Senneth had figured it out. Her gray eyes glanced quickly around the room and she mentally peopled the chairs with noble guests. "I suppose the regent is in the other room with his niece," she said.

Kirra smiled with an effort. "I suppose he is."

Comprehension came to Tayse's face. Not until that moment did he sheathe his weapon. "Well, one thing we know," he said, not sounding at all disgruntled about rushing to a rescue that turned out to be unnecessary, "Cammon can certainly grab our attention when he needs us. That'll work in our favor someday."

Cammon nodded. Senneth took Kirra's arm. "Are you expected in the salon? Or can you come with us?"

Kirra nodded her head toward Cammon. "He came in and announced that you needed me. So I don't think anyone will mind if I disappear with you now."

"Good. Then come back and help me go through all the linens we bought today. You know I'm hopeless with household goods."

Kirra smiled. "That sounds like a marvelous idea."

They turned toward the door to the kitchen, Tayse in the lead, Senneth still keeping one hand firmly on Kirra's arm. But Kirra turned back once to give Cammon a wide-eyed look and mouth the word *thanks*. Senneth also glanced back before she disappeared through the door, but her own expression was narrowed and thoughtful. He had surprised her again, he could tell, and she was annoyed at herself for continuing to be astonished. As the door closed between them, she kept her eyes on his face, and he could practically hear the words in her head: *What else is this boy capable of?*

In the morning, Delt Helven was gone and no new beaux were expected until tomorrow. Milo, clearly disapproving, told Cammon that the princess wanted his company anyway. Cammon donned another clean uniform and hurried to the rose study.

He was surprised to find Donnal leaving just as he arrived. Donnal must have interpreted his expression, for a smile showed through his dark beard.

"What are you doing here?" Cammon asked.

"I always visit the princess whenever Kirra and I first arrive," Donnal replied. "We became friendly last summer when I guarded her rooms, so she likes me to drop by." He shrugged slightly. Donnal was used to obeying the orders of imperious women. It wouldn't occur to him to refuse. "I think she enjoys the company now and then."

It was stupid to feel even the smallest spurt of jealousy. Donnal had only recently become Kirra's lover, but he had been devoted to her most of his life. Lucky for Cammon, Donnal was a shape-shifter, not a reader. "That's kind of you," Cammon said. "I think she's often lonely."

"She has the queen for company," Donnal replied.

Cammon laughed. "I'm not sure Valri is always entertaining."

Donnal nodded expressively and departed. Cammon shook off his mood and pushed open the study door.

Valri was sitting at a desk in the corner, apparently writing out correspondence. She glanced up when Cammon entered, but immediately returned her attention to her letter. Amalie waved him over from where she sat in one of the chairs grouped before the window. On a table nearby rested a whole tray full of after-breakfast treats.

Cammon settled beside her and happily picked out a tart. "What horrible weather," Amalie said in greeting. Instead of the sunshine they had enjoyed for the past few days, lashing winds tossed around low gray clouds, and angry rain spit against the glass.

"Glad I'm not a Rider today," Cammon said with some satisfaction. "These are the days they make it a point to practice outside. Just to prove to themselves weather won't slow them down in a battle."

"That would seem to be a very welcome sort of magic," the princess observed, "the ability to dissipate the weather. Bring on the sun, or call in the rain. Do any mystics have such a gift?"

"Not that I've ever heard," he said. "But that *would* be an excellent gift."

"I don't know much about magic," Amalie said. "What kinds there are—and why some people have it and some people don't."

"Senneth thinks magic is a gift from the gods," he said. "And that there are a dozen or so gods—most of them forgotten. The Bright Mother is the goddess of the sun, and she passes on the ability to call fire, at least that's what Senneth thinks. Kirra has begun to send her prayers to the Wild Mother, who watches over all the beasts."

"That makes sense, because Kirra so often takes animal shape," said Amalie. "What other gods are there?"

"The people of the Lirrens worship the Dark Watcher, or the Black Mother, who apparently offers them all sorts of powers. Justin's wife, Ellynor, is a healer, but she also has the ability to hide herself, literally make herself disappear. She says her brothers can do the same thing. I suppose the Black Mother is a goddess of secrets. Things you whisper in the middle of the night."

Amalie smiled. "I like that. But what about you? Who gives you your power?"

"I have no idea. I can sense things that have intensity and motion. Does that ability come from a god of air or water? I see people's true souls and hear their true thoughts. Perhaps there is a god of mirrors, and whatever glass he holds up only reflects the truth. I don't know."

She put her head to one side, and even without benefit of bright sun, her strawberry hair shone with a captive gold. "I wonder where you might find legends about the ancient gods. Perhaps in the palace library there are old theology books."

Cammon wrinkled his nose. "I don't bother much with reading," he said. "I'd much rather hear someone tell a story."

"I used to read a great deal," she said. "There was nothing else to do."

He found that impossible to understand. "I suppose a princess doesn't really have work to do, but—shopping? riding? entertaining visitors? Anything except reading!"

Amalie glanced at Valri, but the queen appeared deeply engrossed in her letter. "My father was always afraid for my safety," she said. "For years, he didn't want me to leave the palace at all. And even when visitors were here—oh, I almost never got a chance to meet them. Kirra has spent half her life at the palace, you know, and I never spent more than a few hours with her until she joined us at Rappengrass last summer."

"But then—who did you talk to?" Cammon asked. His parents had left him pretty much to his own devices, but it wasn't like they had locked him in a room. He had always struck up acquaintances with the kitchen maids or the carters' sons. He had hated to be alone—still did. He didn't think he would have been able to bear the sort of solitude Amalie described.

"My mother and I were very close, while she was alive," Amalie said. She had dropped her gaze. He had the sudden swift impression that this was something she found difficult to talk about, yet yearned to confide. "And I had nurses and tutors who were kind to me. My old nurse only died a year ago, and I would spend the day with her sometimes. She could hardly see at all by the end, so I would read to her for hours."

He was staring at her, but she had not lifted her eyes. What a terrible existence! Bleak beyond description! "And you never left the palace?" he asked in a quiet voice.

"Not to go shopping in the market. Not to visit friends." She glanced up now, and there was a faint smile on her face, but it was wistful. "My mother and I would go to Merrenstow for weeks at a time, and I always liked that. Uncle Romar was her brother, you know, and he has a wonderful house. Of course, none of my cousins were allowed to visit while I was there, but my grandmother always insisted on coming, and *she* was my favorite person in the world when I was little. She taught me how to bake bread and pluck a chicken. She was Twelfth House, you know, very noble, but she said even a marlady should be able to cook a meal if she had to, and she thought a princess should as well."

So many things to answer in that particular anecdote, but Cammon stupidly found himself asking the most ridiculous question. "You know how to pluck a chicken?"

She dissolved into laughter, and Valri looked over with a frown on her face. Their merriment didn't cause her too much alarm, though, for she instantly went back to her task.

"Not anymore," Amalie said. "I haven't done it in years. But if I was stranded on a deserted farm and there was nothing to eat but a few old hens, I think I could still remember how to do it. If someone wrung its neck for me first."

"I can't imagine you ever being stranded in such a way."

"I could make a loaf of bread, too, if the ingredients were there. After my grandmother died, I was afraid I would forget. So at night I would lie awake and repeat the recipe and the steps out loud. I'm pretty sure it would be lumpy and lopsided, but I bet we could eat it."

He grinned. "We should go down to the kitchens someday. See if the cooks will let you bake. How can they refuse you? You're the princess."

She laughed. "What a good idea. Maybe we should."

He glanced at Valri again, but the queen had pulled out a fresh sheet of paper and was staring down at it as if waiting for it to dictate the proper words. "What happened," he asked, his voice very low, "when your mother died? How did she die?"

Immediately, Amalie's face was very grave, but she did not look angry the subject had been broached. "Fever," she said sadly. "One day she was fine. We had spent the day in the gardens. I remember that we laughed and laughed, but I can't remember what was so funny. I was thirteen. She had been telling me for weeks that she would have the dressmakers in to fit me for a new wardrobe, that soon I would need to attend some small dinners and meet some of the prominent families. I was very excited about the idea. And then the next day she had a fever, and two days later she was dead." Amalie shook her head. "It was so fast—I didn't have time to think about it. I didn't have time to *prepare*." She lifted her dark eyes to his face; she looked as if she was exercising extreme willpower to keep from crying.

"I'm so sorry," he said. He couldn't think of another thing to say.

She shook her head again. "The thing is, I knew she was sick," she said. "Two summers before, she had begun to have these pains. And she had lost weight. We didn't go to Merrenstow that year, and we *always* went to Merrenstow. I knew she was sick, but I didn't realize *how* sick. I didn't realize she could die."

"No," he said. "It never occurred to me, either. That my parents could die. Why would they? It never crossed my mind."

She gave him a swift, tiny smile. "Whereas I've always known my father could die. Since I was quite young, everyone has made it clear that I will take the throne upon his death. But when I was young, I didn't think about it as being an occasion for grief. I imagined how solemn I would be when they put the crown on my head, and I imagined what color dress I would wear to my coronation." Cammon laughed out loud, and her smile grew a little wider. "I imagined what it would be like to be queen, I just didn't imagine what it would be like to lose my father. Once my mother died, I suddenly understood."

"Are you close to your father?" he asked curiously. "It does not seem as if you spend much time with him."

She nodded. "I love him dearly," she said. "He's so busy that I don't see him much, but he usually comes by every morning or every night and spends half an hour just with me. We talk about everything. My mother's death was such a blow to him. I think it was years before he recovered."

Cammon couldn't help himself; he sent one more glance in the queen's direction. "It must have been very strange," he said cautiously, "when he remarried. And someone so young. How soon did Valri come to the palace after your mother died?"

"Oh, she was already here," Amalie said.

He knew that his expression was dumbfounded. "She *what?*"

"She had been living here about a year already. She followed them back from the Lirrens shortly after they visited there—oh, a year or so before my mother died. Valri and my mother had become close friends and my mother invited her to visit."

Cammon's head swiveled between Valri and Amalie. Valri was from the Lirrens? Maybe—maybe—Senneth had actually suspected such a thing once or twice, and of course the queen's affection for the raelynx should have been an unmistakable clue. Then there was the fact that Cammon could not read her, as he could not read Ellynor; there was something impenetrable about Lirrenfolk, or perhaps that was merely the manifestation of their magic. And yet—

"Valri is from the Lirrenlands?" he repeated in a slow voice. "I don't believe that is generally known."

A flash of guilt crossed Amalie's face. "I probably shouldn't have told you, then," she said. "Please don't mention it to Senneth or anyone else. I don't know that it is exactly a secret, and yet my father goes to some pains not to raise any questions about her. People already think Valri is strange, and some of them even think she's a mystic. If they knew she was from the Lirrens as well—"

That was when it fell in place. "Of course. She said she was protecting you. She *is* a mystic, and she has the same kind of magic Ellynor has—the power of concealment. It is a gift of the night goddess, and she is using that power on you."

Amalie stared at him with wide brown eyes and did not answer.

"So your mother knew she was sick," he said slowly, piecing it together as he went. "Did she go to the Lirrenlands hoping to get well? Because there are exceptionally gifted healers across the Lireth Mountains."

"I don't know. Maybe."

"But instead of a healer, she found Valri. And the only thing your mother was more afraid of than dying was what would happen to you once she was dead. And she realized that Valri could protect you—is that it? Keep you hidden away from the king's enemies."

"Something like that."

"And she persuaded Valri to come back to Ghosenhall. But that doesn't work," he broke off. "Ellynor told us how protective her own family is. How they would never let the women of their clans go off and marry outsiders. The Lirrenfolk don't actually consider Baryn their king, as far as I can tell. Sow how did Valri get free of them?"

"She declared herself *bahta-lo*. Like your friend Ellynor," Amalie said. "Above the clan. She said it wasn't easy, and some of her family members have not accepted her choice, but she did it anyway."

Cammon narrowed his eyes. "So, your mother is the one who brought her back here. Specifically to marry your father. I hear all this speculation about why your father married so soon after your mother's death, but it was your mother's idea all along."

Amalie nodded. "They don't even share quarters, my father and Valri. They are very good friends, but all they really have in common is me."

"And Valri has been practically your only friend since your mother died," Cammon said. "I can see why you are so close, but I think it's been hard on both of you."

"Valri worries about me. All the time. She never gets a rest from worrying," Amalie said. "And there are days—oh, I just want to break free!

Run through the palace gates and race through the streets of Ghosenhall, stopping to shake hands with strangers and dance with young men and pick up little girls and twirl them around. I want to—I want to *see* places and try exotic food and meet someone who does not bow to me because he does not know who I am. I was so happy last summer! All those balls! All those wonderful strangers! And yet, for Valri, those were the most terrifying months of her life. Because she was so afraid something would happen to me."

"Well, something almost did happen to you, and more than once," Cammon pointed out. "I don't know that you'll ever be able to go wandering through the city wholly unattended for the rest of your life."

"No," she said dolefully. "I must be proper, and hide behind the palace walls, and sit on the throne, and be very dull."

He could not help but laugh at that. "No, now you are being courted by a couple dozen men, and you will get married, and eventually you will be queen. I would hardly think *that* will be a dull life," he said.

She smiled. "And even Valri seems more relaxed since *you* have joined us," she said. "She trusts you to be able to sense danger before it gets too close. Valri doesn't trust many people, you know, so that is quite a compliment. Perhaps she will trust you enough to let me go shopping in the market someday. Wouldn't that be fun!"

Cammon spared a moment to imagine the cavalcade that would accompany the princess on any expedition into the heart of the city. Riders—ordinary soldiers—himself—and no doubt Valri. He could hardly think any shop was big enough to accommodate them all. But the real challenge would fall to him, trying to open his mind enough to catch any intimation of danger from so many possible sources. It would be like being battered from a thousand directions. How would he be able to deflect all the happy, harmless arrows of attention while identifying the sharp spears of ill intent? "It might be simpler to have merchants bring their merchandise here," he suggested.

"You just don't like to shop," she said.

"I think it might be difficult to keep you entirely safe."

She leaned forward; her eyes suddenly seemed very dark. "Cammon," she said in a soft voice, "who is ever entirely safe?"

CHAPTER
9

SENNETH found herself enjoying Kirra's visit as she had not enjoyed anything in weeks. It was just so frivolous and girlish and—and—*unimportant* to spend the days combing through all the fine merchandise in the Ghosenhall shops, debating over the merits of blond lace or white, picking out rugs and curtains and goblets.

"Ellynor will want to choose some of her household furnishings herself, I'm sure," Senneth said as she held up a beautifully embroidered quilt. "We should hold back a little, perhaps."

"You didn't spend this much time shopping for your *own* house," Kirra retorted. "I've never seen you look at so much frilly stuff in my life."

Senneth smiled. "I don't like bows and ribbons and clutter. But it's making me happy to pick things out for someone else."

Kirra held up a pair of pillowcases, even more elaborately embroidered than the quilt. "Can you picture Justin laying his head on this?" she said, choking back a giggle. "Do you think he's ever used a pillow in his life?"

That made Senneth laugh again, abandoning any notions of restraint.

It had been so long since she had been able to focus on anything that was inconsequential and fun. That had no chance of resulting in someone's death, or the overthrow of the king, or the complete reshaping of the world.

If you were going to spend a day immersing yourself in frivolity, Kirra was the ideal companion.

They shopped and bought, pausing for meals, and then shopped and bought some more. Kirra seemed to have wholly recovered from her distress at seeing Romar Brendyn, though she had made a point of avoiding the formal dinner the previous night.

"While we're buying things for Justin, we might be considering what to give our siblings for their wedding," Kirra said as they sat at a bakery and ate sweets to recover their strength.

"You have given Danalustrous to Casserah. Surely that's enough of a gift?" Senneth said. Kirra was the eldest daughter and by rights should inherit the House, but her father had determined that Casserah would make the better landholder. So he had bestowed the property on his youngest child instead.

"Oh, and I have given her my loyalty. Another expensive present," Kirra said. "You're right. She can't possibly expect anything more."

"And my gift will be my attendance at the event, since I hate affairs like this," Senneth said. "Everyone will be so impressed by that they won't look for a wrapped box with my name on it."

"Did your family present you with any gifts upon the occasion of your own wedding?" Kirra asked. "I'm sure your brothers were disappointed that you chose to elope."

"I'm sure they were relieved," Senneth retorted. "How to explain to the Brassenthwaite vassals that the serramarra is taking a King's Rider for her husband? You know that Nate was mortified just at the thought of such a disastrous alliance. I did them a favor by marrying where no one could witness the humiliation."

Kirra waved this away. "So? Presents?"

Senneth grinned and nodded. "Trinkets and some cash. Not that we needed either, but I suppose the gesture was kind."

"And you like being married?"

"I like it very much indeed."

She could not have such conversations with anyone else—not Tayse, not Cammon, none of the Riders, certainly not the king. Her adventurous life had not left Senneth with an overabundance of close friends, and she had been estranged from her family too long to ever want to confide in her four brothers. But restless, irrepressible, unpredictable Kirra was the one woman in Gillengaria that Senneth absolutely trusted, and that meant she could count on Kirra to fight at her back or give her advice on love.

Strange.

They returned to the palace grounds tired and happy, but once they arrived at the cottage, Senneth learned her day wasn't over. A note from Milo had been slipped under the door. *The king requests your presence at dinner this evening.*

"You've probably got one just like it in your room," Senneth said, showing the invitation to Kirra.

"Well, I'm not going," Kirra said. "I just won't return to the palace. I'll stay here and add our new purchases to Justin's cottage. Oh, sorry, Majesty, I didn't receive the note until too late."

Senneth shook her head. "I don't know why you're one of Baryn's favorites."

Kirra smiled and tossed her gold curls. "I'm so charming that he has to forgive my poor manners."

"But is charm ever really enough?" Senneth asked, with mock solemnity.

"It better be. Because that and hair are all I've got."

Though not interested in attending the meal herself, Kirra supervised Senneth's toilette and even modified the bronze-colored gown Senneth had chosen to wear. Kirra was a shape-shifter, but she could also change anything she put a hand to if she felt like it, and now she traced a finger over the décolletage of Senneth's dress.

"You simply *cannot* go up to the palace with a dress so high-necked it's practically strangling you," Kirra insisted. "There. That's more attractive. Now everyone can see this lovely necklace Tayse gave you and they'll realize you've got a housemark under the pendant. Make them remember you're a serramarra! Make them treat you like one, too."

The gold sphere did indeed fall perfectly over the Brassenthwaite housemark burned into Senneth's skin just above her breasts. She'd spent a good seventeen years of her life wishing she could erase that symbol of her family heritage, and now here she was, living a life where she was forced to flaunt it again.

"That's too low. Change it back," she commanded, but Kirra shook her head.

"I won't. Go up there and flirt with somebody. Give Tayse something to worry about."

Senneth tugged futilely at the neckline, which left her feeling ridiculously exposed. "You're the most wretched girl!" she exclaimed. "I don't have time or I'd put on a different dress."

"And I'd change that one, too. Go! Have a lovely dinner."

Naturally, the meal was not lovely, but it wasn't dreadful, either. Senneth actually ended up being pleased that she had attended, because Ryne Coravann was there with his sister, Lauren. Ryne, of course, was courting Amalie and sat next to her for the meal. He was tall and dark, neither as bulky nor as sensible as his father. Senneth scarcely knew him, but she liked Lauren, and she made it a point to approach the Coravann serramarra as they gathered in the salon after the meal.

"So you have accompanied your brother as he makes his bow to the princess," Senneth greeted her. "Do you find it odd? I was with my brother Will last year as he paid court to Casserah Danalustrous, and it was a most peculiar experience."

Lauren smiled. She was as dark as Ryne and just as attractive, but had a much greater air of self-possession. "I cannot think Amalie will choose him from all her suitors," Lauren said. "He's very wild. But my father wanted him to come, and I jumped at the chance to visit the royal city."

"How are your Lirren relatives?" Senneth asked, for Lauren and Ryne were the rarest of creatures: products of a marriage between a Lirren woman and a Gillengaria man.

"Some of them were arriving just as we left," said Lauren, "and with a most incredible tale! Perhaps you'd heard that two of my cousins were novices at the Lumanen Convent?"

"I did know that."

"And one of them has run away with a King's Rider! They are actually *married*, he said. Do you know how unlikely that is?"

"I lived in the Lirrenlands for a few years. I know," Senneth said, amused. "But I cannot help but think this is an excellent match. I know the Rider, and I met the girl."

"That's more than I've ever done. I've met many of my Lirren relatives, but the younger women rarely travel across the mountains, and I've never seen these two," Lauren said.

"I have been wondering," Senneth said, "how Coralinda Gisseltess took the news? I know she could not have been happy that one of her novices fled the convent. And I know your father holds her in high regard. So, I thought perhaps you might have heard something."

For a moment, Lauren's serene face looked troubled. "She came to Coravann Keep just a week or two ago," she said. "The tale came up. You could tell she was trying to control her temper, but she was still enraged. This girl was a mystic, apparently, and Coralinda had wanted to exorcise the magic from her veins. She did not say how. But the girl eluded her and escaped the convent— Again, Coralinda did not elaborate. I watched her hands as she told the tale. They were clenched so hard I thought her bones must hurt."

"I believe Coralinda was at the Keep last summer when your father held his ball," Senneth said, her voice neutral. "Does she visit you often?"

Lauren had smoothed her face out, but it was clear she was not entirely at ease. "My father thinks of Coralinda Gisseltess as a devout and reverend lady," she said slowly. "He worships the Pale Mother himself and has always worn a moonstone pendant. My father would never harm a mystic—my father in general is the most gentle of men—and he does not seem to believe that Coralinda Gisseltess offers any real threat to anyone, mystics included."

This was interesting. "And you do?"

Lauren raised her dark eyes to Senneth's face. "I hear the rumors, serra. About how she sends her men out to murder mystics in their beds. I do not like her. I do not trust her. I believe she is capable of doing exactly what they say."

Senneth nodded. "And I know she is. Last fall, the king sent a Rider to spy on the convent, and that Rider followed Coralinda's men as they rode to the houses where mystics lay. Her soldiers burned those houses to the ground. She wants to rid the realm of mystics, and she will stop at nothing until they are all dead."

Senneth paused and glanced over at Ryne Coravann, who was standing beside the regent, a glass of wine in his hand. He had apparently already had a few drinks, for his handsome face was flushed and he was laughing immoderately. And Romar Brendyn was not a particularly amusing man.

"Halchon Gisseltess, on the other hand, wants to rid the realm of Baryn and his heirs," Senneth added slowly. "I am not sure it is in your best interests to promote a match between the princess and your brother. I believe Halchon Gisseltess wants to take the country to war in order to win the throne for himself. Anyone who marries Amalie is likely to find himself facing down an assassin before the year is out."

"My father does not believe war will come," the girl said.

Senneth returned her attention to Lauren. In a deliberate voice, she replied, "Your father is wrong."

BARYN wanted Senneth's attendance the following morning—more to trade gossip than anything else, she realized. "What about Ryne Coravann? What do you think?" he asked as they settled in his untidy blue study and sipped hot tea.

Senneth eyed him over the rim of her cup. He looked worn and weary today, she thought. His flyaway gray hair was particularly unkempt this morning, and he had dressed himself in what had to be his oldest and most comfortable clothes. Still, his eyes were bright and sharp, and he waited with eager interest for her reply.

"I think he's immature and hardly fit for marriage with anyone, if what you want is a proper husband for your daughter," she replied bluntly. "If all you're looking for is a bloodline that will satisfy the marlords, he might do. But I cannot imagine he will bring Amalie anything but heartache if she were ever to try to love him."

He seemed neither offended nor alarmed. "I would like to say that love is unimportant, but you have proven in the most flamboyant way that you believe it is the card that trumps all others," he said, his tone mild. "Perhaps I should be looking for advice from other quarters."

She smiled. "Perhaps you should."

"What do you think of Toland Storian? For he will be coming soon to pay court to my daughter."

She almost spit out a mouthful of tea. "I *hate* him. And so does Amalie. He's boorish and arrogant, and we had ample opportunity to observe that for ourselves last summer."

The king was amused. "Yes—I believe there was some incident when you set him on fire?"

"Kirra arranged that," she said hastily. "She provoked him on purpose. He behaved badly, and I had to protect Amalie."

"In truth, I am not eager to see her wed Ryne Coravann *or* Toland Storian," he said. "Let us see what our choices are after all the young men have come courting."

She blew on her tea. "Do you have a favorite?"

He shrugged. "I would like to see her marry a man from Brassenthwaite or Rappengrass or Danalustrous," he said. "A nobleman, of course, but not necessarily a serramar. Someone intelligent and kind, who would allow himself to be influenced by Romar."

"Well, *intelligent*, *kind*, and *easily dominated* are not words that typically describe the men of Brassenthwaite, but I'll ask my brother Kiernan to look around," Senneth said dryly. "There must be some Thirteenth House lords lurking about who would be happy to see their sons marry into royalty."

Baryn tapped the fingers of one hand against his cheek. "There has been more talk," he said. "Of changes to the aristocracy. Soon there may be no Thirteenth House at all."

The noble-born lords and ladies who were not purebred enough to belong to one of the Twelve Houses were all lumped under the rather derisive name of the Thirteenth House. During the past year, some of these lesser nobles had begun to agitate for more power and prestige— including a clear title to the lands they held in trust for the marlords. Many of these vassals had come to Ghosenhall to negotiate in good faith with Baryn. Others had tried to capitalize on the general unrest in the kingdom. Indeed, last year a few rebel lords had attempted more than once to murder the regent.

"What will you do with all the lesser lords, then?" Senneth asked. "Gift them their properties outright? Would you want to see Eighteen

Houses, instead of Twelve? I am no apologist for the aristocracy, but even I find it hard to say such a phrase. Eighteen Houses. Twenty-four. There is no poetry to either."

He smiled at her a little absently. "Another kind of title altogether, perhaps," he said. "We might have both the Twelve Houses and the Twelve Manors. That is pretty enough, don't you think?"

"Very nice. And can you find a property in each of the twelve regions that the marlords would be willing to give up? And would the lords of these manors be satisfied with their new status, or will they want full parity with the marlords?"

"I haven't worked it all out yet," he admitted. "But I believe we might take small steps to change our world, and so perhaps avert a war."

She lifted her eyes and gave him a hard, comprehensive look. "And do you truly think any measures are sufficient to do that?"

He glanced away, for a long time merely looking out the window. Another gray day, though at least there was no rain to contend with this morning. Then he sighed and shook his head, glancing back at her. His face was sad. "No," he said. "But I must do everything in my power to try."

Two days later, Cammon slipped down to the cottage just in time to eat lunch with Kirra and Senneth. "Justin and Ellynor will be here tomorrow," he told them.

"Early or late?" Kirra demanded. "Do we have the day to work, or must we finish everything today?"

"I don't know. If I were you, I'd finish up today."

"Better finish up by this afternoon," Senneth reminded her. "You promised Baryn you would attend the dinner tonight."

Kirra cursed and then laughed. "Well, we're almost done. Let's go over now. What have Tayse and the other Riders cooked up?"

"I believe it involves pelting them with flowers and fruit as they ride up to the cottage for the first time, and then creating a great deal of noise outside their bedroom window in the middle of their first night here."

Kirra grinned. "Everybody loves newlyweds."

Cammon gulped down his meal and then went off to fence with Tayse, while Kirra and Senneth returned to the house set aside for Justin. It was tiny, a mirror image of the one Senneth shared with Tayse—merely one main room that opened into a small kitchen, with a single door leading to a cramped bedroom. Little more than basic privacy and a place to sit before the fire. But Senneth and Kirra had outfitted it with a new bed and several small storage chests, as well as chairs in the main room and dishes for the kitchen. Rugs on the floor to keep out the chill, curtains at the windows to keep out the curious. They had made Cammon and Donnal haul in wood, which was stacked before the fireplace, and Kirra had filched bread and cheese from the palace kitchen.

"What are those?" Senneth said, pointing at a row of terra-cotta planters holding a wilted assortment of scrubby plants. "Those are ugly."

"Give me a minute," Kirra said, and skimmed her hands over the bare, prickly branches. Instantly, the withered leaves turned green; the dried and folded petals were rouged with red.

"Very pretty," Senneth said. "One would almost think you had the gift of growing things."

"No—they're altered, not coaxed," Kirra said.

Senneth glanced around. "I would start a fire in the grate, but who knows how long it will be before they arrive? But I hate to have them come in to a cold house." She leaned her hand against the wall, and the temperature in the rooms began to rise. "Perhaps just a little magic in the stone," she said. "I'll add another touch of heat before we go to bed."

Kirra edged toward the door, pausing to survey the entire scene with a look of satisfaction. Warm, colorful, cozy, the front room had a most inviting feel. "Who wouldn't want to live in such a welcoming place?" she said. "I hope Ellynor is happy here, so far from her family."

Senneth followed her out the door. "Funny—I'm always happiest when my family is farthest away."

"And I when I am either setting out to see them or preparing to leave," Kirra said.

"But then, we're unnatural."

"Mystics," Kirra said darkly. "Never just like everybody else."

CHAPTER

10

THE formal dinner went well enough, though it was as dull to Senneth as most such events were. The regent and his wife were not in attendance, and consequently Kirra was in high spirits. She spent most of the meal attempting to catch Cammon's eye and make him laugh, though he tried hard to hang on to his always precarious dignity. The rest of the time she flirted so boldly with the Fortunalt lord seated to her left that he followed her out of the dining room literally begging to see her again.

"Incorrigible," Senneth murmured to Cammon on her way out the door. "Any news on Justin?"

"Tomorrow morning, I think. Depending on where he spends the night."

"Come down early to help us greet him."

"I will."

Kirra had a similar plan, it turned out, for she and Donnal showed up at Senneth's cottage a couple hours later. "Feed us, house us," Kirra said, pushing past Senneth through the door. Donnal at least sent her an apologetic glance as he stepped inside.

"Why don't you camp outside, like some of the Riders are doing?" Senneth said, leaving the door open suggestively. "See? Tayse and Wen and Coeval and a few others have stationed themselves all around the barracks and halfway to the gate. They have pots and pans and all sorts of noisy items with which to greet our young lovers. Why don't you stay outside with them?"

"Too cold and nasty," Kirra said. "It's going to rain."

"We'll sleep on the floor again," Donnal offered.

Kirra yawned. "*You* can. If Tayse is outside, I'm sleeping in the bed with Senneth."

"Not that you were invited."

"True friends never turn you out, no matter how inconvenient your arrival," Kirra said, wandering to the kitchen. "Heat some water for me, could you? I want something warm to drink."

Senneth grumbled some more, but in truth she had expected them and was a little surprised that Cammon hadn't showed up as well. She poured a mug of cold water, set it to boiling with the touch of her hand, and pointed to the crock containing tea leaves. "But I'm going to bed," she said. "I want to be up early enough to greet them."

They all settled in quickly, though Senneth briefly found it strange to have Kirra's light form beside her instead of Tayse's darker, heavier one. She and Kirra had shared rooms and beds across half of Gillengaria, and there had been a time Senneth never expected to take a lover, let alone a husband, so it should not seem so foreign not to have him next to her; and yet it was. She and Tayse had not slept apart since their wedding. They had scarcely spent a day apart since they met. Even when he hated her, as he had at first, he had watched over her.

Not that she was in danger, here in the well-guarded confines of the king's palace, two mystics in her house and almost fifty Riders within call. Not that Tayse could not be at her side in a minute if she should have need of him. Still. The fact that he was not sleeping close enough for her to touch him with her hand made it hard, at first, for her to sleep at all.

Dawn came, pink-and-white as a porcelain doll, and the three of them rose and dressed with practiced efficiency. Through the windows, Senneth could see frost laying a white-gold gilding over the hard earth and the winter vegetation. Tayse and Wen were already astir, striding down from the general direction of the palace, their hands full of copper pots and big wooden spoons. Their breath showed misty in the cold air. A half dozen other Riders had congregated around the small cottage, either leaning against the walls or making themselves comfortable on the ground. They all looked as if they had rested well and been up for hours.

"Everyone's on the move," Senneth said, letting the curtain fall. "Let's go see if there's any news."

She almost screamed as she opened the door, for Cammon stood just outside, hand raised to knock. "You've been up for an hour," he complained. "What's taking you so long?"

Senneth brushed by him and spoke over her shoulder to Kirra and Donnal, laughing behind her. "Someone turn into a wild animal and kill him for me."

They intersected with Tayse while Wen went off to join the others. "Cold night?" Kirra asked him brightly. "Nice and warm inside your little cabin."

He gave her a lurking half-smile. "A Rider never notices the weather," he said.

"Well, a mystic does." Kirra rubbed her hands briskly over her upper arms and then frowned at Cammon. "So? When are they going to get here?"

Senneth thought Cammon looked the slightest bit uneasy—the expression Cammon always wore when he was trying to keep silent about something. "Well—"

Just then the door to the cottage opened, and Justin stepped outside.

He was dressed in a loose shirt and a pair of breeches that he might have pulled on as he rolled out of bed, and his sandy hair was tousled with sleep. He stretched his arms overhead, manufacturing a big yawn, and then gave a mock start as he noticed the welcoming party. "Oh! Company! I don't know that we're actually ready to receive guests yet, but—"

That was all the further he got. Kirra shrieked, and the whole contingent descended on him in a fury of noise and shouting. The Riders shoved each other aside, one after the other, to beat him on the back or take him in a rough embrace. Kirra actually kissed him and then pushed past him to enter the cottage, calling, "Ellynor? Are you in here?"

Senneth was left staring at Cammon. Who stared back, a stupid grin on his face.

"You told him," she said in an ominous voice.

He nodded happily. "Had to. I told you he was coming. Only fair I told him you were waiting."

"You *told* him!" she shouted, and pounced on him, grabbing him in a headlock and then wrestling him to the ground. He yelped and flailed around, trying to get free, but Cammon was no fighter, and she landed a few hard blows just to teach him a lesson. "I ought to roast your heart in your chest!"

"Ow! Ow! Donnal! Help! Tayse! *Help!*"

Tayse actually came to his rescue, putting a hand under Senneth's arm and pulling them both to their feet. She kept her arm locked around Cammon's throat, though, and another around his waist, but now the grip was more affectionate than punishing. He left off trying to get free and stood tamely in her arms.

Tayse watched Cammon with his eyebrows lifted. "So? What information did you give him? And how?"

"I met them outside the palace gates yesterday afternoon. He knew to wait for me but he didn't know why." He grinned and elbowed Senneth in the ribs, so she briefly squeezed his throat again. When he could speak once more, he said, "He'd guessed, though."

Tayse glanced at the cabin, where Riders were spilling in and out of the door, and a great deal of commotion was being created on the copper-bottomed drums. "And they managed to elude us how? Through Lirren magic?"

Senneth nodded. "That would be my guess. Ellynor snuck them inside the gate—and past a whole gauntlet of Riders. Both of them."

He met her eyes, a certain disquiet in his own. "I find this extremely disturbing."

"Oh, but you can trust Ellynor!" Cammon exclaimed.

Senneth released him and gave him a little shove. "You half-wit, what about her brothers and her cousins and the members of feuding clans?" she demanded. "What about Lirrenfolk who might be siding with Halchon Gisseltess? What if *they* decide to come sneaking into the palace grounds at night? *You* can't sense Ellynor, you've said that before. *Riders* can't see them or hear them. Not Riders guarding the gate, not Riders stationed along a pathway where they *know* one of them is going to come. I find it disturbing myself."

Cammon looked horrified, but Tayse's dark eyes glittered. "And yet, if this is a magic we can harness, I find it very valuable indeed," he said.

"Well," Senneth said. "They've ruined our surprise and scared us to death, but let's go say hello to them anyway."

"Yes," said Tayse, turning to lead the way. "It will be good to have Justin back."

It was maybe two hours before all of the other Riders cleared out. Senneth was not much for playing hostess, but Kirra had hissed at her and grabbed her arm, dragging her to the small kitchen, where Ellynor was standing in some bemusement. The Lirren girl was delicate and pretty, with exceedingly long black hair that just now was piled on top of her head in a hasty knot. She was scarcely more dressed than Justin, though he'd obviously given her time to wash her face and pull on a gown before he went out to taunt the welcoming party.

"Am I supposed to *feed* everybody?" she whispered when the other two joined her. "*Is* there food? What am I supposed to do?"

"They're Riders. You don't have to take care of them," Senneth said, but Kirra had been raised more politely than that.

"We'll go to the barracks and lift some bread and fruit," Kirra said. "I'm not going to cook or anything, but maybe it would be nice to offer them something to eat. Oh, but do you like the plates? Do you like the pans? We picked them out for you, but if you don't like them—"

Ellynor still looked overwhelmed, but now gratitude crossed her fine features. "That was so kind! I've never been to such a big city! I thought *Neft* was an intimidating place, but I'll never be able to find my way around Ghosenhall!"

Senneth laughed. "I don't believe you. If you can track your brothers through the Lirren wilds, you can make your way through the royal city."

Ellynor smiled. "Fewer dangers in the Lirren wilds," she said.

"That's probably true," Kirra said. "But come with us, then, if you want to see the city. Senneth and I can protect anybody."

They made a foray to the barracks and returned with an assortment of food and drinks, Donnal assisting them. Senneth noticed that Ellynor was pleased to see Donnal and reflected that the shy Lirren girl probably found Donnal the least frightening of Justin's friends. But she, at least, was not fooled by Ellynor's soft voice and kind expression. The woman was unyielding if called upon to protect someone she loved; she had literally hauled Justin back from the abyss of death. And she was dense with magic. No, Ellynor was no helpless child dependent on the strength of her husband or her friends.

Although even a mystic might quail at the thought of navigating Ghosenhall on her own.

Eventually the Riders had had their fill of purloined breakfast goods and ribald jokes. Tayse practically pushed Hammond out the door, and Wen was still talking to Justin through the front window. But finally everyone else was gone. Kirra and Cammon flopped onto two of the chairs, Senneth coaxed the hearth fire higher, and Tayse turned the lock on the door.

Cammon looked swiftly around the room, an oddly sweet smile on his face. That was when Senneth realized it: For the first time in more than six weeks, the six of them were together again.

Seven. The seven of them. For Ellynor sat curled next to Justin, who had sprawled on the floor before the fire. Not one of them and yet somehow belonging, somehow seeming to fit right there under the crook of Justin's arm.

Tayse dropped easily to the floor near Justin, while Senneth took one of the other chairs. At some point, Donnal had melted into his familiar shape of a shaggy black dog, and lay with his head across Kirra's dainty feet.

"Let me commend you on your trick," Tayse said. "Very effective."

Justin grinned. "Wasn't sure we could pull it off, not when I saw a Rider every three paces for a quarter of a mile! And then getting through the front door—how to do that so no one saw it open?"

"And how did you?" Kirra asked.

Justin looked down at Ellynor, who answered in her sweet voice. "I made the shadow so deep no one would notice it, and then we slipped inside."

"I'm even more concerned about how you breached the front gate, where I know four Riders were on duty," Tayse said in a calm voice. "How did you manage to open *that* without anyone being the wiser?"

Justin shook his head. "Didn't even try. We came in with another party last night—a group of nobles all dressed up, so I suppose they were arriving for dinner. Ellynor just cloaked us in magic, and we stepped in right behind them."

Tayse nodded. "That's a slight comfort, but very slight. You could bring a whole troop inside the palace grounds if you slipped them in by ones and twos behind other parties."

Justin looked grave. "I wasn't thinking about it that way yesterday, but you're right." His eyes narrowed; he was already considering solutions. "So then—maybe some kind of trip wire—the Lirrenfolk are impossible to *see*, but they still have weight and mass. Though, that won't work—everyone would stumble over that."

"What about dogs?" Kirra asked. She prodded Donnal and he sat up, ears pricked forward. "Or a wolf? Would Donnal have noticed you going by last night?" She glanced at Senneth. "We should have slept outside after all."

"You might have heard or smelled us," Ellynor admitted. "The few times my brothers were caught were when a guard dog raised the alarm. But I can cover almost all trace of our passage. It has to be a pretty smart dog."

"Donnal's an exceptional animal," Kirra drawled. Donnal's black mouth opened in a canine grin.

"Let's try that," Tayse said. "Over the next few days. See how well Ellynor can trick Donnal and what he has to do to catch her. See if Cammon can learn how to sense her, too."

Senneth smiled at Ellynor, who looked a little startled. "He never asks," she said. "He just assumes that everyone is as focused as he is on keeping the palace and all its inhabitants safe."

"Of course—whatever I can do," Ellynor said earnestly, and the rest of them laughed.

"Jerril can help, I bet," Cammon said. To Ellynor he explained, "Jerril's my tutor. He's teaching me how to improve my magic."

"Oh, because you're so weak and useless to us now," Justin said.

But Senneth was nodding. "Good idea."

"You'll like Jerril," Cammon said to Ellynor, who did look just a bit nervous. "He couldn't be nicer."

"Not like the lot of us, you mean," Kirra said lazily. "Unprincipled and ruthless."

"Sounds about right," Justin said with a grin.

"The problem remains," Tayse said, "finding a way to make sure none of Ellynor's friends and cousins—or enemies and uncles—can come stealing into the palace completely undetected. I hardly think we can expect Donnal to spend the remaining days of his life prowling these few acres and trying to scent out trouble."

"Why can't we use real dogs?" Justin said. "*Specifically* on the watch for someone trying to enter the gate by stealth?"

Tayse nodded. "We could do that. The head groom at the royal stables knows an animal trainer. We could work with him."

Senneth glanced at Kirra. "And maybe we could supplement the real dogs with some enchanted ones," she said. "I've been thinking it's time to recruit more mystics."

Kirra straightened in her chair. "Carrebos!" she exclaimed. "We can see who's on hand there."

"I don't have any idea what you're talking about," Justin said.

"City not far from Fortunalt lands that apparently has become a community of mystics," Senneth said. "Maybe some of them would like to come work for the king."

Tayse looked intrigued. For a man who had distrusted magic for most of his life, he had become awfully willing to turn it to his advantage. "You think there might be shape-shifters among them? That would make an interesting contingent to add to the king's troops."

Senneth shrugged. "Won't know till we go investigate. I thought Kirra and I could head down there in a few days and see what we might find." Donnal barked sharply. "Donnal would come with us, of course," Senneth added.

Tayse gave her a quick smile, private despite the fact that five other people could witness it. "So would I," he said. *Because I intend to never be parted from you again.*

Kirra made a tiny cooing sound, but even that didn't keep the slow shiver from tickling down Senneth's spine. "So would you," she agreed softly. *Because I could not bear it if you were.*

CHAPTER

II

IF Cammon had had to describe his emotional state during the next week, he would have called it sublimely content. Justin was back—the others had not yet departed—Amalie wanted to see him every morning—and Jerril was coming to the palace to practice magic. Nothing was missing from his life; every ingredient that he considered essential was solidly in place.

Three more suitors arrived that week, so Cammon had little chance for private conversation with Amalie. Instead, he and Valri and assorted Riders spent an aggregate of hours lurking behind the false walls and eavesdropping on three varieties of wooing. This should have been tedious in the extreme, but somehow it was not. Valri had had a couple of chairs and a small table hauled in, all of them just narrow enough to fit in the secret corridor, and she and Cammon sat there during every interview and silently played cards. When part of the conversation caught their attention, they would look up from their game and either laugh silently, or show their surprise, or roll their eyes and grimace in distaste. This made the hours pass in an entertaining fashion and kept Cammon from thinking too hard about the cold reality underlying the whole exercise: The princess was trying to pick her husband. He didn't know why he so much disliked the idea of her getting married.

One reason, perhaps, was that none of the latest crop of beaux seemed remotely worthy of her. The first one was quite young, rather tongue-tied, and extremely nervous. Amalie was gentle with him, but Cammon didn't need her critique afterward to know she had not considered him appealing. The second was older, very polished, and superficially agreeable, but Cammon found something about him to be repulsive. Maybe it was that Cammon sensed cold calculation in his admiring compliments and honeyed phrases. Maybe it was that Amalie laughed a great deal during their extended and playful conversation.

"You seemed to enjoy your visit with the Tilt lord," Valri remarked once the suitor had gone off to change for dinner.

"He's a toad," Amalie said calmly. "He kept looking around the room as if wondering what it would be like to own the whole palace. And looking at me like—well. Like he was wondering what it would be like to own *me*."

Valri seemed amused. "You've become rather an expert at concealing what you're thinking, then. I couldn't tell you disliked him."

"I find it easier to pretend when I *don't* like someone," she said. "I might be more nervous when I do."

She was not nervous in the presence of the third suitor, a Nocklyn man old enough to be her father. The noble had seated himself, accepted a glass of wine, and traded trivialities for a few moments before he broke off his speech with a laugh.

"I cannot believe a nineteen-year-old girl looks at me and sees a potential husband," he said. "I am here because Mayva Nocklyn asked me to make a case for myself, not because I expect to win your hand. So let me enumerate all the advantages of my rank and station, and you can listen politely. Once that is all out of the way, we can talk of other things. I imagine that will be a much more pleasant way to pass the day."

There was a smile in Amalie's voice. "I imagine it will."

Valri, who had been contemplating her discard when the lord started speaking, paused long enough to listen to this little interchange. Now she glanced at Cammon with her eyebrows raised, as if to ask, *Is he sincere?* Cammon, whose own hand was unplayable, nodded back. There was no lust for power, no lust for a young girl's body, hovering over this middle-aged swain. Cammon saw Valri's face sharpen with interest; she started weighing the advantages of an unpretentious, settled older man who treated his young bride with kindness.

Cammon frowned at her and mouthed, *Too old.* Valri shrugged and pointed at herself. *Look at me,* she meant, married to a man in his sixties. Cammon's frown grew more pronounced. *Different,* he said silently. She gave a half-smile and shook her head. *Not really.* Cammon disagreed, but it was impossible to explain why, given the circumstances.

Amalie seemed to be enjoying her conversation with the amiable Nocklyn lord, which didn't particularly cheer Cammon. The visitor was describing the crops his lands yielded and the markets where he sold them.

"Do you trade with foreign merchants?" she asked, as if she was really interested.

"Sometimes with Sovenfeld," he answered. "I've been looking toward Arberharst, but I'm not sure what they produce there that would be worth the exchange."

Honey spice, Cammon thought, imagining those great fields heavy with bright red flowers.

"Honey spice, perhaps?" Amalie said in the most natural voice.

Cammon laid down his cards and stared at the partition as if he could see right through it. Did she know that? Or had she picked up the thought in his head? Valri looked at him curiously, but he was too focused on the dialogue on the other side of the screen to glance in her direction.

"I've heard of it," the Nocklyn man admitted, "but never tasted it. What's it like?"

Amalie hesitated for a second. Cammon thought, *Richer than cinnamon, and a little rougher.* Amalie said, "It's a little like cinnamon, but the flavor is a bit stronger."

Cammon felt his hands contract into fists.

"So, it's used in baking? Sweets and pastries, that sort of thing?"

And some meat dishes like chicken.

"I believe some people also use it when they're cooking poultry."

"Might be a market for it in the four corners," the Nocklyn man said. Fortunalt, Gisseltess, Brassenthwaite, and Danalustrous were the four Houses on the "corners" of Gillengaria and widely regarded as the most sophisticated of the Twelve.

You can buy it in Ghosenhall, Cammon thought, *but it's expensive.*

"There are a few specialty shops here in the city that carry it, I believe," Amalie said. "If you wanted to try it. You might ask them where they get their supplies and if they would be interested in another source."

There was a smile in the man's voice. "I'll do that—if I decide I want to expand my trading circle over the ocean."

"My father likes the idea of more foreign commerce," Amalie said, and they were off on a topic that she knew better than Cammon did. He took a deep breath, relaxed his shoulders, and turned to look at Valri again.

The queen was watching him closely, her green eyes narrowed to slits. She did not look happy. He wasn't sure what to tell her. But it was clear that, no matter what kind of magic Valri was conjuring to keep Amalie safe, it only worked in one direction. Amalie's thoughts and emotions might be cloaked from the world, hidden so expertly that even a reader like Cammon could not uncover them. But he could communicate with her. He could cast his magic like a net and let it settle invisibly over her shining hair—and Amalie welcomed its arrival, tilted back her head as if to absorb it through her skin. He wasn't sure which Valri would find more alarming—that Amalie was susceptible to enchantment, or that she delighted in it.

The instant Amalie accompanied the Nocklyn lord out of the room and the door shut behind them, Valri clutched Cammon's arm. "What did you do?" she demanded. "Were you putting thoughts in her mind? How can you do that?"

He didn't know how to play this. "I'm not exactly sure," he said cautiously. "She did seem to be picking up on some of the things I was thinking."

Valri shook his arm. "You shouldn't be able to do that. She shouldn't be able to hear you."

"Well—"

The door opened again, and Amalie came bouncing through the concealed opening into their secret corridor. "Cammon!" she exclaimed. "That was so much fun! I could *hear* you!"

Valri's face grew even more set. "Hear him? How, exactly?"

"It was as if he was standing right beside me, talking in a normal tone of voice," Amalie said blithely, while Valri's expression grew blacker. "But I knew he was speaking just to me."

Just then, the two Riders came around the corner of the narrow corridor. There were too many of them bunched inside this tiny space; it was beginning to feel ridiculous. "Majesty, do you have further need of us?" one of them asked.

Valri waved a dismissive hand. "No, thank you, you may go." They bowed, retraced their steps, and disappeared. Valri said, "We need to discuss this. Come back to the parlor with us."

Amalie led the way out, but spoke over her shoulder. "Discuss it? Why? What's wrong?"

"I don't like the notion that people can just—just—put thoughts in your head! Convince you to say any kind of crazy thing!"

Amalie laughed. "Valri, it's *Cammon*," she said. "There's nothing to worry about."

And as they paraded down the gilt hallways to Amalie's favorite room, Cammon had time to reflect on that. Was that a compliment of the highest order, or the worst possible insult?

Inside the rose-and-cream parlor, Valri turned to face the other two as if they were erring children and she a wrathful parent. But Cammon thought her expression owed more to fear than fury, and he lost the irritation that had built up along the way.

"Amalie, it disturbs me that you are open to magic—anyone's magic—even someone as benign as Cammon," she said. "It is what I have given so much of my life to protect you from."

"I can't hear her thoughts, if that's what concerns you," Cammon said. "She's still cloaked in whatever spell you've put on her."

"That's a relief, but only a small one," Valri retorted. "I want her immune from magic. I don't want it to touch her at all."

"Is that what you've been protecting her from all this time?" he asked curiously. "Why did you allow Senneth to accompany her last summer, then? Senneth used fire more than once to keep Amalie safe, and you didn't seem worried then."

"*Princess* Amalie," Valri said sharply.

Cammon felt like he had been slapped. "Princess Amalie," he corrected himself after a moment. "She has been touched by magic more than once already."

Amalie cast him a sympathetic glance but came close enough to put an arm around Valri's shoulders. Amalie was not particularly tall, but she still was bigger than the queen, and she bent her bright head over Valri's dark one as if to offer desperately needed solace. "Valri—don't worry—I just heard a few words he spoke," Amalie said. "Cammon's voice. As if we were talking. Nothing more frightening than that."

Valri was shaking her head, quick little hopeless motions. "It's all frightening," she said. "And it's only going to get worse."

Amalie glanced at Cammon again over the top of Valri's head. "Maybe I should take myself off for the rest of the day," he said.

"That might be best," Amalie said gravely, but her eyes asked for another favor.

Carefully, in case he had misunderstood, he sent a tentative question her way. *Are you angry with me?* A small smile crossed her face. She hugged Valri more tightly to her and shook her head in the negative. *Can we talk about this more later?* Her smile broadened and she nodded.

So it was with a relatively light heart that he left the room, though it had been such a strange afternoon.

H E repeated the entire story that night to the others as they gathered in Senneth and Tayse's cottage after the evening meal.

"I don't know what she's so upset about," Kirra said, unimpressed. "Cammon can make *anyone* hear him. Over great distances. Why is that so terrible? I would think it would be useful, actually, to have a way to communicate with the princess without anyone being able to overhear."

"Valri's afraid of magic," Senneth said.

"No, she isn't," Cammon objected. "Last summer, she was happy enough to have all of us guarding the princess on the road! Donnal took owl form and sat outside Amalie's window almost every night. Valri wasn't afraid then!"

"Maybe she's just afraid of *you*," Justin said with his usual sarcasm. "You're the one *I'd* pick if I had to be afraid of a mystic."

"People don't like the idea that someone else can be inside their minds," Donnal said. "I'm not sure I'd like it, either, if it wasn't Cammon. Someone I trusted."

"Yes, but she *does* trust me."

"I'm not sure a princess can ever trust anyone that much," Donnal said.

"Donnal's right," Senneth said. "All the rules are different with Amalie."

Princess Amalie, Cammon thought with some bitterness.

"I have an idea," Kirra said, eyes sparkling. "You say you can't pick up anything from Valri—can you send *her* thoughts? Maybe if she hears your voice inside her *own* head she'll realize how unalarming you are, and she'll relax."

This was clearly designed to be nothing more than mischief. Tayse gave her a reproving look and said, "I think Cammon has other kinds of magic to spend his energy on. Have you and Donnal had time to work with Ellynor to try and penetrate her shadows?"

"Not yet. Amalie has needed me every day. But Jerril comes tomorrow and we'll practice then."

Kirra said, "I want to watch this."

Tayse looked amused. "Good. All of you. Work out with your magical weapons the way the Riders work out with their blades."

Senneth sighed elaborately. "If only it were that easy."

THE following day was sunny and extremely cold—except where all the mystics had gathered, in a neglected garden overgrown with rustling brown winter vegetation. Kirra, who had been complaining loudly about the chill during the whole walk from the cottage, now pulled off her cloak and threw it dramatically to the ground.

"I *love* being in Senneth's entourage!" she exclaimed, for of course it was Senneth's magic that had warmed the air around them. "I'm like a cat that always wants to sprawl in the sun. I'm not happy in the cold."

Ellynor laughed softly. "I thought maybe we were just sheltered from the wind, and I was grateful. I didn't realize."

"Best winters of my life were the ones Senneth lived with us," Jerril said, smiling in his dreamy way at the memory. "Never had to chop a cord of wood, and the house was warm no matter what the temperature was outside."

Senneth had dropped to the ground and used her own cloak to make a cushion against the stone wall. "I'm just here as a spectator," she said with a grin. "I may as well pay for my entertainment somehow."

"Well, let's get started," Jerril said, nodding his bald head. "Who is participating today?"

Donnal, who had padded to the garden in the guise of a black hound, wagged his tail and offered a short bark. "Donnal. Ellynor. Me," Cammon said. "Kirra?"

She shook her head and settled on the ground next to Senneth, her back to the wall. "Maybe later. First I want to watch."

"We should have brought snacks," Senneth said. "It's like watching a troupe of actors."

"Even more fun, I hope," Kirra said.

Jerril didn't even throw them a look of annoyance, as Cammon did. "Ellynor, forgive me, I don't yet know what you're capable of," the older mystic said. "Why don't you go out the gate, wait a few minutes, and then enter at your leisure—circle the garden once—and see how quickly we're able to spot your presence?"

Ellynor was trying not to smile. "All right."

"Oh, I was wrong," Kirra said. "That doesn't sound fun at all."

Ellynor disappeared through the gate, though she left it standing wide behind her. "We shouldn't watch her entry point," Jerril said. "After all, if she were to come upon us unawares on the street, we would have no idea which direction she would be approaching from."

Cammon obligingly turned his back to the gate but said, "I have a feeling it won't matter." Donnal, who had also faced the other direction, thumped his tail against the ground.

"Should we try to distract them, you think?" Kirra asked. "Tell jokes, sing bawdy songs?"

"I don't know any bawdy songs," Senneth said.

"Oh, I know plenty." Kirra lifted her voice and proceeded to offer what sounded like a sailor's ditty. *"I knew five girls in Fortunalt / Lived by the sea and loved the salt. / One had bosoms flat and thin / Throw her in the water, she couldn't swim—"*

"Why are they always about women, these bawdy songs?" Senneth asked. "Why aren't there awful little melodies about men?"

"Wait. Give me a minute," Kirra said. "*I knew five men from Forten City / Three were dumb and one was pretty. / One said, 'Girl, won't you give me a lick? / I've sprinkled saltwater on—*'"

Senneth slapped her hand over Kirra's mouth. "Just when I think it's safe to introduce you to my friends—"

Jerril, of course, was not offended. "She's a serramarra?" he asked. When Cammon nodded, he added, "She doesn't exhibit the behavior I would expect from the aristocracy."

"Kirra never really does what anybody expects," Cammon replied.

"She has a lot of power, though," Jerril said. "I can sense it. Full of a wild magic."

"'Wild' about covers it," Cammon agreed.

"But I'm having a hard time getting any sense of Ellynor," Jerril added.

"You can when she's in a room with Justin," Cammon said with a grin. "But when Justin's not around—" He shook his head. "She might as well not exist. I can't feel her at all."

"No," Jerril said. "I can't even tell if she's entered the garden yet. I feel certain she has, and yet I cannot pick up any telltale traces of her."

Cammon nudged Donnal with his foot. "Can you scent her?" he asked. Donnal lifted his black nose and sniffed the air, then quirked his ears back. Nothing. "Maybe she's still outside the gate. Maybe she just walked away."

And then it was as if there was a rent in the air—as if the sky itself blinked—and Ellynor was standing right before them. Jerril was so surprised he took a step backward. Donnal yelped and scrambled to his feet, then frisked around her knees, snuffling at her skirt.

"Now that *was* entertaining," Kirra called out.

Cammon was smiling and shaking his head. "How do you *do* that? I'm looking for you, and I can't tell you're there."

She was smiling, pleased with herself. She bent down to stroke Donnal's head. "I used to be able to conceal myself only at night. But now I've found that the magic works in daylight, too." She shrugged. "I don't know why."

Cammon glanced at Jerril. "And I have no idea how to countermand her magic," he said. "How can we even practice?"

Jerril looked intrigued. "This will take some experimentation," he said. "Ellynor, will you indulge us? Can you assume your cloaks as we're standing here watching you?"

She tilted her head to one side. Her long dark hair was braided and wrapped around her head, but here and there Cammon could see the blonder markings of her clan pattern dyed into the black. She looked very neat and compact and serious. "I think so."

"Cammon, focus on her," Jerril directed. "Ellynor—disappear."

Before their very eyes, Ellynor seemed to drop into a well of shadows, which smoothed away and left only ordinary sunlight behind.

"*I* want to do that," Senneth exclaimed. "Next time I'm invited to dinner at the king's table."

Cammon was staring at the place where she'd been but was completely unable to tell if she was still there. Donnal, however, had grown alert. His pointed nose swung in a slow circle as if he tracked a particularly tasty piece of game.

"Donnal, can you find her?" Jerril asked in a quiet voice. "Show us."

Donnal bounded forward and made a low leap, and suddenly he and Ellynor were tussling on the ground. Ellynor was laughing as she tried to dodge his tongue. "That's not fair! I can't outrun him." She pushed Donnal aside and rose gracefully to her feet. "I thought the dog might be more difficult to trick than the mystic."

"But we want Donnal to be able to pick you out even when he doesn't know where you are," Jerril said.

"I can't pick her out even when I do," Cammon said gloomily.

"Concentrate on the spaces around her," Jerril suggested. "When she takes a step, she disturbs the shrubs, the vines—the birds, the squirrels. See if you can sense the disruption she causes in the world, if you can't sense her."

Cammon widened his eyes. "That's awfully subtle."

Jerril smiled. "It's a delicate magic."

They spent the next two hours hunting for Ellynor. Donnal experienced significantly more success than Cammon did, and even he could only find her three times out of seven. Jerril had Ellynor increase her magic by stages, gradually becoming less and less perceptible to the others, and that was a fascinating exercise. Like lifting weights that were successively heavier, Cammon thought. The last round had been possible, so surely the next one should be as well—but there was a point at which he could discern her, and a point at which he could not, and not all his straining changed that.

All of them were exhausted by the end of two hours of effort. Well, not Senneth and Kirra—they had stayed comfortable and lazy against the wall, calling out derision or encouragement as the mood took them.

Jerril finally said, "I think we've had enough for the day. I'll come back tomorrow and the day after that, and we'll work on this some more."

"I want to try one more thing," Cammon said, and he pulled Ellynor over to whisper in her ear. Three minutes later, the Lirren girl had crept invisibly over to the wall and dumped a canteen of water on the other two women.

Kirra shrieked and melted into lioness shape, leaping straight through the dead shrubbery for Cammon. He ran, of course, but she caught him in three steps, and they tumbled on the ground together until she stilled him completely by standing with her great golden paws heavy on his chest. She stared down at him with liquid blue eyes—Kirra's eyes even in the cat's shape, or maybe it was just that Cammon still saw her as Kirra—and yowled in triumph.

"Bite him!" Senneth was shouting. "Have him for dinner!" But, instead, Kirra just dropped her head and ran her rough tongue across his face, practically lifting off his skin. Then she jumped down and loped to Donnal's side.

Jerril helped Cammon up. "She *is* impressive," he said. "One hears stories about Kirra Danalustrous, but to see her up close like that—well."

Cammon brushed off his clothes and grinned. "No one quite like her."

Jerril's eyes wandered thoughtfully over the whole group: Senneth still lounging on the ground, Ellynor now corporeal and kneeling beside her, Kirra and Donnal chasing each other across the width of the garden and back. "It's quite a group of friends you've gathered," the older man said. "With an astonishing array of powers."

"Senneth gathered us," Cammon said. "And Justin and Tayse."

"Yes," Jerril said, "Senneth was always good at knowing what was valuable. She just didn't used to be so good at keeping the things and people that mattered to her. I am glad to see that she has learned to hold on."

Cammon laughed. "Or maybe we're the ones who've learned to hold on to her."

Jerril smiled. "The result is excellent, either way."

CHAPTER

12

ELLYNOR had been at the palace for just over a week before she had an audience with the king. Justin told Cammon that Baryn always made a point of introducing himself to the Riders' brides because, as he said, "If these women are competing with me for my Riders' attention, I should at least know what they look like."

Justin escorted Ellynor to a semiformal room, all dark blue and bright gilt. Cammon followed, curious to see how the meeting would go. The king waited in a high-backed chair only a little less imposing than his throne, and Valri and Amalie sat on either side of him. Baryn and Amalie wore welcoming smiles, but Valri looked brooding and just a little on edge.

Justin shepherded Ellynor to the king's chair and offered a Rider's deep bow, right fist to left shoulder, and pulled Ellynor down in a curtsey beside him. Ellynor looked particularly pretty this day, Cammon thought, for she was wearing a midnight-blue dress that matched her eyes and her face was flushed with color. Her black hair was unbound and flowed down her back so that everyone could see those stylized clan markings dyed into it. Coming to a halt behind Ellynor, Cammon studied the pattern, which looked a bit like a flower, a bird, and a scythe, repeated in rows down the whole river of her hair.

"Liege, may I present to you Ellynor Alowa, of the Domen *sebahta* and the Lahja *sebahta-ris*, and lately made my wife," Justin said, rising. Cammon had heard Justin rehearse this about a hundred times last night, and he didn't mispronounce a single syllable now. "I hope you will welcome her to Ghosenhall."

"And so I do," Baryn said, holding out his hands. Ellynor stepped forward and laid her hands in his, and he kissed them before releasing her. "How is it that you found a way to tame my most ferocious Rider, Ellynor Alowa? I didn't think Justin would ever be won over."

Ellynor blushed and glanced at Justin. "He's won *me* over, sire."

"Ah, well, there is no resisting Justin," Baryn said with a smile. "If he set his heart on you, you would have no choice in the matter." Justin laughed aloud and Ellynor blushed even more deeply. His smile broadening, Baryn made a graceful gesture at Amalie. "Let me also introduce you to my daughter, Amalie, who is just as pleased to meet you as I am."

Ellynor made another curtsey, but Amalie drew her forward and kissed her on the cheek. "I think you're brave to marry a Rider," the princess said. "They're very fierce."

"Justin isn't always fierce," Ellynor replied, and then she blushed again.

Baryn was trying not to laugh. "And let me present Valri, my wife and my queen."

Ellynor's curtsey to Valri was a little more shallow and she did not drop her eyes as she had when she met the other two. Valri's own eyes coolly assessed this new arrival. It struck Cammon now—as it should have struck him before, except he always wasted so little attention on people's outward appearances—that there was a definite similarity between the two women. Not so much their coloring, though they both had black hair, but their essences. They were both watchful and still, secretive and serene. They both looked as if they had been blessed, or burdened, with complex knowledge that was difficult to handle but too sacred to share.

They knew each other. Despite being unable to read either one of them, Cammon could tell that as soon as their eyes met. He picked up a sense of disquiet from Justin, though the Rider kept his face completely impassive. So Justin, too, realized that these women were not strangers to each other. Ellynor had perhaps confided in him something of Valri's history. Which Cammon would dearly love to know—he had no information beyond the fact that Valri was Lirren and *bahta-lo.*

"Ellynor. It is good to see you again," Valri said calmly.

"Yes, and very good to see you, too," Ellynor replied. "You have traveled far from home, but you seem to have prospered."

"Though I miss that home, and all my kin," Valri said. "You shall have to spend an hour with me someday and tell me tales of the land across the mountains."

"So is the secret to be revealed, then?" Baryn asked his queen in a gentle voice. "No more pretense? I know how much you have missed your family and your friends, and to have another Lirren girl nearby—well, I would imagine you would greatly enjoy a chance to make her your friend."

Valri gazed over at him with her bright green eyes. The rest of them stayed absolutely motionless, too surprised to speak. "It is up to you," she said quietly. "Whatever you think is best."

"We have so little reason to continue any fiction about what your background might be," Baryn said. "It seems we will have enemies no matter how carefully you are presented. So let us tell the world you are Lirren-born, and let us see what they make of that."

The permission did not seem to make Valri relax any, Cammon thought. "They will find a way to use the information against you," she said.

"They'll call her a mystic, too," Cammon said, entering the conversation between royals without permission. Justin gave him a minatory look, but Baryn did not seem offended.

Nor did Valri. "They say it already," the queen replied.

"People in Gillengaria don't understand the Lirrenfolk or their powers," Ellynor said. "If some of us have magic, it is not a kind of magic they can grasp. They might call you a mystic but unless you are commanding fire or changing shapes, they will have no idea what exactly you can do. And that may keep you safe."

"That is very good reasoning," Baryn said in an approving voice. "Justin, I like this girl already. Plus, of course, I have to commend your good taste in choosing someone from the Lirrens."

Justin gave the king another deep bow, his right fist pressed to his opposite shoulder. "Sire, I loved her before I knew her heritage."

Some of the habitual darkness left Valri's face as she smiled at the newlywed couple. "So tell us the story of your wooing," she said. "And the happy ending! Such a rare thing for a Lirren girl who looks to take a groom from across the Lireth Mountains."

This was a signal to bring in more chairs and call for refreshments, and soon Justin and Ellynor were vying with each other to repeat the details of their romance. Amalie loved the tale, Cammon could tell, though she was horrified by Justin's very near brush with death. Cammon was more interested in the account of their trip across the mountains for Justin to meet Ellynor's family—particularly her quarrelsome brothers.

Justin was laughing. "Luckily, I had healed up well enough by then, because a couple of times a day someone was challenging me to a duel, or a footrace, or a wrestling match. Ellynor had told me I had to beat everyone at every contest—"

"I didn't say you had to win *every* time."

"So I did, but, let me tell you, I've had workouts with other Riders that weren't as punishing over the course of a week."

Valri, who had seemed to thoroughly enjoy the tale so far, now grew suddenly tense again, or so it seemed to Cammon. "And your family?" she asked Ellynor in a tight voice. "They are all well?"

Cammon noticed that Ellynor met her eyes straightly, seeming to acknowledge some unspoken question. "All of them—my brothers, my cousins, my parents—all the ones you know, all of them healthy and unchanged."

Valri took a quick breath and then folded her lips together as if to keep from speaking. Cammon saw Justin's eyes narrow and thought, *He knows something.* Baryn and Amalie did not seem to notice. The king said, "So you arrived a week or so ago, I believe. Did the Riders welcome you and treat you kindly?"

Justin laughed at that. "Most kindly," he said with a grin. "Quite a welcome."

Baryn smiled. "I suspect a story there," he said.

"None worth telling," Justin replied, still grinning.

The king asked Ellynor, "And what do you make of Ghosenhall?"

"I haven't seen much of the city yet, but I think it's beautiful."

There was a knock on the door and Milo entered, bowed, and gave the king a significant glance. Baryn nodded and rose to his feet. "I have another appointment and I must go. Ellynor, my dear, I am so glad you have joined our family. Justin, of course you realize that officially I am devastated that you have chosen to take a wife, but in private may I say you seem to have made a magnificent choice. Stop by and see Milo before you leave. He will have something to give you—a small gift from me to start you in your wedded life." He kissed Amalie on top of her head, Valri on the cheek. "My dears. I will see you later." And he left the room behind Milo.

Justin was instantly on his feet. "And I must get back to the training yard. I'm still recovering some of the skills I lost on the road. Ellynor—"

"Perhaps she will stay and visit with me awhile," Valri said.

"Gladly."

Even Amalie could tell that the two countrywomen wanted to speak in private. "Cammon," said the princess, "I have something to show you in my study. Why don't you come with me for a moment?"

He did.

And so, for the first time since he had known Amalie, Cammon was alone with the princess.

"W HAT'S in your study?" Cammon asked as they stepped into the room.

"My cloak," Amalie said. "It's cold out and I want to take a walk."

"Without Valri? She won't like that."

Amalie gave him a look that was pure mischief. One of the rare occasions when she looked as young as she really was.

"She will be too delighted to talk to Ellynor to even notice that I'm not in the room. By the time she remembers, I'll be back here, sitting demurely before the fire and confessing to a day of boredom."

Cammon was hardly one to urge anyone to more proper behavior. "Well, let me grab my own coat and we can sneak out the kitchen."

"Meet me back here as quickly as you can."

He did, and found Amalie transformed. She had covered her bright hair with a dull woolen scarf, and her cloak was so plain it could have been borrowed from a maid who possessed neither money nor fashion sense. She had also donned what looked like a pair of her father's spectacles, but she allowed them to perch on the end of her nose so she could peer over the tops of the lenses.

"What do you think?" she asked. "A good disguise?"

He felt his first twinge of unease. "Are you planning to go onto the streets of Ghosenhall? Because I'm not sure that's a good idea."

"I wish I could! But, no, I'll stay safe within the palace walls. I just want to—walk around the grounds a bit without anyone knowing who I am."

"Then let's go."

It was relatively easy for Cammon to get them out of the building unseen. He didn't have Ellynor's trick of concealment, of course, but he had no trouble sensing when the rooms and hallways ahead of them were clear of people and safe to traverse. More than once he had to whisk them into an unoccupied room to avoid a contingent of servants, and on these occasions he and Amalie plastered themselves against the wall and tried to keep from laughing.

Finally they had ducked through a side door to avoid all the cooks in the kitchen and found themselves outside in the cold afternoon sun. "Where to?" Cammon asked.

"The training yard," she answered without hesitation. "I want to watch the Riders working out."

She wasn't the only one. A dozen or so spectators gathered around the fence rails surrounding the yard, watching in fascination as the Riders practiced their swings and blows. The rest of them looked like tourists in the royal city for a special visit—wealthy merchants and their well-dressed wives, their envious sons, their teenage daughters who sighed and giggled over the Riders' splendid physiques. None of them paid any attention to Amalie.

She climbed up the bottom rung of the fence and hung over the top, absorbed in the mock combat. "Tell me who is who," she commanded, so Cammon stepped up beside her and gave a running commentary.

"That's Tir, the oldest of the Riders. Tayse's father. See how he wields the sword? He's not as powerful as he used to be, but he's tricky. Almost no one can beat him. Over there is Wen. She's small and she's not as strong as some of the men, but she's fast. And she can outshoot any of them with a bow. She's fighting with Justin, so she's going to go down in about a minute."

"Does Justin always win?"

"Just about."

"Who's the best? Of all the Riders?"

"Tayse," he answered without hesitation.

"And nobody can beat him?"

"Oh, sure. Now and then someone brings him down—usually Tir or Coeval, and sometimes Justin. But not very often. And never twice in a row."

For a moment she stood in silence, watching over the rims of her spectacles. "I'm supposed to know them all," she said. "My father does. He knows their names and their stories and whether they're married and whether they've been injured and—and—what they're like. Who they are. I only know a few of them, especially those who were with us last summer—Tayse and Justin and Coeval and Hammond. And Senneth."

"Well," Cammon said, "Senneth isn't exactly a Rider."

Amalie pointed to where Senneth was trading blows with Hammond. "She's training with them."

"I've trained with the Riders, too, and that doesn't make me one of them."

She gave him a quick appraising glance out of those lively brown eyes. "Are you any good?"

He laughed. "Not really. But Tayse says I'm getting better."

She returned her attention to the field. "I should get to know them all."

"I'm sure they'd welcome that. I'll ask Tayse to arrange it."

She nodded and then lapsed into silence again. Cammon could feel her intense interest in the activities on the field. Her mind swooped with the swing of a sword blade, dove to the wrestlers in the mud, lifted with the arrows being shot at targets on the other edge of the yard. She was pleased and excited and absorbed and impressed; she saw the activity before her as a combination of poetry and practicality. She missed neither the sheer beauty of the physical motion nor the deadly necessity behind the exercise.

For a moment Cammon's hands tightened on the top rail of the fence. He could sense Amalie. He could *read* her. Valri's cloaking magic had been lifted and Amalie was like a sunlit golden room he could simply stroll inside. He stood at the open doorway, dazzled by what he could glimpse from the threshold. Bright intelligence, swift comprehension, limitless fascination with the world around her. Her mind was like a darting bird too delighted with the bounty before it to want to settle. He could see it, flashing from window to window inside the illuminated chamber of her skull.

He closed his eyes and willed himself to walk away.

This was what Valri was protecting Amalie from, nasty intrusive strangers who would stomp all over those unmarred golden vistas, who would peer inside her and try to read her or try to rearrange her. Valri was protecting Amalie from *him*, from people like him, anyway, readers or, no—people who wanted to invade or dismantle that alluring, untouched space. Amalie was too open, too impressionable, and Valri knew it, and that was why Valri had been so afraid when Amalie could hear the words that Cammon sent her way. What other influences would Amalie succumb to, how could she ever be safe?

Cammon turned his head and put walls up around his own mind and felt himself hunker down behind their shadows.

Amalie touched his arm. "What's wrong?" she asked. Her face was creased with concern.

He made himself smile and shake his head. "Nothing. I'm just hoping Tayse doesn't see me, or he'll want to drag me over the fence and make me practice swordplay. He thinks I don't work out nearly as often as I should."

She smiled, but a trace of worry lingered, as if she knew he was lying. "If that happens, I'll have to throw off my disguise and play the haughty princess. 'I have commanded this man to wait on *me*, Rider, and you will not drag him from my side.'"

"Oh, yes, that tone of voice would make even Tayse back down."

When she had had her fill of watching warfare, they promenaded through a few of the gardens. Despite the sunshine, the cold had chased everyone else inside; they had every path and enclosure to themselves. All the flowers were dead, of course, but some of the hedges retained their color, and the naked trees offered a variety of fantastical shapes with their trailing limbs and supplicating, upraised branches. Cammon and Amalie wandered through the sculpture park, where past kings and queens of Gillengaria struck marble poses and gazed down with forbidding, displeased expressions.

"If I ever have my statue done, it's going to show me smiling," Amalie said. She paused beside a representation of some former queen, whose face could hardly have been more grim, and stretched her arms wide in a welcome gesture. She had taken off her father's glasses so her face was completely bare, completely open, covered only with a smile. "I'm going to be bending down a little, like I'm getting ready to kiss a child on the cheek. I'm going to look *happy*. People will want to come visit *my* statue, and maybe leave offerings for birds and squirrels at my feet."

Cammon couldn't help smiling at that. He was recovering some of his usual insouciance, though he was still being careful to keep his curious mind in check. "Maybe by the time you're old, and you've been ruling for fifty years, you'll be feeling a little more grumpy."

She laughed. "So maybe I should commission my statue now."

Before the war comes, he thought. *While there is still a hope that you will take the throne.*

"I will," she said calmly. "The Riders and the mystics will keep me safe."

He stared at her, completely nonplussed, for it was not a thought he had intended her to overhear. "Majesty—" he said. "I'm sorry."

She placed her fingertips against the smooth bole of a skinny birch, as if feeling for a pulse in its narrow trunk. "Sorry for what? For worrying that war might snatch the crown from my family? You're hardly the only one."

"I shouldn't—I didn't mean—I'm sorry that I didn't keep my thoughts to myself."

She flattened her palm against the tree and looked at him over her shoulder. The wool scarf had slipped a little, and her red-gold hair made a halo around her shrouded face. "But before. When the Nocklyn lord was talking to me. You sent me thoughts on purpose."

"I did *that* time. I haven't tried to do it since! I'm not sure it's a good thing that you can hear me when I don't want to be overheard. Let me see if I can shield my thoughts from you now when I'm really trying."

He shut his mind down, staring at her in concentration. *I wonder what Senneth will make of this conversation*, he thought, willing the words to stay locked inside his own head. *She will not like it any more than Valri would, but I'm certainly not telling the queen.*

Amalie tilted her head as if listening, but looked disappointed. "No. Nothing."

He smiled. "Well, that's a relief."

"Not to me," she said. "I like to hear you thinking. It makes me feel like—like—there is someone else in the world."

He was troubled, and that was a rare state for Cammon. "Majesty, I'm pretty sure the queen would say you should be looking to other people to keep you company."

She tilted her head to one side, considering that. "Valri likes you."

"I think so. But that doesn't mean she thinks I'm suitable to be your friend."

Amalie shrugged, dropped her hand, and started kicking her way down the leaf-strewn path. Cammon fell in step beside her. "But *you* want to be my friend," she said.

He couldn't help himself. He smiled at that. "Oh, I do. But scruffy mystics with no family connections don't get to pick princesses as their friends."

Amalie smiled, too. "But, you see, I *am* the princess. I get to order people to do what I say. And I say, 'Cammon, I want you to be my companion.' What can you do about it? Nothing. You have to obey."

He gave up. He didn't particularly want to keep his distance anyway. "Well, good. And if Valri and Milo tell me I have to stay away, I won't listen to them. Only if *you* tell me."

"So I want you to entertain me at dinner," she said.

"Entertain you how? At the *formal* dinners? With your father and all the nobles present?"

She nodded. "Those dinners. Particularly when one of my suitors is present. I want you to tell me stories." She glanced at him. "With your mind. Put the stories in my head."

He tried not to laugh. "Won't that make it hard for you to concentrate on the conversation?"

"We'll work out a signal. I'll touch my left earring if I'm bored and want you to talk to me, and I'll touch my right earring if I want you to be quiet."

It was a terrible idea. Valri would flay him alive if he agreed, and Senneth would not be even slightly amused. Kirra would think it a delightful plan, but Kirra was hardly a role model for anybody. "Majesty—"

She took a lofty tone. "I command you. You have to do what I say."

He felt, for a moment, like a swimmer resisting a strong current—and then he put his head under and succumbed. "Well, then, I will. I don't know how entertaining any of my stories are, though."

"You can make disparaging comments about my suitors," she said. "Make fun of their hair or their clothes."

"I'm really the wrong one to talk about how other people look."

"And you can let me know when they're lying. Right there at the dinner table."

"And then you'll challenge them, I suppose. 'Not true, ser. You only own half that many horses.'"

She grinned. "You think it would make conversation awkward? I won't say anything. But I'd like to know."

"All right, then. I'll tell you whenever I pick up anything interesting from their thoughts." He glanced at her. "Valri won't like it."

She gave him an angelic smile. "Valri won't know."

He glanced over his shoulder, as if expecting the queen to appear any minute, anxious and scolding. "She's probably looking for you right now. Are you cold? Do you want to go in?"

She shook her head. "I want to see the raelynx."

He was pleased. "You do? I love to visit him. I've never seen you there."

She turned and led him in the direction of the big cat's private enclosure. "I used to go with Valri almost every day. These past few weeks I've scarcely had a moment to myself, so I haven't been. I wonder if he'll have forgotten me."

Someone was coming up the pathway. Cammon touched her arm, put his finger to his lips, and drew her aside. Like children, they hid behind a springy yew until the solitary gardener had passed by, then they grinned at each other and scampered on down the path.

"What does Valri plan to do with him?" he asked. "Does she really think she can keep him here forever?"

Amalie was silent a moment. "I hope so. I've grown attached to him. I would hate to see him returned to the Lirrens, even though that's where he belongs."

"He's not a pet, you know. He can't be gentled like a horse."

"I know. Valri told me."

He glanced at her. "But you'd like to try."

She shrugged and didn't answer.

It took them almost fifteen minutes to cross the compound to the garden where the raelynx was imprisoned. From thirty yards away, Cammon could sense its restless, hungry presence. Violence and motion wrapped in a package of exquisite beauty. It was like fire or wind or something elemental. Not just inhuman—bordering on divine.

It was aware of their approach, too, and by the time they made it to the gate it had padded over to press its square nose against the bars. As when he had been here with Valri, Cammon sensed an unexpected emotion at the forefront of the cat's mind. He strove to identify it while he watched Amalie step up to the gate and circle her fingers around the bars.

Remembrance. Recognition.

"Be careful," he said. "He can bite your hand off."

"He won't," she said, and stroked her index finger down the red fur of his nose.

Hard to believe that there was anyone in the world that *Cammon* would find himself urging to caution. "Majesty. Be *careful.*"

For an answer, she slipped one hand between the rods and scratched under the red chin, extended for just that purpose. With her other hand, she reached through and slowly pulled the tufted ears through her fingers.

Cammon was afraid to move, afraid to startle the creature into sudden brutal movement. "Amalie. Stop. *Amalie.*"

The raelynx began to purr.

It was a dark rumbling sound, so deep and throaty it might almost be a growl of warning. Except its eyes were closed and its flicking tail was stilled and the emotion emanating from its wild heart was even stronger, and even stranger.

Affection.

The raelynx knew the princess and, in the most primitive fashion, loved her.

"Just how much time did you and Valri spend down here in the past year?" he asked in a low voice.

She gave him a quick flashing smile and pulled her hands back, which filled him with overwhelming relief. "All told, days and days," she said. "I thought he would remember me."

And before Cammon truly realized what she was about, she pulled a key from her pocket, opened the locked gate, and stepped inside the garden.

CHAPTER

13

CAMMON was ossified with horror.

Standing there like one of those grim statues of her forebears, he watched Amalie crouch to the ground before the raelynx and rub her fingers over the brushy fur of its face. Its purr intensified; the ground itself seemed to shake with the sound. The raelynx turned its head to catch Amalie's wrist between its teeth, and Cammon's heart exploded, but the cat was playing. It nipped her skin, then ran its rough tongue down the length of her forearm. *That* hurt; Cammon felt Amalie's sudden pain spike through her bubbling delight. But she didn't cry out or jerk away. Instead she bent down and pressed her nose against the cat's and ruffled the fur on either side of its face.

Cammon couldn't even speak, but his mind was frantic. *Amalie. Amalie. He could kill you with a swipe of his paw.*

He had not expected an answer, but it came, wordless but clear, a projection of calm and well-being. She was not afraid. The big animal trusted her, and she trusted it in return. There was nothing to fear.

He stood there, terrified, unmoving, trying to think, trying to determine what to do. Should he call for Senneth? Would she be able to force the raelynx away from the princess, step by snarling step? Should he call for the Riders, send Tayse and Justin racing through the compound with swords uplifted? A raelynx could not be killed by human hands—that was almost axiomatic—but two Riders wielding flashing blades could probably make the creature back away, hissing and shrieking with fury, allowing Amalie time to escape.

Should he push himself through the gate, try to draw attention from Amalie, or would that only excite the beast to sudden violence? He had controlled the raelynx with some success during their trip through Gillengaria last winter. Could he, if the beast suddenly attacked Amalie, regain that control, drive it away from her? Not in time, surely not in time. It would just take a second, a moment of malice, a spurt of rage, and the raelynx could spill Amalie's blood almost without effort.

He must take control now, he must ease the animal away. Slowly, with infinite mental stealth, he crept up on the creature's mind, like a hunter tracking the most devious prey. He would throw the noose of his will around the raelynx's consciousness, tighten it like a choke collar—be prepared for the inevitable furious fight—and hold on. Hold on. He was close, he was almost there, he could slip past those dark and deadly eyes—

But Amalie was there before him. Inside the creature's head. Strolling beside it down a springtime path, an insubstantial leash looped carelessly around one hand.

Not even Senneth had been able to hold the cat so completely in thrall.

"Amalie," he said out loud, his voice strangled, "what have you done?"

She didn't answer, but then, he imagined she was expending all her energy merely to keep the cat quiescent. How had she learned this trick? Through Valri, obviously, but how had she learned it so well? If Valri had the same degree of power over the raelynx, she certainly hadn't demonstrated it the other day. Amalie had an ability that superseded even Senneth's, even the queen's.

The cat had chosen to give her mastery. There was no other explanation. It loved her, and it had submitted.

Cammon hadn't thought such a thing was possible.

Slowly he dropped to his knees on the other side of the gate. Amalie was sitting on the ground now, clearly settled in for a while. The cat butted its red head against her shoulder, demanding more attention. Amalie smiled and began running her hands down its rough fur, picking out burrs and stray bits of bark. "How long has he been like this?" Cammon asked, quietly now, no longer afraid. "How did this happen?"

She glanced at him, half smiling, sensing his change in mood. "I don't know how it happened. One day he didn't care much for me—he would pace and growl and let out this furious scream whenever I came by—"

"I've heard that scream," he said.

"And then one day he liked me. But it was weeks before he allowed me to touch him. And months before I felt safe to come inside. But the first time I did, it was like this. He lay on the ground before me and started this *thunderous* purring. And we have trusted each other ever since." She gave Cammon a serious look. "I'm not sure he *can* go back to the Lirrens now. He's been spoiled—he might not be able to survive. If he doesn't fear me, perhaps he won't fear hunters and other men who wish to harm him. He could be trapped or killed."

"He doesn't seem to have lost any of his basic hatred for other people," Cammon said dryly. "It's only you he trusts."

"It seems like he's not afraid of *you*."

"Maybe not, but he'd eat me if he could."

She laughed softly. "Oh, I couldn't let him do that."

"Does Valri know that you can do this?" he asked.

She shook her head. "She would be almost as afraid as you are. I can't tell you how many times she's warned me—just like you did!—that a raelynx can't be tamed."

"She's probably right. If he wasn't inside that gate—"

"I want to open it and let him out. Just to see."

"*Majesty*. No, no, no, don't even think of it."

She gave him a quick frowning look. "You called me Amalie a moment before."

"I was trying to keep you from getting killed," he said. "When you're not in mortal danger, I think I can remember to use your title."

"I like it when you call me by name."

"Well, Valri doesn't."

"Well, Valri doesn't have to know."

"Then, Amalie, can I just say it would be a very bad idea to let the raelynx out? If you *can't* control it, and you *can't* get it back inside the gate, it could spend the next thirty years slowly killing off all the inhabitants of the palace. Not even the Riders would be able to hunt it. It would survive here till it died a natural death. No one would come to visit for fear of being eaten. Your father would have to abandon the palace and take up residence somewhere else. The Riders would have nowhere to train, and they'd grow fat and sloppy, and pretty soon no one would be afraid of them. And then Halchon Gisseltess would come sweeping in from the south, and take over the whole city, and you'd be forced to marry one of his ugly cousins, and see what you'd have done? Just because you wanted to set the raelynx free?"

His tone had gotten lighter as his threat had gotten sillier, and she was laughing by the time he was done. "I suppose you're right," she said meekly. "He must stay locked up. But I wish he could come keep me company in the palace. I'd like to have him sleeping at my feet at night. I'd be safe then, don't you think? No one would dare try to break in and murder me if the raelynx was watching over me."

He had to agree. But. "That's one of the reasons I'm there," he said. "To make sure trouble doesn't come creeping up on you by night."

She gave the raelynx a final pat on the head, came to her feet, and slipped outside the gate. Cammon had to admit to a profound feeling of relief when she keyed the lock, and the raelynx was still in the enclosure. "Yes," she said, giving him a sunny smile, "I do feel safe knowing you're nearby. Maybe I should keep *you* in a walled garden so you can't ever leave."

The image this conjured up was so vivid that for a moment he couldn't think of how to answer. He glanced down at her, his mouth open as if he would speak, but no words came out. The truth was, he thought, feeling humble, feeling stupid, he didn't think he would mind any more than the raelynx did being kept in perpetual service to the princess. "Men generally don't make very good pets," he said at last, and she went off in a peal of laughter.

"Didn't you say that about the raelynx?" she said.

He managed a grin. "And it's still true, whatever you may think."

They didn't speak for most of the walk back to the palace, being engaged in dodging the attention of servants and soldiers and random couriers off to deliver messages. They made it inside unseen and crept carefully down the passageways toward Amalie's favorite parlor. Valri was inside and sick with worry. It was the first time Cammon had ever been able to pick up her presence without a visual cue, and that underscored for him how alarmed she was to know Amalie had spent the day with him unattended.

"I don't think I should go in," he said in a low voice. "Valri's here, and I don't think she's happy with me."

Amalie nodded but put a hand on his arm to stop him from turning away. "I was only joking, you know," she said.

"About what?"

"I would never try to keep you here against your will. You or anybody. I wouldn't want to."

That brought his grin back, and he attempted to copy the sweeping bow that Justin and Tayse were so good at, right fist to his left shoulder in a gesture of utter fealty. "Majesty," he whispered, "I live to serve."

HE didn't want to tell the story to anybody but Senneth, so he waited until very late before heading down to the Riders' cottages after dinner. She was standing outside, seeming not at all uncomfortable with the late hour, the bitter cold, or the unconventional summons.

"What's wrong?" she asked.

"It's freezing. Can we go inside?"

"Tayse is awake. If you don't mind if he hears—"

He shook his head, shoved his hands in his pockets, and started walking. She fell in step beside him, and almost instantly he started to feel warmer. He felt his shoulders unclench a little as the chill was chased away by her burning magic.

"So tell me what's happened that has you running out in the middle of the night to confide in me," she said. She sounded quite cheerful; clearly she had not had the kind of day *he* had. "I might know the secret already, though, for Justin came back from his audience with the king to tell us that Valri has confessed to being Lirren-born."

"That's not what I came to tell you, but it *was* a pretty interesting moment," Cammon said. "What did Justin say? Was he shocked?"

"Apparently not. Relieved, actually. Ellynor had told him while they were in the Lirrens, but then made him promise not to tell anyone. Justin said he'd never had to keep a secret from Tayse before and wasn't sure how long he could do it."

"Were *you* surprised?"

She waggled her head from side to side to show uncertainty. "Yes and no. Well, there's always been something strange about Valri! And I'll confess that once or twice I wondered if she was from the Lirrens, but it just seemed so improbable that I put the thought aside. Still, it explains so much about her, down to the fact that you've never been able to read her. I confess, to some extent, I was relieved, too. This is the kind of secret I don't mind so much. I have no quarrel with the Lirrenfolk." Still walking, she glanced over at him. "But if that's not what you wanted to tell me, what is it?"

"Well, Valri's part of the story. Remember how, when we were traveling last year, Valri never let Amalie out her sight?"

"Hard to forget that."

"It's still that way. Every time I'm in the room with Amalie, Valri's there. She told me once that she's protecting Amalie. But, of course, we thought *we* were the ones protecting her."

"So Valri's protecting Amalie from something other than physical threats."

He nodded. "I think Valri's afraid someone will see into Amalie's mind," he said. "Uncover a secret."

"What kind of secret?"

"I don't know." He could guess, though, and it terrified him.

"And only someone like *you* would be able to uncover such a thing."

"Maybe. Maybe not. Maybe once we learn what the secret is, we'll realize why Valri thought it would be obvious to everyone if she didn't conceal it."

"Well, unless you've made some grand discovery today—" Senneth said.

"She can control the raelynx."

"Who? Valri? I'm not altogether surprised. I imagine Ellynor can, too."

"Not Valri," he said. "Amalie can handle the raelynx."

That stopped Senneth in her tracks. "She told you that?"

"I saw her do it. We went to see him today."

"Are you sure you weren't controlling it? Not even meaning to?"

"Positive."

She stared at him in the dark. Her pale blond hair drifted around her face like a cap of snow. "How is that possible?"

"I don't know. She doesn't have Lirren blood, does she? Her mother was from Merrenstow, right?"

"I'm sure Romar Brendyn could recite you their ancestry for the past sixteen generations. I can't imagine there was a Lirren bastard anywhere in the line."

"Then I can't explain it." The only other explanation he had come up with was too unsettling to say aloud.

"Are you sure Valri wasn't the one handling the raelynx?" Senneth asked.

"She wasn't with us."

Senneth's chin came up. "You were alone with the princess? How did that happen?"

"Like you said. Valri met Ellynor and suddenly they were talking about family and friends. It was obvious they had a lot to discuss. So, Amalie and I left the room and then—we just—ended up spending the rest of the day together."

"I think perhaps I should be filled with foreboding. What else happened?"

"Well, the bit with the raelynx made me forget it for a while, but before that there was something else that seemed strange. I was thinking something, and she heard me."

"We can all do that," Senneth said.

"I wasn't trying to send her a message. She just picked it up out of my head."

From what he could see in the dark, Senneth's face looked exceptionally grave. "What are you saying?"

"She could hear my thoughts—"

"What's the conclusion you've reached based on these two separate events?" Senneth interrupted. Her mind was a swirl of confusion and dread—and a certain sense of bitter fatalism. *I have feared this for so long.* . . . "Are you saying you think she's a reader? A *mystic?*"

They were absolutely alone on an unwatched pathway under the hard stars, and yet both of them glanced around uneasily as if to search out eavesdroppers. Then they drew closer together so they could lower their voices even more.

"Senneth—I don't know. But I've never seen anyone who *wasn't* a mystic even attempt to control a raelynx. And I've never had *anyone* go into my mind and look around without my knowledge. Jerril can step inside, but he has to knock, and I always know he's there."

"Bright Mother burn me in ashes to the ground," Senneth whispered and shut her eyes. Although she stood absolutely motionless, Cammon felt her regroup, readjust, brace her shoulders for the acquisition of this new burden. "I have hoped so hard that this wasn't true."

"You mean, you suspected it?" he demanded. "You never let on! Ever!"

She shrugged. "It's the one thing that makes all the pieces fit—particularly once it became clear that Valri is from the Lirrens. If Amalie's a mystic, Baryn has had every reason to keep her secluded in the palace all her life. If she's a mystic, Pella had a strong incentive to travel to the Lirrens when she knew she was dying. The queen wasn't looking for a healer to save her own life, but for someone like Valri who would be willing to wrap Amalie in darkness and keep her safe."

"Was Pella a mystic, too?"

Senneth started pacing forward, and Cammon followed her. "I never heard such a rumor. But magic follows bloodlines, so it had to come from the Merrenstow side—since no one has ever called Baryn a mystic, and surely after sixty-five years someone would have mentioned it."

"Then, if it's true, the regent knows of it," Cammon said. "Amalie said she spent a lot of time at Romar Brendyn's estate when she was growing up."

Senneth nodded. "But that makes sense, too. That's just another reason Romar was an excellent choice to name as regent. He would know what else to protect her from. Such as accusations of sorcery."

"It might not be true."

She glanced at him but kept striding forward. "So. You spent the day with her, and Valri was nowhere in sight. Could you read the princess without the Lirren magic to blind you?"

He was silent a moment. "I could have," he said quietly. "I could tell her mind was open and full of wonder. But I didn't want to do it. I didn't want to look inside. It just seemed—unfair. Wrong."

Senneth snorted. "So now you can't answer the question we are both dying to know! A mighty inconvenient time to have scruples, wouldn't you say?"

"Senneth, I didn't sense magic on her, if that's what you want to know. Maybe that's why I was so surprised when she could read my mind. Every mystic I've ever met has just been *caked* in magic—it's like a glow or a scent—I can instantly tell it's there. But I didn't pick that up from Amalie. If she has sorcery, it's buried."

Senneth walked on a few more moments in silence. By now they were almost to the wall that surrounded the compound; soon they would be intersecting with the nightly patrol of guards. Senneth angled her direction a little so that they followed a path parallel to the wall but a few yards away. "You can't read magic on Ellynor or Valri, either."

"Right. Which is why I wondered if Amalie had Lirren blood."

"It just seems impossible. You know how rarely the Lirrenfolk breed with outsiders."

"There's Ellynor. There's Valri. There's Heffel Coravann's wife," he reminded her. "We know of three marriages between Lirren women and men from Gillengaria. So it's not like it's *never* happened. Maybe Pella's mother crossed the Lireth Mountains when she was a girl. Maybe she fell in love with a Lirren boy and came back carrying his child. Maybe not even Romar or the king know how Amalie got her magic—they just know she has it. If she has it."

"If she has it," Senneth echoed. "Maybe we're wrong."

"I don't think I can just ask her."

"No, and I can't ask the king, much as I'd like to. But, Cammon, you can't repeat this to a soul."

"Not even the others?" he said. It was unnecessary to list them. She knew who he meant.

She looked troubled. "I don't know. I'll have to tell Tayse, and he'll surely tell Justin. And I can't not tell Kirra. And what Kirra knows—well, I suppose all of us will know it by sunrise tomorrow." She gave him a serious look, which, in the darkness, he felt more than saw. "But no one else, Cammon. No one. If this secret comes out—"

"I know," he said, feeling somber and afraid as he never had in all his existence. "Amalie could be in the greatest danger of her life."

* * *

HE made his way slowly back across the palace grounds, lost in thought. At this hour, every door was guarded, so even at the kitchen he had to pass a sentry. But that was a good thing, he thought. Let there be soldiers at every door, mystics at every window, dogs and even raelynxes loose in the yard, prowling around, patrolling for interlopers. Let the king invoke every possible measure to keep the princess safe. Cammon was starting to lose the confidence that it was a task he could accomplish on his own.

He could tell, as he made his way up the great stairway to his room, that there were still a couple dozen people scattered throughout the large building who were not yet sleeping. Some were servants, some were soldiers, some were restless souls unable to close their eyes. It gave him a vague sense of comfort to know that part of the world was awake around him. They might all be strangers, but he was not alone.

He pushed open the door to his room and realized with a shock that he still was not alone.

"Valri," he said, for the little queen stood in the middle of the room like a marble statue intended, one day, for the royal sculpture garden. She had not bothered to light a candle. Child of the night goddess, she clearly did not need aid to see in the dark. Only a wavering sconce in the hallway provided enough light for him to identify her.

His own magic had failed him; he had had utterly no idea of her presence.

When she spoke, her voice was hard and angry. "Stay away from the princess when I am not there to chaperone you."

He was instantly antagonized and made no attempt to hide it. "I would never do anything to harm her. You don't need to worry."

"She is the heir to the realm! She cannot be allowed to wander off alone with *any* man! Her reputation is as precious as her life."

"Then you have a strange idea of what's precious," he shot back.

"I think I am better qualified to judge what's important to Amalie than you are."

"And are you better qualified than *she* is?" he said.

"What's that supposed to mean?"

He was angry, a state so rare for him that he almost didn't know what to do or say next. Calm. Senneth would advise him to be calm. Slow down the hot words, bargain for a little time. "Let me light some candles," he said. "I can't even see your face."

He considered closing the door, since she might not want an audience for the conversation, but it probably wasn't good for the *queen's* reputation for her to be alone with other men, either, so he didn't. The candles cast some measure of familiarity back into the room, and he was more serene when he faced Valri again.

"I don't know what you're so afraid of," he said in a quiet voice. "You know I won't hurt the princess. You know that no one regards me as anything more than a servant. I'm not a danger to Amalie *or* her reputation."

"You're the most dangerous man in the city," Valri said deliberately.

"I have no idea why you would say that."

Valri came a step closer. Even in this poor light, her eyes were a spectacular green. "Amalie has so few friends—*friends*, people her own age. None, in fact. Me. And I am hardly anyone's definition of a playmate." She took a deep breath. "And now she has you. And you *are* exactly the kind of person a lonely girl would take to heart. You're kind, you're funny, you're thoughtful, you have wonderful stories to tell, you'll do anything she asks, and you don't particularly care about rules because most of the time you don't even know what the rules *are*. And, oh, yes, you're a young man who is not terrible to look at, and who doesn't covet her throne, and who has been brought into her life specifically to protect her from danger! What do I think you're going to *do*? I think you're going to make her fall in love with you!"

In the following second, Cammon had three radically different yet fully formed thoughts that all managed to occupy his mind simultaneously.

The first one: *Valri's lying. This isn't the real reason she's afraid of me.*

The second one: *Me? Amalie could fall in love with me?*

The third one: *Bright Mother burn me, I could so easily fall in love with Amalie.*

"Majesty," he said, and his voice perfectly conveyed his sense of shock, "you simply can't be serious."

She came closer, and now she frowned and shook her finger at him as if he was an erring schoolboy. "She must marry a high-born noble! You know that! She knows that! It will be a marriage of convenience and, like as not, marked by politeness instead of passion. You can't distract her by being funny and charming and sweet. You can't show her something she cannot have when she *must* have something else."

A fourth thought intruded: *Valri thinks I'm funny and charming and sweet?* "Do you want me to leave the palace?" he asked.

"No! Of course not! We are relying on you and your wretched magic for too many reasons. You have saved the king's life twice and perhaps you will save Amalie's, and I pray to the Great Mother that you will be able to ensure that the husband she picks will offer her a warm heart instead of a cold ambition. You must stay. But you must keep your distance from Amalie. Cammon, you must."

He felt resentful and aggrieved—and just a tiny bit smug, for Valri could not stop him from communicating with Amalie silently even if he had to sit in her presence poker-faced and mute from now until the wedding bells were sounded. And still, under all of that, he remained astonished. *She thinks Amalie could fall in love with* me?

"I don't know what you want me to promise," he said, and even to himself his voice sounded sulky. "If I am cool and unfriendly to her, Amalie will make a scene—you know she will. But if I act the way I have always acted, you will say I am—I am—I don't know what you think I'm doing! Ingratiating myself, I suppose. I never set out to do that. I never set out to do anything except just *be* here like I was asked."

"One thing I do not expect is for you to spend whole days alone with her. If I am not present, you should not be present, either."

He spread his hands. How could he argue? "If that's what you want."

"And—and—you should not think to spend every morning with her, lounging in the parlor and telling her stories."

"I'll stay away, but she'll ask me about it, and she'll insist on an explanation."

"I'll take care of that."

He shrugged. "Then fine. I'll keep my distance. You won't have cause to complain about me again."

Valri nodded once, decisively, as if she was feeling confident and satisfied. But he could tell that she was still distressed, still terrified that something would happen to Amalie and that he would be the cause of it. *What are you really afraid of?* he wanted to ask her. *What truth are you trying to conceal from me by shielding Amalie's mind with your own?*

"Very well," she said. "Then we'll see you tomorrow afternoon when another one of her suitors comes calling."

"I'll meet you by the receiving room."

She nodded again. "Good night. I'm glad you're willing to be reasonable."

She left the room, shutting the door behind her. He stared at it for a long time, wishing he had had the nerve to ask the question he knew she would not answer.

Is Amalie a mystic?

CHAPTER

14

THERE was no real need to supervise Amalie's meeting the next day, for her suitor was Darryn Rappengrass. His mother, Ariane, was one of Baryn's staunchest allies, and Kirra had always considered Darryn the best of the serramar. There was no chance he would suddenly pull a blade and try to slit Amalie's throat. Still, two Riders posed behind the false wall, ready to stop him if he tried.

There was no need for Cammon and Valri to listen in to his courting, but of course they did.

They sat rather stiffly on either side of the card table, hardly on the best of terms after last night's confrontation. Cammon found it difficult to hold a grudge, so he picked up the deck of cards and silently offered to deal. Valri hesitated, then nodded. They were into their second hand when the princess and her visitor entered and settled in for conversation.

At first it was all very superficial, talk about the weather and the roads. Cammon was surprised as everyone else when Amalie said, "So, ser Darryn, tell me! Why are you here?"

Darryn did not allow himself to be nonplussed. He was easygoing and polished, well able to handle himself in any social situation, but Cammon read nothing but good will behind his assured exterior. "I suppose I can't be the first Twelfth House lord to call on you in the past few weeks. I expect you realize we've all come courting."

"But not you," Amalie said, calm as always. "You're betrothed to another girl."

Everyone in the room was astonished at that—Cammon, Valri, the Riders—but Darryn Rappengrass most of all. Cammon could feel his swift, confused reactions: amazement, respect, uncertainty, and a growing desire to tell the truth. "Not betrothed, exactly," he replied in a slow voice. "But I admit I am in love with her and I hope to marry her."

Valri dropped her cards and stared in impotent fury at the thin wall separating them. Cammon had to smother a grin. Surely it was unimaginably rude to tell a princess you preferred another woman.

Amalie, however, did not seem at all distressed. "So, you see I am going to resist any inclination I might have to fall in love with you myself," she said.

Darryn laughed, still a little dazed. "But who has been gossiping with the princess of the realm? Where did you learn this news?"

"Kirra Danalustrous told me."

Valri looked at Cammon and rolled her eyes. *Of course*, she mouthed.

"And how does *she* know?" Darryn asked. "I suppose she got the information from my mother, who is ready to disown me. In fact, the only way I can win myself back into her good graces is to tell her you've agreed to be my bride."

Amalie sounded interested. "So you truly would propose to me, even though your affection was somewhere else? Wouldn't that be risky? What if I accepted?"

Darryn was suddenly all seriousness. "No, Majesty. I planned to come to you, and flirt awhile, and speak of the long-standing bond between Ghosenhall and Rappen Manor. I wouldn't have proposed, but I would have tried to make you enjoy our time together so that you would think of me kindly. And then I would have left and gone back to the arms of the girl I love. All the while hoping, of course, that some worthwhile and sincere young lord had already come calling and won a place in your heart."

"Well, I would much rather you were truthful with me from the outset," she said. "No pretending!"

Valri flung her hands wide in the air as if to say, *The whole world survives on lies and this girl insists on the truth.* But her anger seemed to have faded a little, and she picked up her cards again.

"I will remember that for the future," Darryn said. "I still hope there will be ongoing friendship between the palace and Rappen Manor. We will pledge now to always be honest with each other, and thereby save a great deal of time."

Amalie must have raised her drink in a toast, for there was a slight clinking sound as if two glasses had been touched together. "I will agree to that," she said. "Now tell me about this girl you love. Is she noble-born?"

"No. Yet another reason my mother is displeased with me."

Valri nodded emphatically at the wall. Cammon had to choke back another laugh.

"How did you meet her?" Amalie wanted to know.

There was a rustling sound, as if Darryn had leaned back in his chair and stretched out his legs, preparing to get comfortable. "Oh, now, that's an adventurous tale," he said. "I rescued her on the road—and a few weeks later, she repaid the favor."

So all of them spent the next half hour listening to the story of Darryn Rappengrass's romance with a young vagabond girl. Cammon was inclined to think the girl pretty lucky—Darryn just radiated happiness when he talked about her. If Cammon were ever called on to testify about the serramar's affection, he would have to call it genuine.

"Of course you'll join us for dinner," Amalie said as their visit wound down. "And perhaps stay a day or so?"

"I will be happy to do both," he replied.

Valri waited till they were out of the room and their voices had faded down the hall. "What a waste of time!" she exclaimed. "In love with another girl! And Darryn would be the perfect match for her in so many ways. He's not a firstborn child, and he probably will not become marlord, but a wedding to him would immeasurably strengthen our ties to Rappengrass. And he's such a delightful man! Sophisticated and handsome and at ease in every situation. He would make an excellent husband *and* an excellent king. And he's to throw himself away on this nameless peasant girl!"

"I think you're more upset than Amalie is," Cammon said.

"I have a better idea of what's at stake than she does," was the grim reply.

As he gathered the cards and followed Valri out into the corridor, Cammon found himself glad that the so-perfect Darryn Rappengrass was unavailable to marry the princess. She had to marry someone, of course—he understood that—but he did not mind if it took her another year to find a husband. Or even longer. He would be happy to watch over her for however long the search lasted.

HE had forgotten just how strong-willed the princess could be—and that she might think she had a reason to be angry with him. So he was unprepared for the look of burning reproach she gave him when she entered the dining room that night on the arm of Darryn Rappengrass. He felt his eyes widen and he almost blurted out "What's wrong?" before he remembered that he was supposed to stand immobile and expressionless as any footman. Instead he raised his eyebrows in an expression of wounded innocence, but Amalie just flipped her hair over her shoulder and turned to say something to Darryn. Valri was settling herself in her own seat at the foot of the table and so fortunately missed this interchange.

Ah. Valri. She had forbidden him to join the princess in her parlor this morning, and Amalie apparently was angry that he had not attended her there. Since just the day before he had promised true friendship and unending camaraderie.

Hard to explain this in sentences of simple words that he could convey in silence.

He didn't even try for the first half hour of the meal, which was always very busy, as servants brought in dishes and diners initiated conversations with their tablemates. Kirra and Senneth were both in attendance tonight, Kirra sitting on the other side of Darryn Rappengrass and flirting madly. *That* would be the two you would expect to pair off, if you were going by compatibility and personality, Cammon thought. Both of them noble, born to Houses that were absolutely loyal to the throne— both of them so attractive and appealing that simply watching them together made everyone else smile. Yet Kirra had given her heart to the shape-shifter Donnal, and Darryn Rappengrass loved a nameless girl who seemed to possess nothing except resourcefulness and a will to live.

Senneth sat between the king and Belinda Brendyn and managed to make her way through dinner with only the occasional grimace. Still, he could tell she was both bored and eager to be done with the meal. He sent her mental images of a fire sweeping through the kitchen and racing down the hall toward this very gathering, forcing them all to flee the room. It would, of course, be a fire that she coaxed into life. He knew she received the message, because she pursed her lips together very solemnly to keep from laughing and would not look at him for the rest of the evening.

When the diners had settled into their meals and the pace was a little more relaxed, Cammon sent his first observation to Amalie. *It's not my fault. Valri told me to stay away.*

She gave no sign that she had heard him. She didn't flick her eyes in his direction; she didn't draw her attention away from Darryn Rappengrass. It was possible that Valri had cloaked her in magic so deep that he would not be able to get through to her, but he didn't think that was it. She was so angry she was pretending not to listen.

Valri came to my room last night. She told me I was never to be alone with you again.

Still no response from the princess.

What can I do? She's the queen. And she was truly upset. I told her I would never do anything to harm you, but that didn't reassure her.

Amalie lifted her hand and tugged on her right earring as if it had begun to pinch. Cammon had to think a moment to remember what the signal meant. Oh, yes, she had said she would touch her left ear if she wanted to be entertained, her right ear if she wanted to be left alone.

Well, all right, I'll be quiet, but first tell me you're not angry with me.

Amalie leaned over Darryn to address Kirra. "But weren't you in Nocklyn when that happened?"

"Yes! With Mayva! But Darryn heard about it somehow and then the next time I was in Rappengrass I found he had told his mother, too. I was never so embarrassed to face Ariane!"

Take a sip of your wine if you're not angry with me, Cammon thought.

Amalie toyed with her knife and fork, then picked up a roll and tore off a small piece with her fingers. "I thought you were one of the marlady's favorites."

"Well, she is *now*, because she saved my niece's life," said Darryn. "But there was a time when my mother wasn't so sure about Kirra."

If you don't forgive me, I'm just going to keep talking to you, Cammon said. *I know you can hear me. How can I be your friend if you won't understand that I'm doing the best I can?*

"Your mother sent me the prettiest present," Amalie said to Darryn. "Pieces of sea glass."

"Oh, I love that," Kirra said. "I had a pendant made from blue sea glass when I was a little girl, and I wore it all time. It fell just so—covered my housemark—it's probably still in my jewelry box back home."

"Let me show you what she gave me," Amalie said, and motioned Cammon over.

He tried to keep an impassive expression on his face as he walked stiffly to her side, but he was aware that Valri, Senneth, and Kirra had all gone on alert at the summons. Kirra and Senneth looked merely speculative, but Valri was displeased.

He leaned over and Amalie whispered in his ear. "Stop it! Be quiet! I'll have you sent from the room!"

He could not answer aloud, but he nodded as if she had given him an order he was about to carry out. *I can stand anywhere in the palace and make you hear me. It won't do any good to banish me to the kitchen.*

Her voice was utterly composed. "I've asked Cammon to fetch Ariane's gift from my parlor," she told the others. "He knows right where it is."

Kirra and Senneth exchanged glances at that; Valri's expression looked even more thunderous. Cammon bowed and solemnly marched through the door.

He kept up a running commentary for the entire time it took him to traverse the hallways, climb the stairs, and go rummaging through her bookshelf, which had been rearranged since the time she showed him her treasures. *What if Darryn Rappengrass was an ambitious serramar with designs on your father's throne? What if you sent me from the room and he decided to try to cut your father's throat? Don't you realize that's why I'm supposed to stay in the dining hall when you're entertaining company? You're angry at me, but why put yourself in danger? Didn't you see the look on Senneth's face? She was thinking, "While Cammon's out of the room, I'll have to be paying the utmost attention." I suppose we can trust ser Darryn, but I don't think you should be so careless.*

Box in hand, he returned to the dining hall and presented it to Amalie with a small flourish. She didn't look at him or thank him, but merely opened the hidden door and held the container toword Kirra. "Don't you like these? I was wondering if I should have them made into a bracelet."

You know I'll keep talking all night if you don't say you're not angry with me, he said as he took his position against the wall once more. *Ask Senneth. I can talk long after everyone else wants me to shut up. Just sip from your wine to tell me you forgive me.*

One of the servants was circling the table with a bottle in his hand. "Will you have more wine, Majesty?" he murmured to Amalie.

She lifted her glass and drained what was already in it. "Yes," she said, holding it out to him. "I think I will."

Cammon had to work hard to contain his smile.

It was easier when he realized that Valri was still watching him, a brooding expression on her dainty face.

Easier still when he realized he had caught Senneth's attention, and she didn't look any happier than the queen.

CHAPTER
15

Whenn Senneth returned to the cottage after dinner, she was in such a black humor that Tayse looked up in surprise. He was at ease in a big chair before the fire, playing a casual game of cards with Justin and Donnal, but he picked up her mood instantly.

"What's wrong?" he asked.

"Nothing," she snapped and stalked into the bedroom to change out of her formal dress. She heard the rumble of low voices as the three men tried to guess what had put her in a temper, but none of them seemed alarmed. Well, they knew no danger threatened or Cammon would have summoned them long before this.

Cammon.

Senneth wrenched her dress off and tossed it to the bed, the rational alternative to throwing it on the floor and trampling it. Back into her comfortable trousers, her oversize shirt. Run a hand through her hair to disturb the careful styling Kirra had achieved for her earlier in the evening. Herself again, and a little calmer.

She stepped back into the main room, pulled up a chair, and said, "Deal me in."

Justin shuffled and expertly handed out cards. "Sevens wild."

She glanced around the room. "Where's Ellynor?"

Justin picked up his cards and started arranging them. "Sleeping. She was out all night helping one of the soldier's wives deliver a baby."

"Oh, she doesn't have to do that! There are plenty of physicians in Ghosenhall—mystic *and* ordinary."

"She likes to do it. I think she finds it comforting—a chance to do something she's good at. Something familiar in an unfamiliar place."

"Plenty of other things she's good at," Donnal observed. "As she's been proving to us the past few days."

"Has Cammon improved in his ability to sense her approach?" Tayse asked.

Donnal grinned. "Not as much as he'd like. But more than Ellynor thought he would."

"I suppose that's the definition of success," Tayse said.

Justin seemed pleased at Ellynor's ability. "Cammon doesn't seem to think so."

Senneth slapped a discard onto the table. "But then, Cammon has all sorts of other tricks and skills that keep him happy enough."

There was a short, comprehensive silence. "You're mad at *Cammon?*" Justin asked at last. "That's what this is all about?"

Tayse laid his cards down. "Tell us," he said in his grave fashion.

"Dinner tonight. I'm not sure, but I think Amalie and Cammon were having an argument."

They all looked at her as if she was speaking in an incomprehensible Sovenfeld dialect.

"Silently, I mean. Remember, he told us the other day that he has the ability to put words in her head."

"We know this," Donnal said. "Why are you angry?"

Just then the door opened and Kirra drifted in. "I love Darryn Rappengrass," she said. "He spent twenty minutes telling me about this girl he's so besotted with. Ariane had told me she wasn't even Thirteenth House, but it's even better than that. Senneth, she's a poacher's daughter! Isn't that wonderful? It makes you and me look positively respectable despite our own unconventional choices."

Donnal was grinning broadly, but Tayse showed only a faint smile. "I doubt even ser Darryn's irresponsible behavior can make you seem respectable," Tayse said.

Kirra stuck her tongue out at him and pulled up a chair between Donnal and Justin. "What are we playing? Can I get in the game?"

"We seem to have stopped playing while Senneth explains why she's so angry at Cammon," Donnal said.

"Yes, what was that all about tonight?" Kirra said, picking up Donnal's cards and sorting through them. "Amalie sending Cammon off to get something from her study—I mean, it was a little peculiar."

"Senneth thinks they were having a silent argument," Tayse said.

That did catch Kirra's attention. Her fine eyebrows arched high over her blue eyes. "What were they arguing about?"

"That's not the point," Senneth muttered, her bad mood fully returned.

"We're still trying to understand the point," Justin told Kirra. "It's not obvious to the rest of us."

"The point is, a servant doesn't *argue* with his master or his mistress," Senneth exclaimed. "Would you argue with Baryn? If he gave you an order, you might say, 'Liege, I think that would be a dreadful mistake,' and you would explain why, but if he disagreed with you, you would follow his command anyway. He wouldn't sulk because you had offended him, and you wouldn't stand there trying to defend yourself—in a room full of nobles, might I add!—that is not the relationship you have with him. And that should not be the relationship Cammon has—or thinks he has—with Amalie."

"Well, but, *Cammon*," Kirra said, as if that explained everything. "He treats everybody like a best friend. It's endearing."

Tayse, as always, cut straight through to the heart of the matter. "You think he's crossed the line with her? He's too familiar?"

"I think she's a lonely, isolated girl and he's an outgoing, happy young man, and neither of them realizes they cannot, they *cannot* be friends. And it's not my place to say anything to the princess, but I can damn well tell Cammon to back off."

Kirra's mouth had dropped open. "You think Cammon might fall in love with her? You think *she* might fall in love with Cammon?"

"Surely we have enough other disasters to contend with for that to happen," Senneth said. But she felt glum. Why should this particular disaster hold off? None of the others had.

She was annoyed to see Kirra and Justin exchange glances and then dissolve into laughter. "You were right! You were *right*!" Kirra cried. "Oh, but even you couldn't have predicted this!"

"I cannot imagine what possible amusement you can find in this situation," Senneth said in a cold voice.

Justin tried to stop laughing, but his face was still alight with mirth. "Last year. Kirra and I were remarking on the fact that the six of us seemed to make extraordinarily bad choices when we fell in love," he said. "Picking people we didn't have much chance of ending up with in a happy life. And I said Cammon would outdo all of us."

"But the *princess*! That I would never have anticipated!" Kirra said.

"And this is all premature speculation," Tayse said practically. "He may feel some affection for her, and she for him, but I believe Amalie is very aware of her role and not likely to compromise herself in any foolish fashion."

"Well, she won't compromise herself with Cammon, because I'm going to strangle him," Senneth said.

Kirra looked around. "Where is he, anyway? He always comes down here after dinner."

"I think he's avoiding me," Senneth said. "I made a tactical error."

Justin grinned again. "You gave him a *look*, didn't you? One look, and he decided he would be better off spending the evening up in his room."

"Talk to him tomorrow," Tayse said. "Perhaps you'll be calmer then."

Senneth rubbed the back of her head, where a small ache was beginning to form. She knew better—both great rage and sweeping acts of magic could leave her with debilitating headaches. Magic performed while she was in the grip of fury could produce headaches so severe she was laid low for more than a day. Tayse had the knack of massaging away the agony, but it was stupid to feel so angry over such a trifle and call up a headache to begin with. "Perhaps I will," she said.

Donnal swept all the cards toward him. "Maybe we should start over," he said.

They played for a few moments in companionable silence. "I learned something interesting at dinner tonight," Kirra said presently.

"Some intimate secret of Darryn's?" Senneth inquired. "Because you flirted with him so desperately that I can't imagine you had time to talk to anybody else. I was starting to think Amalie would be jealous—since he came here to see her, after all."

Kirra blinked those blue eyes at her. "Are you just going to go around the table and berate each of us, one by one?" she asked. "In that case, I want to stick around and hear what you say to Tayse. You usually think he's so perfect."

Justin snorted and buried his face in his cards. Tayse tried with a little more success to hide his amusement, but Donnal just laughed out loud. Against her will, Senneth felt her own face lighten in a smile.

"No. No, that will be my last ill-tempered remark of the evening. Though you *were* awfully cozy with Darryn," she couldn't help adding.

"He's always been my favorite flirt," Kirra said, "but even more so now that I know he's in love with another girl. I can say the most outrageous things and know there's no chance he'll take me seriously. It's very freeing."

"I shudder to think what *you* might find outrageous," Tayse said, which caused Justin to laugh again.

"But tell us, do, what you learned tonight while you were trading compliments with Darryn Rappengrass," Senneth said.

"He's leaving for Rappen Manor in a couple of days, and if we want to go to Carrebos, he'll travel most of the distance with us."

Tayse rearranged his hand and threw away two cards. "I didn't know you'd decided to go to Carrebos so soon."

"We hadn't," Senneth said slowly, thinking it over. "But I like the idea of traveling with Darryn. People will see our parties together on the road. It's never a bad idea to reinforce the idea that there is great affection between Rappengrass and the crown."

"I think he's willing to wait a few days but wants to be on the road before the week's out," Kirra said. "And I can't stay much longer, either. If you don't go soon, you'll have to go without me."

"Restless again already?" Tayse said.

"Needed back home," she said. "I promised Casserah I wouldn't be gone long. I'll probably head straight from Carrebos to Danan Hall."

Tayse shrugged. "No reason not to leave Ghosenhall whenever the serramar is ready."

"Well, not until I've killed Cammon," Senneth said.

"Right after that," Tayse said. "We'll be on our way."

BUT Cammon proved elusive the next day. Senneth always just missed him when she searched for him in his room, in Amalie's company, in the kitchens. He was, of course, at his post during the dinner that evening, but somehow she lost track of him as the guests emptied from the room, and he didn't show up at the cottage later that night.

"He's avoiding you," Justin said, seeming to find this hilarious. He and Ellynor had joined Senneth and Tayse after dinner; Kirra and Donnal had been gone all day, and, of course, no one knew where Cammon was. "He can tell you're still mad at him."

"I'm not! I just want to talk to him."

"I'd guess it's pretty hard to approach Cammon by stealth," Tayse observed. "You're never going to be able to corner him."

Ellynor smiled a little wickedly. She was so dainty and small that Senneth was always surprised all over again when she exhibited strength and purpose. "I'll help you," she offered. "I'll hide you so he doesn't know you're coming."

They all liked this idea and spent a couple of minutes discussing the best time and place to trap Cammon.

"I'll have him work out with me and then bring him back to our cabin for some reason," Justin suggested. "You can be lying in wait."

"Would you like me to recruit Coeval and Hammond?" Tayse inquired. "We can help you disembowel him."

"No, no, I think I can kill him all by myself."

THE plan was executed the following afternoon and worked perfectly. Senneth and Ellynor were standing just inside the door when Cammon, talking excitedly, followed Justin inside. His expression of dismay was so comical that Senneth almost forgave him on the spot, but this was too serious. So instead she grabbed him in a headlock and wrestled him to the floor while he flailed about and protested mightily.

"You traitor!" he yelled at Justin. "I warned *you* when people were waiting for you!"

Justin spread his hands. "Senneth," he replied. "I couldn't help it."

"I hate to chase you out of your own house, but I need a few minutes alone with him," Senneth said.

Justin grabbed Ellynor's wrist and pulled her out the door. "We're gone."

When the door shut behind them, Senneth released Cammon, but they both remained on the floor, Cammon ostentatiously rubbing his wrist and throat. "Nobody realizes how *mean* you can be," he said.

"And I never realized how stupid *you* could be," she responded.

He stopped rubbing and gave her a straight look. Cammon's eyes were so unusual, brown eyes flecked with gold spots—the eyes of a seer, or a madman, or a genius. She had never been sure. "Senneth, I haven't *done* anything."

"Then why have you been hiding from me?"

"Well, I didn't want to be set on fire!"

"Seriously."

He threw his hands up, then hunched his knees together and set his chin on top of them. "Valri's already lectured me. Came to my room at midnight to warn me not to be too friendly to the princess. I don't know what everybody's so afraid of. I'm hardly the kind of person—well, I mean, look at me. Then look at somebody like Darryn Rappengrass. Or even Ryne Coravann. They're like purebred horses. I'm a shaggy dog."

"Yet people have been known to become very attached to misbegotten mongrels, especially when they're loyal and affectionate."

"So what am I supposed to do? Valri tells me to stay away. But Amalie is angry when I'm not there. It seems I can't make anybody happy."

"You can behave yourself," Senneth said softly.

He looked mutinous. "What's that supposed to mean?"

"Tell me you weren't carrying on a private conversation with Amalie all during dinner the night before last."

He said nothing.

"Exactly. That's the sort of behavior that creates a certain—emotional intimacy. Yes, you have to attend Amalie when she requests it. No, you certainly don't want to make your liege angry. But you appear to be on the road to becoming Amalie's primary confidante. And that is a very tricky road."

"How stupid do you think I am?" he burst out. "Do you think I'm crazy enough to think that—that—Amalie could fall in love with me? It didn't even cross my mind till Valri said it! I *still* don't think it's possible! But if you keep going on about it—"

"Cammon. You're a delightful young man and all of your friends love you very much. But it has always been clear that you don't really have a sense of boundaries. You've always treated everyone as your equal. And that just won't do when it comes to Amalie. You simply can't be yourself around the princess. You have to be someone else."

He shrugged and looked away. She didn't have to hear the thought in his head to know what he was thinking. *I don't know how to be anyone else.* "I'll try," he said. "But I think you're all overreacting just a little."

"No more secret silent conversations with the princess?"

"All right."

"And no more long days spent roaming the palace grounds with no one to supervise you?"

"I can't imagine Valri would let that happen, anyway."

"That didn't sound like a promise."

"All *right*."

She climbed to her feet and he scrambled up beside her. "You'll have a chance to prove just how good you can be when I'm not watching over you," she said. "I'm leaving for Carrebos in a couple of days. And taking Tayse and Kirra and Donnal as well."

He frowned. "But Justin just got back!"

She was amused. "And how does that have anything to do with this trip?"

"Well, because! We haven't even been together for two weeks!"

Now she was laughing. "I thought sure you'd be relieved to see me go."

He grinned. "I am, of course. I was trying to conceal it."

She laughed, too, and they left the cabin together in perfect amity. But later she thought over this part of the conversation and wondered if she had been duped. True, Cammon was never so happy as when the six of them—the seven of them—were together. And true, for Cammon, a period of ten or fourteen days was not enough time to satisfy his craving for that close connection.

He had showed distress at the thought that four of them were leaving. But had the emotion been genuine? Or had Cammon—the most artless person she'd ever met—had Cammon learned to lie?

CHAPTER
16

CAMMON was miserable for a whole week. Everyone was angry at him, and then everyone was *gone*, and if Justin and Ellynor hadn't been around he would have felt completely lost.

Nominally, he was back on good terms with both Valri and Amalie, and he joined them a couple of mornings in the parlor. But Valri watched him with a darkling expression and—at least for those first two days—Amalie treated him with a brittle coolness. He was tempted more than once to renew his silent diatribes, and now and then he caught a look on her face that made him think she was puzzled that he had not.

But he had promised Senneth that he would be good, and he had decided he would at least *try* to keep his promise. So he was friendly but not intrusive, ran errands when Amalie asked, played card games with the princess and the queen, and was generally unhappy.

He had told Tayse that Amalie wanted to get to know the Riders better, which Tayse thought was a very good idea. The best parts of that week came as the Riders arrived by ones and twos to visit with Amalie. The older ones, like Tir and Hammond, were respectful but hardly loquacious and tended not to stay long. The younger ones were a little more cocky, a little more talkative, and just as curious about the princess as she was about them.

"I've never handled a sword," Amalie confessed when Wen came calling. She was accompanied by Janni, a compact, dark-haired, and infectiously happy young Rider who was Wen's best friend. "Not even a knife, except a dinner knife."

Janni's dagger was in her hand even though she scarcely appeared to move. "Well, *that* we ought to do something about! It's good for everyone to know how to handle a weapon. You never know when you might be required to defend yourself."

Amalie's eyes sparkled. "I agree! What can you show me?"

Cammon glanced at Valri, thinking the queen might not endorse the notion of royalty receiving weapons training, but Valri's face was inscrutable. Janni and Wen gathered around the princess, let her hold their various blades, explained the basic mechanics of edge and weight and reach.

Wen stepped back and eyed Amalie's clothing with disfavor. "You can't really fight when you're wearing a gown," she said. "You see how we're dressed? In trousers and boots? Anything else just gets in the way."

"I don't think anyone would find such attire appropriate for me," Amalie said.

Janni shrugged. "Well, just for an afternoon, maybe. We could come back and show you a few fencing moves."

Amalie was instantly taken with the notion. "Yes! What a wonderful idea! Valri, you don't disapprove, do you?"

Valri shook her head. "No, I think it's a good idea. Not tomorrow, perhaps, because we have a visitor coming, but after that."

"And you ought to have a knife," Wen said. "Something you always carry."

"Sleep with it," Janni said. "I do."

Amalie laughed and gestured down at her skirts. "A weapons belt and a scabbard would look very odd with most of my dresses."

"You need a sheath you can buckle onto your leg," Wen said. "Under your clothes. Thigh or calf. I prefer to have my spare knife right above my ankle, but if you're wearing a dress, it's more likely to be seen."

Amalie's lips parted; Cammon could see she absolutely loved this idea. "Could I wear it while I was dancing?"

"You'd probably have to practice a little so you were used to the way it felt—make sure the buckle didn't rub against your other leg," Janni said. "But once you've worn it for a while, you'll forget it's there."

"And you'll feel strange when you're *not* wearing it," Wen added.

"Where can I get a sheath like this? And a knife? I mean a real weapon."

Wen was grinning. "There're all sorts of spare blades down by the training yard. We'll go through the lot and bring up something good for you." She lifted her hand and spread her fingers. "Here. Show me how big your hand is." Amalie laid her palm against the Rider's and Wen nodded. "All right. I'll find something that'll suit you."

So, that was enjoyable, but those hours were too brief, and some days Valri banished him from the room altogether. Cammon found himself completely at loose ends, particularly once Senneth, Tayse, Kirra, and Donnal rode out. Senneth and Tayse promised to be back in about two weeks, but Cammon felt adrift and abandoned the very first day. If he hadn't been pledged to watch Amalie, he would have insisted on riding out to visit the village of mystics. What could be more fascinating? And wouldn't Cammon be valuable as they met a whole town of people with unpredictable and wondrous powers?

But no. He must remain in Ghosenhall to guard the princess.

Which he would have been more than happy to do if the princess had seemed to care at all that he had stayed behind to serve her.

On days Cammon wasn't needed at all, he hiked into the city to spend time with Jerril. They practiced more tricks to build up mental strength, and these were so exhausting that those nights Cammon tumbled into bed and slept without dreaming. Or maybe he'd been tired out by the labor, since he spent some time chopping wood and clearing out the garden and doing the heavier chores that really required a young body and a strong back. Lynnette fussed over him, making his favorite meals and trimming his hair, which, of course, looked ragged again. Areel drew him aside one day and quizzed him on some of the objects that had been making their way to the palace—jewels and vases and small polished tables—all gifts to Amalie from her various suitors.

"Well, I can take you to the palace someday if you just want to walk around and see things," Cammon offered, and Areel looked as if he'd been offered a gift directly from the Bright Mother herself.

So the next day, Cammon gave him a tour of some of the areas of the palace that weren't generally open to guests, though Milo watched them closely to make sure they didn't disturb anything. Areel seemed more than ordinarily dazed, pausing now and then to lay his hand on a marble bowl or a wooden frame and closing his eyes as if the sensation was almost too great to bear. When Cammon took him home, the old mystic staggered as if he was drunk, but he glowed with glutted satisfaction, so Cammon knew he had enjoyed the outing.

In the evenings, there were invariably guests at the palace, so Cammon always stood watch over the meals. No one showed any inclination to attack the king, and Amalie never summoned Cammon to her side to send him on manufactured errands. Nor did he engage in one-sided debates with her, or make any special effort to communicate. All in all, the meals were long and dull, as the days were long and dull, and life in general was pointless and miserable.

By contrast, the late evenings spent with Ellynor and Justin were a balm to his soul. Justin, who could be so wary and abrasive, was utterly relaxed around Ellynor, even expansive. Ellynor herself was a restful woman, Cammon thought—usually engaged in some small task, but in a serene, methodical way. She often seemed lost in her own thoughts, but always had a smile ready for him and would gladly answer his hundreds of questions about life across the Lireth Mountains.

"You miss it," he said to her once, and she nodded and then she shook her head.

"I miss my family, but I'm happy to be away from them, too," she said. "They're very protective! And I'm too curious about the rest of the world. I spent the past two days in Ghosenhall, just wandering around with my mouth hanging open. What a beautiful city! I love being here—and that makes it easier not to miss my family."

"I've told her she needs to go visit one of the Twelve Houses," Justin said. "If she wants to see wealth and opulence."

"How much time have you spent with the queen?" Cammon asked her.

"A few hours here and there. I think she's more homesick than I am."

"How well did you know her?"

Ellynor glanced at Justin and clearly decided not to say something. "Well enough. She wasn't born to my *sebahta-ris*, but her family had always been on good terms with mine. If there had been a clan war, our *sebahtas* would have been allies."

Obviously there was more to this story and obviously she wasn't going to tell it. "Well, I'm sure she's happy you're here," he said.

In fact, a few days later, Valri got a chance to be extremely grateful for Ellynor's presence. Cammon arrived at the cottage to find Justin alone and Ellynor up at the palace, tending the queen through a nasty stomach ailment.

"So, we're on our own," Justin said. "Want to go into town and get a drink?"

They had more than one drink, as it turned out, at more than one tavern, and enjoyed themselves hugely. Justin wasn't wearing Rider regalia, but all the barkeepers made it a point to recognize the king's most elite fighters, and they weren't allowed to pay for a beer all night. No fewer than five women approached Justin before the evening was over, hinting in ways that ranged from subtle to blatant that they thought the Rider was enormously attractive. Justin, of course, was oblivious.

"What do you mean you didn't *notice* what she was wearing?" Cammon asked in disbelief. "I watched her unlace the front of her gown before she came over to talk to you!"

"She was wearing a moonstone bracelet. I noticed *that*," Justin said. "And her hands were too soft, no calluses, so I'm pretty sure she hasn't been handling any weapons lately. She was short, heavyset, probably easy to put down in a fight. What else am I supposed to notice?"

Cammon laughed into his beer. "It's a mystery to me how you ever managed to realize Ellynor was in the world."

Justin grinned. "Well, I got into a brawl on her behalf. You know me. If it involves fighting, I'm more likely to pay attention." He sipped from his glass. "But feel free to make friends with any of these women who are coming up to the table. Maybe they're really coming over to talk to *you*."

"I don't think so."

"Senneth says you're lovesick over the princess," Justin said with his customary lack of tact.

"Oh, so now she wants *you* to lecture me while she's gone?"

Justin shook his head. "I'm just wondering if it's true."

Cammon used his fingernail to pick at a drop of gravy crusted on the table. "We're a lot alike."

"You and the *princess?*"

"We are. We grew up lonely. We're happiest when there are people around us—some activity going on. You know I hate to be by myself. So does she, except there's no one she can make friends with, so she *is* by herself a lot of the time. It makes me want to— It just makes me want to spend time with her. Chase away the loneliness."

Justin nodded. "You could probably do that, you know, despite what Senneth says. You could be her friend. Maybe she'd turn you into her steward someday. You could be like Milo, always around the palace, someone she could rely on completely. It wouldn't be a bad life."

Cammon felt a sharp well of dissatisfaction at the picture, but couldn't exactly say why. "I *hate* Milo!"

Justin grinned. "He does his job. And Baryn trusts him absolutely. And if the princess trusts you—well, it might be a good fit."

Cammon shrugged, then nodded. It was hard to imagine wanting to hold any position at the palace once Amalie was married. Why would she need him? Why would he want to stay?

"So where are they now?" Justin asked, changing the subject without a transition. But Cammon was used to the question, since Justin had asked it daily. "Are they still in Carrebos?"

"I think so. They seem to be staying put at the moment." He sipped his beer. "And they seem to be pleased with whatever they're doing."

Justin stretched out his long legs and shook back his sandy hair. He looked utterly at ease, almost sleepy. Cammon felt someone in the bar gaze over at them with sharpened attention.

"You haven't had too much to drink, have you?" he asked softly.

Justin gave him a slow grin. "Why? Some hot-blooded young kid with a sword thinking he wants to start a fight with a drunken Rider?"

"Something like that."

Justin seemed to relax even more. "That won't go so well. But thanks for the warning."

"Thoughts of violence are like shouts in my head. I can block out almost everything else, but those always come through."

"What I find interesting is that you always know where we are." Justin never specified "we." It was always clear whom he meant. "Without even thinking about it. We're just there, in your head, all the time."

Cammon nodded. "Pretty much."

"What about Ellynor? Does she register with you the same way?"

Cammon leaned forward and used his finger to make a circle on the table from a few spilled drops of beer. "I can only sense Ellynor when you're with her—and then only because I can feel her effect on you. It's like she pulls part of your attention in her direction." He drew his thumb through the circle to create a short streak of wetness. "So, I can tell if she's with you, but that's the best I can do."

"Still. That's not bad," Justin said. "Who else? Your tutor friend, what's his name?"

"Jerril? I can find him right away if I look for him but he's not always there in my mind like the rest of you are."

"The king?"

"Same."

"The princess?"

Cammon opened his mouth to answer and then jerked his head back and stared at Justin—who stared right back at him, his expression just slightly edged with malice. A trap, and Cammon had fallen into it. Cammon hadn't even realized it, hadn't thought about it, hadn't examined it. But there she was, Amalie, a faint and flickering light on the border of his consciousness. Cammon could leave this bar, head back to the palace, climb any set of stairs, traverse any corridor, and go directly to whatever room held Amalie. He knew where she was, he could *feel* her, she had become one of his constant internal beacons, part of the ordinary and familiar texture of his life.

And this despite Valri's magic.

And this despite the fact that Amalie had scarcely spoken to him in a week.

"That's what I thought," Justin said.

He wasn't sure what to say. "It's not something I have any control over."

"It might not be something you ought to mention too often."

"Don't tell Senneth."

Justin grinned crookedly. "She seems to be working it out for herself."

There wasn't a good answer for that, either, but fortunately there was a distraction as the restless young stranger across the room stood up. "Justin," Cammon said in a low voice. "He's going to try."

Justin's body went even looser. "I suppose he is."

There was a sudden hurtling shape, and the stranger practically dove toward Justin where he lolled back in his chair. Justin's glass went crashing to the floor, and the table legs screeched across the stone. Justin was on his feet before the attacker's first punch landed. He responded with a furious battering of his fists that had the young man tripping backward and holding his arms up, trying to shield his face. Across the bar a woman screamed, and a few of the other patrons were shouting. Cammon sensed a wash of mixed emotions from the foolhardy young man—rage, then pain, then fear—but from Justin, only calm focus and precise, almost mechanical decisions. Justin was born to fight; he was absolutely and completely in control when he faced any kind of opponent. He wasn't even unleashing his full strength on this poor excuse for an assailant. He hadn't drawn a blade and wasn't trying to inflict any damage. A few rough minutes—incontestable proof that he was not to be beaten, at least by this foe—and Justin raised his arms and backed away.

"All done here?" he asked, and the stranger gasped out what was almost a sob and stumbled away. A few of the men who had witnessed the fight offered light applause. Cammon heard one or two of them make derisive comments about the young man's ill-advised attempt to take on a *Rider*.

"Drunk or sober, I'd as soon box with a wildcat," one of them said. "I'd rather take my chances with that raelynx they've got penned up at the palace."

Justin grinned at Cammon, tossed a few coins to the table to pay for any damage, and nodded his head for the door. "I think the night's already been interesting enough," he said. "Let's go home."

CHAPTER

17

IN the morning, Cammon had just slipped into one of his black uniforms when Milo arrived at his door.

"You won't be needed this morning," the steward informed him. "The queen is better but plans to keep to her room today. You are not to attend the princess."

Cammon felt rebellious. "Perhaps I should check with the princess and see if she might want company today after all."

"She is in her parlor," Milo said, giving him a very stern look, "and left strict orders that she was *not* to be disturbed. Particularly by you."

Cammon made a childish face at the door after it had closed behind Milo. Had the steward added that *particularly by you* bit, or had Amalie actually said the words as she stepped into the room that morning?

Cammon's hands stilled midway through the act of undoing his jacket buttons. Except Amalie wasn't in the parlor. She wasn't even in the palace proper. Close—still on the grounds—but out of the building. And alone.

Valri would like that even less than she would like Cammon to spend the day with her.

He quickly rebuttoned his jacket, pulled on his boots and headed out, moving almost blindly through the corridors, following the insistent pull of Amalie's presence. He almost tripped a scullery maid as he cut down a service stairway, which his instincts indicated was part of the shortest route to Amalie. He wasn't even paying attention to what part of the palace he was in and found himself a little surprised when he emerged near the back garden.

That way. As if he could hear a bell clanging or see the smoke of a signal fire, Cammon felt absolutely certain of his direction. He started out at a walk, speeded up to a half-trot, scrambled over obstacles like benches and hedges instead of detouring around them. Past the barracks, past the training yards, past the follies, straight to the walled enclosure that held the raelynx.

She wasn't outside the fence—wasn't just inside the wrought-iron gate—and the raelynx itself was nowhere in sight. But she was there; Cammon could feel her. He tugged on the gate, but it wouldn't open, and a quick inspection convinced him that the lock had been engaged. By the Wild Mother's woolly head, Amalie had locked herself in with the most dangerous creature in the realm.

He closed his hands on the bars as if he might tear them wide enough to admit his body. "Amalie?" he called. "Amalie? I know you're here but please prove to me that you're still alive."

Although he knew that, too—alive and unhurt. Still, he was uneasy. He wanted to see her; he wanted absolute reassurance.

Which he did not get. No reply, no glimpse. "Amalie? Damn. I don't think I can climb this— *Amalie!* If you don't show me you're all right, I'm going to fetch some Riders and breach the walls."

Maybe the threat moved her; maybe she just liked knowing she had alarmed him, but on those words, she strolled slowly into view. She was wearing a black cloak that completely covered her clothing and a black hood that hid her bright hair. The raelynx fluidly paced beside her like so much domesticated fire, its eerie eyes fixed on Cammon, its tail slowly flicking from side to side. Her hand rested lightly in the red fur around its neck. In such a fashion might any noblewoman go out walking with her favorite hound.

"I wasn't sure you'd know where I was," she said, walking straight up to the gate. "But you found me right away. Milo could hardly have left your room ten minutes ago."

For a minute he just watched her in silence. "Did you want me to come looking for you?"

She looked as if she was considering not answering. But then, "Yes," she said, and hunched a shoulder. As if to add, *I don't know why, but there it is.*

"I don't suppose you'd come out of there if I asked you to," he said.

"I like it here."

"I know you think you're safe, but—"

"You could come inside if that would make you feel more secure."

He nodded. "All right."

She looked both surprised and pleased. "Really? You're not afraid?"

"Princess, if he's going to eat one of us, I'd rather it was me."

"He won't eat one of us. He's not even hungry."

Cammon could tell that as well. The big cat was sated from a recent meal. Didn't mean the raelynx might not suddenly develop a taste for human flesh—or a dislike for having its sanctuary invaded. "Let me in."

She turned the lock and he stepped in so quickly the raelynx didn't have time to consider what an open gate might mean. Now, of course, he was only inches away from the great red beast, who examined him with unblinking and unfathomable eyes. Gingerly Cammon reached out to touch its mind, a complex but undefended swirl of thoughts, all of them foreign, all of them brutish and beautiful.

"I don't think I should touch him," he observed presently. "If he's going to give his affection to a human, I think it should only be you."

"You really aren't afraid of him," Amalie said. He thought her voice was admiring.

Cammon shook his head. "We crossed Gillengaria with him in our party last winter. I learned to control him then. Of course, he was just a baby. I'm not sure I could do it now."

"I thought Senneth was the one who held him."

"Most of the time."

She gestured and he saw that there was a lonely bench set deep within the overgrown vegetation of this abandoned garden. The stone was cold under his legs as he sat down, but the sun fell invitingly on his face. Amalie pushed her hood back and her red-gold hair turned to flame.

The raelynx laid its chin across her lap and closed its great eyes. Its tufted ears still twitched from time to time, listening to the sounds around it, but its tail was still, and it radiated peace.

"Now is the time you ask me to forgive you for how badly you have treated me in the past week," Amalie said.

Cammon took a big lungful of air and then expelled it in a rueful sigh. "It seems that no matter what I do these days, someone is displeased with me. And you have to understand, I hate it when people are displeased with me. I can't understand why I suddenly can't seem to make anybody happy. I *always* make people happy. But I am sorry, and I do wish you would forgive me."

She kept her face in profile to him, but she smiled a little. "Valri told me she had warned you to behave more formally with me."

"Senneth, too."

"What are they afraid of? That you'll seduce me?"

He choked and then started laughing. "I suppose that would be the extreme version of it. They say a princess can't make friends with a serving man."

"But I don't have any friends," she said in a small voice.

He didn't even think about it. He just reached out for her hand—the one not buried in the cat's fur—and held it comfortingly in his own. "I think Senneth and Valri have both spent so much of their lives battling other people, fighting to find their own ways, that they didn't spend much time thinking about whether they needed other people," he said. "Senneth wanted to be free of her own family—"

"Valri, too," Amalie interposed.

"I think they were both strong enough to achieve their goals wholly on their own. But I'm not. I don't want to be. I *require* people around me. Maybe it's because I'm a reader and I am so attuned to the voices of other people. If there aren't people, if there aren't voices, I feel like I'm dead." He glanced at her and then glanced away. Her hand was still in his, her fingers cold. She wasn't wearing any gloves. "I don't think Valri and Senneth understand what that's like."

She nodded. "That's not exactly what it's like for me, but it's similar. Since my mother died, I'm just so *lonely*. I want to be around people all the time. And it seems I am so seldom around them."

"Well," he said, smiling a little, "you've had quite an assortment of suitors lately."

She laughed. "And I have enjoyed that sometimes! And sometimes not. I like the ones like Darryn Rappengrass, with whom I do not have to pretend. The rest of them—oh, who knows what they want from me? Why they want to marry me? It makes me wary and uncomfortable. Though that's better than being solitary and sad, I suppose."

"Have you truly liked any of the lords who've come to visit?"

She shrugged. "I found a few of them agreeable, but enough to marry them? Cammon, it is so strange to sit there with a man, and talk about stupid things like weather and travel and trade routes, and the whole time be looking at his face and thinking, 'Are you the one I shall make my husband? Will you be the man I take to my bed? Shall I name you king of Gillengaria?' Sometimes it's hard to concentrate on the conversation because I'm thinking of all the things we're *not* saying."

"They're probably wondering the same things."

"Yes! Which makes it even worse! And, of course, knowing that you and Valri and a couple Riders are listening to every word we say just makes it even more peculiar."

"Riders don't care about things like that," he said with a grin. "They're just waiting to see whether or not they should run in and kill somebody. And Valri and I sit there and play cards. I'm not always listening to the words, to tell you the truth. I'm listening to what they're not saying—trying to read violence in their hearts, you know, or greed, or cruelty."

Her hand moved in his, but she did not pull it away. Part of him remained astonished by that fact, and part of him remained delighted. There was no detail of this scenario he had envisioned this morning when he woke up. "And you'll tell me if any of my suitors would be unkind to me," she said.

"As far as I'm able to judge."

"But there's more you can tell me."

"About the men who come calling? Like what?"

"About men in general. And what they will expect me to know."

"Know about their family fortunes? I thought Milo briefed you about that."

"Of course I'm familiar with their estates and their connections," she said. "It's just that I—well, I'm a princess. There are things people haven't thought to tell me. Even Valri."

He was mystified. "What things?"

She took a deep breath and stared straight in front of her. "I don't know what happens once I'm married," she said. "I've never even seen a man's naked body." A tiny hesitation and then, "I'm sorry if that embarrasses you. I just—I don't know what they will want from me."

He was thoughtful, not embarrassed, and he let enough of that emotion flow over to her so that some of her tension eased away. "Not even statues?" he asked presently. "Not even books? You said you spent a great deal of time in your father's library."

She laughed, but the sound was slightly strained. "Well, *those* books were locked up, apparently, or else I could never find them! I mean, I know their bodies are different, I just don't—I haven't seen—and then I don't know the rest of it. How they fit together. It seems mysterious and—well, a little frightening, to tell you the truth."

Cammon considered it. "I can tell you how it goes."

The relief poured from her in waves. "You've made love to a girl?"

He nodded. "When I lived in Sovenfeld. I was seventeen. My father lived in one town for three whole months, and that's when I got to know Murrie."

He could tell that just the rhythm of his voice was calming her down. She was feeling both relaxed and hopeful. *Cammon will help me.* It wasn't an articulated thought so much as an unshakable belief. She felt secure enough to allow some of her curiosity to surface. "Were you in love with her?"

He grinned. "Well—she was about ten years older than I was, and mostly bored, and she thought I was a funny kid. So I don't know that I loved her. But I sure liked her a lot. We were silly together. I made her laugh and she made me feel good." He felt his grin grow a little lopsided. "So I don't know. Maybe you don't ask too much more of love than that."

"So?" she said. "How does it go?"

He paused, trying to figure out the words. "Well, you'd have to know what a man looks like. I don't suppose you have drawing paper with you. I could sketch in the mud, I suppose."

"You could show me," she suggested.

He nodded. "I could, if you wanted. You realize I'll be hanged if anybody sees me taking off my clothes in front of you."

"Nobody ever comes down here except Valri and me. And the groom who brings fresh game, but he was here yesterday."

If he was going to strip in front of the princess, Cammon wanted to be a lot more certain that no one would accidentally witness the event. He expanded his consciousness outward by feet and yards, searching for other souls wandering nearby. The Riders were the closest but they were acres away, focused on their mock battles. Farther still were gardeners, servants, grooms—the hundreds of people who lived and worked at the palace—but none were close enough to come upon him unawares.

With Valri on her sickbed and Ellynor in attendance, Cammon didn't think he even needed to worry about Lirrenfolk creeping up on him at a time he most desired no audience.

Slipping his hand free, he stood up and began unlacing his pants. "It's pretty cold, so that's going to have an effect, but you'll get the general idea," he said. "Do you want me to take off *all* my clothes, or just my trousers?"

"All of them," she said. "If you wouldn't mind."

So three minutes later he was standing naked before Princess Amalie, heiress to the throne of Gillengaria, explaining how a man's body worked and how it could be used to pleasure a woman's. She listened intently, asked a dozen questions, made him turn around, and sought clarification on a couple of points. The raelynx lifted his head as if Cammon might smell a little more appetizing now that his pale skin was uncovered, but it showed no inclination to attack. Cammon was freezing by the time Amalie was satisfied enough for him to put his clothes back on, and he hopped in place for a few minutes just to get his blood warmed back up.

"Thank you," she said. "I'm still not sure I'm looking forward to this, but at least I know what to expect."

He grinned and settled next to her on the bench again. There didn't seem to be any casual way to retrieve her hand. "Murrie liked it," he answered. "She said most girls did. So maybe you will, too."

"Maybe it depends on the man you're with."

"Maybe," he said. "So be careful who you pick."

She gave him a sideways glance through a fall of bright hair. "That's why I need you," she said. "To help me make the right choice."

It was Cammon, not Amalie, who insisted that they return to the palace. "Majesty, they will send me away from Ghosenhall altogether if they think I am becoming too familiar," he said, and that, apparently, was a threat that worked. So she sniffed, and let them out of the garden, and preceded him to the palace so that no one would see them together. He returned to his room to await his summons, and soon Milo had reappeared at his door.

"It seems the princess desires your attendance after all," the steward said. "She is in the parlor."

But Valri had roused herself from her sickbed enough to make sure Amalie had a chaperone, and Cammon arrived in Amalie's favorite room to find Belinda Brendyn already in place. Amalie shot him a warning look, but he knew better than to pull up a chair and instantly deal out a hand of cards.

"Majesty? My lady? Milo said you might have need of me."

"The regent's wife mentioned that she knew very little about mystics, and I said you would be willing to tell us stories to pass the time," the princess said.

Belinda smiled. She was small and dark-haired and growing round with pregnancy, and she simply glowed with goodwill and happiness. "Well, I know that some of them are exceptional healers, and I was hoping one of them might be on hand when my baby comes," she said. "It's my first child, and I'm a little nervous."

"You can't count on Kirra being anywhere nearby when you need her, but there's a Rider who's just married a mystic, and she's a gifted healer," Cammon said. "I'm sure Ellynor would be happy to meet with you anytime you wanted."

He didn't stay long, and over dinner that night he only sent one or two comments Amalie's way when something in the conversation struck him as odd or humorous. But it didn't matter. He was sublimely happy. Amalie was no longer angry with him. And the whole world was glorious.

CHAPTER

18

Two days later, Valri was fully recovered, Senneth and Tayse were a day into their return journey, Kirra and Donnal were headed for Danalustrous, and Toland Storian came calling.

Amalie had spent the morning combating her dread. "But I hate him, Valri," she said every time the queen reminded her to treat him with friendliness. "He's a pig."

"Hey, maybe Kirra could really turn him into a pig," Cammon suggested. Amalie looked amenable to the idea, but Valri frowned.

"Storian is an important ally."

"Storian has been trading with Fortunalt and Gisseltess and may in fact be contemplating an assault on the throne," Amalie retorted.

"That's why it's so important that you be amiable to ser Toland. If he believes he has a chance to wed you, he might persuade his father to hold back from war."

Despite her misgivings, Amalie managed to be perfectly gracious to Toland while the two of them sat in the receiving room, engaged in the opening round of their courtship. Cammon thought the serramar was boastful, arrogant, and a little too familiar (though he realized he had no right to criticize on that last point), but Amalie handled him deftly.

"Of course you'll join us for dinner tonight," she said, as she always said.

"Of course I will. I was hoping there might be dancing as well." Cammon imagined the leer on Toland's aristocratic face. "We danced together at a number of Houses last summer, and I enjoyed those times very much."

"No, I don't think we have such entertainments planned."

"Too bad. I would like a chance to hold you in my arms again."

The heavy gallantry made Valri grimace—and made Cammon want to rip through the false wall and punch the proud noble in the face. Of course, just imagining what would happen next—Riders bursting through

right behind him, Valri launching into a furious tirade—made him want
to smile again.

He had not intended to send Amalie that picture, but somehow she
had caught it, for he heard the lilt in her voice. "Now, ser Toland. You
don't want to press too hard or appear overeager. I have many defenders
and one of them is likely to take offense."

Bright Mother burn me, Cammon thought. Valri looked at him curiously but he did not meet her eyes. He was going to have to be a lot more
careful about what he thought if Amalie was going to be able to read him
so easily.

"Well, of course you have defenders," Toland said smoothly. "But I
wager if you spend a little more time alone with me you might find you
don't want them interfering as we get to know each other."

Now Valri was scowling at the wall. She turned to Cammon and
mouthed, *What an ass*. He nodded emphatically.

Amalie, surprisingly, did not seem at all offended. "Perhaps you're
right. I assume you are planning to stay a day or two? Let's go for a walk
tomorrow morning, just around the palace grounds. I can show you some
of the prettiest gardens and you can tell me a great deal more about yourself. I'm sure we will enjoy ourselves immensely."

Valri and Cammon exchanged startled glances, but Toland was
deeply pleased. He said, "Majesty, it will be an honor."

ACCORDINGLY, the next morning, a small procession set out to stroll
through the royal lawns. Toland did not seem delighted to realize that his
romantic outing with the princess would be attended by two Riders, the
queen, and a serving man, but he offered Amalie his arm and escorted her
down the path to the sculpture gardens.

"How much will you wager that before the hour is out he'll put his
arm around her waist or take her hand?" Valri said.

"Nothing," Cammon replied. "I'm sure he will."

"Why is she encouraging him this way?"

"*You're* the one who told her to be nice to him!"

"Amalie never does what I say."

That made him grin. "Maybe she's really testing us. Seeing how much
we can stand when we see her with an idiot like Toland."

"If he tries to kiss her, I'll have one of the Riders run him through."

Cammon was amazed at how furious he suddenly was. "*Kiss* her?
Surely not! With so many people watching?"

"You wait and see. He'll find a way to get her behind a tree or around a corner, and he'll kiss her. He's the type."

Amalie, be careful with him, Cammon sent out to her. *Valri thinks he'll try to take liberties. Turn around at any point and go back inside. You don't have to placate Storian quite so much.*

But Amalie's mind was completely closed to him. He couldn't even tell if she heard him, and she certainly didn't respond.

So he fretted for the next thirty minutes, every time a bend of the path or the stoop of a tree momentarily hid the princess and her swain from view. Even Justin and Coeval, a few feet behind, must have lost sight of their quarry now and then, Cammon was sure. Once, as Amalie and Toland slipped past a dairy house, they disappeared for a good fifteen seconds, and when Cammon could see them again, Amalie looked flushed and Toland smug.

"He kissed her," Cammon whispered to the queen. "I'm sure of it."

"Why doesn't she look more upset?"

Cammon felt a profound and bitter blackness settle over him. "I don't know. Maybe she likes him after all. Maybe she was just pretending before."

"Well, he *is* handsome in a sort of hearty and stupid way."

His mood grew even darker, and he made no answer.

Cammon had been so absorbed in watching the suitor and trying to guess Amalie's response that he hadn't paid much attention to where they were heading. But a small exclamation from Valri made him realize Amalie had led them all the way to the far end of the compound where the raelynx made its home.

"Why bring him here?" the queen murmured.

Amalie said something indistinguishable to Toland, and he caught her hand in his, lifting it to his heart. Suddenly the still winter air was shattered by a blood-chilling and inhuman sound—the wailing shriek of a raelynx, rising and rising, increasing in intensity, until it was abruptly cut off.

Toland dropped Amalie's hand and whirled around, fingers on his dress sword, eyes wide and frightened. Cammon saw his lips move. *What was that?* Justin and Coeval had drawn their weapons and taken defensive postures—though Justin, at least, recognized the sound of a raelynx and knew there was no defense against one.

Amalie's clear voice was distinct in the sudden silence. "That's my raelynx. One of my many defenders."

She twisted the key in the lock and flung wide the gate.

The raelyx bounded out.

For a moment, everyone was frozen. Cammon caught Valri's sudden silent scream of horror, felt Justin's wicked spike of fear—those two knew what a raelynx was capable of, how impossible it was to contain. Toland's fright was more elemental and uninformed. He just knew that this large, feral, unfamiliar creature was stalking in his direction with its hot eyes fixed unwaveringly on his face.

"It's going to kill that boy," Valri whispered, and suddenly both of them were running. *Toward* the big cat, which was insane, hoping to save the serramar, hoping to save the princess. Cammon felt Valri's mind open up as she reached out for the raelynx—felt her utter astonishment when she realized that the cat was under someone else's control.

Justin and Coeval were also on the move but, without looking at them, Amalie held up her hand to keep them at bay. Cammon and Valri skidded to a halt beside the Riders, and Justin gave Cammon one quick, wide-eyed glance. But no one spoke. No one moved except Amalie, who took two steps closer to Toland and buried her hand in the fur of the raelynx's neck.

The raelynx released another of those preternatural cries. Only Amalie seemed unaffected.

"One of my protectors," she repeated to Toland in a tranquil voice. "I told you I had many."

"What—what *is* it? Will it eat me?"

"He's a raelynx. Imported from the Lirrenlands. He would most definitely eat you if he was hungry. And if I wasn't here to stop him. He responds to my will and to my moods. He knows that you have upset me a little with your behavior—and you see, that's upset him as well."

"I didn't! I—I didn't know and he—he—what are you going to do with him? Put him back! Lock him up!"

Amalie stroked the cat's fur. "I don't think so. He's been locked up too long as it is. I believe I'll take him back with me to the palace tonight."

That was so outrageous that suddenly all of them found their voices, Toland, Valri, and Justin all simultaneously begging Amalie to change her mind, to not be ridiculous, to think of the danger, Majesty, think of the panic. Cammon said nothing aloud but he put a question directly in her head. *Are you serious?*

This time she replied, a single word, but he heard it distinctly. *Yes.*

By the Bright Mother's red eye. "She can control it," he whispered to Valri. "I've seen her do it. Better than you or I can."

"Can you take it away from her? I'm trying, and I can't."

He shook his head. "I think we have to trust her."

"It's madness!"

For the life of him, he couldn't repress a grin. "I know."

Amalie was smiling impartially at the whole group as if they weren't all regarding her with varying degrees of terror and despair. "I think ser Toland is getting a little chilled. Shall we all head back inside?"

Justin, living up to his reputation for reckless bravery, actually gainsaid her. "Majesty. Think a moment about the chaos you will unleash throughout the palace if you try to bring that creature inside."

"Yes," she said. "I'm sure there will be some consternation until people get used to him. But he responds to my direction. There is no need to fear."

Justin held his ground. "But there *will* be fear. If nothing else, let someone return in advance of you to warn the inhabitants what danger is on its way."

Amalie tilted her chin at him, clearly not liking this suggestion. It was the first time Cammon realized that she was blazingly furious and that only the most iron will was allowing her to keep her anger in check. Sweet gods, if she lost that control, the raelynx would slip away from her, and then there would be a reckoning such as she could never have imagined.

"I would never do anything to endanger my people," she said loftily.

"Then return the raelynx to his cell and bring him out some other day when his appearance will not be so terrifying."

Amalie hesitated—then glanced at Cammon. Half of him thought it would be marvelous to have Amalie parade the wild cat across the compound and show the entire city what strange and potent resources she commanded. Half of him desperately wished to see the raelynx safely behind a barred gate. This was not the time to give in to his more adventurous impulses. He nodded slowly.

Amalie seemed to deflate slightly. "Very well. Since you are all so worried. I will return him to his pen for now. But I will release him on some future date, and you will see then how well he minds me."

Justin bowed very low, his fist against his shoulder. "Majesty, that will be a most memorable day."

Amalie's hand tightened in the cat's fur, and she seemed to tug it toward the fence. "Come," she said in a soft voice. "Just a taste of freedom after all."

For a moment, the raelynx resisted, and the rest of them all grew motionless again. But then, growling with protest, the big cat turned under her hand and slunk back into the garden. In a moment, the gate was shut, the lock was thrown, and Amalie was giving them all that sunny smile.

"Well?" she said. "Shall we head back?"

Toland drew a shuddering breath and stumbled up the path toward the palace without waiting for anyone else to move. Valri sagged against Cammon, clutching his arm as if she might fall to the ground without his support. Justin gave Cammon a very serious look—and then, the smallest grin. Coeval said nothing, just sheathed his weapon.

"Yes, Amalie," Valri said, straightening up and pulling free of Cammon. "I think we *should* head back. And you and I shall walk in front of the others so I can tell you *exactly* what I think of this little escapade."

The queen pulled the princess ahead of her and began a low diatribe in a dark voice. The other three followed more slowly, but it was impossible not to realize that Amalie was receiving the tongue-lashing of her life.

"I'll be off to the barracks," Coeval said, and parted from them at the first branching of the pathways.

Justin continued alongside Cammon, his grin growing wider. "Damn," he said a few times. "That took cool nerve, didn't it? *Damn!* Senneth will fall down in a faint when she hears the story."

"Guess we don't have to worry any more about Toland Storian wanting to marry the princess," Cammon said. That thought was cheering him up so much that he was quickly overcoming his shock.

"It would tend to dampen your ardor if you thought your wife could loose a wild animal on you," Justin agreed.

"Ellynor could probably call up a raelynx to maul *you*," Cammon scoffed.

Justin nodded. "She probably could. But she hasn't produced one lately, so I'm just not that worried about it. But *damn*. I can't believe she did that." He cut his eyes over at Cammon. "Makes me wonder what she might try next. I'm thinking the princess might keep surprising all of us."

Cammon nodded. "She keeps surprising *me*."

It was exhilarating and spectacular, but unnerving and terrifying at the same time. Cammon was out of his depth, and he was fairly certain Valri was fast coming to the same conclusion.

Senneth, he thought, sending the message halfway across Gillengaria. *I wish you were here now.*

CHAPTER
19

THE trip to Carrebos had been quick and free of trouble. Tayse was a most efficient traveler, and Senneth never required any particular amenities on the road. Kirra and Donnal had elected to make the journey in animal shape, although Kirra, at least, always took human form when they stopped for the night. Donnal sometimes joined them as a black dog, sometimes as a white-faced wolf, but never as a man. Senneth wondered if that was because Darryn Rappengrass was present, and Donnal was rarely at ease around any nobility except Kirra and Senneth.

Darryn, as always, was delightful company, humorous and charming. He only turned serious when talk turned to war, and they spent part of every evening running over the same fears and possibilities. Was Halchon Gisseltess still a prisoner on his own lands at Gissel Plain, or had he escaped the king's men who were guarding him—as he had managed to do more than once in the past? Was Rayson Fortunalt helping him raise an army? Which other marlords had he recruited? If they planned to attack, what signal were they waiting for? Would they send another assassin to Ghosenhall to try to murder the king?

"And what of Coralinda Gisseltess?" Senneth demanded the night before they arrived in Carrebos. "She has been so quiet lately! Surely she is plotting something as well?"

"I wouldn't doubt it," Darryn agreed. He ran a hand through his chestnut hair and allowed a frown to settle across his pleasant features. "My mother is convinced that Halchon and Rayson are only awaiting the coming of good weather before they launch an assault. Her spies tell her there has been increased activity at all the southern ports as Gisseltess and Fortunalt import supplies to support an army."

"Makes sense," Senneth said gloomily. "Does your mother feel prepared to defend her own borders?"

"As prepared as she can be. But I think she lives in constant worry."

"As do we all."

Kirra was tired of war talk. "So, Darryn! Why haven't you abandoned us yet?" she asked. "I thought you would turn toward Rappen Manor at least a day ago."

He gave her a casual smile. "I thought I would accompany you to Carrebos instead. I find it a most intriguing city."

"You've been there?" Senneth asked.

"Many times." He dropped his gaze. "She lives there. Sosinetta. The woman you have heard me speak of."

"Your ladylove!" Kirra crooned. "Oh, Darryn, will you introduce us?"

"I'm afraid she might be overwhelmed. You're very grand."

Senneth glanced down at her travel-stained trousers and her long-sleeved shirt, rather the worse for wear. "I don't think that's an adjective that applies to me. And Kirra can look like an urchin, you know."

"Even better. I'll shift into a friendly little dog," Kirra offered. "I'll just frisk around and lick her hand and she won't be at all intimidated."

Darryn laughed. "I'll think about it."

"There's no *thinking about it*," Kirra said. "Now that we know she lives in Carrebos, we won't rest until we've seen her! Why didn't you tell us before?"

He groaned and dropped his head in his hands. "For precisely that reason. I'm a fool."

Senneth grinned at Kirra. "Now I'm even more excited about arriving tomorrow."

THE weather was nasty as they pulled into the city around noon. Icy droplets were pelting in straight from the roiling sea, so they were not particularly focused on watching for young ladies who might run up to offer Darryn ecstatic greetings. They headed for the nearest inn, gratefully turned over their horses, and gathered in the taproom once they had changed to dry clothes. Kirra, Senneth, and Tayse slid into a booth; Donnal settled under the table at Kirra's feet.

"Ser Darryn has disappeared," Tayse observed.

"We'll find him," Kirra said. "Don't worry about that."

"What we need to find now is a mystic," Senneth said.

In a town like Carrebos, that task proved simple to accomplish. Their server was a boy of about sixteen, gangly and thin, with unkempt black hair falling into his eyes. He had taken their orders so negligently that Senneth did not repose much faith in receiving the meal she'd requested, but when he returned she saw he had found a novel way of carrying several dinner platters at once. They were levitated in front of him, one stacked above the other, supported by nothing but air and willpower. Three glasses of beer hovered near his shoulder.

Senneth couldn't look at Kirra, who was clearly on the verge of erupting into laughter. "Thank you," she said gravely as the boy settled everything on the table without a single spill. "I have to suppose you possess a little magical skill."

He nodded carelessly. "Makes the job easier, that's for certain."

"I know this is a city where many mystics live," Senneth said. "How do I go about meeting all of them?"

Now his face turned closed and suspicious. So he'd been scarred by fear or malice a time or two, Senneth guessed. "Why would you want to do that?"

She held her hand out, palm up, and allowed fire to dance between her fingers, all the while keeping her eyes on his face. "No need to fear me," she said quietly. "I am a mystic myself. I am on a mission for the king."

The boy's eyes darted from Senneth's burning hand to the faces of her companions. "You're all mystics?" he said.

"Not him. He's a soldier," Senneth said, because naming Tayse a Rider might create more distrust in this particular community. "The rest of us." Donnal poked his black nose out from under the table and offered a short bark.

The serving boy seemed reassured. "I'll ask Ward. He owns the place." He gave her a quick grin. "He's a reader, so if you're lying, he'll throw you out."

The boy departed and Kirra said, "He'll *try* to throw us out. No one's ever managed that yet."

"I don't think he'll even try, since we are who we say. Sweet gods, I'm hungry."

They all dug in, happy to have a meal that hadn't been prepared on the road. Senneth hadn't quite cleaned her plate when they were approached by a rather large man—big bellied, round faced, and nearly bald. He wore a filthy apron over his clothes and carried a rather large butcher knife in one hand, so Senneth guessed he was both owner and chief cook—and defender of the premises.

He pulled out a chair, reversed it, laid his knife on the table, and introduced himself. "I'm Ward. What is a King's Rider and a group of mystics doing at my inn?"

So much for anonymity. Kirra was giggling again, but Senneth actually liked having a reader in the mix. Everyone was forced to be honest.

"Trying to raise an army," she said. "And wondering if we might find a few sorcerous recruits in Carrebos."

Ward scratched the back of his head. "Way I hear it, king's already got an army."

"Ordinary men," Senneth said. Her gaze flicked to Tayse, who was smiling slightly. Very well, the Riders were hardly ordinary. "We hope to augment them with extraordinary ones. Shape-shifters. Readers. Healers. Those who can call fire. I fear we may have need of all their magical skills if we truly are drawn into war."

"King hasn't done much to protect mystics from people who hate them," Ward said.

"Not true," Tayse interposed. "He has made Ghosenhall a haven for them and fined the marlords who allow mystics to be persecuted on their lands. There is little the king can do to guard mystics who live in remote hamlets far from the royal city."

Ward shrugged. "Maybe. But not everyone feels kindly toward the king."

"Do you feel kindly toward Coralinda Gisseltess?" Kirra asked. "Because if war comes and the king is defeated, she will be free to spread her gospel of hatred across the realm. No mystic will be safe then, not even in enclaves like Carrebos."

"We can defend ourselves," Ward said. "Done it for months now. There was only one time the Pale Mother's soldiers came here, and we defeated them all."

"Which is exactly why I would wish some of you to join the king," Senneth said. "To help us defeat enemies who want to strip magic from the land."

Ward scratched the back of his head again. "I'll mention it to a few people," he said. He hauled himself up and pushed his way back toward the kitchen.

"Not sure we can count on him for unconditional support," Kirra observed.

"We'll make the rounds tomorrow morning. Drop by the other inns and restaurants," Senneth said. "Word will get out. We'll see if anyone's interested."

THE weather was better the following day, for which Senneth was grateful. She didn't mind heat, didn't mind cold, but she hated ice and snow. All was well with the world as long as there was sunshine.

Even in winter, Carrebos was a pretty little town, a crowded collection of mismatched but well-tended buildings mostly grouped along a few major streets. It was nestled right up against the sea, so the smells of salt and fish were very strong, and the view of the sparkling water added to the pleasures of the sunny day.

Senneth had decided that a smaller group might have better success, so she and Kirra began to canvass the other eating establishments in Carrebos. Donnal conducted investigations in his own fashion, nosing around kitchens and street corners; Tayse said he wanted to patrol the town and get a sense of its size, makeup, and fortifications. He disliked being in unfamiliar territory and always welcomed a chance to study new terrain.

Senneth and Kirra were at their third stop when, most unexpectedly, they encountered someone they knew. They were sitting in a back booth at an inviting tavern where they were the only customers of the morning. Having already consumed two breakfasts, they'd decided they should just order tea and hope the proprietor didn't grumble. Their waitress was a young woman with dark hair piled in a bun and an air of smooth competence.

"Good morning, I hope you're well," she greeted them—and then she flung out her arms so wide that the towel in her hand went flying.

"*Senneth?* Can it be you? Oh, and *Kirra!* I can't believe it!"

Senneth stared, at first absolutely blank. "I'm sorry, I don't—"

The young woman was almost dancing where she stood. "I'm Sosie! You probably never even looked at my face, you were so busy with Annie, but I'm the one—"

"Sosie!" Senneth exclaimed and jumped to her feet to give the girl a hug. "I never thought to see you again. And Annie is well? And the baby?" She glanced around. "Are they here?"

Kirra was on her feet, too, predictably delighted. "I remember you!" she said. "Your sister is the one who was having the mystic baby that night we were in your village. And no one would help her except us."

Sosie nodded vigorously. "We left our father's house three weeks later and went to Rappengrass. Then we heard about Carrebos and we thought it might be safer here."

Senneth was drawing her down beside her in the booth. "Can you sit a moment? The place doesn't look too busy. Can you talk? Tell us what's happened to you and your sister."

Sosie laughed. "We're all doing quite well. Kinnon—that's the baby, you know—he's a year old now and *so* much trouble. Those first few weeks he would just fling stuff about! While we traveled, he sometimes could make trees shake and stones start tumbling. I can tell you, I thought we would never survive the trip. But Annie learned to control him, and now she and Ned are married, and, of course, Ned can keep Kinnon in check—"

"Who's Ned?" Kirra asked.

"Oh! Kinnon's father! He was in Carrebos when we arrived! Doing tricks with the acrobatic troupe, but he's got a better job now."

"And you?" Senneth asked. "You look well and happy. You like being here among all the mystics? It might be a little strange for someone with no power of her own."

"It is strange sometimes," she admitted. "Sometimes I wonder if the rest of them despise me a little because I don't have any magic. But then I think how odd it must be for *them* when they live someplace where they're the only ones who are different. And then I don't mind so much."

"And you've found a job. This seems like a nice place—do you like it?"

"Very much! I have a room off the kitchen. Annie and Ned have built their own house and I stay with them sometimes, but there's more privacy here."

"Why do you need privacy?" Kirra inquired. "Do you have a young man?"

Sosie blushed deeply, and smiled, and looked very pretty. She had been thin and anxious that dreadful night when Kinnon was brought roughly into the world, but she had filled out and gained a great deal of confidence since then, Senneth thought.

"Well—yes—at least—I don't know how serious he is," Sosie said. "But I see him when he's in town and I miss him when he's not, so—" She shrugged. "But tell me about the two of you! You have no idea how often I have thought of you and wished I could tell you how much it meant to us to have you there that night. You saved our lives and you gave us courage." She tugged at a cord hidden under her gown and pulled out an amulet made of faded silk. "I wear this every day. It has helped me so many times."

Senneth had no idea what it was. "What's inside the bag?"

Sosie laughed and opened her eyes wide. "The piece of quartz that you enchanted for me! You told me it would give me strength."

Senneth felt Kirra's eyes on her. It had been—oh, not exactly a bit of trickery—more a wild hope that she could transfer a bit of her magic to an inanimate object and then hand it over to someone who might be able to draw on its reflected power. "I'm so glad I was able to give you that much help," she said quietly. "Being able to save Annie and Kinnon meant more to me than I think I can explain to you. Magic had cost me so much at that point in my life. I needed to know that it could pay back in some appreciable measure as well."

Sosie nodded. "I think the same thing sometimes. Magic almost cost Kinnon his life—almost cost Annie her life. It had better be worth the price."

The door to the tavern opened and a lone man stepped inside. "Oh, no, looks like you're going to have to wait on customers," Kirra said. "Well, get him settled right away and then come back and talk to us."

Sosie glanced over and her blush suddenly returned. "No, that's Darryn. He'll wait for me. I saw him last night."

Senneth's eyes flew to Kirra, whose face was alight with divine mischief. Obviously, they had solved the mystery of Darryn's peasant lover. "Darryn? Darryn Rappengrass?" Senneth said faintly. The visitor had his back to them, for he had paused to say a word to a man who had stepped out from the kitchen.

Sosie's face was even brighter. "Do you know him? He's a great noble."

"Why, yes, we've met ser Darryn a few times," Kirra said in an affable voice. "You wouldn't think it to look at us, but Senneth and I are fine nobles, too, and many's the ball we've attended where we took a turn dancing a waltz with the serramar."

Sosie looked uncertainly from one to the other. "Are you joking?" she asked.

"She's not, but don't be nervous," Senneth said, laying her hand on Sosie's arm. "We're about as disreputable as nobles can be, and both of our families have practically disowned us."

"And you know Darryn?" Sosie repeated, clearly trying to decide how alarmed she should be.

"Know him! We traveled with him here from Ghosenhall!" Kirra said. She was utterly gleeful; this was a situation that irresistibly appealed to her sense of devilry. "And while he had mentioned that he'd fallen in love with a girl, not until we were almost at the city limits did he tell us her name or the fact that she lived in Carrebos."

"Though he didn't call you Sosie," Senneth said. "What was it? Something else."

"Sosinetta? Sosabelle?" the girl said faintly. "He is always making up new names for me."

"Well, I think you can believe that he truly loves you, if that's something you were worried about," Kirra said. "For he tried not to talk of you too often, but it was clear you were constantly on his mind—and, oh, perhaps this might convince you," she said, as if just now struck by the thought. "He's turned down a chance to wed Princess Amalie, who's a pretty girl with lovely manners and a kingdom to inherit. But ser Darryn says he's in love with *you.*"

Sosie gasped and then clapped her hands to her hot cheeks. "The *princess*! No! But he—I mean, he— I love him so much, but I know he—"

Kirra put her elbows on the table and leaned forward in a confiding manner. "Senneth and I rather like it when two people make an unequal match," she said. "Our own romances have been so unconventional."

Senneth patted Sosie on the shoulder. "Don't let her tease you. We're really quite pleased to see you again—and we really do know Darryn—and he really did tell us how much he loves you. There, that's a present better than magic any day, isn't it? Proof of love?"

"You should let him know we're here," Kirra said. "Just bring him right over."

"I—I think I will," Sosie said, and scrambled away from the table.

Kirra looked over at Senneth and laughed outright. "I think this must be the best trip we've ever had."

Senneth was watching Sosie run up to Darryn, saw him kiss her quickly, listen intently, and then glance over at the booth in something like dismay. She waved, and Kirra blew him a kiss. "Well," Senneth said, "today has certainly been fun."

THE rest of the day was a little less fun but definitely more productive. The owner of the tavern where Sosie worked—a thin, fretful man named Eddie—was much more amenable to the notion of army recruiters than Ward had been, and he agreed to let Senneth and Kirra stay in his place all day, presenting their case to residents. His wife turned out to be a reader as well, and she sat beside them most of the day, giving them quick biographies of the mystics who approached them and her assessment of their reliability.

Before day's end, Senneth guessed that they'd talked to thirty or forty mystics with a range of powers and varying degrees of amiability. A few she liked instantly and hoped to bring back to Ghosenhall right away. A few others seemed only mildly interested in her proposition but agreed to join up with the royal army if war really did sweep across Gillengaria.

One or two struck her as being too furtive or too damaged to be of much use, no matter how desperate the battle became. These were mystics who had been beaten or threatened or abused so often that they had little strength and no trust left in them, and their power, if any remained, was buried and hard to summon.

These were the mystics, in some sense, who most deserved to have a war fought in their defense.

Ward came by late in the day, sneering a little. He was accompanied by a boy who might have been twelve years old, slight and reedy and freckle-faced. He had badly combed hair, impish eyes, and an air of guileless excitement.

"Lot of people seem to be interested in this story you're telling about the king needing an army of mystics," Ward said. He was so big he seemed to be crowding them back into the booth, though he didn't actually try to sit.

"It's the truth, as—with your ability—you surely know," Senneth replied.

"Might be true, but people need a reason to follow someone like you. A total stranger," Ward said. "Maybe you don't have any power of your own, or not much, anyway. People want to know how strong *you* are."

"Other people want to know, or just you?" Kirra inquired sweetly.

Senneth ignored her. "I'm a fire mystic. I'd be pleased to demonstrate my ability. Would you like me to burn Carrebos to the ground? I can do that, but I doubt it would make anybody truly happy."

Ward put his hand on his companion's shoulder. "Jase here's a fire mystic, too," Ward says. "We've all seen him call up flame—and settle it down, too, when a house was about to burn. Maybe you could have a sort of competition with Jase—show us what you can do that he can't. People might be impressed by that. If you were better."

"Oh, a duel!" Kirra said, clapping her hands together. "What fun!"

Senneth didn't even look at her. "It's not remotely fair," she said quietly. "I'm twenty years older than he is and far stronger than you realize. He has no chance of besting me."

Ward shrugged. "Well, if you're afraid to try—"

Kirra strangled a laugh. Senneth dropped her eyes to Jase's face. "How old are you?" she asked him.

"Thirteen a week ago."

"You're pretty good with fire."

He shrugged, but his eyes were blazing with excitement, so she guessed he had a nice combustible power. "Well, Jase, I tell you this just so you know what to expect. I've never met a mystic who's stronger than

I am, no matter what his skill. And I can see I'm going to have to show off a little to prove a point to your friend here. So don't be upset if I don't hold back. Don't let it discourage you."

He grinned. "All right."

"When shall we have our little contest?" she asked Ward. "Do you need time to alert the town?"

"How about right after dinner?" he said. "Sky'll be dark. Fire'll show up real pretty then."

"Agreed," she said. "Let's meet out on the main street in about two hours."

Tayse was back about an hour later, Donnal at his heels, so they ate a surprisingly delicious meal in Eddie's tavern. Darryn joined them and endured their teasing until talk turned to the upcoming competition.

"How do I play this?" Senneth asked Tayse, the consummate tactician. "Start small and build, or just open with conflagration?"

He considered. "Open big, but save something for a final showdown. Awe them, and then terrify them."

"Any chance the boy could really be better than Senneth?" Darryn asked.

"No," Senneth, Kirra, and Tayse all answered in unison.

Senneth laughed. "And if he is, then I'm certainly bringing him back to Ghosenhall, whether or not he wants to come! Anyone with more power than me should definitely be in service to the king."

When it was full dark, Senneth and her party emerged from Eddie's tavern to find a sizable portion of Carrebos's population already lining the main street. An iron brazier had been set in the middle of the road. Ward and Jase stood right in front of it, tending a small fire, while the townspeople waited a respectful distance back. Senneth made her way through the crowd with quite a contingent following her—Tayse, Kirra, Donnal-the-dog, Darryn, Sosie, Eddie, and Eddie's wife. None of the spectators appeared worried, Senneth thought. They all looked like they had come out for an evening of rare entertainment.

She couldn't imagine another city in Gillengaria that would be so complacent at the notion of witnessing a duel between mystics.

She stepped up to the brazier and smiled at Jase. "Do you require a little fire to begin with? To get your own fires going?"

He eyed her uncertainly. "I don't know. I've never tried to start one on my own. But I can put *out* any fire that's set."

"Let's see, then," Senneth said. She held up her hand, closed her fingers, and tamped out the blaze.

There was a small ripple of response from the crowd, but she wasn't done yet. She raised her arm and offered a quick twist of her wrist, and every window of every building in town went dark. Candles blown out, hearth fires extinguished, light and heat smothered at every source. The murmuring of the crowd grew louder.

"Ah, but we need a bit of fire, don't we, just to see what we're doing," she said. Pivoting slowly on one foot, she pointed at building after building—the taverns, the shops, the cottages—and reignited each separate flame inside each one. Then she made the circle one more time, spinning a little faster, setting fire to objects that had never been meant to be torches. A short pole holding a merchant's sign. The tall chimney of a two-story boardinghouse. A bare, scrubby tree lurking on one side of the road. A cart. A wine barrel. The coals in the brazier sprang back to life.

Undaunted, Jase whirled around just a second or two behind her, dousing each unnatural blaze, leaving the hearth fires unmolested and the candles primly flickering.

She had to laugh. "Very good," she approved. "Now, can you put this one out?"

She set herself on fire.

"Mercy!" someone shouted, and she felt the whole crowd shift back. She viewed the world through a wall of violent colors, orange and red and yellow and black. Her clothes writhed with flame, her short hair was a crackling wick. She felt the tickling heat on her skin, breathed the scorched air—she knew she was burning—but she felt relaxed, familiar, ordinary. She was always a degree or two away from combustion anyway; she harbored fire in her heart, felt it running always through her veins. Sometimes it surprised her to think she didn't always exist surrounded by a prismatic inferno.

She felt Jase's magic tugging at the flames, dampening them to short little licks of fire. She let him succeed for a few minutes, enough for the crowd to notice, enough for Jase himself to feel a little thrill of accomplishment. Then she flung her arms upward and a column of flame shot above her head, reaching so high no one on the ground could see the end of it. She pivoted again, more quickly this time, and gestured. *Here. Here. This place. Here.* And each time she pointed her fingers, something else erupted into fire. Eddie's tavern. Ward's inn. The house of some poor on-looker, who instantly started wailing. The whole street was hemmed in with heat; every intent face was illuminated by the erratic, dramatic light.

Jase gamely stabbed his own hands toward a few burning buildings, and the fires went cold. But for every one he put out, Senneth started two more. He waved his arms and scrambled around her, but he could not keep up. Another house consumed by fire—another. She made one broad sweeping gesture, and every structure in the town suddenly burst into flame.

This audience knew magic, but even they were beginning to grow fearful. And she wasn't done yet. Make it spectacular, Tayse had said. So Senneth reached out—not laying her hand on a soul—and one by one set spectators on fire. Jase. Ward. Eddie. Sosie. Anyone who stepped too close.

Then she raised her voice over the excited consternation of the crowd. "You must realize by now that anything I touch with sorcerous flame will only burn if I want it to," she said. Indeed, Sosie and a young man at the front of the crowd both appeared utterly delighted, lifting up their incendiary hands and turning them this way and that. "Yet I hope you will believe me when I say I could bring this whole town down in a matter of minutes and no one—not even this talented boy—could stop me."

Abruptly she lowered her arms and all the fires vanished, except the small one twinkling in the brazier and an uneven halo glittering around her own fair head. "I truly possess a great deal of power, and I have the absolute confidence of the king. Anyone who wants to travel to Ghosenhall would be welcome to leave with us when we return. We would be glad to have you in our army. We know just how formidable a weapon magic can be."

Of course, that unleashed a maelstrom of conversation as everyone in the crowd began speaking at once—though most of them were talking to their neighbors about the extraordinary sights they had just seen. A few pressed closer to speak with Senneth herself, but she turned first to Jase, who had darted to her side the minute fire fell away from his body.

"I hope you aren't too disappointed," she began, but he was skipping in place.

"I want to learn that!" he exclaimed. "Can you show me? How do you make it burn without burning? Without hurting?"

She laughed but had no time to explain before others pushed between them. "Come see me tomorrow," she called to Jase. "I'll show you some basic exercises."

Then she was swallowed by the people of Carrebos, who seemed, for the most part, to be thrilled by her exhibition and suddenly willing to share with her their own tricks and abilities. Even the hostile Ward came up to clap her on the back and express his admiration. *It doesn't make sense to me,* she thought as she smiled and nodded. *When I want to be convinced a person is worthwhile, I want to listen to his arguments and understand his mind. I don't suddenly trust him because he's put on a gaudy display of power and might.* But Tayse had counseled her correctly, and it was just such a gaudy display that had won her friends throughout the town of Carrebos.

CHAPTER

20

THE next day Senneth and Kirra spoke to even more mystics, all of them suddenly eager to hear about the opportunities in Ghosenhall.

"I'm jealous," Kirra said. "Perhaps I should challenge a shape-shifter to see who can take the most forms in the shortest amount of time."

"You'd lose that one," Senneth observed. "Donnal's faster than you are. Maybe *he* should run that competition."

Kirra pretended to be insulted. "Well, then, I'll see who else can transform another human to animal shape," she said. "I'll bet I'm the only mystic who can do *that*."

"I'll bet you are. And tolerant of magic though the townspeople seem to be, perhaps that's not a skill you should put on display, since it's generally considered an abomination," Senneth said. "You might have the distinction of being the first mystic stoned to death in Carrebos."

"I live to earn such distinctions," Kirra replied.

But Kirra was just as popular as Senneth was with a party that visited Eddie's right before lunch. The group consisted of an attractive young woman, her squirming toddler, and a fair-haired man with dreamy eyes. Kirra recognized the woman first and jumped up to give her a hug.

"Annie!" she said. "Look at you! The last time I saw you, you were on the threshold of death. Oh, and this must be Kinnon. What a troublesome boy you were the night you were born."

Annie laughed, introduced her husband, and thanked them as earnestly as Sosie had for saving both her baby and herself. "We were glad to do it," Kirra said merrily. "Always delighted to show off our magic to a town full of people who hate mystics! And Senneth got to set a bunch of people on fire, so that made her especially happy. So tell me about the little one! He seemed awfully willful as he was coming into the world. Is it too much to hope that he's gotten easier to handle?"

They only chatted a few minutes before more strangers showed up, looking for an audience with Senneth. It was late before there was a break in the stream of visitors, and by then, Senneth and Kirra were starving. Tayse and Donnal had joined them, so Sosie brought meals to all of them, putting a bowl of stew on the floor for Donnal. They'd just finished eating when Sosie returned, wrapping a towel around her hands and glancing back toward the kitchen door.

"Would you be willing to go to the kitchen a moment?" she asked in a diffident voice. "There's someone you might want to meet, but she's shy and she's strange and I don't think she'll come to the front room."

Senneth and Kirra exchanged glances and quickly rose to their feet. Tayse and Donnal followed them through the door, too curious to stay behind.

A young woman was moving through the small kitchen as if she didn't really see the layout of table and oven and baker's rack. Her muddy green eyes were focused on something invisible to the rest of them; her hands were half lifted as if to catch something that might be tossed her way. Her hair was tangled, her face was none too clean, and Senneth noted with astonishment that her feet were bare. Yet a faint fragrance clung to her of roses or lilies or irises. Kirra caught it, too, for Senneth saw her sniff and look around as if trying to locate an unseasonal bouquet.

Sosie touched the woman's arm to catch her attention. "Lara," she said, and then repeated the name. "Lara, remember I wanted you to meet Senneth."

Lara's strange eyes passed unseeingly over Senneth's face and went to Kirra. She nodded silently and then turned her gaze toward the window.

"Are you a mystic?" Senneth tried.

Lara said nothing, so Sosie answered for her. "She is, though I don't really understand her power. She's a healer of some kind. I've seen her bring people back from the brink of death, but it's not the kind of power that Kirra has. And she can make anything grow—she can touch a tree and ripen fruit two months out of season. It's as if her power was spring, or maybe life itself." Sosie smiled, as if that sounded foolish. "Or maybe her power is hope."

Kirra's voice sounded behind her, quiet and unalarming. "Surely there must be a goddess of growing things," Kirra said. "Such a one would claim a woman like this."

"Can she hear us?" Senneth said.

"I don't know. Sometimes she participates in conversations, but I'm never sure of what she does and doesn't hear. She's only here rarely—I think she just wanders barefoot around Gillengaria most of the year."

"Well, Lara, I hope you wander to Ghosenhall someday soon," Senneth said in a friendly way. "I'm sure we will need all the healers we can accumulate if war really does descend on us."

For a moment, it seemed as though Senneth's voice penetrated the other woman's abstraction. Lara's eyes rested on Senneth's face. "War," she repeated.

"Though I hope not," Senneth added.

Lara's attention drifted back to Kirra, down to Donnal, and over to Tayse—and then suddenly sharpened. She took in his stance, his weapons, the gold lions embroidered on his sash. "King's Rider," she said distinctly.

They all froze, and then Tayse said quietly, "Yes, I'm a Rider. How do you know of such as me?"

"Justin," Lara said.

Now they were all astonished and having no luck hiding it. "You know Justin?" Tayse repeated.

"Cammon," the strange woman added.

"Justin and *Cammon?*" Kirra said. "Wait—are you the mystic they rescued last fall when Justin was on his way to Neft?"

Lara turned her attention back to Senneth. "I will help you," she said, "if war comes." Before they could recover from their amazement, she turned to Sosie, gave the other girl a quick embrace, and slipped out the back door, making no noise with her bare feet.

They all stared after her, though Sosie was choking on a giggle. "And that's a fairly typical conversation with Lara," she said at last. "But I thought you should meet her if you got a chance. She is—I think she's very good. But she's not like anyone I've ever met."

"Can anyone else smell roses?" Kirra demanded.

"Sosie's right," Senneth said. "Her power is spring."

"Well, spring is coming, and war might be coming with it," Tayse said. "I would be relieved if it came wearing Lara's face instead of Halchon Gisseltess's countenance."

Senneth gave a last glance at the door where Lara had disappeared and offered a sigh. "Maybe it will come wearing both."

SHORTLY afterward, Jase dropped by for lessons. By the time Senneth had spent an hour with him, he was able to manufacture fire from his own body heat and keep a piece of paper from burning even though it was red with flame. "If you come to Ghosenhall, there's a man who would love to tutor you," Senneth told him, writing Jerril's name and address on a piece of paper.

He pocketed it carefully but shook his head. "Probably not anytime soon. My folks brought me here to keep me safe and I don't think they like the idea of leaving just yet."

"And we hardly want to strip the place of all its magic," Kirra added to Senneth after he'd left and they had settled back into the booth. "How strange to have a town of mystics if all the mystics have fled."

Senneth grinned. "I'd guess only a handful will come to Ghosenhall now—the adventurous ones who are starting to chafe at the safe but dull existence they're leading," she said. "Well, think about it! Neither you nor I would have been able to live here more than a month or two without suddenly feeling the urge to wander off and explore the world again."

"Mystics are restless," Kirra agreed. "Hard to believe that this many of them could have settled down long enough to actually form a town."

Senneth was watching two men enter the tavern, a younger one supporting an older one who appeared to be both blind and physically weak. "What I think," she said slowly, "is that enough of them were in danger enough times that they were willing to trade their love of adventure for a sense of security. They'd had their fill of back-alley beatings and midnight escapes. Life in Carrebos might not be exciting—but excitement can sometimes mean death."

The two strangers approached the booth and Senneth and Kirra both rose to show their respect for the older man. He looked to be in his mid-eighties, with thin white hair rather wildly styled and huge blue eyes that were cloudy with age. Brown spots dotted the wrinkled skin of his face and his mouth hung open as if he had found that was the most convenient way to breathe.

"Good afternoon, serras," his companion said. The younger man might have been fifty, a little plump, a little weary, but his round face held a look of peace that Senneth instantly liked. "My uncle wanted to meet you. I hope you don't mind."

"Not at all," Senneth said. "Is he a mystic? Would he like to offer us help in protecting the kingdom?"

Both men laughed, the younger one looking rueful and the older one delighted. "I'm afraid my uncle Virdon isn't in good enough shape to travel so far as Ghosenhall," he said. "But he does have power and you would surely find it useful."

Senneth slipped around the table to join Kirra and gestured at the other side of the booth. "Sit. Tell us about your uncle."

It took a certain amount of shuffling and guidance, but eventually Virdon and his nephew were situated. "I'm Chake, by the way," the nephew said. "My uncle was most impressed with how you flung fire about last night. I'm not sure he would have come to see you otherwise, but the elemental magic appeals to him."

"Can he call fire?" she asked.

Old man Virdon spoke up for the first time in a gruff and thready voice. "Water," he said. "It speaks to me."

"Really?" Senneth said politely.

Chake nodded. "It doesn't just speak to him, it obeys him. When he was younger, he could call rain down on the sunniest day. I've seen him put his palm to dry ground and draw water up from some deep underground source. There was a boy once who almost drowned in a river. And my uncle waded into the water and put his hands down in the current and just *pushed* that water back. It stopped flowing, serra, long enough for the boy's mother to rush out through the muddy riverbed and snatch up her child. There are other stories that my mother told, but those I saw for myself."

"Those are quite impressive," Senneth said. "You make me sorry that he is too weak to travel. Did you inherit any power?"

"None to speak of," Chake said. He cupped his hand over Senneth's glass and a drop of water broke free of the greater mass and leapt upward into his palm. He turned his hand over and back, over and back, and the droplet rolled like a pearl across the upturned surface of his skin. Then he wove it between his fingers like a coin that he had pulled out to do tricks for children. "This is about the extent of my skill. But my uncle is truly gifted."

Virdon leaned forward, his blind eyes turned toward Senneth. "Ocean talks to me," he wheezed. "Tells me a strange story."

"And what story might that be?" she asked.

He waved his hands as if to indicate the sea not so far from the tavern door. "Boats," he said. "Hundreds of boats. Lined up in the waters outside of Forten City."

Senneth stared at him and felt every vein in her body turn icy. Beside her, Kirra grew rigid. "What else can you tell me about these boats?" she said in a soft voice. "How big are they? What's their cargo?"

"Big," he said. "Heavy in the water. Don't know what they carry, but every day they're fouling the currents with excrement and piss."

"Troop ships," Kirra breathed.

Senneth nodded slightly. "Do you know—can you tell where they're from?"

Virdon shook his head, and his voice was a little petulant. "Usually the ocean tells me everything, talks about the wood in the hulls and the cargo in the holds. Tells me about the fish in the water, how many there are, where they're swimming. But it's keeping secrets from me, the ocean is. It only tells me that those boats are there and they're waiting."

"Foreign ships," Kirra whispered in Senneth's ear. "That's why he can't pick up much detail about them."

She nodded and whispered back, "So, how can he know anything about them at all?"

The faintest smile crossed Kirra's lips. "The water tells him. And the water isn't happy."

Senneth addressed Virdon again. "Do you know how long they've been there?"

"Some started arriving about a month ago. More come every day."

"Are more on the way?"

"I don't know. I think so. Too far away—the water won't let me know."

"Well, the water has given you plenty of valuable information, and I thank you with the utmost sincerity," Senneth said. She glanced at Chake, trying to assess his economic status. Would he be pleased or offended if she offered him money for Virdon's information? "Is there some way I can show appreciation to your uncle for sharing this news with me?"

"No payment required," Chake said. "But my uncle is never so delighted as when he gets a chance to see someone else's magic at work."

Senneth glanced at Kirra, for a shape-shifter's effects could be far more long-lasting than those of a fire mystic. "Hand me that knife," Kirra said, and the old man passed over an unused bread knife from their afternoon meal. She balanced it between her palms and concentrated fiercely for a moment. Suddenly it fell to the table with a jangle and revealed itself to be a silver bracelet made of heavy, interconnected links. Kirra picked it up and passed it over to the old man, whose hand was already outstretched.

"Perhaps you might like to wear this as a remembrance of the afternoon you talked magic with Senneth Brassenthwaite and Kirra Danalustrous," Kirra said grandly. "And it will remind you of how grateful we were to learn your news."

Chake smiled. "Thank you. We won't take up any more of your time. Thank you again."

They left just as Tayse and Donnal were returning. Darryn was a few steps behind and instantly joined them when Kirra waved him over. Senneth slumped on the bench next to Kirra while the men slipped into the booth across from them. Donnal settled under the table at Kirra's feet.

"What's wrong?" Tayse said. "What did you learn?"

"That old man who just left. A mystic who apparently communicates with the ocean. I never heard of such a thing, but I believed him," Senneth said.

"I believed him, too," Kirra added.

"He says there's a fleet of ships right outside of Forten City, just sitting in the water, waiting. Big ships. Sounded like they were crammed with men. He couldn't say how many, but more are coming every day."

Tayse instantly analyzed the information. "Soldiers from outside Gillengaria being imported to fight this war?" he said.

Darryn looked stricken. "Has to be."

"Makes sense," Tayse said. "Explains the gold."

"What gold?" Darryn demanded.

"We heard rumors last year," Tayse replied. "That Coralinda Gisseltess had a fortune in gold piled up in the convent. Probably gathering it to help her brother and Rayson Fortunalt pay for an army of foreign mercenaries."

"I feel sick," Kirra said.

"Also explains why they've waited so long to launch their attack," Tayse continued. "It takes a while to recruit soldiers from overseas."

"I thought they were just waiting for spring," Senneth said.

"Now they are. But we've heard rumors of war for a year. Why didn't they attack *last* spring? It didn't make sense—until you realize they were raising foreign troops."

Senneth appealed to Darryn. "Why didn't your mother alert us? Surely she's got trade ships sailing out toward Arberharst and Sovenfeld. Surely one of her merchant captains would have seen something?"

He shook his head. "Maybe not. My mother's been so worried about war these past few months that she's practically closed the borders. All the sea captains that normally engage in trade have been pressed into service to guard the coasts. Rappengrass has always had good land soldiers, but we've never had much of a military force on the water. She's doing what she can to make us less vulnerable there."

"Then you need to get to Rappen Manor right away," Kirra said. "And tell her there's a navy piling up not too far from her ports."

He nodded. "I was planning on leaving tomorrow."

"This is horrifying," Senneth said. "We were already worried that we wouldn't have the numbers—that more Houses would rise up in rebellion than would stay loyal to the crown. But if they've hired outsiders as well—"

Tayse nodded. "It tilts the odds against us significantly."

"*Senneth,*" Kirra said. "It's worse than that! If Rayson and Halchon bring in foreign troops, we'll be helpless! You and I and *all* the mystics— our magic won't work against anyone not born in Gillengaria!"

"Bright Mother burn me in ashes to the ground," Senneth swore. But Tayse offered her a small, calm smile.

"You can still battle the native-born traitors," he said softly. "But Riders don't need magic to defend the king. We will fight as we have always fought, with sword and spear and bow and bare hands. This changes nothing for us."

"Except that you will face more enemies!" Senneth exclaimed. "Except that you are more likely to be defeated!"

Now he laughed outright. "We might face more foes," he said, "but we will not be overcome."

THERE was no need to stay longer in Carrebos, and the next day, anxious and unsettled, Senneth packed for home. A group of twenty mystics from Carrebos had agreed to come with her to the royal city, a selection of shape-shifters, healers, readers, fire-callers, and a few with powers she couldn't quite name but nonetheless respected.

"What in the world are you going to do with them when you get back?" Kirra asked. She wasn't bothering to pack. She was going to change herself to a hawk and fly for Danan Hall alongside Donnal, and she planned to leave behind all the clothes she had manufactured for herself during their brief stay.

"I'm going to find a makeshift barracks for them somewhere in the city and make Jerril responsible for training them all," she said. "Except for the shape-shifters, whom I plan to bring to the palace grounds so they can roam around sniffing for trouble. It will be very strange. I have no idea how we'll control them all. I just know that I want them nearby and feeling friendly toward me."

"Well, don't forget that you have to be at Danan Hall in something under three weeks," Kirra said. "Make your trip to Ghosenhall quickly, then head out as soon as you can. If you're not there for Casserah's wedding to Will—"

"Kiernan will be there, surely, and Nate and Harris," Senneth said. "If Will has all his brothers there, he won't mind if I miss the event."

"But I'll mind," Kirra said. "How will I endure if I am there by myself?"

"Don't go," Senneth advised. "Then there will be nothing to endure."

But that was not an option for Kirra—not an option for Senneth, either, if she wanted to maintain the fragile good relations she had established with her brothers this past year.

"I just had a thought!" Kirra exclaimed. "Will Nate bring Sabina Gisseltess along? How odd that will be! And yet you know my father would not turn her away."

Sabina Gisseltess had run away from her husband, Halchon, last year and had been offered sanctuary at Brassen Court. It had quickly become clear to Senneth that Sabina and the insufferable Nate had been in love with each other all this time—Imagine! Someone pining for Nate for fifteen years!—which made her wish even more passionately that something would happen to strike Halchon Gisseltess dead. Not that Senneth could blame Sabina for wanting to escape her husband, for Halchon had made it very clear his frail wife had become an encumbrance he was prepared to shed. He wanted to be free to make an alliance with a powerful serramarra who might join him in Ghosenhall to rule Gillengaria, once he had wrested the throne from Baryn.

He wanted to marry Senneth. And Senneth would rather die herself than come close enough to touch the fingers of his hand.

"That's certainly a reason for me to be there," Senneth agreed. "To watch Sabina explain her presence in Kiernan's household. I will try to come."

Kirra and Donnal were gone within the hour. It took rather more time for Senneth to round up her recruits, make sure they all had horses and provisions, and urge them to keep in a close formation on the road once they set out. They didn't get as far as she would have liked before nightfall, and the second day was just about as disorganized as the first.

"It looks like our return trip will be far less efficient than our outbound journey," she said to Tayse as they made camp that second night.

"At least we're well guarded at night," he said. "Hard to surprise a party of readers and shape-shifters."

"I feel the need to hurry, though," she said. "I have the feeling that Cammon is distressed about something."

Tayse instantly looked solemn. "How distressed? Does he want us back immediately? We could force the pace harder tomorrow."

She shook her head. "No—I don't get the sense that there's terrible trouble. Just that he's out of his depth."

Tayse relaxed a little. "Guarding a princess and arguing with a queen," he said. "Yes, I imagine he is."

The third day was a little smoother, as they got into the rhythm of the trip. All the mystics continued to be somewhat in fear of Tayse; their primary interaction with soldiers in the past had usually been violent as civil guards and Coralinda Gisseltess's men had hunted them down. So they gave him a wide berth and scrambled to do his bidding whenever he made the mildest suggestion. Senneth sighed to watch them. She hadn't gathered much of an army if her recruits were afraid of one lone Rider.

They were a little afraid of her as well, though that didn't bother her as much; she was used to others eyeing her askance. It wasn't her magic that impressed this group, she thought, but her self-confidence, her refusal to offer any kind of apology for her ability. They had spent so long hiding their skills and suffering because of their magic. They couldn't understand Senneth's calm acceptance of her gift.

The thought made her want to offer a bitter smile. The Bright Mother alone knew how much magic had cost her. She was damned if she would repudiate it now.

Of course, there was another reason this motley troop of mystics looked at her with wide and uncertain eyes. She wore a moonstone bracelet on her wrist and seemed not to feel it burn her—or care if it did. More than once as she was talking with some of her new companions, she saw their eyes drift down toward her left hand. Their attention would fasten on the softly glowing stones that encircled her wrist and they would completely lose the thread of the conversation. None of them could touch a moonstone, of course. Even Kirra would yelp in pain if one of those gems came in contact with her skin. A mystic bound with moonstones was helpless, stripped of power.

Coralinda Gisseltess and her followers all draped themselves in moonstones. The Pale Mother had taken the jewel as her own—and the Pale Mother hated mystics.

Long ago Senneth had determined that nothing, *nothing*, would be denied to her simply because of the magic in her veins. She was stronger than hatred, than intolerance, than fear; she could survive punishment, banishment, despair. She would not be afraid of a few pretty rocks, malicious though they might be. She would wear moonstones, and the slight, constant tingle of fire at her wrist would simply remind her that the outside world was as full of heat and turmoil as her soul.

"You're not afraid of anything, are you?" one of the recruits asked her that night after they had made an untidy camp. The speaker was a young man, maybe Cammon's age, a fluid shape-shifter with a sad, hunted face. He had asked the question because she had showed no alarm at a quick scuffle between two of the other mystics, though the threat of conflict had sent this young man cowering to the other side of the fire.

Senneth glanced at him. "I'm afraid of more things than I could name in an hour just sitting here counting them off," she said.

"You don't act like it," he said, half admiring and half resentful.

She smiled and fed another branch into the flames. "Because what I'm most afraid of is having fear control me," she said. "And so I will not give in to it, no matter what that costs me."

He was still mulling her words over that night when they all took to their bedrolls and slept.

Senneth's magic made the warmth of the fire extend all around the camp, but as they set out in the morning, they instantly encountered deep chill and ground frozen so hard that the horses' hooves rang against it. Tayse picked up the pace just to keep them all warm. Even so, they were barely halfway through the return journey when they made camp that night. Senneth wished, not for the first time, she had a shape-shifter's skills and could fly the remaining distance to Ghosenhall in a day.

It was still cold the following day, and they continued their faster rate of travel. They were an hour or two past their noontime break when a sudden, sharp cry had Senneth reining back hard. She looked around swiftly, but no one in her party seemed disturbed—seemed even to have heard anything. Tayse, riding some distance in the lead, hadn't even turned around, and there was no chance Tayse would have failed to react to such a call of distress.

Heart pounding, she slowed her horse still more, then closed her eyes and opened her mind. There it was again, just as urgent, but a little more clear. Cammon's voice, Cammon's words.

Senneth! I need you!

CHAPTER
21

AFTER what Justin liked to call "the raelynx incident," they had two days of relative calm at the palace. Cammon found himself in Amalie's presence most of that time, though they were never for a minute unchaperoned, and he was fairly careful not to communicate with her silently, either by accident or by design.

But there had been a subtle shift of power, and he and Valri, at least, were aware of it. Amalie was more sure of herself, a little less willing to be guided by the queen. It was hard to pinpoint the change, exactly, because in those two days Amalie did not engage in any overt act of mutiny and never showed Valri the slightest impoliteness. But there was a certain set to her jaw, a speculative expression in her eyes. She looked like a cat that was considering a jump to a high wall, not sure if she could make the leap but almost determined to try.

Valri watched her both days with a close and silent attention, and her mood seemed to grow darker by the hour.

Cammon found himself worrying about both of them.

He tried to articulate his thoughts to Justin, who merely shrugged. "Not your business," Justin said. "Your role is easy. You're there to make sure no one dies. It doesn't matter what else breaks around you."

"What if Valri tries to murder Amalie?" Cammon said glumly, but Justin only grinned.

"You protect the princess from the queen," the Rider said. "See? It's still easy. You have one task. Focus on that task."

Ellynor was more sympathetic. "Valri has done hard things before," she said. She was lightly kneading the back of Cammon's neck, since the tension of the past two days had given him a rare headache. The pain had dissolved with her first touch, but her hands were so soothing he didn't want her to stop. "You don't need to be concerned about her. And Amalie is only doing what every young girl must do—figuring out what she is capable of and throwing off the restraints her parents have put around her." She stopped rubbing his neck, tousled his hair, and sat next to him at the table.

"It's probably even harder for Amalie than it is for a Lirren girl to break free of her protectors," Ellynor added. "From what you've said, Amalie has been so carefully guarded her whole life that she might have been smothered in care. I think it's a good sign that she is starting to test her power."

Justin laughed. "You say that because you're a rebel yourself."

She smiled at him but said, "She is to be *queen*. Surely she needs to start developing her own instincts before she is suddenly sitting on the throne."

"Well, but her instincts made her want to set the raelynx free!" Cammon said.

Justin shook his head. "Damn. Never saw anything like that."

"And what did you learn then? Two things," Ellynor reminded Cammon. "She *can* control it. And she heeded the words of an advisor she trusted. Both of those things ought to reassure you at least a little."

"You mark my words," Justin said. "One day that raelynx *is* going to be out. And nothing I say, or Valri says, or Cammon says, or Senneth says, will make her put it back in its pen."

"Maybe," Ellynor said. "But wait until that day comes before you decide whether or not she's done a foolish thing."

In the morning, despite Valri's protests, Amalie had another weapons session with Wen and Janni—in the Riders' training yard.

"I'm perfectly happy to have her learn how to wield a knife, but let her learn inside! Where it's safe and it's *warm*!" Valri exclaimed as she and Cammon hung on the fence rails, watching.

The day was bitterly cold, though at least there was neither wind nor snow. Cammon imagined that the combatants on the field were plenty warm, though he and Valri were freezing.

He grinned. "Can't imagine she could be safer anywhere than in a field surrounded by Riders," he said. "Even if Halchon Gisseltess came bursting through the gates this very minute with an army at his back."

Valri shivered. "Don't say that."

Cammon watched as Amalie dodged a blow from Janni and went tumbling to the ground. The princess's cheeks were streaked with mud, and her borrowed clothes—a close-fitting vest and leather pants tucked into sturdy boots—were already filthy. Yet she had a very businesslike air about her. She had braided back her red-gold hair, pulled on the proffered gloves, and listened to the day's instructions with calm intentness. She hadn't done a half-bad job, either, he thought. She would have been dead only four out of the five times Janni had attacked her this morning. Pretty good record for the rawest of recruits.

"Maybe you could stand a little training, too," he said. "Learn how to use a knife."

Valri gave him a scornful look. "You think I don't know how to cut a man's throat?"

He was so surprised that he stared back at her a moment and then he burst out laughing. "I suppose you do. You're fierce enough. And you come from fierce enough people. Do you have brothers like Ellynor's? Do they constantly make war with other clans? All I know is that you were born in the Lirrens and you left. I don't know what your life was like before."

She had turned her moody gaze back to the field, where Amalie was circling Janni, her own blade upraised. "If Ellynor has told you much about her life, she has essentially described my own. Except I was wilder than Ellynor, more dissatisfied. I schemed and schemed about getting free. Running away. While I was still a child, I dreamed about declaring myself *bahta-lo* and walking away from the clans. It was no surprise to anyone that I did it."

"But it seems to me," he said softly, "that you are even more confined now than you were in the Lirrens. Tied to the king, tied to his daughter. You named yourself *bahta-lo* and you crossed the Lireth Mountains, but you are hardly free."

Her smile was a little grim. "You're right. And I knew it before I agreed to follow Pella back here. I was trading one kind of prison for another. But at least it was a prison I chose."

He shook his head. "It still doesn't really make sense to me. That you would choose this life. The Lirrenfolk barely even acknowledge Baryn as king. Why would you care if his daughter lived or died? Then, I mean," he added hastily. "Now I'm sure that you love Amalie and are willing to do anything you can to protect her."

Still watching the field, Valri nodded slowly. "Yes. I will do everything in my power to guard her. But I crossed the mountains for Pella's sake—I had not even met Amalie at that point. I don't know if I can explain it to you. Pella was almost a stranger to me. She looked nothing like me or anyone I knew, for she had bright gold hair and that open smile, just like Amalie's. And yet I recognized her. She was in some way a sister.

I felt that she had come to the Lirrens specifically to find me." Valri glanced at Cammon and glanced away. "I thought the Great Mother— who counts every soul, who knows where every one of her sons and daughters lies sleeping at night—I thought *she* had directed Pella to me. I thought the goddess had given me this task. And so I accepted it."

Ellynor, too, seemed to have a direct and personal relationship with that night goddess who watched over Lirrenfolk. It did not surprise Cammon nearly as much as Valri might think to hear that she followed the will of the deity. He asked, "And have you been sorry that you gave up so much to come here? Or glad?"

Valri made a sound that might almost have been a laugh, except it wasn't. "Sorry every day. I miss them more than I thought I possibly could—my sisters, my brothers, my cousins, my—everyone. And glad every day. Convinced that my presence has saved Amalie from both grief and danger. And sorry again, as I find grief and danger creeping closer anyway, and I think I have no way of keeping them away from her." She turned her head to survey him. "And glad again, when I think she has other friends besides me to stand at her side."

Her words gave him a little glow, especially since the last time Valri had talked to him about Amalie she had been warning him to keep his distance. She must have recovered some of her faith in him. "What will you do, once Amalie is named queen?" he asked curiously. "We hope that will be years from now, of course! But you will be widowed then, I suppose. Will you go back to the Lirrens? Will you stay in Ghosenhall?"

"I will stay as long as she needs me. But after that—I'm not sure. I may go back. I may travel. I may leave Gillengaria altogether, who knows? But I would like to see the Lirrens again someday. I miss them, I miss—" She shrugged and closed her mouth.

He didn't know what made him say it. Maybe there was an image in her mind, and her emotion was sharp enough that he could sense it, though normally she was so adept at cloaking her thoughts. "You could marry again."

She gave him a swift look in which he read a sudden surge of pain. "If anyone I cared for would have me."

He caught his breath. "Did you leave someone behind in the Lirrens?"

She hesitated and then she nodded. "We were both young, of course. I was about the age Amalie is now. But I loved him. I thought it would kill me to leave him. Yet I survived, and he survived, and now I am married to the king."

"You're still young," Cammon pointed out. "If something were to happen—well—of course I don't want anything to happen, but if it did—"

"You think he will have waited for me?"

"*I* would have, if it were me," he said.

The words hung between them for a moment, both of them surprised. He thought Valri softened toward him in that instant, lost just the tiniest edge of her diamond hardness. "Ellynor says he has not yet taken a bride," Valri said in a low voice. "But that he does not speak of me."

"Does *everyone* in the Lirrens know everyone else?" he demanded. "I know you're all part of these complicated clans, but—"

"He is Ellynor's cousin. I believe your friend Justin actually met him during his stay." She gave him a smile, but he thought it was forced. "So, you see, I have fewer secrets every day."

He didn't know how to say how honored he was that she had trusted him with a few of those secrets, nonetheless. Instead he smiled and spoke lightly. "I'm guessing you still have a few left."

Her own face was sad. "Unfortunately, you're right."

V ALRI'S last and worst secret was revealed that very afternoon.

Amalie had cleaned up and changed clothes and now sat in the rose parlor looking the very picture of demure royalty. The three of them had settled in their customary chairs before the window, hoping to absorb the sunlight, while Valri went through Amalie's correspondence. None of the letters were calculated to please Cammon, since they were all from young lords or their fathers, all desirous of seeing Amalie make a connection with their Houses.

"Here's a young man from Coravann who plans to be in the city next week," Valri said, scanning a few pages that were accompanied by a long, slim box tied with gold ribbon. "He has sent you a small gift as his envoy—that's a nice way to put it, don't you think? Anyway, he hopes you will accept it and possibly wear it when he comes to call."

"I thought the princess had already entertained a suitor from Coravann," Cammon said.

"Yes, the marlord's son," Valri said. "But other high-ranking nobles will of course come to pay court. It is not always politic for a princess to marry the heir to a House. Sometimes a lesser lord is a better prospect, as he would know." She glanced at Amalie. "I'm guessing he's sent you jewelry, don't you think?"

Amalie was untying the ribbon. "Probably. I hope it's not hideous, or I won't want to wear it."

"Surely something made with lapis lazuli," Valri said. "Isn't that the gemstone of Coravann?"

"Or the royal lion," Amalie guessed.

But they were both wrong. When Amalie opened the box, she revealed a creamy white moonstone nestled on a bed of black silk. A heavy silver chain coiled around it like a protective serpent.

"Oooh, very pretty," Amalie said, lifting it from the box and holding it up by the clasp. The moonstone, swinging languidly at the end of the chain, held an internal phosphorescence that seemed unaffected by the sunlight—no brighter, no duller. Just the sight of it made Cammon's skin prickle; he knew it would sear his hand if he touched it.

"Looks like the chain's just the right length," Valri observed. "The moonstone will cover your housemark if you put it on."

If you are truly a mystic, I will discover it now, Cammon thought. *For you will scream aloud as soon as it lies against your skin.*

Amalie quickly took off the pendant she habitually wore, consisting of ribbons of gold woven together and studded with the gemstones of the Twelve Houses. When she fastened the gift necklace around her neck, the moonstone fell perfectly on the small red mark centered just above her breasts.

She did not cry out, but Cammon did.

He felt as if a giant hand had closed over his body and clawed hard, carelessly stripping away his flesh. He felt as if a malevolent spirit had put its mouth against his and sucked the air from his lungs with one disastrous kiss. He felt as if his mind had been darkened, his eyes had been blinded, all his senses shut down and replaced by pain. Choking and dazed, he toppled to the floor, where he crouched and coughed for breath. Through a roaring in his ears he heard Amalie call his name, heard Valri exclaim, *Take it off! Take it off!* Felt Amalie's hand on his shoulder, Valri's palm against his cheek.

Then, just as abruptly, the world righted itself again. Pain gone, sight clear, hearing perfect.

Cammon glanced around to find Amalie and Valri kneeling on the floor beside him, Amalie still with her hand on his shoulder. She had yanked off the necklace without even bothering to undo the clasp, so now it lay, twisted and broken, halfway across the room where she had thrown it.

"Cammon!" she repeated, her eyes wide with fright. "What happened? Are you all right?"

He stared back at her and felt the world start to wobble again, because he had a terrible suspicion about what had just happened and it struck at the foundations of everything he knew.

"When you wore the moonstone," he said, his voice sounding a little scraped, as if he had been screaming. "When it touched your skin. It stole my power. It stole my magic, and fed all of it to you."

Amalie dropped her hand and didn't say anything. Cammon leveled an accusing stare at Valri.

"*This* is what you have been hiding, all this time," he said. "She's a mystic."

"Amalie is—"

He didn't let her finish. "A mystic. But not just any mystic. She has thieving magic. If there is a goddess who watches over her, it's the goddess who only knows how to rob from others—the moon goddess, who takes light from the sun." He pointed across the room. "That's why she can wear a moonstone and it doesn't burn her skin. It's not stealing from *her*, it's stealing from any other mystic in the room."

"I never heard anyone say that moonstones steal a mystic's power," Valri said. "Only that they burn a mystic's skin."

He pushed himself to his feet, feeling shaky, feeling betrayed, feeling stupid. The others stood when he did, but they just watched him as he took a few clumsy steps away and began pacing. "I don't think anyone ever realized *why* the moonstones burned us," he said, trying to think it through. "And I've touched moonstones before and never had a reaction like that." He gave Amalie one quick, hard look, but she didn't meet his gaze. Her eyes were downcast and her face was shuttered. "Maybe moonstones themselves don't have much power. They're like—like—leeches that bite our skin and try to feed on our energy. But they're not truly harmful to us unless we touch them in the presence of someone who can use them. Who can reach through them as if they were portals and try to drain us of every drop of magic we possess."

Amalie spoke to the floor. "I didn't try to do that. I've never held a moonstone before. I didn't know what would happen."

"I suppose most people who wear moonstones are just ordinary folks, and they can't use the jewels against us," Cammon said. "But someone with thief magic—" He abruptly halted in his pacing. "Coralinda Gisseltess," he whispered.

"Are you saying *she* is a mystic?" Valri asked in an acid voice. "I've never heard *that* before."

"She must be," he said, resuming his pacing as his agitation increased. *Senneth!* he called, a single almost witless cry. He needed her to help him sort this out. "She's the one who is covered with moonstones. *She's* the one who wants them handed out all over Gillengaria. She's using them to draw away our power. And feed it to herself." He stumbled against a chair, so blind with sudden knowledge that he couldn't properly navigate the room. "This changes everything we know about Coralinda Gisseltess."

Neither of them replied to that, and neither did Senneth, to whom he sent another pleading message. He was halfway around the room now, and he whirled around to face them across the intervening distance.

"But *you*," he said, and he knew that his confusion and his sense of hurt were naked on his face. "Both of you. You have known this awful secret for years now, and you didn't even tell me, tell *us*, the people who were there to keep you *safe*. Don't you think we should have known? Last summer when we were at every House in Gillengaria? Don't you think that we might have needed this information in order to protect the princess?"

"And don't you think that this is the most terrible secret anyone in the kingdom can possibly know?" Valri shot back. Amalie just stood there looking miserable and stricken, her hands in fists at her sides. "Don't you think it has cost me something every day to conceal it? I have kept it to myself too long to be offering it up to every random acquaintance, whether mystic or king's guard! Who can be trusted? The heir to the kingdom is a mystic! Surely that would bring war down on us if nothing else would! And you wanted me to tell you? I have been afraid you would discover Amalie's secret from the day you first met her! And now that you know, I'm even *more* afraid!"

It was deliberately unkind. Cammon stood straighter, trying to make his expression stern, not wounded. "Who else knows?" he asked in a dignified way.

"No one," Valri said. "Except the king."

"Not even her uncle?"

"No," Valri said, and Amalie shook her head.

"I find that hard to believe," Cammon replied. "She told me she spent months at his house when she was a child. Surely he noticed something then."

Finally Amalie looked at him, and her expression was lost and sad. "No," she said. "My mother and my grandmother were always there, and they kept my magic in check. And they were always very secretive about their own powers. I'm not sure he ever realized what they were capable of."

"Pella was a mystic, too? Like this?" Senneth had been right in her speculations—though neither of them had suspected the whole truth.

Amalie made a small hopeless gesture. "She didn't have much power, not nearly as much as my grandmother did. And my grandmother never considered it magic—at least, she didn't talk about it that way. I don't think my mother actually realized that she *was* a mystic until she came to Ghosenhall and began to understand what magic was, and how much people hated it."

"So what could she do?" Cammon asked.

Amalie shrugged. "Small things. It's hard to explain. Mostly she could learn quickly. Like you said, it's a thieving kind of magic. It puts on other people's colors. The funniest thing my mother could do was learn accents. She could spend five minutes with someone and perfectly copy his patterns of speech. When I was a little girl, I loved to hear her talk like the maid from Fortunalt or the lord from Brassenthwaite. She could imitate anyone."

"And what can *you* do?" he asked in a rather hostile voice.

She lifted her eyes, huge and brown and pleading, and for a moment he felt cruel. That shocked him, because he was never cruel. But he crossed his arms and awaited her answer, for it was desperately important to know.

"I don't think you have the right to question the princess in that tone of voice," Valri said.

But Amalie answered. "I'm a mockingbird," she said. "I can repeat magic. From Valri, I learned how to control the raelynx. From you I've learned how to communicate without words. I haven't been around Kirra and Donnal enough to learn shape-shifting, but watch—" Her face screwed up in concentration, and suddenly her red-gold hair turned a dull and listless brown. Valri's exclamation of distress led Cammon to believe this was the first time the queen had witnessed that particular trick. "I can't call fire, though," Amalie added, allowing her hair to revert to its normal color. "Maybe Senneth is too strong for me—she resists without even knowing it."

"Maybe if you wore that moonstone necklace you'd be able to steal anything you wanted," Cammon said, still in a hard voice. He had to admit part of him was impressed, though. What a versatile skill! Justin and Tayse would already be figuring out how to turn it into a fine weapon. "What about ordinary people? Can you steal from them?"

Amalie flinched a little at the word, even though she had used it herself just a moment ago. "I think so, yes. Janni and Wen told me today how quickly I was learning self-defense—although perhaps they were just praising me because I'm the princess—"

"No, you seemed to be catching on faster than most people would," Cammon admitted. "Although, who knows? Maybe there's a god of war who watches over gifted fighters. Justin says he's starting to believe it, anyway. You may have been imitating more magic, you just didn't realize it."

Amalie offered a tentative smile. "It didn't seem like Janni and Wen were touched with magic, but I might believe it of Justin. And Tayse. And Tir."

Cammon shook his head and began pacing again. "I don't know what to think. I don't know what to say. This changes everything."

"It changes nothing," Valri said sharply. "No one else must know."

Cammon gave her an incredulous look and just kept walking.

"I mean it," the queen insisted. "*No one* must know. None of your special friends among the Riders! Not Senneth—no one."

"If you cannot trust Senneth, if you cannot trust the Riders, then you might as well set the princess outside the gates of Ghosenhall and let her be murdered by the first Gisseltess soldier who rides into the city," Cammon said. "Do you expect to keep this secret forever? For her whole life?"

"Perhaps."

"Then you certainly need allies, because once she is queen she will need far more protection than you are able to offer. Do you think you'll keep this a secret from her *husband?*"

Valri was silent.

"Well, then, you'd better choose even more wisely than you had planned, because it will have to be an awfully stupid man who doesn't find it strange that you are hovering behind his wife night and day, never leaving him alone with her for a moment! *There's* a fine way to make sure Amalie bears the next heir to Gillengaria!"

He hadn't meant it to be funny, but Amalie laughed, and even Valri permitted herself a wintry smile. "Perhaps her husband will have to know," Valri admitted. "But—"

"And Senneth will have to know, and Tayse," Cammon said. "I'll let them decide who else is informed."

"Cammon, you cannot—"

"I cannot keep this secret myself! It's too big for me! I don't know what to *do*! But what I do know is that this secret puts Amalie in greater danger than ever before. And I know—" *Thank you, Justin, for this insight.* "I know that *my* task is to keep the princess safe. And I cannot do it alone."

"Cammon, the more people who know, the greater danger she is in," Valri said sharply, taking a few steps across the room toward him. "Please. Say nothing to them."

"Tell them," Amalie said in a soft voice, and both of them swiveled to stare at her. She looked pale but decisive. "Tell them. Cammon's right. They are my defenders, and they deserve to know what they're defending me from."

"Amalie—" Valri began.

But the princess nodded firmly. "And what they learn about me may help them understand Coralinda Gisseltess, who is an enemy to all of us," she added. "Valri, we will keep the secret longer if we can—but not from those who must know."

Valri rubbed her hand along her forehead. She suddenly looked, Cammon thought, very young and very troubled. What a burden for her, all these years! No wonder she had been so fretful, so afraid, during their whole journey last summer. She had had even more to fear than the rest of them realized.

"What about that benighted necklace?" the queen demanded almost petulantly. "You'll have to wear it when the young lord comes calling. But that means Cammon will have to be a mile away from here, or he'll be on his knees vomiting from the shock!"

Both Amalie and Cammon laughed aloud at that. Suddenly he was back in a good humor. "Perhaps if we practice a little in the next few days, I will learn how to shield myself from your rapacious magic, or you will learn how to hold it at bay," he said. "Not today, though. I'm not up to the task." He was struck by a sudden thought. "But if you want to learn how to control your magic better, my friend Jerril—"

"No," Valri said sharply. "No. A fine and discreet person, I'm sure, but we cannot have outsiders running tame at the palace—or known mystics coming in to tutor the princess! What kind of secret would we have left then?"

This time he agreed with her. "Well, then," he said. "You'll just have to make do with the rest of us."

Amalie gave him a hopeful smile. "And I think, with your help, I will manage very well."

CHAPTER

22

CAMMON spent the rest of the day and most of the night trying to absorb everything he'd learned. He was essentially useless at the formal dinner that evening, so it was fortunate that no one made any attempt on the king's life, and he skipped his usual nightly visit to Justin and Ellynor. He didn't think he could conceal his shock from them, and it was impossible to put Justin off with vague references to "something I'd rather not discuss."

The secret about Amalie was enormous all on its own, but what it meant about Coralinda Gisseltess might be even more staggering. Did she realize she was a mystic? Had her persecution of them been the most monstrous act of hypocrisy? Or had she truly believed magic was evil, not understanding that the power she wielded came from the very same source?

There was no way to expose Coralinda without exposing the princess, that was certain. Cammon had seen enough instances of violence directed against mystics to blanch at the thought of revealing Amalie's ability. Yet could this secret truly be kept from more than a few close advisors? Pella had managed the trick—would Amalie be able to do so as well?

Should she?

If a mystic sat on the throne, would the people of Gillengaria begin to lose their fear of magic? Would they set aside their hatred and embrace their strange brethren? Was that idealistic and unrealistic thinking, or was it the only hope the kingdom had?

Cammon rubbed his eyes. Not a decision he was equipped to make. *Sweet gods, bring Senneth home soon.* Only a day or so away now, he could tell, and moving quickly. She knew he needed her.

He had gone to his room immediately after dinner, so exhausted from the day's excesses he wanted to go straight to bed. But now, perhaps an hour before midnight, he found himself restless again. Pacing his room. Staring out the window at the dark lawns unrolling from the castle walls. Needing to talk to someone.

Needing to talk to Amalie.

As soon as he had the thought, he was filled with an absolute conviction. Amalie wanted to talk with him as well. He put his head to one side, thinking. He could hardly go to her room in the middle of the night. Where might they safely rendezvous? Even as he was considering the options, he realized Amalie was on the move. She was gliding along the hallways, stepping down a set of stairs. Heading away from the parlor where she spent most of her days.

He smiled. She was on her way to the kitchens. Even a princess might plead hunger in the middle of the night, if someone saw her ghosting through the halls. Even a serving man. No great scandal if they were to be discovered talking before the enormous banked fire of the central ovens, munching on leftover bread.

He threw his jacket back on and hurried downstairs to meet her.

He was ahead of her by a minute, long enough to make sure no one was lurking in the larder. He had stirred up the fire, fetched plates and glasses from the drying rack, and set out bread and cheese and a pitcher of water, before she slipped through the heavy door. She was dressed in a long white nightdress covered with an embroidered white robe, and her strawberry-blond hair was unbound down her back. Her eyes sparkled with mischief, and she put a finger to her lips as she settled onto the stool beside him. He nodded. He had already sensed the presence of the butler making one last circuit of the great hallway before going off to seek his own bed.

They cut off thick slices of bread and layered them with equally thick slices of cheese, eating for a while in companionable silence. Then, "He's gone," Cammon said, keeping his voice low.

"I'm glad you were willing to come meet me," she said straightaway. "I couldn't bear to have you angry at me all night. I knew I wouldn't be able to sleep."

He poured glasses of water for both of them. "It's not my place to be angry at the things you tell and don't tell. I should be apologizing for behaving badly. But I'm still—it's a lot to try to understand all at once."

"You think I have a terrible kind of magic," she said.

He was astonished and turned to stare at her by the rosy light of the half-dead fire. "What? What kind of thing is that to say?"

She nodded. "You do! Magic that steals from other people. What sort of power is that? It's mean and spiteful, that's what."

He took a bite of his bread and chewed it, considering. "Is that what *you* think?" he said at last.

She hunched her shoulders and looked down at her plate. "Maybe. It doesn't seem very pretty—like Senneth's magic, or Kirra's. It just seems— I don't want to be a thief! I don't want people to be afraid of me! People already keep their distance from me because I'm the princess. If they think I'll *take* things from them, just borrow their power whenever I want to—well, no one will be comfortable with me. No one will want to be near me." She hesitated and then, in a small voice, added, "Particularly mystics."

It was a reasonable fear, he thought. And yet . . . "To my knowledge, no mystics have ever been allowed to choose their magic," Cammon replied. "They were endowed with it, or forced to accept it, no matter what they wanted. So mystics will understand this is not a power you sought out—merely a power you need to comprehend."

"I think they will hate me," Amalie said, still in that soft voice. "As they hate Coralinda Gisseltess. As they hate the Pale Mother. I have been touched by the wrong god."

Cammon cut another slice of bread. "As to that, you might talk to Ellynor—once you've decided it's safe to discuss secrets. She lived at Lumanen Convent for a year and worshipped the Pale Mother along with the other novices. I think she's rather fond of the Silver Lady, to tell you the truth. She might be able to tell you some tales that will make you a little happier to fall under her protection."

Amalie glanced over at him, her face showing the first stirrings of hope. "Do you think so? Because right now I don't think I could ever honor the same goddess that Coralinda Gisseltess loves."

He wasn't sure how to phrase this. "Have you been—do you think— have you found yourself hating yourself a little because of the magic in your blood?"

She nodded vigorously. "Yes! Ever since I realized how strong my own magic was. And today I hate it even more because I realize Coralinda Gisseltess possesses the same kind of power. If she's evil—"

"It doesn't necessarily follow that *you* are," he said swiftly. "Though I have to say it makes everything more complicated."

She brooded a moment. "I wanted to tell you," she said at last. "Valri was so afraid you would find out, but I wanted to tell you. It's just been— it's so *heavy*. Knowing that there is something deep in your heart that will make people despise you, waiting for the day when they learn it—the day they turn away from you in horror. I—I wanted you to find out." She gave him one fleeting glance and looked away again. "I did foolish things, to give you clues."

"The raelynx."

She nodded. "I had to know. What face you would show me when you discovered the truth."

"I'm sorry it was such a shocked face today, then," he said, instantly full of remorse. "But—it *hurt*—and there was so much to understand, all at once—"

She laughed softly. "Oh, I thought you would curse me and run from the room. The fact that you stayed and were willing to *talk* to me—I never hoped for so much."

Sweet gods, what a desperately lonely life she had led. She had no concept of how much strain the bonds of friendship could bear. Without thinking about it, he reached over and laid his hand on her wrist. "Amalie," he said. "Nothing you do or say or *are* could ever turn me against you."

She twisted her hand so she could take hold of his, but she didn't look at him. "I don't think that's true," she said. "People turn against their friends all the time. I don't know the reasons. Maybe I'll do something at some point to disgust you or repulse you, and then you'll leave. That could happen."

He laughed back in his throat. "I think it's more likely to work the other way. You'll get tired of me or annoyed with me and send me away."

"No, I won't."

"Or your husband will. He might not like to have me loitering about the palace all the time, scowling every time I see him."

That made her smile, and she gave him a sideways glance. "Why would you be scowling?"

"Because I'll be jealous of him, of course! Married to you!" He said it lightly but his stomach twisted. It was the first time he had admitted the thought out loud, though it had dwelt at the back of his mind for weeks.

She shrugged a little and her fingers tightened. "Maybe I won't find a husband right away."

That made his heart leap, though he sternly told it to hunker back down. "I think you're supposed to. I think that's what everyone wants you to do."

She straightened her posture and tossed back a lock of hair. She was recovering some of her habitual poise and a little of her playfulness. "Maybe it's not what *I* want. Maybe I won't do what everyone tells me to do."

"That's something I've noticed," he said. "Lots of times you don't."

"So will you stay then?"

He gave her as much of a bow as he could muster while sitting on a stool and holding her hand in his. "Majesty, I am yours to command."

She finally turned to face him, frowning a little. "No, I *mean* it. Will you stay as long as I'm not married?"

For a moment, he simply stared at her, and she stared back. They were still handfast; the warm, shadowy kitchen seemed a place of comfort and ease, a place to share secrets. "Amalie, I will stay as long as you want me to," he replied slowly. "But you should not let—let—your friendship for me stop you from making an advantageous match. Valri and Senneth would banish me from Ghosenhall altogether if they thought that."

Her dark eyes were extremely wide. "I wouldn't say it was because of you. I would just say that I don't want to get married right now."

He felt a brief smile come to his lips. "They might not find that a very good reason."

She whispered, "But I *don't* want to get married just now."

She was still watching him, and now the expression on her face was half-pleading, half-afraid. Afraid he would not be able to tell what she wanted. Ah, but he was a reader, after all, and she had dismantled her safeguards. He could feel the confused tumble of her emotions—hope, longing, affection, nervousness, curiosity, daring, desire—and knew that he should drop her hand and leave the room. She was so young, she was so precious, and she was even more inexperienced than he was; he was the one who should walk away.

He leaned forward and kissed her.

Immediately he was awash in her feelings as well as his own. He felt as if he had been enfolded in gold, as if the air shimmered when he drew in breath. His own pleasure and excitement were added to hers and multiplied; both of them experienced both of their reactions. She liked the kiss, no doubt about that, and so he continued kissing her, lifting his free hand to draw her closer, bring her into a half-embrace made ridiculously awkward by the placement of their stools. The air grew even more golden; he was enveloped in a haze that replicated, in a translucent fashion, the precise color of Amalie's hair. He was flushed with heat and tingling with delight—or she was—or they both were.

Kissing Murrie had never been like this.

Kissing Murrie had led to—

Shocked, he lifted his head and stared down at her again. The gold mist abruptly evaporated, and so did Amalie's feelings of warm satisfaction. She was afraid again.

"What?" she said. "What did I do wrong?"

He pushed himself back on his stool, resettled himself, but didn't release her hand as he absolutely should have, except she looked so woebegone. "Not you. Me," he said with emphasis. "I can't be kissing the princess in the kitchens! And—and thinking all kinds of things! Amalie, I'm sorry."

Now she pouted. "I wanted you to kiss me." And then a little sideways smile. "And I liked it."

He strangled on what should have been a laugh. "Well, yes, so did I, but—by the Bright Mother's burning eye! It's practically a treasonable offense."

"I'm sure my father kissed plenty of girls before he married my mother," she said.

"You know it's not the same thing. You could probably kiss any number of serramar, too, and no one would think a thing."

"Toland Storian," she said in a provocative tone. "He kissed me."

Cammon felt himself glowering. "I thought he did. I wished I could have punched him."

"But I didn't like it when *he* kissed me."

She didn't add the obvious corollary. Cammon put his free hand to his forehead and tried not to laugh. "You don't understand," he said. "I'm not very good at knowing how to do the proper thing. The expected thing. I don't comprehend—" He waved his hand as if to indicate the whole kitchen, but he really meant to refer to the entire country. "About nobles and peasants, lords and ordinary people. What's the difference between them? So part of me doesn't understand why it is that I'm not good enough to kiss a princess." He glanced over at her, still rubbing his fingers against his forehead. "And part of me does."

She assumed her loftiest expression and touched his shoulder with the fingers of her right hand. "If your princess commands you—"

He released her hand and stood up, trying to smile. "Nobody is going to think that's a good enough reason for me to act so badly."

She stood up, too, looking a little lost, trying to hide it by smoothing down her nightdress and glancing around the kitchen. Her distress was clear to him, though, and he wanted to put his arms around her again. How was it possible that *he* had to be the one to preach propriety? He was the oblivious and feckless one too blithe to anticipate consequences. Why did *he* have to be the one to behave?

"I guess this is the reason Valri didn't think I should spend too much time alone with you," he said, attempting to speak lightly.

She gave a little shrug. "I think she was more afraid of what you would find out about my magic." She was completely depressed.

He couldn't bear it. "Amalie." When she didn't look at him, he put his hand under her chin and tilted her face up. "Amalie. You're wrong in what you're thinking."

She jerked her head away. "You don't know what I'm thinking."

"Oh, yes, I do."

And, because it was so much easier not to say the words aloud, he let them reach her silently. *You're embarrassed. You're afraid I think you're silly. You're afraid I don't like you. You wish you knew what I was thinking, because maybe I do like you. You wish you weren't the princess. You wish that I was somebody else.*

"No," she said. The rest of his words had only made her blush, but this last sentence made her speak up. "No. I want you to be exactly who you are."

He smiled. *Maybe that was me, wishing I was somebody else. Someone who had a right to court a princess.*

She turned away, blushing still, but a little less forlorn. "I can't do that," she said. "I can hear you, but I can't put thoughts in your head that clearly."

Whatever else you take away from this night, you should know at least two things, he said. *I never, never, never want to hurt you. And I am pretty sure you're going to break my heart.*

Her chin went up at that. "Why would I? And say it out loud."

He smiled, shrugged, looked away, smiled again. "Because one day pretty soon, you're going to marry one of those serramar after all."

That made her happy. His wretchedness and jealousy chased away her own insecurities, and now she was just another pretty girl who'd been kissed by a man she liked more than she wanted to admit. She smiled, ducked her head, failed to keep another blush at bay, and suddenly whirled around and headed for the door. He didn't follow. She paused with her hand on the frame and gave him one quick look over her shoulder. Her words came to him, shaky and tentative and not entirely intelligible.

Maybe I won't.

And then she giggled and swept through the door, into the dark corridor.

Cammon stood there a long moment, wondering exactly what she'd meant.

Maybe she wouldn't marry? Or maybe she wouldn't break his heart?

HE met Senneth and Tayse on the outskirts of Ghosenhall two days later. He had borrowed a horse and gone riding toward their small party, grinning at the exasperation Senneth was feeling toward her fresh recruits. Tayse exuded far more patience, though Cammon guessed it hadn't been an easy trip for any of them. He could pick up a motley impression of their varied companions, full of awe and excitement and the sheer love of change that was inherent in every mystic. The city loomed before them, dazzling with promise. All of them were both eager and uneasy at the thought of stepping through the gates.

"A good trip, I take it," Cammon greeted them as he pulled his horse around to ride alongside Senneth.

She gave him one quick, irascible look and decided not to answer. Tayse said, "We had a few inconveniences along the way."

Cammon grinned. Just having them nearby was righting his sense of balance, seriously off-center for the past two days. "Why don't you introduce me to everybody?"

Senneth arched her eyebrows at him, clearly asking why he had called her back to Ghosenhall so urgently if he was just going to engage in small talk when she arrived. "Do you have a few moments?" she asked pointedly.

He nodded. "Yes, of course. Though I have something I need to tell you."

"I can take this lot to Jerril's house," Tayse offered.

"All right," Senneth said. She turned in her saddle and began motioning people forward. "This is Baxter, he's a shape-shifter."

It took about fifteen minutes to go through the roster. Cammon picked up significant reserves of power from three of the mystics and made it a point to memorize their names. The others had a range of talents that would come in useful, but not as much ability as those three.

"Cammon's a reader," Senneth finished up. "So only think kind thoughts when he's around."

He grinned. "Something she herself never bothers to do."

Tayse put up his right hand and motioned the others forward. They were nearly at the city gates now, and they were encountering all sorts of traffic. "Come with me. I'll take you to the house where you'll be boarding."

Cammon and Senneth reined their own horses to a walk as the mystics pulled away. "You got a few really good ones," he said. "That redheaded girl? She's strong."

"Really? She was so quiet on the whole journey that I began to wonder if I should even have brought her along."

"Oh, I think so."

"Now, what's going on here? Why did you call me?"

So many parts to this tale. And the parts that would shock her most he wasn't even going to share. "We were right. Amalie *is* a mystic. And so was her mother."

Senneth took a deep breath. "How did you find out? Did she confide in you?"

"It gets much worse. So stay calm."

"Just tell me."

"Some young lord from Coravann is going to come calling next week, and he sent her a gift in advance. A moonstone necklace. She put it on and—"

"And it burned her skin? Bright Mother strike me blind. She's going to be in all sorts of situations where people wearing moonstones will approach her and take her hand—"

"That's not what happened," he said quietly. "It burned *me*."

She pulled her horse to a stop. "I don't understand."

"You remember that little lioness charm that Kirra carries around with her? I could take it in my hand and I could use it to pour some of my power into her. You remember that?"

Senneth was clearly bewildered. "Yes, but—"

"The moonstone is like that, I think. It can channel power. Or, more truly, it can steal power. Take it from a mystic and give it to whoever is wearing the charm."

Now she was frowning. "But that can't be true. I've been around plenty of people who were wearing moonstones and they didn't seem to pull any power from me."

"Well, you're different anyway. You can *wear* a moonstone and it scarcely bothers you. But the real reason those people couldn't pull power from you, I think, was because they weren't mystics, too."

"That makes even less sense! Kirra and Donnal can't touch a moonstone, let alone use it to—"

Her voice trailed off. She was staring at him. He nodded. "It only works for a certain kind of mystic. A *true* Daughter of the Pale Mother."

"Coralinda Gisseltess," Senneth whispered.

"A thief mystic," Cammon said. "Just like Amalie."

"By all the forgotten gods." She took a moment to absorb the information, turn it over in her mind, seek out the logical implications. She urged her horse forward again and Cammon rode beside her in silence while she worked it out. "Does Coralinda know she's a mystic? Has this whole persecution been a sham?"

"Only she could tell us that. But I think she's a sincere fanatic. You remember, I met her when we were in Coravann. She's awfully powerful, so she could have been shielding, but I didn't pick up anything from her but blazing righteousness."

"Well, you didn't pick up magic, either, so obviously you weren't reading her entirely right."

He gave her a hurt look. "It doesn't read like other kinds of magic. It's the *opposite* of magic."

"Wait a minute," Senneth said. "When we were in Coravann. You escorted Coralinda across the room. She took your arm. She was dripping with moonstones. And that didn't bother you? That didn't burn your skin?"

He shook his head. "No. But when she touched Kirra, Kirra was desperately in pain." He shrugged. "Maybe it's easier for thief mystics to steal from some than from others. Maybe Amalie's stronger than Coralinda and can pull power from farther away." *Maybe I am more attuned to Amalie and thus she finds it easier to rifle through the pockets of my soul.*

"Oh, I don't even want to *think* about what this means!" Senneth groaned. "It was too complicated before!"

He smiled briefly. "And it might be even more complicated."

She gave him a suspicious look. "Why's that?"

"I keep wondering. If the moonstones feed the energy of other mystics to Coralinda, why does she want them dead? That just eliminates her source of power."

"But if she doesn't realize she's a mystic, she doesn't understand what she's doing to herself," Senneth pointed out.

"I guess that could be the reason."

"You have a different theory."

"Well. She hates us so much. She believes so passionately that she's right to hate us. I have to assume that every time a mystic dies, she feels an intense sense of satisfaction—a validation of what she's done. A sense of well-being . . ."

He let his voice trail off as he watched understanding come to her face. Understanding and horror. "You think she feeds off death? *That's* what boosts her power?"

"I think it's possible. She might feed off of torture as well."

"Bright Mother burn me," Senneth said. "I think I'm going to be sick. And *this* is the power that Amalie carries? This dreadful kind of magic?"

"Don't say that!" he cried.

Senneth looked surprised. "Well, I wouldn't. Not to her. But—"

"She had that very thought herself, and she was so upset, but it's *not* the same! Magic responds to the will of the man—Jerril taught me that, and I have to guess he taught you, too. Coralinda has chosen to twist and misuse her power, but Amalie won't. Amalie will make something good and useful out of it. But not if people—especially other mystics, who ought to know better!—treat her like she's corrupt and evil!"

Senneth's eyes had widened at this impassioned defense. "Of course I don't believe Amalie is evil. But to learn that the heir to the realm is another Daughter of the Pale Mother— Cammon, I have to admit that gives me pause. That gives me *nightmares*."

"The Pale Mother is not evil, either," he said stiffly.

"She rejoices when she sees mystics burned to death!"

He shook his head. "No. Coralinda does. Not the goddess."

"You can't possibly know that! You might be a powerful reader, but I don't think you can scan the minds of the *gods*."

"Ask Ellynor," he said. "She knows more of the Silver Lady than any of us do. Except—well, you can't ask Ellynor because Valri made me swear to tell no one about Amalie."

"I'm glad you didn't keep *that* promise!"

"I told her there was no way I could try to keep the secret from you. And that you wouldn't keep it from Tayse, but that we would tell no one else. At least right now."

Senneth sighed and slumped in her saddle. "And I thought the trip was the hard part. I thought life would get easier once I was back in Ghosenhall. Though I have bad news of my own."

"I could tell something went wrong," he said, "but I couldn't tell what."

"Old mystic from Carrebos. Couldn't travel with us but he came in to show off his magic. He has some control over water, it appears. He said the ocean revealed to him that there is a fleet of ships gathering off the coast of Fortunalt. Sounded like warships, full of foreign soldiers."

Cammon felt alarm register separately in his skull, his stomach, his elbows, and his knees. "Come to war on Gillengaria?"

"That's what it looks like. Imported by our rebel southern Houses."

"Then—why haven't they landed and come to attack us?"

"Tayse says they're waiting for spring." She held a hand up as if to test for reprieve in the air. "And it's not that far off. A month, maybe less, and this hard weather will be over."

Cammon swallowed against a lump of fear. "Senneth—what do we do?"

She gave him a grim smile. "We prepare for war."

CHAPTER

23

OVERNIGHT the city was transformed. Soldiers who had been in training in the more rural districts outside of Ghosenhall were brought in and deployed in a ring all around the city. Reserve soldiers, housed for months on property in Merrenstow and Storian, were sent for, and accommodations for them were hastily built on the outskirts of town. Shopkeepers and tavern owners suddenly had to truncate their hours of operation; residents were ordered to adhere to an early curfew. The number of night watchmen tripled, but they roamed streets that were practically empty.

"I can't go to Danalustrous," Senneth said to the king. "My brother will just have to get married without me. I got married without him, after all."

"Go," Baryn said. He looked oddly relaxed for a man who believed his home could be attacked at any minute. "When our customs and civilities are most under siege is the time we most need to observe them."

"Sire, I'm not sure I can persuade Tayse to stay behind. He knows his first duty is to you, but he—"

"I am the one who commanded him to protect you, and he obeys me very well," the king said, his eyes crinkling up with laughter. "I require you to defend the realm, and therefore I require him to keep you safe. There is no conflict here."

"I am not comfortable leaving you behind without either of us in your arsenal."

"I believe that my safety can be reasonably assured by forty-nine Riders, several thousand soldiers, and this highly unusual troop of mystics you have assembled for my protection."

That made her groan. "Oh, those mystics from Carrebos! Two of the shape-shifters have proved to be quite talented, and they prowl around the palace grounds all day, sniffing for trouble, but the rest of them are a very mixed blessing. Jerril and Areel have rented another house and turned it into a dormitory of sorts, and I believe Jerril is actually enjoying himself, but training a mystic is like trying to train a raelynx. It pretty much does what it wants to, no matter what you tell it—and it's dangerous even when you think it's tame."

"I quite like having them here. Amalie tells me she has met them all. She has become most interested in magic, you know."

He looked at her over the tops of his spectacles, and she was forced to laugh. "You know I have learned Amalie's secret."

"And you are very shocked."

"Yes."

He picked up a quill pen in his right hand and lightly brushed the feathers across the back of his left hand. "Pella's magic was a true gift to her," he said quietly. "It enabled her to analyze any situation, fit into any group, put anyone at ease. It was as if she could almost instantly become anyone else for just as long as she needed to. It made her very popular—everyone loved her."

"I think Amalie's gift is a little different. But since I'm not sure even she knows the extent of it yet, it is hard to gauge."

"I have spent her whole life concealing it from others," the king said. "This does not seem to be the time to announce to the world that she is a mystic."

"No! But I would want your permission to tell a select few—those I trust the most—those of us *you* trusted to guard her last summer."

"I will tell Tayse he may inform the Riders. I assume you wish to give the news to Kirra."

"And Donnal. And Ellynor. No one else."

He regarded her a moment, his face grown sad. "And do you think even such a small group will be able to keep the secret?"

"The mystics won't tell. Only you can gauge the loyalty of the other Riders, but Tayse and Justin are safe."

He sighed. "Any one of the fifty would defend me to the death if *I* suddenly claimed to have sorcerous blood. They are bound to me—their loyalty is more important to them than their own lives. But they are not so bound to Amalie. Their oaths were not made to *her*. They will defend her because she is mine, and as such, she represents the throne. If they know that she is a mystic, I do not know if that fealty will extend to her after I am dead."

"Which we hope will not be for a very long time."

He looked suddenly tired. "I pray the gods at least let me survive this war. At least let me give her that much—a kingdom that is whole, if wounded."

"I think I should stay in Ghosenhall," Senneth said.

"And I say you should go to Danan Hall," Baryn replied. "Attend your brother's wedding. Your king commands you."

ACCORDINGLY, five days after they had returned from Carrebos, Senneth and Tayse were traveling again. A much different journey this time, she thought. With just two of them to consider, they moved speedily and with utter efficiency. They were accustomed to each other's strengths by now, so they never had to discuss where to make camp (Tayse always chose some easily defended site) or who would make the fire (Senneth merely had to glance at a pile of kindling). They could, if they needed to, communicate merely with glances and gestures, and whenever they came upon other travelers on the road, they always agreed by some wordless communion whether to pause and share information or simply ride on by.

Both of them were capable of long stretches of utter silence. Senneth found it easy to lose herself in her thoughts, and Tayse was always so interested in the terrain around them that he never seemed to lack for occupation. So they could have passed the entire journey without exchanging a word—but instead, they talked for almost every mile.

Tayse wanted to know if she was nervous about seeing her brothers again. *Oh, I think I got past both nervousness and rage sometime last summer. But I wouldn't say I'm excited at the prospect. Except, of course, for seeing Will.* She asked how the Riders had taken the news of Amalie's magical heritage. *Quietly. I think some of them don't care and some of them are still deciding how they feel, but not one of them would desert the king at this hour because of it.* He wanted an update on Jerril's success with the recruits from Carrebos; she asked if he thought the regent would be the commanding officer on the field when war finally swept into Ghosenhall.

They talked about Ellynor. "She seems cautiously happy to be here," Tayse remarked. "As if she still thinks she might be dreaming the whole thing, or there might be a monster lurking somewhere in one of the shadows, but otherwise mighty pleased with her new life."

They talked about Valri. "I've guarded some pretty dangerous secrets in my time, but I couldn't have kept this one for so long," Senneth confessed. "It makes me respect her more but also fear her a little. What strength of will she has! Anyone with that kind of determination is dangerous."

They talked about Amalie. "She's too young to bear the burdens that will be thrust on her if war comes," Tayse said. "But there's something unbreakable about her. I would be the first Rider to swear fealty to her if Baryn died."

They talked about Cammon. "Something happened to him while we were gone," Senneth said. "And I don't know what."

They were on Danalustrous land by now, having survived a very thorough inspection at the border, and needed only half a day to arrive at the Hall. *Which is good,* Senneth thought, *since the wedding is tomorrow.*

Tayse gave her a questioning look. "You think Cammon was physically hurt?"

"No. Something struck him to the heart."

"Something more than the startling revelation about his princess and his enemy?" Tayse said in an ironic voice.

She laughed. "Something more."

"Why do you think it?"

"Because he avoided me the whole time we were there—once he'd told me his great news, of course. You know Cammon. Usually he's always underfoot, and even more so if any of us have been absent for any length of time. But we were gone more than two weeks and preparing to ride out again, and we only saw him for a few minutes now and then."

Tayse reviewed his own recent history. "I hadn't realized it, but you're right."

"And Justin said Cammon avoided *him* those last few days before you and I got back. And you can always find Cammon somewhere in Justin's vicinity."

"Do you think he's hiding something that he doesn't want you to discover? That he did something you would condemn?"

In a very soft voice she replied, "I think he's falling in love with Amalie, and he can't help it, and he doesn't want me to know."

Tayse shrugged. "So a mystic becomes devoted to the princess. That's not such a terrible thing. If he loves her, he will serve her with all his heart."

She gave him a wide-eyed stare. "I'm even more afraid that Amalie is falling in love with him. And he knows that, too."

Tayse's eyes narrowed. "Do you seriously think she would take him as her lover?"

"I think that both Amalie and Cammon have led such unconventional lives that something that seems impossible to us does not seem particularly consequential to them."

He smiled. "Many men have dared to love women whom they had no reasonable hope of winning."

She laughed, but grew instantly grave. "This is a little more outrageous than a serramarra and a King's Rider! She will be queen, and he is *nobody*. You hold a respectable position that my brothers can admire, but Cammon can't even claim that distinction."

Tayse didn't seem nearly as concerned as she was, which she found both calming and exasperating. "Say it happens. She takes him to her bed. What are you afraid of? That she will bear his child?"

"Sweet gods, I hadn't even gotten that far in my calculations! No, I'm afraid that a number of her noble-born suitors might decline to marry her if it was discovered she had taken a lover."

"You're strangely moralistic for a woman who has defied every law of her own society," he commented.

She exhaled a breath of laughter. "I am, am I not? Does that make me hypocritical? It is just that the laws I disregarded myself seem to have been *designed* to apply to Amalie."

"And I would say she can contravene them with even more impunity. So she has a lover. So she has a dozen. Does that truly ruin her marriage prospects? A man who loved her, or a man who wished to be king, wouldn't care at all."

Senneth had never thought of it that way. "I suppose you're right. But there are plenty of serramar who might care less about virginity and more about her choice of bedmates. If Cammon were of noble blood, they might not cavil so much. And if she has fewer candidates to choose from, I think it will be harder for her to find the right husband."

He turned his head to give her a long, half-smiling appraisal. "And tell me again, please, why it is so critical that Amalie marries?"

She practically stared at him. "Because the whole kingdom is watching her and wondering if she is suitable to be queen! Because a stable alliance with a strong House will mollify the marlords—we hope—and help us stave off the possibility of war."

"We are already going to war," he pointed out. "There is a navy collecting outside of Forten City. Marry her off tomorrow, and Ghosenhall will still be under attack. *Why* does she need to wed?"

She absolutely had no answer for that. It had seemed to make such perfect sense, back when she and Valri and Baryn were talking strategy. Find Amalie a husband, show the marlords that she was a fit and fertile princess, strengthen the alliances, avert war. But if war were to come anyway . . .

"If you are so determined to get her a bridegroom, wait till the war is over," Tayse recommended. "Reward some House that shows exemplary service to the crown. But I see no need for Amalie to marry where she has no inclination. At this stage, a husband could divide her loyalties and scheme to influence her in ways that you do not desire. She is young, yes, but she is already surrounded by advisors who are utterly faithful and united in their views. Why bring in another voice? Why bother with a husband at all?"

"There is still the matter of heirs," Senneth said faintly. "Eventually, she must produce a few of those."

His smile was even broader. "She wouldn't need a husband for that, either."

She couldn't bite back a laugh. "But this is too amusing!" she exclaimed. "You have always been far stricter than I have about the boundaries of class! And now you would upend everything! Just for the pleasure of the debate? Or is this how you truly feel?"

"I never understood why Amalie was being rushed toward a wedding. I *do* understand why you want her to marry within her own rank and station, but I am not worried that a liaison with Cammon will harm her." He shrugged. "In fact, the opposite."

"You think it would be a *good* idea for her to fall in love with Cammon?" Senneth demanded. "Oh, no, surely not!"

"If he is lying in bed beside her at night, no assassin will be able to reach her in stealth," Tayse said deliberately. "My first goal is to keep her alive. Everything else bends to that imperative."

Senneth caught her breath. Yes, Tayse always saw life in the starkest and most absolute terms. It was something she had had the skill for at one point—when her own life had been simplified to the most drastic choices of survival or death. She had lost her way a little in these past months, as she had reentered the social circles she had scorned for so long. She had gotten muddled. She had lost her focus.

"I am *not* going to encourage him, even on those grounds," she said. "In fact, I still want to wring his neck for being so heedless and—and *stupid*. But you might be right. Perhaps. Some small part of your argument might have merit. I will think it over."

His lurking smile was back. He placed his right fist against his left shoulder and bowed from the saddle. "Serra, that is all I ask."

DANAN Hall was festive with bridal decorations, but they had to work their way through a half dozen checkpoints to get a glimpse of the bouquets and garlands. Senneth could tell that Tayse approved of the soldiers massed around the city that surrounded the Hall; more guards patrolled the grounds of the manor itself. Trust Malcolm Danalustrous to protect his own.

Kirra met them in the great foyer while they were still being interrogated by the steward. "Carlo, of course you remember Senneth!" Kirra exclaimed, flinging her arms around first Senneth and then Tayse. "She used to live here! Though, of course, it was a long time ago."

"Yes, serra, and she and her escort were here last fall," Carlo replied. He was a thin, precise, well-dressed man who was a little vain about his appearance. "But your father has instructed me to ascertain that everyone who crosses the threshold is, in fact, on the list of expected guests."

Kirra had taken hold of Senneth's arm and was pulling her toward the gracious, polished staircase. "Well, both of them are," she said over her shoulder. She glanced at Tayse. "At least, I think so. Are you going to attend the wedding? Or are you going to spout some nonsense about Riders not being fit to participate in the celebrations of the nobility?"

"No, Tayse is in quite an iconoclastic mood these days," Senneth said. "Topple the social conventions! Let peasants mingle with princesses! We shall all be equals."

"I think I'll need to hear the rest of this story later," Kirra said, herding them upstairs. "But I'm glad you're here. I was afraid you'd decide not to come."

"Well, with the news about ships at Forten City, I wanted to stay in Ghosenhall," Senneth replied. "But Baryn insisted we come."

Kirra turned off at the landing on the second floor and tugged Senneth forward again, down the main corridor. The ceiling arched high over their heads and banners fluttered on the walls. Danan Hall was so beautiful and so restful that it scarcely allowed a visitor to entertain thoughts about something as ugly as war.

"Baryn has called in his reserve troops. We're readying for an onslaught," Tayse said.

Kirra stopped at a room not far from the stairwell and pushed open the door. The room was decorated in dark maroon shades lightened by accents of pale wood, washed gold, and pale green. "This is where you'll stay. Isn't it pretty? I've put you in the family wing, so you might stumble over my father or my stepmother when you come and go. But you're right down the hall from me, which should be convenient. I hope our new egalitarian Tayse isn't going to insist on sleeping in the stables."

Grinning, Tayse dropped his saddlebags to the floor beside the bed. "I slept inside the walls at Brassen Court," he said. "I suppose I can do Danan Hall the same honor."

Kirra's laughter pealed out. "And, of course, it *is* an honor to have a Rider staying under our roof again!"

"Who else is here?" Senneth asked. "All the Houses?"

Kirra shook her head, suddenly sober. "My father and Kiernan decided it would be unfair to ask marlords and marladies to leave their own properties when the realm is in such turmoil. Well, can you imagine? Ariane certainly wouldn't want to desert Rappen Manor at a time like this! So they have sent out announcements proclaiming the wedding will be this day but saying that they have decided upon a private ceremony. That way, no one has to turn them down."

"Good strategy," Tayse said.

"Are all my brothers here?"

Kirra shook her head again. "Only Kiernan and Harris. Nate stayed behind. Officially, he is ill, but Kiernan told my father honestly that he wanted to leave one of his brothers in place in case there should be trouble."

"And that neatly solves the problem of whether or not to bring Sabina Gisseltess with him," Senneth said. "More excellent strategic thinking!"

"I would not want to match wits with Kiernan," Kirra confessed. "I like Will so much better!"

"Though Will is not stupid, either," Senneth warned. "He just doesn't have Kiernan's ruthlessness."

"No, Casserah will supply that," Kirra said.

"What's on the schedule? Does something happen tonight?"

"Just a dinner for everyone staying in the manor. The wedding will be tomorrow at noon. There might be a hundred people present—vassals from Brassenthwaite who made the journey, and some of our own lesser lords."

"So we can leave tomorrow afternoon?" Senneth said. Tayse laughed, but Kirra was horrified.

"Of course you can't! How rude! There will be another dinner tomorrow night, and of course there will be dancing afterward, and I must see you take a turn around the ballroom in Kiernan's arms! And then the following day there will be a breakfast, and I think there will be a hunt for those who can't force themselves to leave, but I would think you could be on your way as soon as the breakfast is over."

"I want to get back to Ghosenhall with all speed," Senneth said.

"Did something else happen?"

Tayse didn't quite laugh. "It's a long tale," he said. "Where's Donnal? I'll leave Senneth to fill you in."

Kirra immediately settled herself in the middle of the maroon bed-spread. "Yes. Sit down. We have at least an hour before we have to dress for dinner. Tell me everything."

THE meal was lavish, delicious, and surprisingly informal. Forty people sat at the two long tables, but they were all the most trusted vassals of two friendly Houses, and so there was little pomp, little posturing. Then, too, Senneth reflected, neither Malcolm Danalustrous nor her brother Kiernan had much use for frills or ostentation. If Kiernan had had his way, no doubt he would have seen Will and Casserah married in some hasty ceremony in a back parlor with only a handful of close friends in attendance, and he would have sent them out the door the very next day to go on with the unromantic business of ordinary life.

Much the way Senneth herself had gotten married.

Though it actually *had* been the most romantic evening of her life.

She found herself given the chair next to Malcolm Danalustrous, a high honor. Customarily, a husband and wife were not seated together, so she looked around to see where poor Tayse had landed. Ah—he had been well-placed between Kiernan's wife, Chelley, who was quite kind and who liked Tayse, and Malcolm's vassal Erin Sohta. Erin was a silly and fawning sort of woman, but she fancied herself an intimate of the mar-lord's and always loved to be granted special privileges. She was just the sort of woman who would be delighted at a chance to be seated next to a King's Rider at a dinner party and then gossip about it for the next two years.

Heartlessly, Senneth ignored both Tayse and the Brassenthwaite lord sitting on her other side, and talked to her host the entire night. Malcolm was the man she respected most, after the king; his House was the one she would have taken sanctuary in, if she had ever needed it. He was stern, stubborn, willful, fair-minded, and absolutely devoted to the land he owned. Kirra said his veins ran with Danalustrous river water and his heart was made from a curiously animate lump of Danalustrous clay. He had bequeathed his blue eyes, his black hair, his iron will, and his fierce commitment to the land to his daughter Casserah. Neither of them was comfortable to talk to. Both of them were easy to understand. Respect Danalustrous, or be gone.

"Tell me the news," he said. "Kirra says war is on the doorstep."

So she repeated everything she had told Kirra—except the parts about Amalie and Cammon, which were more interesting in their way but less important from Malcolm's point of view. He listened intently, asked sharp questions, and shook his head when she asked if he planned to raise an army for the king.

"I want to close the borders," he said. "And once my esteemed guests are gone, that is exactly what I plan to do."

She toyed with her wineglass. "I don't know how you think you can do that. You have miles of coastline, and you cannot possibly defend every inch. Your soldiers line every road that leads into Danalustrous, I'm assuming, but there are so many places a small troop could creep across the border in stealth! Your boundaries are porous, Malcolm."

He gave her a faint smile. "And you don't think I would know if hostile forces came stepping across those boundaries, no matter how secret their approach? You underestimate me, Senneth. I feel every footstep as it falls on Danalustrous soil. I will not be surprised by strangers."

She sat back in her chair and regarded him with her head tilted to one side. "And do you still believe," she said in a soft voice, "that Kirra inherited her magic from her *mother*? I have always thought you had some kind of mystical connection to your land. Maybe you're the one with sorcery. If what you say is true."

His smiled widened. "If so, then every marlord in Gillengaria, including your brother, has been touched by magic," he said. "For they all have that same sense of kinship with their property. Talk to Heffel Coravann sometime if you don't believe me. Talk to Ariane."

She laughed back at him. "And if that is true, then how ironic it is that so many marlords have joined the campaign to eradicate mystics! My father, for instance. Banished me from Brassen Court when he could have been accused of the very same crime!"

Malcolm nodded. "And did you never wonder why Kiernan wished to reconcile with you after your father died? He had come to understand that he was attuned to Brassenthwaite in a way that could not be explained away by anything other than magic. That he was no different than you were—no, and your father had not been, either."

"Bright Mother burn me in ashes to the ground," she swore.

"I don't expect he'd ever admit it, though," Malcolm added.

She laughed again. "And I don't expect I'll ever ask."

She did make her way to Kiernan's side after the meal, though, and found him with her brother Harris. They all exchanged cool but civil greetings. Kiernan had the same sort of stubbornness she had always seen in Malcolm, but less charm and less humor. Still, in the past year she had been forced to admit that his virtues—loyalty, intelligence, and a passion for justice—outweighed most of his flaws, and they had cautiously rebuilt

a relationship of sorts. She still had no patience for her brother Nate, and
Harris was practically a stranger. But Kiernan she respected, if grudgingly
so. He was a powerfully built man with heavy features partially obscured
by a neat beard; his eyes betrayed nothing but a watchful shrewdness.

"What's the news from Ghosenhall?" Kiernan asked.

She gave him the same recital she had given Malcolm, edited a little.
He seemed equally unsurprised, though his response was different. "I'll
send troops from Brassenthwaite as soon as I'm back at the Court," he
said. "We've been training them against the day they would be needed."

"Malcolm won't send his men to battle," she said.

Kiernan glanced over to where the marlord was making conversation
with a Brassenthwaite vassal and her daughter. "Malcolm may change his
mind," he said. "He may decide that he does not like to see his nearest
neighbors fighting over scraps of land that lie awfully close to his borders.
He may decide Danalustrous's best hope of remaining strong is making
sure Gillengaria itself survives."

She didn't need to reply to that, for they were joined just then by the
bridal couple. "Casserah," Senneth said, embracing Kirra's sister. The
presumed excitement of the event didn't seem to weigh much with
Casserah. Her wide-set blue eyes still showed their habitual abstracted
expression. Will stood beside her, lanky and smiling, his face familiar to
Senneth because it looked so much like her own. "And, Will! I was so
afraid I would not be able to make it for the wedding."

"I was surprised to hear you'd arrived," Will said, giving her a smile
and a hard hug. "I was sure you'd find some excuse for staying away."

She laughed. "The welfare of the kingdom? Would that have been a
good enough reason?"

"Of course it would," Casserah said, her voice as composed as always.
"You didn't need to come. I would not have been at all offended."

Senneth couldn't help grinning. Never anything less than the absolute truth from Casserah. "Then you won't be offended to learn I do not
plan to stay long after the ceremony concludes. I am uneasy being away
from Ghosenhall. I think my place is there."

"Perhaps the bride does not wish to talk of war on the eve of her wedding," Harris said.

"It doesn't bother me," Casserah said. "Talk of whatever you like."

The group broke up relatively soon after dinner; everyone wanted
plenty of time to rest and refresh themselves before the morrow. When
Senneth and Tayse returned to their room, they found Donnal there,
shaped like a black hound, sleeping in front of the fire.

"Change to human form, and I'll deal the cards," Tayse invited him, and so the three of them were deep in a game when Kirra arrived half an hour later.

"Everyone off to bed and the bride settled in for the night," she said with a sigh, pulling up a chair and motioning Senneth to include her in the next round. "I'm exhausted but I can't sleep yet."

Senneth felt her laughter bubble up. "Your sister does not seem to be a nervous bride."

"No! Cold-blooded as ever. But she and Will deal together extraordinarily well. I think he finds her entertaining, and she considers him useful. I suppose there are worse ways to make a match."

They played cards, talking idly, until well past midnight, when all of them were finally yawning. "Shall I come dress you in the morning or do you feel able to handle that task yourself?" Kirra asked Senneth on the way out.

"I think I can manage, thank you."

"Then I'll see you tomorrow."

CHAPTER
24

In the morning, the house was filled with all the bustle of a grand event, so Senneth and Tayse didn't look for much interaction with Kirra. Tayse rose and left the room while she was still half asleep; she was certain he had gone to work out with some of Malcolm's house guards. But he returned in plenty of time to bathe and change into his Rider regalia—a formal uniform of black and gold, topped by a sash embroidered with the king's gold lions.

"You look very handsome," Senneth said. She was wearing a long-sleeved dress of deep blue, embroidered at the cuffs and hem and bodice with a complex border of gold. The necklace Tayse had given her hung just above the neckline, perfectly covering her Brassenthwaite house-mark. She had made some effort with her hair, threading blue and gold ribbons through it, and touched up her pale cheeks with a hint of rouge.

"And you, serra. Extremely beautiful."

"I will be glad when this is over and we can be on our way."

He grinned, and bowed her out of the room.

The wedding guests were beginning to assemble in a large, formal hall on the first floor. Columns, archways, and topiary had been decorated with intertwined ribbons of Brassenthwaite blue and Danalustrous red, and someone had coaxed red chrysanthemums and blue delphinium to bloom out of season, for vases of the cut flowers were scattered throughout the room. Kiernan and Harris were standing in a group of Brassenthwaite men, holding what looked like a serious conversation. Senneth nodded their way but did not bother to join them. A harpist and a flautist sat in a corner, offering light music; servants circulated with trays of drinks. Sunlight streamed in through the eight huge windows that lined the east side of the room.

"A pretty day to be married," Tayse observed.

"And then a pretty day to travel," she replied. He laughed at her silently.

Finally, finally, all the guests had gathered. A small red bird with a black tail swooped in through the high doorway, circled the room once, and landed on one of the beribboned plants. Senneth supposed it was Donnal. He rarely attended even informal dinners at Danan Hall, for he was peasant-born and not comfortable in the company of nobles, but clearly this was an occasion he wanted to observe. She waved and he dipped his head in acknowledgment.

He was the last to arrive. Now the music changed, sending a cue to the bridal party. Malcolm entered with Kirra on one arm and his wife, Jannis, on the other, and strode to the front of the hall where a magistrate stood waiting. Casserah and Will were only a few steps behind. She wore deep red; her dark hair was unbound down her back. Will wore blue with touches of scarlet. He had attached a red blossom to his jacket with a ruby stickpin. Kiernan and Chelley and Harris went to stand beside Will while Malcolm, Jannis, and Kirra arranged themselves around Casserah.

The magistrate raised his hand to quiet the last mutterings of the crowd. He was tall and big-boned, with a shock of white hair and a lined, handsome face. Senneth judged that he had observed pretty much everything the world had to offer. "Those who have chosen to marry step forward. Tell me your names and your stations," he intoned.

Senneth took a quick sip of breath and glanced up at Tayse. In almost the same words, a magistrate had married them last fall. He smiled down at her and put his hand on the small of her back.

"I am Casserah Danalustrous, serramarra," the bride said, speaking with utmost confidence. "Daughter of Malcolm and Jannis Danalustrous and heir to all their property."

"I am Will Brassenthwaite, serramar . . ."

It was clear that this ceremony was going to take a little longer than the one that had united Tayse and Senneth, so she let her mind wander a bit. Therefore, she was not paying attention when Tayse nudged her and nodded toward the front of the hall. He raised his eyebrows as if to ask what was wrong.

She focused on the wedding party. The cleric was speaking, but Casserah was not attending. She had turned to look at her father and he was staring back at her. After a moment, he nodded, and Casserah faced the magistrate again. Senneth saw her hands ball up at her sides.

Standing next to her sister, Kirra carefully turned her head, searching the crowd for Senneth; her eyes asked a question. Senneth lifted her hands in a gesture that signified ignorance. But the black-tailed songbird had taken wing. He fluttered out the archway and disappeared.

"Something's happening," Senneth breathed to Tayse.

He nodded and put his hand surreptitiously to his sword. Most of the men present had buckled on dress swords, if they bothered with weapons at all, but Tayse, as always, was armed as if he might have to go into combat at any moment.

No one else seemed to realize there might be trouble. Even Kiernan looked stolid and just a little bored, his arms crossed on his broad chest, his eyes fixed on his brother while his mind probably was busy calculating tax rates or land yields. The cleric, who was now deep in some kind of homily, continued speaking in a deep and solemn voice.

It was less than ten minutes before Donnal returned, arrowing in through the doorway and straight to Kirra. He landed on her shoulder, which caused one or two people in the audience to murmur and laugh, but Senneth knew he did not have Cammon's ability to put his thoughts directly into someone's head. As unobtrusively as possible, Kirra stepped away from the bridal party, the bird still on her shoulder, and ducked into a doorway leading to a servant's hall.

This Kiernan noticed. He unfolded his arms and gave Malcolm an inquiring look. And when, a minute later, Kirra hurried back in and headed straight for her father, Kiernan took five long steps over to join her. They stood there briefly, conferring, while the crowd began to mutter and the magistrate's sonorous voice stuttered to a halt.

"Marlord, is there a problem?" the cleric asked.

Malcolm spoke up calmly. "Finish the ceremony."

"What's wrong?" Will asked Casserah.

Malcolm's voice was a little louder. "Finish the ceremony. Bind them in marriage. Perhaps finish it more quickly than you planned."

Will appealed to Kiernan, who was still standing beside Malcolm. "What's wrong?"

At that moment, Senneth heard the thrumming sound of hundreds of booted feet, as if all of Malcolm's house guards had suddenly been called to formation. They must be outside and some distance away, but there were enough of them that the noise carried. Even farther away there was the silver call of a bugle and a man's voice raised in what was clearly an order to march out.

"Danan Hall is under siege," Malcolm said coolly. "Finalize the wedding. Let them speak their vows."

Now the crowd was alive with agitation, and a few people fled for the door. But Kiernan and Malcolm stood fast, both of them watching the cleric, and Casserah took Will's hand.

"Yes," she said, serene as ever. "Finish this."

"Then—then—" the magistrate stammered, leafing through his book to the final pages. He looked quite pale, and his deep voice was suddenly breathy. "Bound together in friendship, bound together before witnesses, bound together in marriage," he rattled off. "From this day forward, you will be known to all as husband and wife."

"That's done, then," Kiernan said, loudly enough for everyone to hear, and the whole crowd fell apart.

Kirra spun on one heel, lifted her arms above her head, and collected herself into a dark winged shape. Flinging herself into the air, she skimmed over the heads of the visitors and ducked out the great door. She barely beat Tayse, who had sprinted for the threshold the instant the magistrate's last words had sounded. Senneth turned to follow but got caught up in the milling crowd. People were crying, reaching out to grab each other, calling out questions, edging for the door, edging back.

Malcolm strode through the mob, Kiernan close at his heels, then turned at the door to address his guests. "You are probably safest if you stay here," he said. "Those with weapons who wish to use them are welcome to join the defense." And he disappeared out the door.

A hand caught Senneth's arm; she turned to find Will and Casserah beside her. "Will you stay or will you fight?" Casserah asked. Senneth was impressed at her iron control. She clearly realized the situation was dangerous but was not about to melt into a puddle of fear.

"Fight," Senneth said, "though I'm hardly dressed for it."

"I have a sword in my room," Will said.

Senneth shook her head. "No. You and Casserah stay here. The point of this whole day was to unite Danalustrous and Brassenthwaite. It's why Malcolm wanted the ceremony concluded. The two of you must be safe no matter who else falls."

Will glanced at his new bride. "Do you have any idea who would attack? Has Halchon Gisseltess decided to open his war on Danan Hall?"

Casserah shook her head. "No one crossed the borders. This is local trouble."

Senneth's eyes narrowed. So Casserah, like her father, could sense when the boundaries of the land were breached. "Who would wish you so ill on your wedding day?"

"I'm only guessing. But I suspect Thirteenth House lords who have been dissatisfied with the distribution of property." She thought a moment. "There is one young lord in particular who dislikes me. Chalfrey Mallon. He would be especially glad to see me wounded on what should be my happiest day."

Senneth felt rage race through her; her temperature was rising, dangerously high. "Cruel and stupid," she said in a harsh voice. "To try to bring pain where there should be joy."

"He is cruel and stupid," Casserah agreed. "And so we have death instead."

Senneth stalked toward the door, her dark blue dress swirling around her ankles. "Well, Danalustrous and Brassenthwaite defend their own."

As soon as she was in the hallway, she started running, following the scurry of servants, the sounds of combat. Casserah was right. No foreign force could have gotten this close to the Hall without Malcolm being aware of it. Whoever these invaders were, they had come cloaked in Danalustrous colors. How many troops could such malcontents have raised? Enough to overrun Malcolm's personal guard?

She burst through the front door and came upon a melee. It was almost impossible to tell who was fighting on what side, since the majority of the combatants were wearing red. But the invaders were on horseback and the defenders mostly on foot, a bad matchup for the Hall. There were terrible sounds of shouting men, screaming horses, clashing blades. She could see Tayse off to her right, unexpectedly mounted—he must have wrenched a horse from one of the assailants. He laid about him with a furious and brutal efficiency, cutting a swath through the oncoming soldiers. A phalanx of soldiers in blue and red waded behind him, emboldened by his charge, dispatching enemies with a righteous fervor.

But there. Near the garden. A line of invaders was weaving through the ornamental hedges, creeping toward the manor as if to slip in the back way and wreak havoc in the halls. Two civil guardsmen spotted them and let out yells as they ran to engage them, but there were already twenty enemies almost at the house.

Senneth flung a hand out, and the whole maze of hedges burst into flames. Two invaders cried out in pain, saw their trousers catch fire, and dropped to the ground. A dozen of their companions broke free of the sizzling shrubbery and headed toward the house at a dead run. Another eight or ten backed up, away from the flames, away from the battle, and watched indecisively.

Senneth snapped her wrist. The first of the oncoming soldiers ignited and screamed in agony. She splayed her hand again and two more men started blazing. Again. Again. Mad with pain and terror, the enemy fighters shrieked and flung themselves to the ground, rolling on the brown grass. The soldiers who had held back now turned on their heels and sped away.

Senneth felt the heat licking through her veins; her eyes were misted with a fine red. She might have been on fire herself, or perhaps it was just fury that consumed her. She swung her attention back to the main fray and ran forward to cast herself into the middle of it, heedless of swinging blades and trampling horses. Who was loyal, who traitorous? When she was sure, she placed her torrid hand on a soldier's arm, on his back, and heard him scream as his clothes caught fire. Ten men burned as she darted through the grunting, battling squads. Twenty. Thirty.

But more were coming. How many more? How far away were they? She snatched a blade up from a fallen combatant, and hewed her way through the mass of men. Her blue dress was covered in dirt, spattered with blood, ripped at the knees, and, *gods*, was it inconvenient. She hacked and kicked and burned her way through the crowd and finally was clear of the first ring of attackers.

She stood on the outer lawns of Danan Hall, breathing hard, staring around her, wondering where the next assault might come from.

A hawk plummeted from above, talons outstretched. As soon as he touched down, he took Donnal's shape. His feet were bare and covered with blood.

"How many?" she demanded. "How far away?"

"Maybe a thousand advancing from south and west," he said, pointing. "The marlord's reserve soldiers are on the run from the north. But the enemy will arrive first."

"How many in the marlord's troops?"

"Easily two thousand. There's another several thousand that can be summoned, but they're housed on property a day's ride from here."

"How quickly will reinforcements arrive?"

"Maybe an hour."

"And the advancing troops?"

But she could hear them herself, the thunder of hooves, the shouts of men. "Now," Donnal whispered just as the first men broke across the horizon line and charged straight for the embattled Hall.

Senneth spun around, flung her arms wide before her, and called up a monstrous wall of flame. It was taller than an oak tree and raced a mile from either side of her; she felt her own skin blister from its roaring heat. At least fifty men cantered through it, unable to pull up their horses in time. They were shrieking in pain, and their mounts snorted and reared and threw them to the ground. Through the wicked crackle of the flames she could hear shouts and cries on the other side, questions flung out, orders issued, orders remanded. One or two more soldiers braved the barrier and came through, livid with fire.

Senneth spread her fingers as wide as they would go, extended her arms before her, and *pushed*. The whole long wall of fire crept slowly away from her, leaving a charred band of black in the grass. More cries and yelping on the other side as the attackers realized the conflagration was advancing. She heard a confusion of horse hooves retreating, more shouts, more cursing.

She took a long breath, gathered her strength, and pushed again.

Step by blazing step, she forced the opposing forces backward, till she was crunching through a broad swath of cinders as she crossed her own original line. Donnal gathered himself back into a bird shape and darted away to reconnoiter, returning a few minutes later to report.

"They're spreading out in both directions," he said. "Trying to find a way around the flame."

Senneth nodded. She gathered her fingers into points and stretched her arms wide, extending the wall of fire another quarter mile on each side, another half mile. It was taking all her energy, all her strength, but she could enclose the entire Hall in a circle of flame if she had to. "Where are our reinforcements now?" she asked in a tight voice.

"Another half an hour away. The battle on the inside is nearly won— only a few attackers are still fighting for their lives."

"Tell the others to gather at the edges of the fire and await any who try to break through."

She could hear what was almost a smile in Donnal's voice, though she couldn't break her concentration enough to look at him. "Tayse has already organized them to do so. He wants to know how long you can hold the wall?"

"Till dawn, if necessary."

"I don't think the fight will last that long," Donnal said. A rustle, a shadow; he had changed and flown away.

Senneth stood where he had left her, spine stretched up, head tipped back, arms still spread as wide as they would go, and fed her soul to the fire. She was alive with magic; a liquid fever careened through her veins. Her fingertips were candlewicks, and flames danced at the end of each one. Each individual strand of her hair was on fire; her eyebrows had been singed. There was nothing in the world except heat and energy and rage. Noises had fallen away, time had ceased to pass or matter. She was an elemental in a primitive state, and she could burn forever.

It was Tayse's voice that brought her back to a sense of humanity, a sense of self. "Senneth," he named her, his voice both compelling and soft. "Senneth. Drop your arms. Let the fire die. We have vanquished them. The Hall is safe."

He said the whole speech three times before his words actually registered. Slowly she opened her eyes, tilted her head forward, allowed her arms to fall to her sides. Instantly, the fire went out. Just as instantly, she was flooded with a multitude of pains. Her back ached, her arms were sore, and Bright Mother of the burning sky, her head hurt so badly she thought it might shatter. She looked around in wonderment a moment, orienting herself. Still daylight, though the sun was low on the horizon. Before her, a scattering of charred and broken bodies littered the ground. Behind her, a grim and efficient cleanup was under way, as servants and soldiers moved through the dead and wounded, searching for friends, carrying away the bodies of enemy and comrade alike.

"What were our costs?" she asked in a hoarse voice.

"More than seventy dead. Mostly Danalustrous men, though a few Brassenthwaite soldiers fell in the defense. The assailants lost four times that number and eventually retreated. Some of Malcolm's soldiers are pursuing."

She put a shaky hand up to the back of her neck. Every small movement was agony. Her bones felt brittle and scored by heat. Surely someone had taken a chisel and hammered a thousand holes in her skull. "Who attacked? Could he tell?"

"It appears to be the work of three malcontent vassal lords who had been left out of the negotiations to inherit property outright." He shrugged. "Now their sons and daughters will inherit nothing but shame."

He took her arm and she leaned on him heavily as he escorted her back toward the manor house. So many bodies—such a dreadful sight on Malcolm Danalustrous's well-manicured lawns. "Tell them," she said. "If they gather up the bodies, I can make a pyre."

"I think they can make a pyre of their own with more traditional methods," he said firmly. "You need to rest. You look the color of ash—gray and white. And just as likely to disintegrate."

"My head hurts," she said.

"I'll help you as soon as we get to the room."

They came upon a pile of fallen bodies; no easy task to pick a way through. Tayse simply lifted Senneth up and carried her around them. She knew she should protest that she was perfectly fine, but she felt utterly dreadful. She leaned her head against his shoulder and listened to the rumble of his voice from deep in his chest. "Your brother is anxious to make sure all is well in Brassenthwaite. He plans to set out for home first thing in the morning."

"We should leave for Ghosenhall tonight," she muttered.

"We'll leave in the morning," he said. "If your headache is better."

She wanted to lift a hand to rub her temple, but she couldn't make the effort. "It'll take us almost a week to get back."

"We might be able to push that."

"I wish we hadn't come!"

They were almost at the broad, gracious front entrance of the manor, just now stained with blood and piled high with discarded weaponry. Tayse bent to kiss her gently on the forehead. "You saved the Hall," he said. "They all might be dead if you had not been here."

That silenced her for the whole trek through the foyer, up the stairs, and down the corridor to their room. There was no fire in the grate and the air was cool, for which Senneth was grateful. Her skin was still heated; her pulse was too high, too fast, too thick.

Tayse settled on the bed beside her, arranging her so that her back was to his chest but she was leaning away from him. On their very first journey together, he had learned the trick of chasing away her headaches. No one else had the physical strength or reach to command all the pressure points at once. Now, very gently, he placed the thumb of one hand on a bone partway down her spine. With the other hand, he cupped the back of her neck. Senneth braced her fists against the bed.

"I'm ready," she said.

His hand closed around her neck; his thumb bored into her back. She gasped with a sensation that was both pain and the cessation of pain. It was as if his hands were as ferocious and unbreachable as her own wall of fire. It was as if they made a barrier that misery could not cross. Still, the suffocating hold was difficult to endure. She invariably had spectacular bruises the day after a cure like this, but the alternative was three days or more of migraine.

"All right—enough," she breathed, and he slowly released her. They both waited in silence a moment to see if the pain would come washing back, but Senneth felt nothing now except hollow exhaustion. "I think that's done it. What a gift you have for healing me."

"The gift I treasure most," he said solemnly. His hand pushed her down so she was lying on the bed. "Sleep now. I'll go hear the councils of war."

"I need to talk to Kirra," she said drowsily.

"I'm sure she'll be by as soon as she's taken care of details of her own."

"And my dress is covered with blood."

"You can take it off later. Sleep now." He leaned over and brushed his mouth across hers. The light kiss made her smile. She was asleep before he left the room.

CHAPTER
25

IT was full dark when Senneth woke, feeling physically refreshed but emotionally drained. Sitting up cautiously, to make sure no pain woke up with her, she touched a few of the candles on the bedside table, and light wavered through the room. A glance at the fire sent the coals leaping with fire. Sweet gods, she was filthy. And starving.

She had changed into a more comfortable—and much cleaner—shirt and trousers, and was washing her face in the basin, when a quiet knock sounded on the door. "I'm up," she called, and Tayse, Kirra, and Donnal filed in. Kirra was carrying a tray of food. "Oh, you most thoughtful girl," Senneth said, immediately pulling up a chair beside a small table. "I was thinking about chewing some firewood, I was so hungry."

Kirra sat beside her at the table. Donnal settled in his customary place on the floor before the hearth, even though he was shaped like a man tonight. Tayse dropped to the window seat so he could monitor any activity occurring outside.

"Everyone in Danan Hall sends you gratitude and adoration," Kirra informed her, sneaking a slice of potato off Senneth's plate. "And your brothers have been struck almost speechless by your display of power. You have done what you always hoped to do—earned their respect."

"And it only cost the lives of several hundred men," Senneth said between bites. "Hardly a steep price at all."

"Still, it was most impressive, even for you," Kirra said. "Though you look dreadful, I must say. How's your head?"

"Better. But I'm sick at heart. Tell me the extent of the damage and what your father plans to do next."

"The Hall itself is mostly unharmed. Except the lawns are completely destroyed, but who cares about that? We lost a little over eighty men, and my father and Casserah are devastated by that. They are also both furious—that a man of Danalustrous would betray the land. I think they care less that *they* were attacked. They would give their own lives for the House."

"Are they prepared to defend themselves if a bigger army convenes?"

"They are. The reserve troops will be here tomorrow. But my father doesn't seem to believe there will be another assault. He is busy collecting renewed oaths of fealty from the vassals who did *not* participate in the uprising. It seems that only three lesser lords were responsible for the mutiny."

"Your sister mentioned Chalfrey Mallon? I think I met a Mallon or two many years ago when I lived here."

Kirra looked deeply depressed. "It is my fault he hates the Hall. He despises mystics, and Casserah made it clear to him that she would choose me over him. He has been nursing a grudge for months, I suppose."

Donnal stirred on the hearth. "Or found that incident a convenient excuse to turn against your father now."

Tayse spoke from the bench at the window. "Does this change your father's attitude about joining the battle on behalf of the king?"

Kirra's laugh was bitter. "No! Indeed, it makes him more adamant that he will not send soldiers away from Danalustrous when it is clear Danalustrous needs defense. I cannot entirely blame him—except I do blame him. If Gillengaria is torn apart, Danalustrous will be trampled in turn. I don't understand how he can fail to see that. It is so short-sighted, so *blind*, to care only about your own small patch of land. If we do not stand together, we will all fall. Gillengaria *must* supersede Danalustrous."

Senneth smiled at her. "And this, I believe, is the reason your sister will be marlady, and not you."

"It is indeed."

Senneth finished the last of the bread and wished there were more. "We leave for Ghosenhall in the morning," she said. "Will you stay here or come with us?"

"My father wants me to stay, but I can't," Kirra said. "There is obviously a great deal to do here—but—I have to put myself in the king's service. I have to."

Senneth glanced at Donnal, and he nodded. "Even if Kirra wanted to stay, I would go," he said quietly. "All of us are needed. All of us who have some ability to defend the throne."

Senneth tapped an impatient hand against the table. "Still, it will take so long to get to the city! And this is news that should go fast. Perhaps you two should fly on ahead and tell Baryn what happened."

Kirra locked eyes with Donnal and he grinned. "As to that," Kirra said. "There might be a way. To get you to Ghosenhall faster."

Senneth sat up straighter in the chair. "Why am I filled suddenly with apprehension?"

Kirra smiled, but only briefly. "I could change you, you know. Both of you. To something small and furry, perhaps mice. Donnal and I could take hawk shape and carry the two of you across Gillengaria. Not comfortable, and not fun, but we could do it."

Senneth just stared at her. Tayse had slewed around at her first words, losing all interest in whatever might be unfolding on the grounds. "I'm not sure I have the heart for that," Senneth said faintly.

"No. I thought you might not. And I don't blame you. I wouldn't exactly relish being set on fire by you, even if it was ultimately something that would aid me."

Donnal's voice was casual. "Justin would do it. *He's* not afraid."

"Justin's recklessness is legendary," Senneth shot back.

"And I'm not *entirely* certain I can change you," Kirra said. "Last fall, I altered all those people on Dorrin Isle who were sick, but none of them was a mystic. Maybe the magic in your veins will keep *my* magic out." She shrugged. "It's the reason I didn't try to change Ellynor last year when she had to be rescued. The situation was too dire for me to try something that might go seriously awry."

"You realize such a confession makes me even less eager to subject myself to your spells!" Senneth exclaimed.

"Yes, but I really think I can do it," Kirra said. She managed another smile. "And I should have no problem changing Tayse."

"Could you change my sword? And my knives?" Tayse asked.

Kirra's face brightened even more. "Yes, my valiant Rider, I could change your weaponry right along with your body. And change them back the minute we touched down in Ghosenhall."

Now Senneth was staring at him. "You can't seriously be considering—"

He grinned at her. "Justin would do it. Justin *has* done it."

"Justin has never been my guide for behavior."

"And there's more you might not like," Kirra added. Her expression was impish, but Senneth could tell she was utterly serious. About the offer, anyway. "The trip will still take us about two days—we cannot fly all that way, carrying you, without stopping to sleep. It would be easiest for me to *not* change you back to human form overnight, then change you again in the morning. But you might find it too disconcerting to stay altered for so long."

Senneth just opened her mouth and didn't answer.

Kirra went off into gales of laughter. "Oh, look at you! You're trying to decide if I'm joking! I'm not, truly I'm not. Senneth, I believe I can do this, and it would cut the trip easily in half. But it would be strange and probably unsettling. And if we had flown half a day and you were too petrified to continue, we'd be in the middle of the country with no horses and no gear, and it would take you even longer to get back to the royal city."

Donnal shrugged. "We'd change ourselves into horses for the rest of the trip," he said. "We'd still have gained a day or two."

"And you want to turn me into a *mouse?*" Senneth demanded, finding her voice.

Kirra nodded. "A very small one. Easy to carry."

"Are you sure you wouldn't forget and accidentally *eat* me?"

Kirra bubbled with laughter again. "Of course I wouldn't forget! Do you ever accidentally set something on fire?"

"I think we should do it," Tayse said.

She looked at him helplessly. "How can you not be afraid? How can you not be *repulsed?* I don't want to be a mouse flying above the earth in the talons of a predator!"

"I never thought to see you unnerved by magic," he said, amused.

She shuddered. "It's not the magic that frightens me so much as the loss of control," she said. "I would think the same thing would weigh with you."

"I'm practical, and this is a practical solution," he said. "But we will not do it if you cannot endure it. We will send Donnal and Kirra ahead, and make our way with all speed by more conventional means."

How was this possible? That Tayse, who had distrusted sorcery with all his heart when she first met him, was now willing to abandon himself utterly to witchery? While she, whose life had been shaped in every particular by the power in her hands, was hesitant and afraid to submit to enchantment? She took a deep breath.

"We must have some kind of agreement," she said. "After the first hour of flight. You must stop, and set us down, and ask us if we can tolerate more of this unnatural existence. And if we say we cannot—"

"Well, you won't be able to *say* anything," Kirra pointed out. "You'll still be a mouse."

"I realize that! But you will ask, and you will give me a task to do to indicate that I am or am not willing to continue. And if I am, then you can gather me up in your claws again and carry me away for as long as your strength holds up."

Kirra practically bounced in her chair. "Most excellent! I am proud of both of you. Sleep well tonight. We leave on quite an adventure in the morning."

THE entire manor house was awake by dawn, for their own small party was not the only one anxious to return home. Senneth met all three of her brothers in the dining hall and said good-byes over a hasty breakfast. She waved off Will's wild enthusiasm about her magic and Harris's somewhat less hearty appreciation, and she gave Kiernan a sober look.

"When I see you again, it may be on another battlefield," she said.

"Count on it," he said. "I will ride out with the army I send to Ghosenhall."

"Travel safely back to Brassen Court. You have to assume there is unrest across all the northern Houses. I would avoid Tilt, if I were you."

He smiled grimly. "Yes, I believe I will. You, too—take care in your travels."

He had no idea how completely she planned to disregard that admonition.

It was still early morning when she and Tayse, Kirra and Donnal gathered in a little garden not far from the kitchens. Tayse made a pile of the items he wanted to bring with him back to Ghosenhall—his various blades, his uniform, his sash with the royal lions—but Senneth had very little she cared to salvage from her outbound journey. The blue dress was ruined. Her pendant, Kirra had assured her, was small enough to change along with her body. She added nothing to the pile.

"All right," she said, taking a deep breath and sinking to the ground, "change me if you can."

Kirra knelt beside her and put her hands on Senneth's face. The blue eyes were intent and serious as they watched Senneth; the beautiful face was furrowed in concentration. Senneth closed her eyes and felt the sharp tingle of magic along her cheekbones, down the back of her throat, in her hips, her knees, her toes. Her head felt suddenly bound with pressure, which abruptly faded. Her fingers involuntarily splayed and flexed. Her heart was beating so fast it should have made her breathless, but the pulse seemed strangely unalarming. She sniffed and thought how rich and spicy the air had suddenly become.

"Open your eyes. And give yourself a moment to adjust."

Oh, how the world had changed.

She was in a forest of high, brown grass; nuts as large as her head littered the ground. Huge, ungainly creatures were grouped around her, so big they were impossible to see. Below her, the ground stretched on forever, loose soil full of hidden treasures, pockets of mud safe for burrowing into. Her feet were pink and dainty, perfect for scratching through dirt. She could feel her nose twitching, sifting through the laden air, picking out scents for food and danger.

In a lifetime of magic, Senneth had never experienced such a strange spell. She lifted one of the four-toed feet and patted her cheek, trying to get a sense of her face and fur. She was herself, all her thought processes familiar and intact, and yet she wasn't. Fine-honed instincts not her own hovered at the back of her mind. Even now, knowing that the monsters around her were beloved friends, she was poised to run should they suddenly turn capricious. She was calculating the distance to safety; she was distracted by the presence of a dried berry on a nearby shrub.

One of the gigantic humans flattened to the ground, its face inches away. Senneth recognized Kirra but it took all her willpower to keep from chittering and scurrying away. "How are you tolerating this so far?" Kirra asked, her voice very loud and quite distinct. "If you don't think you can bear it another moment, just stay right there and I'll change you back. If you think you can manage, take a few steps over toward Donnal."

Well, which one was Donnal? Senneth turned in a half circle to locate him, kneeling a few feet away, his outstretched hand lying on the ground. She minced over and scrabbled into his palm, thinking how different the texture of skin was compared to grass and dirt.

She felt a moment's panic when his fingers closed around her and he lifted her up, but she sternly suppressed her fear. She blinked her little eyes as she found herself staring into Donnal's large ones.

"She'll do," he said. He was grinning through his beard.

A rustle and a thump as Tayse dropped to the ground. "Then change me, and let's be off."

Senneth didn't really get a good view of that alteration, for Donnal held her and stroked her back until it was over. But a few minutes later he set her on the ground face-to-face with a sleek black mouse with bristling white whiskers and inquisitive black eyes. Tayse. He took a few tentative steps forward, lifted his feet one at a time as if to gauge how they worked, then came close enough to touch Senneth's nose with his own.

It was so strange. It was Tayse. She could almost see his mind working, hear him assessing how he felt, what his strengths and weaknesses
might be in this particular form. He didn't seem nearly as disconcerted as
she felt. Indeed, after only a moment of self-exploration he whipped
around in a circle so tight that his long tail almost snapped across Senneth's face. He was looking at Kirra, and his stance plainly communi-
cated his message: *No more wasting time. Let us leave now.*

Kirra laughed and looked over at Donnal. "Successful so far," she said.
"Do you want to be responsible for the Rider or the mystic?"

"I'll take Tayse," he said. "Let's be on our way."

Senneth had to fight back a moment of abject terror when Kirra and
Donnal, suddenly, became two great hawks stalking majestically through
the grass. *Kirra and Donnal,* she reminded herself. *Kirra and Donnal.* But
the hawks looked ferocious, sharp-beaked, and evil. Her little heart was
hammering inside her tiny chest.

And, oh, didn't *that* get suddenly worse when the nearest one closed
its talons around her round brown body and carried her off into the fath-
omless air.

Senneth shuddered in Kirra's careful grip, trying not to shake too
much for fear the claws would open and send her tumbling to the ground.
For the first ten minutes of the flight, Senneth couldn't even bear to look
down. She just concentrated on calming her terror and reminding herself
who she was. When she did finally try to peer through the talons to the
ground below, she felt another surge of fright. There was nothing—just
patches of white that must be bits of cloud, and a blur of dark so far away
it had no distinguishing features. They could not possibly be so high in
the air; this foolish little creature must simply have eyesight that could
not see very far.

Senneth did not know whether to be sorry or grateful.

They flew for what seemed like forever. Once her fear faded, and she
realized she couldn't even entertain herself by watching the landscape,
Senneth started to get bored. Two days of this? No conversation, no distraction, nothing but wind and existence? How in the world would she
endure? The only real option was sleep, and that was easy enough to
achieve, despite the truly extraordinary circumstances. She closed her
eyes and let herself be lulled by motion.

Twice during that day, Kirra and Donnal landed and let them attend
to their needs. Food was sparse, but they were in agricultural country, so
there were seeds to nibble on and water was easy to find. At each stop,
Tayse scurried over to nuzzle at Senneth's ear, checking that she was still

whole. At each stop, Kirra conserved her energy by staying a hawk, but Donnal shifted into human shape and asked if either of them wished to be changed back.

Neither of them found that necessary.

They flew on until nightfall, then made a neat landing and a rough camp. Both Kirra and Donnal took human form to lay out bedrolls and hunt for water.

"Feels like it's going to be a cold night. I think I'll have Donnal start a fire when he gets back," Kirra told the mice when Donnal had gone off foraging. "Should be safe enough—I haven't seen a homestead or another traveler for miles."

Senneth wrinkled her nose and picked her way off the smooth boulder where Kirra and Donnal had deposited her and Tayse. She used her tiny hands to gather a handful of twigs and pile them together. Could she do this with such an unfamiliar body? Wasn't the magic an intrinsic part of her? Surely it could not have been changed, actually erased?

"I don't believe this," Kirra said and settled on the ground nearby. Tayse had jumped off the boulder and come over to watch, his dark eyes curious. "Even you—"

Senneth patted the kindling with her small, nervous fingers. Her body heat was so high already when she wore this shape; how hard could it be to summon fever, summon sparks? She tapped the twigs again.

A yellow flame licked through the scraps of wood. Senneth backed up on quick legs to get far enough away and then teased the flame higher, hotter. It was hard to gauge from this unfamiliar size. Was that a normal campfire, or too big? Too small?

Kirra was laughing. "How is that possible? Gods, no wonder people hate mystics. The little mouse who could set fire to a house! Who wouldn't be afraid of such a creature? Senneth, you're amazing."

Donnal was back a few moments later, water in one hand and a dead rabbit in the other. He looked at the fire a moment before glancing at Senneth and then over at Kirra. "Did you build it or did she?" he asked.

Kirra was still laughing. "She did! And I assume it will burn all night, no other fuel required!"

Donnal grinned. "Well, then. Let's cook dinner."

THE second day was much easier than the first. The fear was completely gone, and all that was left was impatience. On the other hand, Senneth was actually enjoying the chance to simply sleep the day away. She couldn't remember the last time she had ever been so idle.

"If we continue after dark, we can make Ghosenhall tonight," Donnal informed them as they took a break in the afternoon. "Do you want to be human before you return or shall we take you straight to your own cottage and change you there?"

Kirra-the-hawk uttered a sharp cry and danced on her thin legs, but no one could understand her. It was important enough to her that she spent the energy to transform herself to human. "We'll take them to *Justin's* cottage," she said, her face alight with mischief. "Don't you think Justin would love to see Senneth and Tayse as mice?"

"Cammon's the one who would make this interesting," Donnal said.

Kirra actually clapped her hands together. "Yes! We won't change them till Cammon has seen them! Will he recognize them, do you think?"

"He always recognizes *us*."

"Surely this is different. Oh, I hope it won't take us too long to find Cammon once we get back."

Donnal was grinning and shaking his head. "You know he knows we're on the way. He'll probably be at Justin's place, waiting for us to touch down."

"Then let's go! No more time to waste!"

Kirra and Donnal each took owl shape so they could see well enough for the nighttime flight. It was full dark and then some when they finally made it to Ghosenhall. Senneth was awake now, and once again trying to see through the prison of Kirra's talons. They were close enough to the ground that she could make out buildings and spires—unbelievably huge structures—everything half-lit with exterior torches or interior candles. They glided across the guarded walls, and no Rider thought to halt them. They dipped even lower, wingtips almost brushing the rooftop of a long building that had to be the barracks. Lower—silently banking—and toward a boxlike structure that had to be a cottage. Kirra settled to the ground and released her burden, and Senneth came tumbling out into a familiar and utterly alien world. One very large man was just now bursting through the door; two other shapes hurtled after him. Cammon, followed by Justin and Ellynor.

"Look!" Cammon cried. "Kirra and Donnal are back, and they've brought Tayse and Senneth!"

CHAPTER
26

CAMMON had actually been a little glad that Senneth would be gone for nearly two weeks. Her absence, he'd hoped, would make it easier for him to steal time alone with Amalie. But he had reckoned without Valri, who became more watchful than ever during the time that Senneth was gone. It was as if Valri knew about the kiss.

During this time, the queen did not allow Cammon and Amalie any time alone at all. If she couldn't be present whenever Cammon was expected in the room, she made sure Belinda Brendyn was on hand. If the regent's wife was unavailable, Wen and Janni were sure to show up, prepared to offer the princess another lesson in self-defense.

Wen had brought Amalie a wicked little dagger with a carved bone hilt and taught her how to use it. Now not a day went by that Cammon didn't see Amalie absentmindedly touch her hand to her left knee, where the slim sheath had been buckled on just above the bend of bone.

"Sleep with it, too," Wen advised one day shortly after Tayse and Senneth had departed. "Only take it off when you're bathing—and even then, keep it close to hand."

"Well, she might want to take it off when she's—you know—I mean, her husband—" Janni said, floundering past what she was originally going to say when she realized that the princess probably had never taken a lover.

Wen gave her a look of exaggerated surprise. "You remove all your weapons *then*? That's when you need them most."

The Riders erupted into laughter. Amalie was delighted—she loved it that the other women didn't guard their tongues around her. Valri, who was present today, tolerated the raillery, though she clearly disliked it. "And these men you spend time with," Amalie asked, trying to keep her voice grave. "Are they also armed when you are—intimate?"

"The Riders are," Janni said, still laughing. "But other men? Sometimes I'm amazed at how unprotected they allow themselves to be."

"But then, who'd want any man but a Rider?" Wen asked. The smile abruptly left her face and Cammon felt her well-worn flare of misery. *But what if the Rider doesn't want you?* she was thinking. And then, so clearly that he could not have blocked the thought if he tried: *Justin.*

Amalie folded her hands in her lap and looked decorous. "I don't believe a Rider will be my fate," she said. "So what else should I know in order to protect myself from my husband if he becomes unpleasant?"

"Majesty," Valri said in a sharp voice. She was sitting halfway across the room, frowning over some correspondence, but this turn in the conversation had caught her attention.

"It's a fair question," Janni said, clearly not intimidated by royalty. "Myself, I'd wait till he was asleep, then slit his throat."

"But if he's turned violent and wants to hurt her, she can't wait," Wen said.

"Please!" Valri exclaimed. "Amalie's husband will not offer her harm! And if he does, he'll be imprisoned for treason!"

Wen put her fingers around Amalie's wrist and pulled the princess to her feet. She was completely ignoring Valri. "I'm going to show you a nice trick," she said. "Pretend I'm your brutish husband. Now, when I grab your arm—"

Valri flung her hands in the air, watched a moment, and then returned her attention to her letters. Cammon spared her a glance, remembering what she'd said to him more than a week ago. *You think I don't know how to cut a man's throat?* He would put his money on Valri, despite her small size, if he had to wager on who would win a fight between an assailant and the queen.

He sighed. She had certainly won this particular contest between the two of them. He wanted to see Amalie, and Valri wanted him to keep his distance. So far, Valri had prevailed.

There had been no more midnight trysts in the kitchen, no more unchaperoned strolls down to the lair of the raelynx. Sometimes, late at night as he walked back up from Justin's cottage, Cammon let himself hope that Amalie would sneak from her rooms and come meet him on the back lawn. But even though he allowed some of his longing to escape, to whisper in her ear, he never sensed her moving from the upper reaches of the palace down to the public rooms and gardens. He knew she wanted to see him as much as he wanted to see her. But Valri had developed a habit of coming to Amalie's room at night to discuss the events of the day. On these nights the queen would fall asleep curled up in her chair—too close for Amalie to creep past her without waking her.

At first, Cammon was annoyed and resentful when he realized that Valri was deliberately staying in Amalie's room to keep her from any secret assignations with him.

Then he was astonished when he realized that Valri had become one of the people whose presence always registered in his consciousness.

He knew when she was in the breakfast room with the king. He could tell when she had gone down to the kitchens to confer with the cooks. He knew when she was in the gardens with the princess, for he could sense them both, a bright shape of gold, a dense shape of shadow, side by side, slowly pacing.

When had that happened? He still could not break through the Lirren magic when she chose to conceal her thoughts, or Amalie's. He suspected that, if she tried, she could render her body invisible to him while they were sitting in the same room. But he would still be able to close his eyes and know exactly where she was. She had become a part of him, important to him. Her existence had become ingrained into the daily routine of his own.

He didn't know how to interpret that. Didn't know why it had happened. But she was there now, along with the others, indispensable and integral. And so he knew where she spent her nights, and he knew he could expect no more stolen moments with Amalie.

They had, of course, other ways to communicate.

You're getting very good at this, he told her when she wrestled with Wen and Janni. *But use your magic. Steal their thoughts from them. If you can tell where they're going to strike next, you can block them even more effectively.*

Or: *Have you convinced Valri that it's safe to tell Ellynor your secret? I know she'd come talk to you about the Silver Lady.*

And: *I wish you could meet me tonight very late.*

And: *I hated that Kianlever lord who came calling.*

And: *I miss you.*

She was right there in the room. But he missed her anyway.

She did not often try to reply in the same way, though now and then he would receive hesitant and incomplete messages in return. One day when Valri was deep in conversation with the regent's wife, Amalie touched her fingers to her mouth, silently told him, *Kitchen—kiss,* and gave him a private smile. But she did not escape to meet him there that night. *Miss you* was something she could send him, though, and so she did, at least once a day. It was as if those two words were the abbreviation for everything else she wanted to tell him.

He wasn't in the room when she persuaded Valri that it was safe to tell Ellynor her astonishing news, but he was there when the Lirren girl presented herself one morning. Her knock on the door caught him totally by surprise, and he scowled when she stepped in to join them.

"I hate it that you can do that," he said. "After all the times I've practiced listening for your approach!"

She smiled. "Maybe you've stopped listening."

"Maybe you know she's not dangerous," Amalie suggested.

"Everyone is dangerous," Valri said in her dark way.

Cammon sighed.

But it was hard to imagine anyone less threatening than Ellynor that day as she curled up on the chair beside Amalie and began telling stories about the Pale Mother. She was not as small as Valri, but she was dainty and feminine, with a certain innate grace and warmth. The sort of person you might run to when you were hurt and crying.

"So I understand the Silver Lady has taken you under her protection," Ellynor said in her gentle voice.

Amalie grimaced. "That's what everybody thinks. And I don't feel blessed at all. I feel cursed. I'm afraid she's an evil goddess."

"Oh, not at all," Ellynor said, and she spoke with such certainty that Cammon saw Amalie instantly relax. "She's a complex lady, easy to misunderstand, but she is beautiful and she offers unexpected gifts."

Amalie looked hopeful. "But she steals magic. And she's deceitful."

Ellynor smiled. "It's true that she's curious about everything, and she looks in private windows and rummages through furtive souls, and it's true she likes to keep what she finds. But it's even more true that she reflects, rather than steals. What she loves most is to be bathed in praise and affection. She offers much to those who offer a great deal to her first. The more she is given, the more beautiful—and bountiful—she becomes."

Now Amalie's expression was thoughtful. "But Coralinda Gisseltess—"

"I believe that the Lestra has misinterpreted the will of the goddess," Ellynor said sadly. Not until then did Cammon remember that *Lestra* was the title Coralinda Gisseltess had bestowed upon herself when she founded the Daughters of the Pale Mother. "She is so filled with hatred for mystics that she believes she sees that same hatred mirrored in the Pale Mother."

Valri looked over. She and Cammon were sitting nearby, listening. "If she can't control her followers any better than that, she's a weak goddess," the queen said contemptuously. "The Dark Watcher does not let any of us behave so badly in her name."

"She's not weak," Ellynor answered. "But she is, to a large extent, at the mercy of those who worship her. She can only give back what they give to her. If Coralinda radiates hatred and greed, hatred and greed are all the Silver Lady has to offer." She paused a moment to think something over, and then smiled. "When I was in the Lumanen Convent, I grew to truly love the Pale Mother. I saw that she could be changeable and moody, and yet at the same time I learned that she could always be relied on. The moon shifts through its phases, but you know what those phases will be. They do not alter. If the moon makes you a promise, she will keep it in her own time."

"I *am* starting to like her a little," Amalie said cautiously. "If what you say is true."

"She helped me on the most terrifying night of my life," Ellynor said.

"Tell me!"

"You remember that we told you about the right Justin was hurt, and I had to go to the nearest town to ask for help. I needed to find one man in that whole city, and all I knew was his name. And she guided me to the very building he was in, and made him cross the room to ask me if I needed aid."

Valri looked unconvinced. "That might have been extraordinary luck, but you can't be sure it was a goddess at work."

Ellynor nodded. "It was. She is the giver of extreme and unexpected gifts. I know her hand was on me that night."

"And now I like her even *better*," Amalie said. "So what must I do? To show her honor?"

"She likes moonstones."

Amalie glanced at Cammon and he rolled his eyes. "It seems a little disruptive when I put one on."

"You might carry one with you and only let it touch your skin when you want a stronger connection with the goddess," Ellynor suggested.

"That's a good idea. What else should I do?"

Ellynor smiled. "She likes music. I'll teach you the prayers that we would offer up every night. You could almost feel her preening when the songs reached her ears."

"I don't sing very well."

"That doesn't matter. And she likes it when you are mindful. When you know where she is in the sky, when she is scheduled to rise, what phase she will show. She is vain, it's true, but she's also generous. Pay attention to her, and she will most definitely pay attention to you."

"I wouldn't have patience for such a goddess," Valri said.

"No, but you don't have to," Cammon said. "You follow the Dark Watcher, and she's served you pretty well. I think maybe all of us are drawn to different gods for different reasons. Maybe that's why there are so many gods."

Valri looked skeptical. "Then why are there so many forgotten gods?"

"Because people got careless and arrogant," Ellynor said. "They started to think that they were doing everything themselves. They didn't realize that the gods still watched over them, even though they stopped honoring the gods."

"Maybe that's why the gods created mystics," Amalie said. "To remind us that they're powerful—and that they can interfere in our lives."

"If, indeed, the gods created mystics," Valri said. "I think that's just a theory of Senneth's."

Cammon shrugged. "It makes sense," he said. "It seems to explain the range of magic."

"The only goddess I am certain of is the Black Mother," Valri said.

"I know there is at least one more," Ellynor said softly. "And sometimes she's powerful, and sometimes she's lonely, and she is always beautiful." She smiled at the princess. "And I believe she likes you. And I believe you will be safe in her hands."

AMALIE cheered up considerably after that conference. Cammon could see Valri visibly restraining her desire to scoff when Amalie practiced the prayers that Ellynor taught her. Valri would never be particularly open-minded about the deities, but even she could tell that Amalie needed to make peace with her goddess, and so she held her tongue.

You stayed up last night and sang that to the moon, Cammon thought when Amalie completed one of the prettier songs.

She smiled and answered indirectly, because Valri was sitting right there. "That's my favorite one, I think," she said. "Ellynor says it's most beautiful when there is a whole chorus of singers, although *some* of the prayers are meant to be sung by only a few voices."

"Well, I'm not sure we should be inviting acolytes of the Pale Mother to take up residence here and harmonize with you," Valri said, with a touch of humor. "And surely we should not be sending you to the Lumanen Convent to pray with all the Daughters."

Amalie answered, but Cammon lost the thread of the conversation. For the past few minutes, he had been feeling dense with uneasiness, and now suddenly the sensation intensified. Donnal had seen something that distressed him—Donnal was in motion to Kirra's side. A few moments later he felt Kirra's sharp concern knife through him, and then Senneth was on guard, then Tayse.

A hand touched his arm and he almost shivered. Amalie. "Cammon? Are you all right? Cammon?"

He must look as if he had fallen into a trance. His sensibilities were divided; part of him felt like he was hundreds of miles away, viewing a large, crowded hall from four perspectives. Part of him was sitting in this cozy room, with Amalie's grave eyes on him and Valri's face a study in worry. It was hard to speak coherently. "Something's wrong. In Danalustrous," he said. "I can't tell what."

"Something's happened to Senneth?" Valri said sharply.

"Or one of the others?" Amalie added.

"No. They're all just—worried—afraid—grim." He couldn't find the right words. "Tayse is preparing for battle."

"Battle? In Danalustrous? At a *wedding?*" Valri exclaimed.

"I can't explain it. There's a mood that settles over him when he thinks he's going to have to fight. It's very distinct." Tayse was preparing for combat, but Kirra was the one who was most upset. *Danalustrous, Danalustrous, Danalustrous!* "They're under siege," he said abruptly. "Someone's attacking the Hall."

Valri jumped to her feet. "I'll tell Baryn."

So, after all, he and Amalie had a moment alone, but it wasn't likely to do them any good. Cammon couldn't draw his attention away from his distant friends, couldn't relax or focus on anything else while they were in danger. He could feel Kirra and Donnal taking the shapes of great winged predators and diving into the fray from above, gouging out eyes, slashing open faces. His arm was heavy with Tayse's sword, relentless and unfaltering. His hands burned with the heat of Senneth's fire.

"Cammon." That was Amalie's voice, curiously disembodied, strangely distant. "Cammon, I'm worried about you. You seem to have disappeared. Should I send for Justin? Or Jerril?"

He managed to shake his head. "No, I'll be all right. When Justin was hurt, I felt like a knife had gone through my heart, and it took me a couple of hours to recover. But this is—there are four of them, all at once—there's so much emotion I can't push it back. But I think it'll be all right. I think it'll fade. I'll be fine."

In truth, he wasn't so certain he *would* be fine. He had never been buffeted by so many intense emotions simultaneously. Jerril would certainly tell him he needed to pull back, to throw his mental shields up, to conserve his own strength. But he couldn't. Not while they were so passionately engaged, not while they were in such danger. They were all, in their ways, splendid fighters, but any man could be felled on a battle-field. Any mystic could be cut down by a sword.

Amalie stood up, drawing her hand away. He felt an instant sense of loss that momentarily jerked his attention back to this room, and he saw her hurrying over to her bookcase of treasures. But then Senneth called forth an incredible burst of power and he was right back in Danalustrous, behind a roaring, impregnable wall of flame. Gods, he could feel the backlash of her power; she could set the entire country on fire.

Amalie circled his wrist with her hand, and for a moment the world went black.

No fire. No battlefield. No parlor. Just a blank and empty spasm of existence.

He gasped for air and reality shifted back into place. He was in the pretty rose-and-cream parlor, sitting in an upholstered chair, facing a window that looked out over the sunny lawns of the palace. Amalie was beside him, her earnest face creased with worry. Danalustrous and his four friends who were defending it were still there at the edge of his mind, but in a muted and shadowy fashion. He could monitor the fight while still existing in his true environment.

Her hand was still closed over his wrist, and he could feel the sharp prickle of magic in her touch. "What did you do?" he whispered.

She opened her other hand to show him the moonstone pendant she had been given by the Coravann lord. "I wanted to see if I could steal some of your visions away," she said. She looked a little nervous, as if she thought he might wrench out of her hold or yell in fury. She also looked stubborn and determined, as if she would yell right back.

He swallowed. "You succeeded."

Now she looked anxious. "And is it all right? Should I let you go? It's just that—you seemed so far away—and it seemed dangerous. I was afraid you would slip away completely, and I didn't know how you would get back."

"I don't know. That's never happened before, but it's never been so intense before," he said, his voice a shade closer to normal. "Now—I can still feel them, but it's a little more bearable." He attempted a smile. "That's a trick I would use on somebody. How did you learn it?"

Her smile was timid. "I don't know. I just thought I'd try."

With his free hand, he gestured at the moonstone. "And how did you keep it from burning me this time?"

She shook her head. "I just tried to. I didn't know if that would work, either."

Despite his pressing worry, despite his continued abstraction, he felt a tremendous excitement begin to build up in his chest. "Amalie," he said. "Do you realize what you're doing? You're teaching yourself to use your magic. And you're using it to help and to heal. You've been afraid of it, but Ellynor was right. You can make it benevolent. And you can figure it out completely on your own."

Now her smile widened. She was pleased that he was pleased with her. "And I helped you come back? I made you feel better?"

He put his free hand on the back of her neck and drew her forward so that their foreheads were touching. She released his wrist, but only so she could lace her fingers with his. The conflict at Danan Hall was still playing out on the edge of his vision, but Tayse was convinced of victory, and even Kirra had grown calmer. "You made me feel wonderful," he said.

That was how they were sitting when Valri came back in the room and found them.

CHAPTER
27

THE afternoon passed in a tangled blur. Baryn wanted whatever details Cammon could supply, and Cammon had to repeat them all to Tir when the older Rider came in for a briefing. They were already armed for war. There was little else they could do to prepare for an assault on the palace, should one be coming, but everyone was shocked at the news from Danalustrous.

More bad news was to follow. As the day wore on, Cammon became oppressed by other intimations of hostility, and he spread his attention outward toward all the borders of Gillengaria. Violence had always been what registered most sharply in his consciousness, and violence was unfolding throughout the Houses. He had never been good at geography, never been able to tell exactly where something was occurring, but he could tell that blood was being shed in multiple locations throughout the realm.

After all, Amalie brought Justin into her study. The Rider unrolled a huge map on the floor and weighted its four corners. Then he made Cammon stand on the spot marked as Ghosenhall and face the northern border. "Give me directions," he demanded.

Cammon waved to his right. "That way. Not very close to us."

"Kianlever," Justin guessed, placing a rock on Kianlever Court. "Where else?"

"That way. East. But farther up. North, I guess."

Justin's voice was grim. He placed another stone. "Brassenthwaite."

"Although it's not as intense there," Cammon added. "I think the battle is already over. Maybe it was just a skirmish."

"Where else?"

Cammon pointed behind him. "Pretty far. Almost at the edge of what I can sense, so maybe at the coastline."

"Rappengrass."

"And that way. Toward the Lireth Mountains."

"Coravann." Justin's voice was cold with fury. "Uprisings at all the loyal Houses, timed to occur on the same day. To make the marlords think twice about sending any reinforcements to the palace once they learn that Ghosenhall is under attack."

"Merrenstow's a loyal House," Amalie said. She and Valri had watched this whole exercise.

Justin laughed mirthlessly. "Royal forces have been bivouacked on Merrenstow land for the last six months. It would be difficult to plan an uprising there."

Valri was on her feet and pacing. "So does this mean that the Houses where there have *not* been confrontations are Houses that are not loyal to the crown? So many of them! We always knew that Fortunalt and Gisseltess were against us, and Nocklyn and Tilt have been questionable for a long time, but Storian? Helven?"

Justin looked grave. "I don't know. Perhaps those Houses have maintained better relations between the marlords and their vassals."

Valri pressed her hands to her cheeks. "Baryn must know."

Justin nodded. "I'm assuming the marlords will send word as soon as they can to confirm Cammon's suspicions."

"They're not *suspicions*," Cammon said.

Justin's face almost relaxed into a smile. "I know. You're always right." He sighed. "I wish Senneth and Tayse were here."

So does Senneth, Cammon thought. "They'll be on their way tomorrow."

THE next day, Cammon was briefly confused by the pace at which Senneth and Tayse were covering the ground on their return journey, for he could tell they were keeping up with Kirra and Donnal, which was hard to do.

"They've been *changed*," he told Justin that night. Just the thought of it had given him his first true smile of the day. "*Tayse* let Kirra change him! Can you imagine?"

"Are they birds, then?" Justin wanted to know. "Because that's fast, but, gods! It's a tricky body to master."

"I can't tell what they are. Just that they're all together and they should be here tomorrow night."

"Finally you have *good* news."

Ellynor made him bundle up for the long walk back from the cottage to the palace. It was almost spring, but the nights were still uncomfortably cold, and Cammon moved as briskly as he could without actually breaking into a run. By habit, he let his mind search the palace to locate the people who mattered to him. For once, Valri did not seem to be in the same room as Amalie; he thought she was with the king, for he could catch the stately aura that he associated with Baryn.

I'm on my way back to the palace, Cammon sent hopefully to Amalie. *If you're alone and you'd like to meet me somewhere.* But she stayed stationary in her room, and he sighed. She might be asleep already. She might—with the kingdom in such turmoil already—be unwilling to add any more drama to her life. He couldn't say he blamed her.

But as he entered the palace and climbed the stairs, it became clear that each step was bringing him closer to Amalie. As he turned down the hallway toward his own room, he felt her presence more strongly still. His pace quickened; he was almost running as he reached his door and pulled it open.

Amalie stood inside.

Even more hastily, he shut the door behind him.

Then he turned to stare. She was wearing a long white nightdress and holding a single white candle. There was no other light in the room. She looked like a column of moonlight topped with a halo of sculpted fire.

"How long have you been here?" he demanded.

"Maybe an hour."

"If I'd known that, I would have come back much sooner!"

She smiled. It occurred to him that she was a little nervous. "I hope you don't mind. I couldn't exactly ask you."

"Of course I don't mind! But are you sure Valri won't come looking for you?"

"She was pretty tired. I think she's had so much else to occupy her thoughts in the past few days that she's forgotten to pay as much attention to me."

But she still seemed tentative. He went straight up to her, pushing aside the hand holding the candle, and kissed her soundly. That made her smile; that made all her uncertainty disappear. The glow that seemed to emanate from her very skin intensified.

"I like that so much," she exclaimed in a low voice.

He laughed. "Time to put the candle aside, I think."

She blew it out and let it fall to the floor with a clatter. Now they were both laughing. He put his arms around her and gathered her close, his mind again filled with imagery of moonbeams and reflected fire. She lifted her face and responded to his kisses with curiosity and delight and awakening desire. He was being careful, keeping his hands primly around her shoulders, but she was starting to explore. Her hands slipped under his shirt and flattened against his back. He could feel how much she liked the sensation of skin on skin, how marvelous it seemed to her, how extraordinary. Every kiss seemed to turn her a little brighter, as if she was absorbing all of his own sensations and turning them luminous.

"This feels wonderful," she murmured against his mouth.

"A little too wonderful. We need to stop a moment."

She clutched him tighter. "No. No, not yet."

He kissed her. "I just want to build up the fire. It's freezing in here."

So he knelt at the hearth, blew on the coals, and built a fine fire that would burn a good long time. He could hear Amalie moving around the room, and before he could stand up, she had dragged over a thick blanket and began spreading it before the grate.

"Let's sit and watch the flames," she suggested, and dropped down beside him. He put his arm around her and felt heat from all directions—from the fire, from her skin, from his own body.

"More kisses," she whispered, and twined her arms around his neck.

Easy to comply; easy to toss aside thoughts about what anyone else might think of such an assignation. She was so pleased to be with him that his own happiness multiplied. They could have been mirrors, each endlessly replicating what they found inside the other. She was like the moon itself, he thought, taking whatever he had to offer and making it visible, reflecting it back to him. And she liked all of this, every touch, every murmured word, every caress.

"When do I take off my nightdress?" she whispered against his mouth. "I will even take off the sheath with my knife in it, but I will mind Wen's instructions and leave it nearby."

He laughed against her lips. "I think you don't take off the nightdress *or* the weapon," he said. "And I don't take off my clothes. And soon you go back to your room."

Now she pouted. Instantly, much of the light faded from the room. "You don't want to make love to me?" she asked.

He sucked in his breath, caught completely off guard. "Amalie! I didn't—you—is that why you came here tonight?"

She pulled back, affecting haughtiness to hide her disappointment. "Naturally not. I simply came to your room because I was bored."

He caught her and drew her closer, giving her one hard squeeze and dropping a kiss on the top of her head. Surely it was his imagination that even such a small mark of affection could make some of that glow return to her skin. "Don't be hurt. Don't be offended. You have to speak plainly. This is risky for so many reasons. I need to know what you want from me."

She peered up at him through red-gold hair that was rather mussed and disordered. "But what if I say something and you don't like it?"

"Well, that happens between people all the time. And sometimes it turns them awkward with each other, and sometimes it makes them angry, but unless they tell the truth it's all just guessing and mistakes anyway." He pressed his lips against her cheek. "But I don't think anything you say will make me angry."

She leaned into him, comforted but still unsure. "I am terrified that war is coming, but a very small part of me is glad, too," she said in a soft voice. "Because there will be no more lords arriving at the palace to court me. And there will be no time to arrange for my wedding. And I don't want to get married."

"You don't ever want to get married? Or just not now?"

She spoke slowly and deliberately. "I'm pretty sure I'll marry someday for the sake of the throne. But I want to know what it's like to love a man before I end up married to one I don't love for the rest of my life."

"You might end up loving the man you take as a husband," he pointed out.

"Not if I have to pick from the ones I've seen so far."

"There must be dozens of eligible men who haven't made it to Ghosenhall yet."

"I want my first lover to be someone who isn't thinking about a throne when we fall into bed. I want him to be thinking about me."

"Speaking for myself," he said, "I find it hard to think about anything *but* you."

She shifted in his arms to look him more fully in the face. "You don't sound shocked."

"Nothing shocks me," he said.

She lifted her hands to put them on his shoulders, watching him intently. "But you're not sure this is something you want to do."

He kissed her; in a very short time, he had learned that a kiss would always please her. "I'm trying to decide if what you think you want is what you really want—"

"It is!"

"And even if it is, whether it might be so harmful to you that I just can't do it anyway."

She was still watching him. "You didn't say whether this is something *you* would want," she said presently.

Of course *that* needed to be answered with a kiss as well. "I adore you," he said simply. "You're in my thoughts night and day. I always know where you are, and I always look for ways to be beside you. I don't know that much about how men and women fall in love. I don't know what would have happened by now if you were just an ordinary girl." He smiled, imagining it. "If you were a shopkeeper's daughter, I probably just would have showed up at your door every day, asking you silly questions or bringing you stupid presents."

"Presents aren't stupid," she murmured.

"But I would have brought you shoe buckles and coins that had been smashed into funny patterns by carriage wheels, and maybe bird feathers. Not *real* presents," he said. "And every time I left, your father would have said, 'What's that strange boy doing, hanging about here so much? What's he after?' And you'd have said, 'I don't *know*. He makes calf-eyes at me, but he never flirts or gives me pretty compliments.' And your father would say, 'Well, is he courting you or isn't he?' And you'd say, 'I don't know! I can't even tell if he likes me!' Because I wouldn't know how to go about it, you know. What to say. How to tell you that I thought about you every day."

She was giggling now. "If I were a shopkeeper's daughter, I'd wait till the next time you came by. And I'd invite you in and say, 'Come to the back room with me, I have something to show you.' And my father would be shaking his head, but you'd follow me, and when we were alone I'd put my hands on my hips, and I'd say, 'Well? Do you like what you see or don't you? Do you want me? Because if you do, I'll take you, young man, but if you don't, stop cluttering up my father's shop.'"

"You probably would," he said. "And you'd probably have to! Because I'd be so clumsy and tongue-tied I wouldn't know how to say the words myself."

She slipped out of his hold, rearranged herself so she was kneeling in front of him, her hands on her hips. On her face was an expression that was part exasperation, part sassiness. "Well? Do you like what you see, or don't you?" she said softly. "Do you want me? Because if you do, I'll take you."

"I want you," he answered quietly. "But you're not a shopkeeper's daughter."

Now she put her arms around his neck and leaned in for the kiss he could not have refused her to save his own life. "And shouldn't a princess get what she wants at least as often as a merchant girl?"

"A princess has so much more to lose," he said. But his own hands had come up to wrap around her back, to draw her closer.

"I don't think so," she whispered. "I think it's all the same." She kissed him hard; her hands tightened, and the two of them tumbled back onto the blanket. "Love me, Cammon," she said. "Please show me how it goes."

And so he showed her. Or at least he showed her the little that he knew, though they both rapidly learned new tricks and pleasures. Amalie's skin glowed white in the darkness; her hair was radiant. The fire died down but the incandescence of her body brightened the longer that he loved her. The whole room was bathed in the soft light of her content-ment. Or maybe it was just that he could see nothing but Amalie, and his eyes had been bespelled by love.

CHAPTER
28

A messenger from Halchon Gisseltess arrived in the morning, and every key member of the royal household spent the day huddled in conferences. Milo told Cammon that he would not be needed until the evening and he should find some useful way to employ his time.

"What did the messenger say?" Cammon wanted to know, but Milo, of course, would not repeat it.

So Cammon headed down to the training yards, where the Riders were engaged in mock combat. It took a while to isolate Justin, who was deep in a furious battle against Coeval, while just a few paces away, Hammond and Wen tried to cut each other down. All the Riders were strung tight with tension. More than one, Cammon could tell, wished war was upon them already. *Enough of this damn waiting! Time to fight! We're ready!*

But no one was ever really ready for war, Cammon thought.

Justin was covered with sweat, despite the chill, when he finally took a break. He pushed back his sandy hair, wet and ragged, and accepted the canteen of water Cammon handed him. "What was the message from Halchon Gisseltess?" Cammon asked.

Justin downed the entire contents of the canteen in five swallows. "He offered to meet with Baryn a week from now to discuss a 'peaceful settlement of our differences.' "

"Will the king do it?"

"No. Too much danger in leaving the palace and heading to a rendezvous with a man who's already said he wants you dead. The marlord would have nothing to lose by killing the king without a parley."

"Does that mean the Gisseltess forces will attack us at the end of the week?"

Justin gave him a sober look. "Or before. The deadline may have been set to make us believe we had that much time." He handed back the empty canteen. "Spies in Fortunalt tell us the foreign soldiers have landed, all of them dressed in Arberharst colors. A small force could make it to Ghosenhall in a week, though it would take longer to march a full army this far."

Cammon shuddered. "I kept thinking that war wouldn't really come."

"But it has," Justin said. "When will Tayse and Senneth be back?"

"Tonight, I think. Or tomorrow morning."

Justin grasped his sword again. "Well, war better not strike until they return."

Cammon watched the workout a while longer, declined the opportunity to join in, and drifted back toward the palace. But Amalie was still closeted with her father. There was no hope of seeing her, even in a public setting. He sent a thought to her, just a remembrance, to let her know he was thinking about her. He caught her start of happiness when she perceived it.

Oh, she was the easiest girl in the whole world to love, because she took such delight in it; and he would never be able to love anyone else so much; and surely she would break his heart in so many tiny pieces that not the brightest display of moonlight would be able to pick them out and infuse them with remembered brilliance. But despite all that, he could not wish last night undone—despite all that, he could not stop hoping there would be other nights ahead just like it.

He was too restless and too close to miserable to linger around the palace. He left the grounds and spent part of the day helping Lynnette with chores while Jerril was away training the Carrebos mystics. He spent another hour just prowling through the city. He had some vague idea of buying Amalie a gift, but what could she possibly want from him, this girl who received fabulous presents from serramar across the kingdom? It was sheer luck that drew his attention to a glitter of metal in the street, and he stooped down to retrieve a very paltry treasure indeed—a silver coin crushed and reshaped by the wheels of a passing carriage. Smiling, he pocketed it and went whistling down the street.

DINNER was a small and grim affair, with no true outsiders at the table, but Cammon took his accustomed place among the footmen because no one had told him otherwise. Before the diners arrived, he tucked the ruined coin under the plate at Amalie's place, and as soon as she sat down, he silently bade her to look for it. She bit her lip to keep from smiling as she slipped it into her pocket.

Tonight? he asked. She replied in a wavering but clearly disappointed negative.

Soon, then, he said, and that made her smile again.

She disappeared with Valri, Baryn, and Romar Brendyn once the meal was over. Cammon headed down to Justin's to await the arrival of Senneth and the others.

"Senneth will be interested to hear that one of her new mystics caught Ellynor this morning," Justin said.

"Turned himself into a raelynx," Ellynor confirmed. "He couldn't find me when he was in any other shape."

"Makes sense," Cammon said. "Become a Lirren animal to catch a Lirren woman."

"But the true question is, what kind of animals would catch spies from overseas?" Justin asked. "Since we're not as worried about Lirrenfolk at the moment."

"Oh, now I suppose you want me to remember some kind of bird or dog that can only be found in Arberharst," Cammon said.

"Well, you might try to make yourself useful once in a while," Justin answered with a grin.

"The princess says there's a library full of books at the palace," Cammon answered. "Maybe we can find some with pictures of exotic creatures."

Ellynor settled next to Justin. "Will a mystic from Gillengaria be able to take the shape of an animal from another country?" she asked.

"Maybe not," Cammon said. "But it might be worth a try."

They kicked around other ideas, tried to guess what Halchon Gisseltess's next move would be, and wondered what his sister, Coralinda, would be up to now.

"She's not just sitting quietly in the convent," Ellynor said positively. "She hates mystics too much. She's planning to join this fight."

"Then we have to plan how to stop her," Justin said.

During their entire conversation, Cammon was tracking the progress of the travelers. He wasn't good with geography or distance, but he could tell they were steadily drawing nearer. "Almost here," he said when they crossed into the city and began angling down for a landing. Passing the wall that surrounded the palace grounds, gliding low over the barracks. He flung open the door and dashed out as two owls softly landed and deposited small burdens to the ground.

And then Senneth and Tayse were standing there, and Kirra and Donnal. All seven of them, gathered together again. For a moment, Cammon almost felt whole.

Till he realized there was a part of him that was now missing, and would always be missing, unless Amalie was in the room, too, and that for the rest of his life he would be incomplete, no matter how close he could hold the rest of his friends.

Senneth had spent the morning with the king, relaying her story. Cammon waited for her outside the study door, and he followed her the rest of the day. There was a great deal to tell her, though, of course, he didn't repeat the most important news. *Senneth, I've become Amalie's lover.* No, he told her how he had watched the battle at Danan Hall through four sets of eyes, how he had felt similar skirmishes unfolding across the kingdom. Indeed, the messengers from Kianlever and Coravann had already arrived bearing the grim news. Slaughter at the Houses, followed immediately by outrage and fear. Eloise Kianlever had sustained heavy losses but reported that some of her most loyal vassals had ridden to her aid.

"And she says she'll be sending troops to Ghosenhall," Senneth added. "And part of me thinks, 'Defend yourself! Even if the royal city falls!' It's what Malcolm would tell her. But I'm afraid we'll need her troops."

"Don't leave again," Cammon said to her.

She gave him a sad smile. "Not to save Brassen Court itself. I am here till the city surrenders or triumphs."

They spent part of the afternoon with Jerril and some of the shapeshifters Senneth had recruited from Carrebos. Jerril was pleased with their progress and told Senneth three times how they had sniffed out Ellynor even when she was cloaked deep in Lirren magic. "What about the others?" she asked him. "Are they trainable?"

Jerril gave her an affable smile. "Indeed, they have both ability and eagerness. If I had a year—"

"You might have three days," she interrupted.

"They will be at your disposal whenever you need them."

Cammon had spent some energy cloaking his own thoughts from Jerril, but that didn't stop the older mystic from giving him a few curious looks. Jerril was sensitive enough to pick up the gist of the story, Cammon thought—and smart enough not to ask questions in front of Senneth.

"I'm not entirely sure how one deploys a mystic army," Senneth said.

"I imagine you tell them broadly what you wish they would accomplish, and then let them go," Jerril replied. "It's not like you can send them into battle in formation."

"What do you think about this?" Senneth asked him, and launched into a discussion of strategy.

Cammon stopped paying attention. He heard a door open on the far side of Ghosenhall. Or—not exactly. He felt a brush of wind as if someone had walked past him at a rapid pace. That wasn't it, either. There was a moment of silence in a crowded room. There was a glint of metal from a weapon smoothly drawn.

There was nothing. No sound, no movement. Just a cool day on a brown field where a few green stalks of grass were pushing their way up through the hard ground.

When Cammon focused on his surroundings again, Jerril was watching him strangely. "What is it?" the other mystic asked.

Cammon shook his head. "I don't know."

Jerril's question had caught Senneth's attention. "What? Did you sense something?"

"Not exactly. At least—I can't identify it."

"Danger?" she asked. "A new assassin come to town? That would make sense, from Halchon's point of view."

Cammon spread his hands. "Usually I can sense violent intent, but— did a stranger just ride into Ghosenhall? I don't know. Something *slipped*, that's all I can tell you. Something shifted."

"Something magical?" Jerril asked.

"I don't think so."

"Something anti-magical, perhaps," Senneth said. "That's what happens when Halchon Gisseltess touches me. I lose all my power. It's like he cancels me out. Maybe something like that?"

"Maybe," Cammon said uncertainly. He looked at Jerril. "Did you feel anything?"

Jerril shook his head. "You're far stronger than I am. If you can't read it—"

"But you have more experience than I do! Just concentrate. It seemed like—a door opened. Or closed. Or someone walked by. Somewhere in the city."

Jerril turned his hands palm upward, then took a deep breath and let his mind expand. Cammon mentally followed that journey, tagging along beside the older mystic, peering around the corners and down the alleys that caught Jerril's attention. There it was again—a silence that filled with echoes, a scent that dissipated too quickly to be analyzed.

"That," Cammon whispered. "Did you catch it?"

Jerril nodded and let his mind snap back. Senneth was watching both of them with her gray eyes narrowed. "I don't know what it is," Jerril admitted. "I don't even know if it's dangerous." He glanced at Senneth. "If I were a hare, I'd say the shadow of a hawk had passed over the ground."

"I'm telling Tayse that something alarming has come into the city, but nobody knows what," she said, already striding off. "We will act as if the city is full of enemies."

Cammon was left staring at Jerril. "But it might not be."

Jerril shrugged. "But it will be soon enough."

WITHIN the hour, the Riders had mobilized. Two each had been assigned to stand over Baryn, Valri, and Amalie; twenty had been dispatched to roam the streets of Ghosenhall, looking for anything untoward. The rest of them roved over the palace grounds like guard dogs let loose, randomly and ceaselessly patrolling.

Naturally, it was impossible for Cammon to creep to Amalie's room or hope she might sneak up to his when she was being constantly guarded by Coeval and Janni. Janni even spent the night inside Amalie's room, wide awake, watching at the window.

Everyone was edgy the following morning, even the imperturbable Milo. "Make yourself useful in some fashion," Milo said when Cammon asked for orders, and then he stalked off.

Cammon found Valri, Amalie, Belinda Brendyn, Justin, and three other Riders preserving an uneasy silence in the rose parlor. Amalie sent him a look of mute appeal when he stepped inside, but Cammon stopped first to speak to Justin.

"Nothing happened? No news?"

Justin shook his head. "Tayse walked the grounds all night and found nothing but your shape-shifters awake. He's sleeping for a few hours now, but he'll be up again around noon."

"Maybe I imagined something. Maybe—I just can't tell."

Now Justin gave him that cocky grin. "You saying trouble might be coming is like Donnal saying he can turn himself into a wolf. It's true. It's guaranteed."

"Who's with Baryn?"

"Tir and Wen."

"Are you guarding Valri or Amalie?"

"The princess."

"Maybe we could go outside. Walk around the grounds for a bit."

Amalie heard that and broke off a low conversation with Belinda to answer. "Oh, yes, please, can we go outside? I think I'll start screaming if I just sit here any longer, imagining terrors."

"They're not imaginary, Majesty," Justin said.

"The real ones could hardly be worse than the ones in my head."

Amalie fetched a cloak while Justin eyed Cammon with disapproval. "Where are your weapons?"

"I don't keep a sword. I always borrow one from the Riders."

"Well, you need to be armed. All the time. Even in the palace."

Amalie arrived in time to hear that. "Then let's head down toward the barracks."

Hammond led the way, while Justin and Cammon marched on either side of Amalie as they picked their way through the sunshine toward the training yard. It was strange to be so close to the yard and not hear the incessant sound of blades striking and voices shouting. But all the Riders were either on duty or resting after their watches the night before.

Cammon fastened on a sword and selected a backup dagger as Amalie lifted her skirts to show the Riders the sheath belted at her knee. "Let me see you use it," Justin said, so she feinted at him with one quick lunge. "Not bad," he said. "A little more force, if you can manage it, or you won't kill an attacker outright."

"She just has to slow him down long enough for a Rider to arrive," Hammond said.

"Sometimes help isn't as close as you'd like," Justin said. "Show me again."

Soon enough they were back outside, heading toward the sculpture gardens. "Look, you can see it's *almost* spring," Amalie said. "There are buds on some of the trees, and there are whole patches of green grass where the lawn is always in sunlight."

Justin didn't voice his thought, but Cammon caught it anyway. *This year, spring means war.* Amalie bent down to brush aside dead weeds that covered the curled leaves of a crocus, poking its way up through the hard ground. Still leaning over, she turned her head to give them all a lovely smile. "Almost spring," she repeated.

Cammon heard a sound. Felt a flutter. He jerked around to peer behind him, swung his head as if to discover the source of an unpleasant odor.

"What is it?" Justin demanded.

"I don't know. I think—Justin, I think someone has breached the walls."

Instantly, Justin's sword was in his hand and Hammond had half-drawn his. The soldiers crowded closer to Amalie. "Back toward the palace," Justin ordered, and the four of them hustled through the ranks of scowling marble royalty. "Cammon, wake Tayse. Call in the other Riders."

"I don't know if the others can hear me," Cammon said breathlessly, jogging alongside Justin.

"Just do it. Send an alarm. Even if they can't *hear* you, they'll be uneasy enough that they'll come in from the city. Riders are used to following their instincts."

Cammon glanced around. They were free of the gardens now and could see the wide expanse of the front lawns, empty and serene, rolling straight to the high stone walls surrounding the palace. "It might be nothing—"

"Do it."

Cammon flung his thoughts out like water tossed from a half-filled cup. He felt Tayse start from a sound sleep and roll to his feet, his weapon in his hand before he had even put on his boots. He felt the other Riders startle, pause, look around, and then set out running. Those already on the palace grounds headed for the main building. Those quartering the streets of Ghosenhall raced back for the compound.

Those guarding Baryn and Valri pulled their blades and shifted closer to their charges.

Senneth, Cammon called. *Kirra. Donnal. Trouble is coming. I can't tell what. But trouble is coming.*

Almost as soon as he thought the words, a runner of fire darted along the very top of the wall, till the whole stone fence was topped by a ragged crown of flame. Justin slowed to a walk, looking pleased.

He said, "Well, that'll stop anyone who—"

And three men slipped through the partition of fire and dropped gracefully to the ground.

CHAPTER
29

THE intruders were dressed in black, from their closely hooded heads to their polished boots; they moved like dancers. Each of them carried a long blade in one hand and a short blade in the other, and their belts were heavy with an array of other weapons.

Justin loosed an inarticulate cry, and ten Riders raced toward the wall with their swords held high. "To the palace!" Justin cried.

Before they could take another step, twenty more invaders glided through Senneth's fire and landed on the palace lawn. Motion caught Cammon's eye and he swiveled around to see another ten—another twenty—swarming up the walls of the palace itself, breaking through panes of glass and diving through windows. Another dozen were storming the main door. From inside came the sounds of hysterical voices and clattering metal. More Riders charged in through the gates and instantly engaged the attackers. Cammon could hardly breathe. The odds against the defenders were horrible.

"No!" Amalie shrieked and picked up her skirts to run. Justin grabbed her arm and jerked her back.

"There's no safety in the palace!" he shouted in her ear. "Back to the gardens! We have to hide you."

Amalie kicked at him, beating his chest with her free hand. "No! No! My father's in there! Let me go! I have to find him!"

Justin didn't sheathe his sword but, one-handed, he shook Amalie so hard her hair tumbled in her face, and then he started dragging her very fast back toward the sculpture park. Hammond and Cammon loped along beside him. "Majesty! My orders are to protect *you*! Whatever happens to anyone else, I must keep *you* alive."

Amalie moaned and twisted in his hold. Cammon caught her other arm and helped Justin half carry her toward what was only the most dubious kind of safety. "Amalie, he's right," Cammon said quietly. "There are others protecting your father and Valri. We must keep you alive."

They ran, but all of them kept looking back over their shoulders. More of the black-hooded attackers—*more*. "At least two hundred," Hammond estimated as they ducked inside the sculpture park and lost sight of the battle. "More coming."

Justin strode through the lines of statuary, looking for a place to hide or a place to make a stand. "Foreigners," he said. "That's why Cammon couldn't feel them, that's why Senneth's fire didn't stop them. Impervious to our kind of magic."

"Not impervious to Kirra," Cammon said with a dark kind of gladness. "She just ripped someone's throat out." Even as he spoke, he could feel Donnal make a leap for an enemy soldier and bring them both crashing to the ground. "Not impervious to Donnal."

"Good." Justin had found a spot that appealed to him, a giant curved slab of white marble carved to resemble a shell. Before it, a black granite pedestal held an oversized and extremely forbidding woman carved out of more white marble. "Majesty, you stand with your back to the wall. Cammon, in front of her." He and Hammond took up stations on either side of the stone queen. "They'll have to kill us to get to you, and they'll have to come at us one at a time," Justin said. "We can hold off an attack for a good long while."

"Can you tell what's happening?" Hammond asked Cammon.

He nodded numbly. He was trying very hard not to get sucked into the vortex of the action through the eyes of his friends—he needed to keep his focus *here* in case the battle turned their way. But he couldn't help absorbing some of their rage and fear and ceaseless motion.

"Three Riders have fallen, but I can't tell which ones," he said. "Not Tayse. There are close battles up and down the halls of the palace, and it's hard to tell who's winning. Kirra and Donnal and the other shape-shifters are tackling the ones who are still outside, trying to prevent them from getting into the palace. A few Riders are still on the lawns, too."

"My father?" Amalie demanded. "Valri?"

"Alive," Cammon said.

"Senneth?" Justin asked.

"Fighting with a sword instead of fire."

"Where's the city guard?" Hammond asked.

"Massed on the outskirts of the city to keep away an army," Justin replied. "I'm guessing no one had time to run for them. But the fire on the walls should alert them that there's something wrong! They're probably on their way."

"Why didn't—red and silver hell!" Hammond exclaimed. He pointed with his sword. "One of them just peered around that statue and saw me. Probably saw the princess's hair. He ran off, but I'm betting he'll be back with friends."

Justin nodded curtly and shifted his stance.

In less than two minutes, they heard the sound of running feet, and more than a dozen invaders came weaving through the statues. They moved with a curious and well-trained grace; they held their swords as if the heavy weapons weighed hardly anything. As they drew closer, Cammon could see that their black hoods were really close-fitting caps sewn with scales of metal. Their chests were covered with similar protective garments, gleaming blackly in the sun.

"Hard to kill," Justin commented.

"One at a time," Hammond said.

The enemies descended.

Amalie screamed as the blades engaged. Cammon's own sword was out, but Justin and Hammond beat back the first wave of attackers with relative ease. Still, it was clear that they would soon be overmatched. The slim black-clad soldiers pushed closer, attacked in pairs, tried to squeeze past the tall statue. One of them had leapt to the pedestal and was climbing up the queen's skirts as if he would scale the statue and launch himself at Amalie from above. It didn't take much imagination to picture two or three others swarming up the back of the marble shell with the same intention. Justin thrust his sword straight through one attacker's armor-plated throat and shoved him aside. A new one leapt over the growing pile of bodies and presented a fresh blade.

Cammon was awash in Amalie's terror, could practically feel the smooth cold stone against her hands as she pressed her body to the wall. He was almost dizzy with so much motion, so much blood. He could sense every swing of Tayse's sword, every thrust of Senneth's, even as he watched Justin and Hammond strike and hammer. Kirra swooped; Donnal leapt. Everywhere was violence, danger, and destruction.

Hammond cried out and staggered to one side, and an attacker charged through.

Amalie shrieked. Cammon didn't even feel his sword hand come down as he severed the soldier's head at the shoulder. There was a spray of blood, then the falling body, jingling with metal as it crashed to the ground. Hammond had forced himself upright and was now wielding his sword with his left hand, but he was gravely wounded. Cammon doubted he would be able to fight another ten minutes, even another five.

Justin cut down another soldier and instantly took on the next.

"Hammond!" Justin shouted. "Hammond, what's your damage?"

"Deep," the other Rider shouted back.

"Cammon, you'll have to take his place!"

The soldier who had climbed the statue now swung over the queen's head and dropped lightly to his feet right in front of Cammon. This time there was no single lucky blow. This time, Cammon had to slash and parry and slash again, panic and adrenaline making him crazed. He had never been a skilled swordsman; he had always relied on his uncanny intuition to know where his opponent was going to land the next blow. But he could read nothing from this man's mind, had no advantage whatsoever except a year's worth of intermittent training with the best fighters in the country.

It was enough, at least this time. Cammon thrust suddenly and hard, breaking through the protective layer and opening the man's heart. With a strangled cry, the soldier fell. Cammon stepped back, gasping for breath.

"Bright Mother burn me," Justin said in a voice so quiet it was the most frightening tone he could have used. Cammon peered around the Rider's flashing sword to see another ten soldiers streaming into the garden. Hammond was fading fast; it was a miracle he was still on his feet, still wielding a sword. Justin could not possibly hold off another ten men.

"Sweet gods," Cammon whispered, and felt black despair swamp his heart. "We cannot save her."

Just then the air was split with a sound that made his blood spoil in his veins.

For a second, everyone froze—Justin, Hammond, their attackers, the new invaders darting through the statuary. The unearthly sound came again, so venomous, so menacing, that it was impossible not to start shaking with fear.

Even though Cammon knew what it was.

One of the attackers uttered a shaky curse and lifted his sword again. But before he could swing his blade, a dark red shape erupted into the sunny garden, announcing its presence with a third horrifying shriek.

And then it leapt for the nearest black-clad soldier and cleanly ripped his head off.

Justin started fighting like a madman. "The raelynx!" he cried. He didn't add the one clear thought he had in his head. *Maybe if it kills off the invaders, it will be too tired to go after the rest of us.* He just accepted it as the gift from the gods that it truly was and went after his enemies with fresh vigor.

Hammond was done for, falling against the edge of the marble shell in a dead faint of blood loss and exhaustion. Cammon surged forward, his sword uplifted, but the opponent who faced him could not concentrate when the men behind him were screaming in agony and panic. Emitting a range of truly terrifying cries, the raelynx bounded between enemy soldiers with a fierce abandon, dragging down one, then another, in a bloodthirsty frenzy. In two minutes, it had killed five men. It licked its red mouth, looked around, and leapt. Six men.

Cammon took advantage of his opponent's inattention and gouged him through the neck. Burbling and choking, the man fell to the ground. Cammon felt Justin's intense satisfaction as his own opponent fell.

The raelynx screeched again and brought down its seventh victim.

There were only four invaders left now and it was clear they realized their situation had grown perilous. Two of them began to run, and the raelynx went straight after them, catching one before he had gone six paces. The man's wild yells of pain and fear were abruptly silenced, and the raelynx bounded after his companion.

Justin charged over the bodies at his feet and descended upon the last attackers, who stood transfixed with horror. One of them turned to make a fight of it, but his fellow stumbled away, hoping to escape. Justin pulled his bloody blade from the soldier's throat and turned to locate his last enemy. Just then the raelynx sailed over a low stone bench and knocked the fleeing man to the ground. There was an unholy sound of ripping, a cry of utter desolation—and then a spine-chilling noise from the raelynx, who lifted his red mouth and loosed a primitive howl of triumph.

Now the only ones left alive in the garden were Justin, Cammon, Amalie, and Hammond, and Hammond was as near death as made no difference. Cammon saw Justin make a quick assessment and shift his mental focus. *My human enemies are dead. Now I must face this feral creature.* Circling just a little, so his back was to Amalie, Justin gathered his sword in both hands and dropped into a crouch of readiness.

Cammon called out in a low voice. "Justin. No. He won't harm any of us."

Justin relaxed, but not completely. "Is it Donnal, then? I didn't think, even in animal form, Donnal could move so fast."

"No," said Cammon. "It's the wild raelynx." He glanced at Amalie, who had dropped to the ground next to Hammond. "The princess called him."

Justin risked one quick look over his shoulder at Cammon. "How did it get out of the enclosure?" Not, *How did she call him?* Justin had seen the mystical connection between Amalie and the big cat. He could accept miracles, but his mind always ran on practical matters.

"I think it leapt the wall."

Justin backed up slowly toward the marble shell, picking his way carefully through fallen bodies. "If it could do that, why didn't it ever try before?"

"I guess it didn't want to badly enough."

"You keep an eye on it," Justin commanded, pushing past Cammon to kneel beside Hammond. "How is he?" he asked Amalie.

"I'm not sure. I don't know much about injuries. I think he's lost a lot of blood."

"Someone taught you how to bind a wound," Justin commented. "We can't do anything else for him until we get help."

Amalie came to her feet, slowly, shakily. She put her hand out and Cammon took it. She was so cold she was trembling. Or maybe she was trembling with fear and shock. But she was trying hard to remain calm, to not fall to pieces. "What's happening now?" she asked Cammon, and her voice was almost steady. "What do we do next?"

Cammon pulled Amalie closer, into a true hug, but kept part of his attention on the raelynx. The big cat seemed to have lost its bloodlust and was now consumed with curiosity. It trotted from corpse to corpse, sniffing at its fallen foes and occasionally licking down a bright swath of blood. "Do you have complete control of him?" he asked her quietly. "Or should he be our next point of concern?"

"He's fine," she said with a touch of impatience. "What's happening at the palace? Can you tell?"

There had been so much action here the past few minutes that Cammon had had no attention to spare for the rest of the compound, but now he let his mind skip through the palace grounds, seeking information. Instantly, he picked up good news. "The city guard is here!" he exclaimed. "Five hundred men. All the attackers are dead or disabled, but Tayse and the other soldiers are going through the palace, double-checking." He grimaced. "Bodies everywhere."

"What about our losses?" Justin demanded as he rose to his feet.

"I can't tell. None of *us* have fallen." He could pick up clear, if weary, signals from Tayse, Senneth, Kirra, and Donnal, and he sent them all a strong message in return. *Justin and Amalie and I all live.*

"Ellynor?" Justin asked fearfully.

Normally he wouldn't be able to answer that question, but Senneth had apparently anticipated his need to know. She had grabbed hold of someone's arm and tried to convey a single word of reassurance. "She's with Senneth."

Amalie stirred in his arms, tilting her head back. "My father? Valri? My uncle?"

"Valri's alive," he said—and then hesitated, because Valri had crumpled into misery. Now he felt alarm from Senneth and a sudden deep stab of grief from Tayse. He pulled Amalie so close that she had to struggle for breath, and he shared a look of utter dread with Justin.

"Tir is dead," he whispered. "And the king with him."

CHAPTER
30

SENNETH had never in her life seen a sight so strange as that of Amalie running across the lawns of the palace after the skirmish was over. The princess was filthy, spattered with dirt and blood; her beautiful hair was a tangled mess of color. Ahead of her strode Justin, his sword still in his hand, his face as grim as ever Tayse's could be. Cammon hurried next to her, holding her hand tightly in his—perhaps just to help her over the corpses littering the field, perhaps to fill her with whatever comfort he could muster.

The red raelynx loped lazily beside her, his body so close to hers that his fur brushed against her soiled dress. He looked around with bright interest, sniffed the air, noted every fallen body, located every living soul. Even on this day of so much loss and destruction, there was something spellbinding about him, something mesmerizing. Senneth's head was ringing with pain and for a moment she thought she might be imagining the presence of this feral creature, so unexpected, so unlikely. She stared at him, briefly losing track of everything else in the dazzle of his elemental beauty.

Then Amalie came closer, and Senneth could see the tears streaking the princess's dirty cheeks, and she realized that the awful message she had come forward to convey had already been delivered. She had never been so grateful for Cammon's ability; these were words she had not wanted to be the first to speak.

She should have greeted the princess as *majesty*. She should have placed her fist against her shoulder as a mark of reverence and respect. Instead, Senneth gathered the girl in a close embrace and whispered in her ear, "Amalie, Amalie, I am so sorry."

For a moment, Amalie clung to her, and then she pushed away. Her face was pale, her lips bitten through, but she wore an expression of proud determination. "What happened?"

"Too many attackers, and he was in an open room," Senneth said, but she could hardly take her eyes off the raelynx. It had dropped to his haunches and was staring up at her with an unwinking gaze. Was Cammon holding it? Was Amalie? How had it gotten free? Was it safe? Was that blood on its whiskers? "Wen went down—though she's alive—and Tir battled so hard. Coeval and I fought our way into the room, but there were so many of them." She took a deep breath. "Once Tir was dead, the king fell. But only once Tir was dead."

Justin nodded at the fresh soldiers roving the field, seeking for the wounded among the fallen, identifying friends, making sure that enemies were dead. "What alerted the city guard? Your fire on the walls?"

Senneth almost smiled at that. "Your wife. No one saw her as she slipped out of the gates and ran for help."

Justin only nodded, but Senneth saw pride in his eyes. "And she's safe?"

"Unharmed. As are Kirra and Donnal. Kirra's with Wen, and Ellynor has been called to the ballroom, where they are bringing in our wounded men. We do not have nearly enough healers."

"Hammond's in the sculpture garden. He might be—he was alive when we left. Someone must go to him."

Senneth nodded. "I'll tell Milo."

"Where's my father?" Amalie asked.

Senneth gave her a compassionate look. "Valri is with him. You might not—"

Amalie's voice was almost cold. "I will go to him."

"I'll take her," Cammon said in a soft voice. As soon as Amalie had pulled free of Senneth's hug, Cammon had taken her hand again. He had the ability to keep despair at bay—Senneth had seen him do it—but she was not sure even Cammon's magic was enough to buoy Amalie through the next few hours, the next few days. "Where is he?"

"Where he fell. The great dining hall."

Amalie nodded regally and swept forward, still flanked by Cammon and the raelynx. Senneth stared after them and then turned to Justin.

"What in the silver hell happened?" she demanded.

He shook his head. He had pulled out a cloth and was wiping blood from his blade but he didn't look like, even once it was clean, he planned to sheathe it anytime soon. "We took shelter in this little alcove in the sculpture garden. About a dozen men stormed us—we were in a good position and able to fend them off until Hammond got hurt. And then more came." He shrugged, but Senneth could imagine the grimness of the scene. "I knew I would not be able to keep them at bay much longer. Cammon was fighting in Hammond's place—"

"Cammon? He's never killed a man in his life."

"Well, he killed three today. But he's no Rider. I knew we would all be dead within minutes. And then—that creature came howling into the garden." He shook his head. "You think you've heard it, when we were traveling on the road or when you were walking by its enclosure some afternoon when it was hunting. But, Senneth, you *never* heard anything like this. It went after those men, one after the other—just slaughtered them and moved on. I knew the attackers would all be done for, but I thought we might be, too."

"Cammon says she can control it."

"Well, it sure looked that way to me."

"So—now—well, *what?*" she demanded. "She thinks to keep it out of its garden? She thinks to keep it by her side like some kind of lapdog? Or to let it roam the palace grounds at will?"

Justin gave her a ghost of his familiar grin. "Doesn't sound like a bad idea. We might lose a Rider here and there, or maybe a servant or two, but the princess will be safe."

Senneth caught her breath. "The queen."

THEY found Tayse in the ballroom, checking on the condition of the fallen Riders. His face was utterly set, his expression remote, and Senneth ached for him as much as she ached for Amalie. He had lost his father; he had lost his king. The man he loved, the man he served. Even in the greater turmoil of a kingdom in chaos, these two losses would hit the strongest man hard enough to make him stagger.

Justin went straight up to Ellynor and took her in a tight embrace. They stood together and whispered, repeating their own tales of this dreadful day. Tayse nodded to Justin, a simple acknowledgment of a job well done, and came toward Senneth.

"I want to hug you, but I don't know if that will harm you," she said to him in a low voice.

He immediately put his arms around her. She could feel his weariness finally battering down his rage. "How could it harm me?"

Her voice was muffled against his shirt. "Love might seem like a kind of weakness during a time when you cannot afford anything but strength."

He kissed the top of her head and dropped his arms. "You give me strength," he said quietly.

She glanced toward the middle of the room, where ten or twelve men lay on pallets on the floor. Milo, the housekeeper, and a handful of servants moved between them, administering herbs and binding up injuries. Two footmen had just been dispatched to find Hammond, but there were plenty of others who also needed serious attention.

"What's the tally among the Riders?" Senneth asked.

"Five dead, twelve badly wounded. The rest of us all have injuries but nothing severe." His own chest was bound with a thick layer of cloth, white except where the blood had seeped through, and his left arm was also wrapped from wrist to elbow. Senneth had only minor cuts and scrapes, though she was fairly certain she should have someone check out a persistent burning sensation on her right leg. She might have taken a blow there; she couldn't remember.

She didn't want to remember.

"I have seen Riders fight before," she said softly. "But today I saw them die. I have never seen such bravery and skill in all my life."

He nodded, accepting that compliment on behalf of all Riders, but did not answer it directly. Instead, he said, "Where's Amalie?"

"With her father."

He compressed his lips and did not reply.

Senneth added, "And Cammon. And the raelynx."

That *did* startle an expression onto his face. "Someone freed it? Is it safe?"

"Apparently it freed itself when she was in gravest danger. Justin says it saved all of their lives."

"Another weapon in her arsenal," he commented. "She has many."

"Tayse," Senneth said urgently, "she is queen now. Should there be a ceremony? A coronation? In the midst of all this bloodshed?"

"Her uncle will know the answer to that," Tayse said. He took her hand. "Let us go find the queen."

AMALIE was in the great dining hall where Baryn had so often entertained high-ranking visitors from across the realm. Now the king's body had been laid on a bench at one end of the room. Ten yards away, his inner circle of family and advisors clustered around the end of a long, polished table and discussed strategy. Senneth noted that someone had covered Baryn with a purple blanket embroidered with the royal lions. Someone else had set up a half-circle of votive candles around his bier.

Amalie sat in such a way that all she had to do was lift her eyes and she could see him.

Cammon sat next to her, Romar and Valri across from her. The captain of Romar's guard stood stiffly behind the regent, and the Rider Janni, looking even worse than some of the dead, had taken up a place behind Amalie. Kirra was sitting next to Cammon, trying hard not to look at Romar. Senneth glanced around for Donnal, and saw a small spring hawk perched on one of the upper beams of the high-ceilinged room.

The raelynx lay on the floor a few feet away from Amalie, its chin pillowed on its outstretched forepaws, but its eyes still wide and curious. Everyone in the room occasionally sent the creature a look of fear or marvel, and Senneth had to guess that it had caused no little consternation as Amalie paced through the palace. But for now, it was quiescent. *For now,* Senneth thought, *it has earned its place among us.*

"Sen!" Kirra called, and waved them over. Senneth headed directly for the table, but Tayse strode first toward Baryn's body. As Senneth slipped in place beside Valri, she watched over her shoulder to see Tayse drop to one knee and bow his head. Making his farewell to his king.

"Serra," Romar greeted her. "Please share your thoughts. We are debating whether to hold a hasty coronation and name Amalie queen. Will that inflame the warring marlords or call the loyal ones to more decisive action?"

"There was always the fear that the marlords wouldn't accept a nineteen-year-old girl on the throne. That's why the king named a regent to begin with," Kirra pointed out, addressing Senneth instead of Romar.

"I would still serve beside her. My title would just change from regent to advisor."

Tayse came to stand behind Senneth as she addressed Amalie. "Majesty, what do you want to do?"

Amalie shifted in her seat. One of her hands was under the table, and Senneth was pretty sure it was caught in both of Cammon's. "I think we need to worry about war first, and then titles," she said in her soft voice. "Put our energy into battle."

"More than one nation has gone to war over titles before," Romar said.

Amalie shrugged a little. "Then I say we announce that I will remain princess for one year, with you at my side as regent. At the end of that time—assuming there is still a throne of Gillengaria to be had—we will have a ceremony to name me queen."

Kirra was nodding. "That's good. That offers a hope of continuity without a sense of fevered rushing. It shows judgment and a focus on priorities."

Tayse spoke up in a heavy voice. "Majesty, there is something you cannot wait a year to do. You must release all the Riders from your employ."

Senneth jerked around to stare at him, and everyone else let loose exclamations of surprise and dismay. Everyone except Janni, who was nodding.

"This is not the time to be casting off the finest fighting force in the kingdom!" Romar exclaimed.

"She has to," Janni said. "Our vows are made only to the king. He is dead, and we have no fealty."

"But none of you would harm Amalie!" Senneth said.

"Of course not," Tayse said. "But the king—or the queen—selects his or her own Riders. There is a personal and close connection between the soldier and his liege. That connection does not transfer. Amalie must choose her own Riders—and they must choose her."

In Amalie's place, Senneth thought, she would have wailed, *But I want all of you!* But Amalie merely nodded, her tight face a little tighter, and said, "Then I release you, Tayse and Janni. You are free to serve any master or mistress you choose."

At the same instant, both Riders dropped to their knees, bowing their heads and slapping their fists to their shoulders. "Majesty," Janni said in a quiet voice. "If you will have me, I will serve you with my life. I will be loyal to you above all others—I will defend you against all dangers. I will not betray you till the end of the world itself."

Amalie leaned forward and pressed her free hand to Janni's shoulder. "Yes. I accept your vow. I welcome your fealty. I will trust you without reservation."

"Majesty," Tayse said. "If you will have me, I will offer you my life, my loyalty, my sword, my steadfastness. I will not betray you, and I will not fail you."

He stayed where he was, head down, so Amalie shook herself free of Cammon's hold, stood up, and circled the table to place her hand on Tayse's head. "I accept your vow, I welcome your fealty, I will trust you without reservation." She glanced between them. "You are now Queen's Riders, and I will deliver my life into your keeping."

Senneth felt her throat thicken as she strove to keep from weeping. She glanced at Kirra, who wasn't even trying. Her blue eyes were huge with tears and her cheeks were wet with them. Such sad poetry on a day of such ugliness. The vows were like miniscule candles held up on a limitless field of black—the smallest, most hopeless attempts to beat back the night. Senneth glanced at Amalie as the princess took her seat again. She thought there was a touch more color in Amalie's cheeks now, as if these protestations of faith had supplied the princess with an indefinable source of strength. Or maybe Amalie's face just reflected the pale glow from the late afternoon sunlight, streaming in at an almost horizontal angle through the high windows, and had nothing at all to do with those gifts of love.

THEY stayed another hour in the makeshift funeral chapel, discussing options, reviewing losses. Romar's captain, a dour man named Colton, and some of the other Riders had pieced together a theory of how the attack had been launched. The city guard had been deployed in a ring outside the city to keep an army from marching on the palace. But these foreign assassins had slipped into the city in ones and twos, over the course of a few days, dressed as ordinary Gillengaria merchants. They were already through the protective ring before the day had even dawned. Still wearing their regular wools and linens, they had slowly spread themselves around the palace walls, loitering until some agreed-upon hour. Then they cast off their disguises and climbed into the compound.

"We found hundreds of jackets and cloaks lying on the ground just outside the palace," Colton told them.

It made sense, but it was hardly any comfort. And it was only the barest comfort that the Riders and the motley array of mystics had managed to hold off a force about four times their size until reinforcements arrived.

"Did any of the attackers survive?" Senneth said. "Are they being questioned?"

Romar nodded. "About a dozen. And yes. Two of them have already given us names—but the names are hardly surprising."

"Halchon Gisseltess," Senneth said wearily. She rubbed the back of her skull. Her head was pounding. She had not employed much of her magic today, since it had proved so ineffectual, but rage—oh, that had sung through her body like a form of ecstasy. Her worst headaches tended to come from a combination of sorcery and anger, but this one was bad enough. "And Rayson Fortunalt."

Romar nodded again. "I think it's time we reply to the letter marlord Halchon sent, asking for a conference with the king. We can tell him the princess is not interested in any terms and she will not yield her throne to him. That will let him know she is alive still."

Senneth gave him a grave look. "It will be his signal to go to war."

Romar shook his head. "He has already gone to war. It will merely signal that we are prepared to fight back."

Kirra said, "We need to know where his armies are. And if any of our allies have more troops to send us."

Romar nodded. "I thought perhaps you and some of your mystic friends might take wing and carry messages across the kingdom."

"I won't," Kirra said instantly. "I'm staying here. But I'm sure Donnal will be willing, and some of Senneth's recruits."

"Because now," Romar said, "we need information almost as much as we need reinforcements. And we desperately need both."

At last it seemed there was nothing left to discuss, and continued speculation was not benefiting them at all. By this time it was dark, though whether early or late dark Senneth could not tell. She was so weary she would not have been surprised to learn they had passed the last year in the dining hall, talking, after spending an entire year in battle.

"I think, for all of us, food and rest," Senneth said, feeling her whole body protest as she came to her feet.

"First Amalie must release the Riders," Tayse said. "And we must determine a schedule for the night watch."

"No night watch for *you*," she protested. "You patrolled last night."

He gave her a steady look from those dark eyes. "I am whole, and too many are not," he said. "I will sleep early and take the later shift."

If he considered it his duty to pursue that course, nothing she said would dissuade him. She sighed silently and followed the others from the room.

They encountered Justin in the hall, fetching supplies for Ellynor. Before Amalie had even opened her mouth, he dropped to his knees and offered his oath.

"Is it a mere formality, then?" Senneth whispered to Tayse as they proceeded. "All Riders pledge themselves to the new monarch?"

"No. In fact, there have been many instances in which virtually no Riders aligned themselves with a new ruler—and when a new ruler did not invite any standing Riders to ride under his banner. Those usually were cases when there was some tension between the king and his heir, for instance, or when most of the Riders actively disliked the new king or queen. But there are always some Riders who do not want to continue, for whatever reason. They are tired of the role, they are weary of the responsibility, they want to live a calmer life, or marry, or travel. There is no dishonor in declining to serve a new ruler. There is no shame in not being asked back to the royal court."

"Sweet gods, I hope no one refuses Amalie today. I don't know if we can spare another sword."

He gave her an exceedingly sober smile. "No one will desert her. But some of them might relinquish their titles as Riders. They will stay till they are no longer needed, but they will no longer dedicate their lives to her protection."

He was right, of course. They found about half of the Riders in the makeshift infirmary—the injured lying on their pallets or attempting to sit up, their healthier comrades doing what they could to ease them. Amalie glanced uncertainly at Tayse as they entered. He leaned down and murmured, "Approach them one by one. They will know why you are here."

So she did, supported by Cammon and trailed by the raelynx. Senneth stayed by the door, leaning her aching head against the wall. She could not hear what passed between Amalie and the soldiers, but it was easy to tell how each case unfolded. Most of the Riders instantly swore their fealty to the princess. Even the hurt ones, those who could not kneel and bow their heads, put their shaky hands to their shoulders and whispered their oaths. But there were three or four who bowed their heads, and clasped their hands behind their backs, and gave Amalie a different answer.

"Will some of them change their minds?" Senneth asked Tayse. "Are they giving conditional responses?"

"Perhaps. We will know more once this war is over."

She turned her head slightly to watch him. "So how does she find new Riders?"

"The news gets out among soldiers and civil guards—even mercenaries—and those who are interested will wend their way to the palace. Usually candidates are first assessed by other Riders before they are allowed to approach the king or queen. But sometimes royalty makes choices without any advice at all."

"Yes, but—I mean, how? Amalie will be giving these people power over her *life*. She will allow them free run of the palace. How can she possibly know, after a few minutes' conversation, if a stranger is someone she can trust?"

His smile was faint. "Ah, perhaps that is the magic inherent in the crown. In all the history of Gillengaria, there is no story about a king or a queen who has chosen Riders unwisely. Is it that only honorable men and women seek the office of Rider? Is the monarch blessed by the gods with some supernatural powers of perception?"

"Are the stories truly complete?" she asked with some acerbity.

His smile widened. "I like to believe they are." His gaze went to the princess and her small entourage. "In Amalie's case, she will have Cammon to guide her. I cannot imagine she will chose ill."

Senneth shook her head. "One more hard task that falls to her all at once. I hope she is not crushed under her responsibilities."

"We are here to support her," he said softly. "But I think she is strong enough to survive it."

ONCE they had toured the sickroom, Senneth insisted Amalie come to the smaller dining hall for a rather slapdash meal. Some of the servants had died in the day's assault, and the rest were understandably traumatized, and Senneth was grateful that the cooks managed to assemble a meal at all. It was a simple buffet, and there were signs that Valri, Romar, and a few others had been at the table before them.

Riders continued to seek them out for the next half hour, presenting themselves, being released from service, and then either offering their fealty or calmly stating that they planned to leave once the princess had found their replacements.

"That's everyone," Tayse said when Coeval exited after swearing his loyalty. Apparently Tayse had had better luck keeping track of the numbers than Senneth had. "Except the three who were too injured to speak. Majesty, ask them again tomorrow."

Amalie nodded. She looked so tired Senneth thought she might tip over and bury her face in her platter of food. "And then? Tomorrow? What else must I do?"

"We will know when tomorrow arrives," Senneth said gently. She tugged on Amalie's shoulder. "Come. To bed with you. If you don't think you will be able to sleep, Kirra can make up a potion."

"She'll sleep," Cammon said.

Senneth glanced at him. He had not been more than a step away from the princess since they came running back from the garden with the raelynx in tow. Clearly the connection between them had intensified during the days Senneth had been gone, but she found herself deeply reluctant to discover how far their relationship had progressed. She kept remembering Tayse's comment: Amalie would be safe if Cammon were sleeping by her side. After today, Amalie's safety mattered much more than Amalie's virginity.

"I will be grateful if you, indeed, will use your magic to help her relax," Senneth said. "But what of the raelynx? Are we to attempt to cage him again for the night?"

"No," Amalie said. "He will stay with me."

Of course she should protest, Senneth thought, but the raelynx had certainly earned its right to freedom today. And if danger *did* manage to force its way through Amalie's door, the raelynx would almost certainly pounce on it and kill it. And eat it.

"Then, Majesty, I will see you in the morning."

True to his word, Tayse accompanied Senneth back to the cottage to sleep at least some portion of the night. She had overheard him making murmured plans with his fellow Riders, dividing up the shifts. There had never been a hope he would be comfortable allowing ordinary soldiers the solemn responsibility of guarding the palace.

At the cottage, they had water enough to bathe, and Senneth heated it to the point where it almost blistered the skin. In silence, they took turns discarding their ruined clothing, washing themselves thoroughly, and climbing into bed. Not until Tayse put his arms around her did Senneth feel she could find even the most fleeting moment of real peace.

"In the morning, you will have to tell your mother that Tir is dead," she said. "And tell your sisters."

"And let them know the city is not safe. They can take refuge with my aunt."

"Your mother will be heartbroken, I think. I am convinced she still loved him, despite the fact that she left him so long ago."

She felt him shrug slightly. He was a dutiful son, but his mother exerted no pull on him, as she had exerted no pull on Tir after the first few years of their doomed marriage. Tayse changed the subject. "How's your head?"

"Hurts," she said. "How's your heart?"

"Hurts."

"If I'm not better in the morning, I'll ask you to scare away my headache," she said. "But Tayse, my love, my dearest one, I do not know how to scare away your pain."

"These are losses too great for magic to heal," he said. "I know my father's only regret about his death would be that it did not save the king. If it had, he would have gladly given his life."

"And that is how you want to die someday, is it not?" she murmured into his chest. "Defending Amalie? Or her son or daughter?"

He was silent a moment. "Once that would have been true," he said. "Now I want to live as long as you are alive, and die when you are not. And if I do not fall in battle, but instead die when I am an old man, bent and crippled and useless, except that you still love me, then I will consider that a better death than my father's."

She was so stunned she almost could not answer. Tayse was so much a soldier that she had always accepted she had been grafted onto his life. Important to him, essential even—transcendent—but only a part of his life, not the center, not the whole. "Oh, then I have to hope that is what happens," she whispered. "That you are ancient and demented and *blind*, and everyone despises you, and laughs at you behind your back, and cannot believe you have lived so long. But *I* will still love you. *I* will be glad to see you, every time your scowling face comes into view."

That made him smile, as she hoped it would. "And you will be a doddering old woman yourself, mumbling around the house, constantly setting small unintentional fires and causing the curtains to go up in flames. We will have to live in a house of stone, so it doesn't burn down around our heads. We will be buying new furnishings every week and my eyebrows will be singed off my face. But I will still love you."

Now she was giggling, and laughter felt so good, so hopeful, when weighed against all the misery of the day. She tightened her arms around him, felt the strength of his body even through his exhaustion and sadness. "War will come, and heartache and betrayal, and friends will die and all of Gillengaria may be lost, and I will still love you," she said against his mouth. "And if I accidentally set your hair on fire in a few years' time, well, let me just say now that I didn't mean to do it. Unless you made me angry, of course, but even then I will only make a *little* fire. Hardly enough to hurt you."

"And who could mind that?" he said. "I look forward to a happy old age."

She snuggled against him even more closely. "I hope we live to see it."

CHAPTER
31

CAMMON had lived through some wretched days, but none as bad as the ones that followed the king's death.

There was just so much grief. So much anxiety. Fear and tension and anticipation of violence. It lashed against him from all directions, impossible to block out. He tried to close his mind, concentrate only on the people who desperately mattered to him—but those were some of the people who were suffering most.

In public, Amalie maintained a steely calm that had everyone marveling. She listened closely to advice, made sometimes surprising decisions, exhibited only a decorous grief, and seemed ready to assume the heaviest burdens of government.

But at night, in her room, she broke down and wept so hard that she sometimes threw up whatever meal she had forced herself to eat last. Cammon could calm her—more quickly as the days went on, as he learned the trick of it—but sometimes she didn't want him to touch her, didn't want to be comforted.

That was especially true two days after the attack, when they had spent the morning burying bodies. Baryn and his fallen Riders had been interred in a cemetery on the palace grounds not far from the raelynx's old haunt. Ghosenhall residents had not been allowed past the gates, but thousands of mourners had gathered around the walls, offering prayers and songs and leaving behind small tokens. It was not nearly the grand farewell a king deserved, but they did not have time for pomp. They did not dare parade the princess down the city streets as she followed her father's casket through weeping crowds. They were forced to keep the ceremony small, private, and secure.

But that had not made it any easier for Amalie. She had been pale but tranquil at the graveside, quiet but functional as she made the day's decisions, but as soon as she stepped into her room that night, she broke down completely. When Cammon tried to take her in his arms, she pushed him away.

"I want to get it *out* of me," she sobbed. "All this sadness. I want to cry it away. Magic isn't enough. I have to let it go."

So he let her weep unrestrainedly for half an hour and then, when she was too tired to resist, he lay beside her on the bed and gathered her close. Still sobbing, she turned in his arms and buried her face against his shoulder. She let his hands play across her back, let his magic coax away her frenzy. The grief stayed inside her, black and silver and razor sharp, but he sprinkled it with peace, he blunted down its cruelest edges. He didn't think he could take it away from her, didn't think he *should*, but he could make it bearable, at least long enough for her to sleep.

Tayse, too, endured the funeral day with little outward emotion, though Cammon could tell that the Rider carried a heavy stone of sadness. But Cammon could practically see the marks of Senneth's hands on Tayse's heart; if there was healing that could be done there, Senneth was doing it.

Valri's grief was just as deep and more unexpected. The day after the funeral, Cammon woke in the middle of the night with his stomach so tight he felt he had been dealt a physical blow. For a moment he thought *he* would be the one to start vomiting, but then he realized the pain was not his own. He kissed Amalie on the cheek and left her sleeping, though the raelynx lifted its head to watch him slip through the door. He need have no fear about leaving Amalie unguarded.

The pain was so strong that, at first, Cammon could not attach a person to it; he just held up his candle and followed the beacon of woe. But he recognized the door to Valri's room and hesitated before he knocked. So many reasons not to seek out the widowed queen in the middle of the night, in her bedroom, unchaperoned. But then he rapped his knuckles against the wood.

"Valri? It's Cammon. I know you're awake. Let me in."

He could feel her surprise and hesitation, but in a minute she opened the door. She had been crying; her porcelain face was blotched and red, her short black hair wild. "What's wrong?" she asked in a low voice, raspy with tears.

"I came to see what's wrong with *you*," he replied, and stepped inside without an invitation.

Again she hesitated, then she shut the door and followed him inside. Like Amalie's, her room was tasteful but luxurious. It was spacious enough to practically be two rooms, with a grouping of furniture on one side creating a sitting area, while the bed and dresser were arranged on the other side. Plush rugs on the floor held back the chill; the curtains and bed linens were colored in soft mauves and pinks and grays. Valri wore a dark green robe over a long nightdress but it was clear she had not yet been to bed.

"I thought you could not sense the Lirrenfolk and their emotions," she said, sinking down into a well-padded armchair. He took a seat across from her.

"I can sense yours," he said simply. "And you're so distressed that you woke me from a sound sleep."

She laughed shortly. "Now must be an uncomfortable time for a man with magic like yours."

"It is," he acknowledged. "I can't even tell how much grief I might be feeling on my own, because everyone else's is pressing so hard against me."

She leaned her head against the back of the chair. "And yet you could still feel mine."

"I don't mean to be rude," he said quietly. "I didn't realize you loved Baryn so much."

"I was not in love with him, no, but I loved a great deal about him," Valri said. "I would have done anything he asked. I believed that while he was in the world, there was goodness and justice and order. Now I'm not sure any of those things still exist." She flung up a hand as he started to answer. "And Baryn's death makes me remember Pella's, and remembering Pella, I remember all the things I left behind to be with her. And so loss piles upon loss and it becomes too much to bear. Do not worry about me, Cammon. I am touched that you heard my despair and came to comfort me, but I am not your burden. I will mourn, and I will recover, and you will need to do nothing for me at all."

"It's just that I don't think you have anyone to comfort you," he said. "And that makes you even more lost."

She did not answer for a moment, just surveyed him. Against her red-rimmed lids, her eyes were even more impossibly green. "Who comforted you, when everyone you loved died?" she asked. "I heard the stories you told Amalie. No one cared for you. And yet you survived."

"I did not survive very well."

She shook her head slightly. "Do not try to take me on, Cammon. I am too dark for you. I want you to pour all your light and all your goodness into Amalie. I don't want you to spare any of it for me."

He smiled slightly. "That's an odd way to hear oneself described. As being full of light and goodness."

"You are, though. And that's what she needs most at this moment."

"I thought you wanted me to keep a proper distance from her." Cammon did not particularly want to be discussing Amalie with Valri right now, but the conversation distracted her, eased some of her grief, and so he didn't try to change the subject.

Valri lifted a hand and began picking at the fabric of the chair where her head rested against the upholstery. "You can't marry her, of course," she said, almost absently. "But I think I don't mind if you love her for a while. She is happy when you are nearby, and fretful when you're not. There is something about you that gives her peace. And right now, Amalie deserves to hold on to anything that gives her joy."

"I love her," Cammon said. "And I know you care for her as much as I do."

"I love her as if she was my sister's child. I didn't think I would. I came here for Pella's sake, and because my goddess asked me to. I thought I would find Amalie a duty, not a delight."

"But you're thinking of leaving her," he said.

Now she narrowed her eyes and watched him silently a moment. "I don't think I like how easily you are picking thoughts out of my head," she said at last. "Clearly you have learned to break through the shroud of Lirren magic."

"Only yours. But, yes, to some extent I can read your thoughts and feelings. And I know that you are planning to leave Amalie once you think she is settled."

Valri made a helpless gesture with the hand that had been picking at threads on the chair. "A dowager queen—and such a strange queen as I have been!—is more an encumbrance than an advantage. Amalie will have plenty of other problems to deal with. I am not going to add to her troubles." He started to speak and she kept talking over his words. "Besides, I have been tied to Ghosenhall too long. I want to see my family. I want to see the land I left behind. I want to see what else I might make of my life, when I might make my life about me."

"Will you go back to him?"

She gave him an icy look, but he could tell she was unnerved. "Back to whom?"

"That man in the Lirrens who loves you."

She turned her head away. "Who may still love me."

"Will you seek him out?"

She was silent a long time, her head still turned to the side. "I will try to discover if his heart is still unclaimed. And if it is . . . I may look for him. I may travel to wherever he is. I'll try not to hope he still loves me. But I'll try to discover if he does."

"And are you too dark for *him*?" he couldn't stop himself from asking.

That made her smile, barely, thinking about this man she loved. "Oh, he is like winter, in a way. He has a still beauty all his own. Sometimes when I would come to him at night, he would seem to glow like moonlight against snow. I don't think my darkness would trouble him at all."

Anyone who could talk like that about a man she hadn't seen in six years certainly deserved to hope he had waited for her the whole time they had been apart. But. "Don't leave Amalie too soon. Don't assume she doesn't need you, just because so many people are clamoring for her time now," he said. "But I think, once the war is over, you should definitely go searching for this man."

"His name is Arrol," she said. "And I will."

He straightened in his chair, ready to stand up. "Do you think you will be able to sleep now?"

She turned her head to look at him again, and the expression on her face was both puzzled and sweet. As if she had been surprised by benevolence. "Yes. Thank you. You have done me a great kindness, Cammon."

"I don't want you to think you have to be alone, even when you're sad."

She watched him rise to his feet but made no move to get up herself. "Then I won't be. I'll know you are worrying about me, and that will lift my spirits."

He wanted to give her a hug, or take her hand, or in some physical way make a farewell; he wanted to infuse just a whisper of his magic into her veins, diffuse just a little of her remaining heaviness. But she merely settled more deeply in her chair, her arms along the armrests, and watched him pick up his candle and shuffle to the door. With his hand on the knob, he turned to give her one last look.

"You're sure you're all right?"

"Don't divide your loyalties," she said softly. "Give Amalie your whole heart."

"Nobody's heart is whole," he said.

"No," she said, "but don't squander love."

He opened the door and stepped into the hall. "I don't think I ever have," he said quietly. "I don't think it was ever wasted."

She was smiling again as he shut the door between them.

CHAPTER

32

IN the morning, messengers arrived from all directions. From Brassenthwaite and Rappengrass came brief reports of uprisings at their Houses and promises of troops on the way. Ariane Rappengrass's note contained additional dire news: "My spies have seen armies forming in Fortunalt and Gisseltess. Majesty, they have described hundreds of foreign soldiers disembarking in Forten City. If they do not turn toward Rappen Manor, I am certain they will come for Ghosenhall. Prepare yourself."

Romar's cousin, the marlord of Merrenstow, had sent more than a letter—he had sent thousands of troops, in addition to the royal soldiers who had been quartered on Merrenstow land for the past six months. The promised troops from Kianlever also arrived, and a small contingent from Helven showed up with a brief note from marlord Martin: "I cannot spare any more. I see the dust of Fortunalt armies headed my way." Heffel Coravann did not send any men to swell the royal army but did relay a message to Ghosenhall: "I am restoring order to my own House. We will not war with either faction."

There was no word from Tilt. No word from Nocklyn or Storian.

Donnal and two of the Carrebos shape-shifters had returned from reconnaissance missions flown over the southern half of the kingdom. The news was worse than they had feared. Yes, there was an army cutting northeast from Fortunalt. Half of its soldiers marched under the pearl-sewn flag of Fortunalt, half under the blue triple pendant of Arberharst. And yes, there was an army from Gisseltess, wending its way between Nocklyn and Coravann. Every soldier in the ranks wore the Gisseltess standard, a black hawk carrying a red flower in its talons.

But there was a third army, smaller, more nimble, roving just ahead of Halchon Gisseltess's forces. These riders wore black and silver and rode under a flag emblazoned with phases of the moon. Coralinda Gisseltess was riding alongside her brother, bringing her soldiers to war against the crown.

"Why? What can she offer on a battlefield?" Senneth demanded. They were holding a conference in the smaller dining hall, which was big enough to hold everyone who might need to consult but small enough to allow them to do so comfortably. Today the group held Amalie, Cammon, Kirra, Romar, Tayse, and Senneth. Someone had tacked a large map of Gillengaria to the wall. The long table was covered with papers and messenger's pouches and letters full of promises or bad news. "Her few hundred men are not enough to affect the outcome—unless they are much better than I think they are."

"Justin and I defeated four of them last fall," Cammon said. "And then a few weeks later he defeated five all by himself. So I don't think they can be *that* good."

"Then perhaps she believes she herself will be the advantage on the battlefield, and the soldiers accompany her merely to give her consequence," Tayse said.

Kirra snorted. "She comes to bring *magic* to the battlefield," she said. "The magic she claims she doesn't have."

Senneth nodded. "I think that's what we have to assume. Though I'm not sure how she intends to wield it."

Everyone sent sideways glances in Amalie's direction. The princess widened her eyes and said, "I have no idea how such magic could be used! It is pointless to ask me."

"Then we cannot plan how to defeat it," Romar said briskly. He was always the one who kept any conversation going forward, pushing aside fruitless debates and focusing on the major problems. "We need to look instead at the forces we understand."

"Tilt worries me, because everyone forgets about Tilt," Kirra said.

"Tilt's army is scarcely bigger than Coralinda's guard," Romar said dismissively. "Whether they send men to aid us or attack us, it will hardly matter either way."

"And it is just that attitude that makes them dangerous," Kirra muttered.

Cammon could tell she was surprised when Tayse agreed with her. "Kirra's right. Tilt men could easily come upon us from the north, a direction from which we do not expect danger, and enact sabotage."

Romar shrugged. "I will ask my cousin to step up patrols between the Merrenstow borders and Tilt," he said. "If trouble comes from that direction, he will let us know."

"We have to assume Storian and Nocklyn have joined the rebels," Senneth said. "And that the ranks of the armies will be swelled by their soldiers as they pass through."

Romar nodded. "I have sent messengers to Rafe Storian and Mayva Nocklyn and gotten no word in reply," he said. "I am greatly afraid you're right."

"Well, there was never a prayer Mayva would be strong enough to oppose her husband—and he's Halchon's cousin, so of course he will war against us," Kirra said. "But I admit I kept hoping her father would rise up from his sickbed and wrest back control of Nocklyn Towers. I'm sorry it hasn't happened."

"And I admit I kept expecting better of Rafe Storian," Senneth said. "For him to side with Rayson Fortunalt! How could he do it?"

"That matters less to me than the number of additional men he may offer to our enemies," Romar said. "For now, if the shape-shifters have estimated correctly, there will be nearly ten thousand soldiers arrayed against us. Assuming Brassenthwaite and Kianlever send the men they've promised, we will muster only about seven thousand."

"Then we should pick our ground, for whatever advantage that affords us," Tayse said.

"You do not think we are wiser to stay in Ghosenhall, where we can withstand a siege?" Romar asked.

"I think in Ghosenhall we have enemies on multiple sides," Tayse said, standing up and moving toward the map. "Tilt to the north of us, Storian to the southwest, and armies from the south. If we move here"—he indicated a spot in the middle of unaligned territory between Brassenthwaite, Merrenstow, and Kianlever—"it will be harder for enemies to surround us. And if Amalie needs to flee, she will have two escape routes to the oceans, and one over the mountains."

"The mountains!" Romar repeated. "You'd send her to the Lirrenlands?"

"With her Lirren stepmother. I would." He glanced briefly at Amalie, and Cammon could just barely see his smile. "I would send her now, before battle is joined, except that I do not think she would go."

"No, I most certainly would not!" Amalie declared. "If you are fighting for me, I will stand beside you."

Romar gave her a serious look. "But Tayse is right. The entire war is pointless unless we are able to secure your safety. If it becomes clear that we are overmatched and we fear for your life—will you promise then to seek refuge? In the Lirrens with Valri, or wherever else we determine is your best hope for safe haven?"

She didn't even hesitate. "I will."

"Then perhaps Tayse is right, and we should engage these rebel armies on ground of our choosing. Leave Ghosenhall behind."

"The city's already half empty," Kirra said. "Ever since the attack, people have been abandoning their shops and houses."

"I would wish the whole city deserted before the armies arrive," Amalie said. "Send criers out—let them know war is upon us."

Romar nodded. Cammon knew that the regent had already sent his own wife back to Merrenstow, though she might find only a relative safety even there. "We have done so," Romar said. "But some people won't leave. They're more afraid of looters left behind than soldiers marching through."

"Their choice," Amalie said. "But they need to know how quickly danger comes."

The debate went on but Cammon did not follow it closely. He was not a strategist; he was not particularly good at considering the future and how he might improve its bleak picture. What he knew was that the people in this room, and a few of them outside it, the ones he cared about most in the world, were about to fling themselves headlong into danger. And he had enough experience with calamity to know that devastation could blight the most ordinary day. He could not imagine how it might come calling when times were so desperate.

AMALIE had been thinking somewhat along the same lines, as became clear that night when they finally made their way to her bedroom. The raelynx preceded them down the hallway, sniffing at promising corners and pausing every once in a while to look over its shoulder and make sure they were still following. Nonetheless, it seemed to lose all interest in them as soon as they pushed through Amalie's door. It headed to its favorite spot beside the freshly built fire and curled up to sleep.

Amalie went to stand at the window and look out over the sloping lawns. The moon was small and high; the grass mustered a subdued sparkle under its light. At this time of night, it was impossible to tell how green the lawns had become in just a few days. They had pulled away bodies and found new grass underneath.

"When armies ride to war, death rides with them," she said. "I love so few people in this world, and any of them could lose their lives in this endeavor."

Cammon settled in one of the extremely comfortable chairs and watched the back of her head. "I had the identical thought."

"I wonder if it might be better to abandon Ghosenhall, indeed, but not so we could make a stand in another place. Cede the palace, cede the crown, spare all these lives."

He was silent a moment. "There is probably not a single one of your friends who would agree that is a good idea."

"Even you?"

"I'm hardly qualified to advise."

"But you can tell me your opinion."

"My opinion is that war will follow you wherever you go. If you hide in the Lirrens, Halchon Gisseltess will track you down there. If you are alive, you are a threat to him. He would prefer to see you dead or in his power."

She reflected a moment. "And if I were dead?"

"*Amalie!*"

"I'm just asking. I'm not planning to kill myself."

"If you were dead and he could take the throne—yes, I suppose it would avert a great deal of bloodshed. Every mystic in the country would be put to death, though. And I suspect the rebels would still war against Merrenstow and Rappengrass and the Houses that have shown loyalty to the throne. And I have to believe that Halchon Gisseltess would make a bad king—unjust and violent. His sons would rule after him and be equally brutal. Is that the legacy you would leave for Gillengaria?"

She sighed. "It is just that I do not want anyone to die."

"I know," he said. "I don't know how to keep them all safe. I don't even know how to keep safe the ones I care about the most."

She stared out the window during another short silence. "Valri is grieving over my father's death," she said presently.

"I know," he said again.

"She thinks he didn't know that she loved him. She thinks if she had told him so, she would not be so distraught now."

"I always thought your father knew everything," Cammon said with a touch of humor. "I'd be surprised if he hadn't realized it."

"Still, you should *tell* people the important things, while you can," she said, turning away from the window and coming straight for him across the room. Before he could stir from the chair, she dropped to her knees, clasped his hand, and cradled it against her cheek. "I love you," she whispered. "I have let you think that I am merely playing at love when I am with you, learning things I need to know, but that's all been pretense. I truly do love you. I don't know how I'm going to give you up when the time comes that I am supposed to do so."

His heart, at the same time, compressed with grief and expanded with joy. "*Amalie,*" he said urgently, trying to pull her off her knees, into his lap, but she would not budge. So he slipped from the chair and joined her on the floor, drawing her into his arms. "Amalie, you won't have to give me up. We'll think of something. I'll stay on as a footman or a groom—I'll work in the wine cellars or the gardens. Maybe I'll have Kirra do some magic, change my face. No one but you will even know that I'm still here." She laughed against his chest, as if he had been joking, and he added, "I'm *serious*."

"I don't think that will be good enough for me," she said unsteadily.

He stroked her hair. "I haven't been able to bear to think about it," he said. "I sat there all those days when the serramar of Gillengaria came courting you! Knowing that one of them would marry you, and how would I be able to stand it? I was already wondering where I should go once you were married. Except where *would* I go? Justin and Tayse and Senneth are here, and no one ever knows where Kirra and Donnal will be, and I have no one else. But I have been afraid to let myself love you too much, because I don't know how to walk away from love. I don't know how to let it go. But what do I do with that love if I don't have you in my life?"

She lifted her head, and so, of course, he kissed her. She had started crying, but the kiss made her smile. "And I have been afraid that once you left the palace, you would forget all about me."

He gave a little snort. "That doesn't seem to be how it works for me. When they're gone—Senneth and the others—I can still feel them. I know if they're safe, if they're afraid, if they're hurt. It doesn't matter how far away they are. As long as they're in Gillengaria, I can hear them." He kissed her again. "I was thinking I would have to sail to Arberharst if I wanted to get you out of my heart. Or, well, not Arberharst anymore, I suppose. Karyndein or Sovenfeld. Somewhere so distant that even your memories couldn't follow me."

"I don't want you to go that far," she said. "I don't want you to go at all."

He hugged her closer, feeling both elated and hopeless. *She loves me* warred with *I still can't have her*. "There are no answers, not now," he said quietly. "Maybe when the war ends, the world will have changed. Or maybe we will both just be so glad to be alive that we will be able to stand it better, whatever happens next. But, Amalie, as long as you want me with you, I will stay. And if ever you want me to go, I will go. I love you. For now, at least, maybe that's enough."

For her it was. She lifted her mouth and kissed him again, straining against him as if trying to meld her body to his. Death and destruction loomed immediately ahead; separation and heartbreak lay inevitably beyond. But, for tonight, there was no course open to them but to prove their fealty by making love. They feverishly pulled off their own clothes and each other's—laughed to see Amalie's dagger still tightly buckled to her leg—and sprawled on the floor, tangled together, swearing vows and whispering each other's names. The moon watched through the window; the raelynx, asleep at the hearth, did not seem to notice at all. But Cammon wondered, just before he fell asleep, how many other gods had tiptoed through the room, offering or withholding their blessings. Surely whichever goddess watched over him must be celebrating tonight; surely she was moved by honest emotion and unguarded passion. Surely she would want to grant her most dutiful acolyte his heart's desire.

IN the morning, the troops moved out, ranks of royal soldiers marching beside borrowed fighters from Merrenstow, Kianlever, and Helven. Amalie rode at the head of the army, Cammon and Valri on either side of her, Riders in a ring around them. Romar Brendyn, acting as commander, followed shortly behind her. The raelynx traveled near Amalie, sometimes roaming far ahead, always returning when she called it to her side. Sometimes Cammon saw three raelynxes bounding along beside them— sometimes a raelynx, a wolf, and a lion. Donnal and Kirra, choosing to accompany the army in animal form.

The lead Rider carried a two-tiered standard: the royal flag, a gold lion splashed on a black field; and a new device that Amalie had adopted as her own, a red raelynx rampant on a gold background. The Queen's Riders wore new sashes that alternated lions and raelynxes. Even some of the common soldiers had tied scarlet scarves around their arms or braided crimson ribbons into the manes of their horses. They were the princess's army; they were riding to protect her.

A small regiment had stayed behind under the command of Tayse, to engage and distract the enemy troops as they advanced on Ghosenhall. Justin and two other Riders had also joined this perilous venture.

Senneth and Ellynor waited with them.

CHAPTER
33

$\mathcal{S}$ENNETH knew it was risky, of course. They might all die. But Justin and Tayse had spent hours planning an ambush, an escape route, and an alternate plan. They seemed to think they could inflict some damage on the oncoming army, then whisk their troops away with a minimum of loss.

Tayse had been less than thrilled with Senneth's plan to confront Halchon Gisseltess.

"I won't let him near enough to touch me," she said. Something about his skin, his body, was anathema to her. She could not call fire, she almost could not summon rational thought, if he had any physical contact with her. She wondered sometimes if he possessed a peculiar magic, a kind that rendered other kinds of magic inoperable, and if so, what kind of strange god might watch over such a man. "But I think we need to take one last chance to try to bargain with him."

Predictably, Justin's comment had been, "The only bargain he understands is a blade through the heart."

"It will come to that, no doubt," she said. "But I feel compelled to try."

They had learned quite by accident that the Arberharst men were not immune to Lirren magic. Only a handful of attackers had survived the assault on the palace, and a few had been so wounded that they could not be expected to live through the night. Kirra had been unable to heal them, but Ellynor had brought two of them back from the brink of death. She had then made herself invisible in order to eavesdrop on the manner in which Romar Brendyn questioned the enemy soldiers. "Because if he tortured them, I wasn't going to help him again, and I'd let him know that," she confessed to Senneth. Romar hadn't seen her there—but neither had the soldiers from Arberharst.

And that had gotten Senneth to thinking.

They laid their trap a few miles outside the city limits, on a low stretch of road that Justin called a natural ambush, since it passed between high ridges on either side. They had barely a day to wait before their scout came racing back to pant out that the armies were only a few hours behind him.

Senneth didn't think she had quite prepared herself for the sight of ten thousand men advancing to war.

They made one undulating, multicolored river of motion, ten men across and a thousand men deep. The three armies had blended into one, but she could still discern pockets of soldiers who rode with hundreds of their fellows—Lumanen guards dressed in black and silver, for instance, or Gisseltess men in black and red. It was no surprise, she thought, to find among the enemy troops rows of men wearing the topaz sash of Storian. The blue uniforms of the Arberharst soldiers, several thousand all told, were scattered throughout the Gillengaria masses. A deliberate move on Halchon's part, Senneth thought with grudging admiration; he knew the foreign recruits were much less likely to be affected by homegrown magic.

But today that decision would work against them.

Senneth, Tayse, and their small force hid on top of the northern-most hill, watching the army march closer. An advance guard of perhaps twenty men led the way, carrying the flags of all three armies. Behind them rode the heads of this villainous alliance: Rayson Fortunalt, a florid, heavyset man with small eyes and a perpetually sneering expression; Halchon Gisseltess, square-faced, dark-haired, powerfully built, and purpose-ful; and Coralinda Gisseltess, whose black-and-silver hair mirrored her flag, her cloak, the colors of her goddess. She looked like an older, smaller version of her brother—no less purposeful, no less powerful. Senneth could not remember the last time she had seen them together, though she vividly recalled her last few meetings with each of them, and none of those memories gave her pleasure.

Senneth could pick out the small red flowers on Halchon's vest before Tayse turned to her and gave a small nod. *Now.*

She balled her hands into fists, then spread her fingers wide. A wall of flame leapt up in the middle of the road.

Horses screamed; men shouted. There was a terrific clamor of confu-sion. Above it all she could hear Halchon's voice calling out, "Stay calm! It is sorcery! Halt your horses! Stay calm!"

As if she was lifting a long, unwieldy boulder, Senneth slowly raised her arms, palms upward, fingers splayed. The flames whipped higher and began to travel, racing back along both sides of the massed men, follow-ing that endless line of oncoming soldiers. More shrieks, more sounds of struggling horses. It was impossible to see through the coruscating flame, but she could hear the clang of swords and shields. Blades drawn, no enemy to fight but fire.

A line of blue-clad soldiers galloped through the orange wall, weapons raised, bodies unharmed. Emboldened, a few Gillengaria men attempted to follow. Senneth heard their shouts of pain, the wild stomping of their horses' hooves. Three of them burst through the fire, their uniforms alight, their horses wild with terror. They each used one hand to beat out the flames, one hand to grasp their swords.

The defenders flowed downhill from their hiding place. Every enemy who broke through the wall was met head-on by a Rider or a royal soldier.

The conflicts were quick and decisive, always favoring the defenders, for, while combatants trickled through, royal soldiers had the numerical advantage. Senneth could hear Halchon shouting again, hear Rayson's furious questions. "What's happening? Who's fighting? Call them back!" But still more Arberharst soldiers worked their way past the fire. About fifteen cantered up from the rear ranks of the army, ready to engage. A few more Gillengaria soldiers staggered through, scorched but determined.

All of them were cut down.

Finally, after a bloody hour of combat, no more soldiers attempted to breach the wall. The Riders and the royal soldiers still sprawled across the road, waiting for another assault, but for the moment, all was quiet.

Senneth cupped her hands around her mouth and called out, "Marlord Halchon! I would have a conference with you!"

There was a moment of silence while she imagined Halchon first cursing her name, then wondering how he might turn this confrontation to his advantage. "Serra Senneth," he shouted back. "I would be delighted to parley. I do not particularly wish to be incinerated in my attempts to communicate with you, however."

"If you will agree to meet under a flag of truce, I will rescind my flame. There is a place two miles ahead of you on this road. Come alone to meet me there in one hour. Leave the rest of your army where it stands."

"I am not fool enough to come by myself."

Tayse had practically scripted this for her. "How many men will make you feel safe?"

"How many are in your army?"

"Bring no more than twenty," she said. "Otherwise, we have no deal."

"I will agree to that. When do you put out the fire? Our horses are ready to bolt."

"I will douse the flames when we have withdrawn to our position."

"I will see you in one hour, then," he said.

This first part had been tricky; the next part would be trickier still. Coeval led most of their troops toward an agreed-upon rendezvous some distance past Ghosenhall. Tayse, Justin, Senneth, Ellynor, and about twenty men moved up the road to the second spot they had chosen. Again, they had commandeered the high ground, arranging themselves on a hillock that brushed against the road. Still on horseback, Senneth took a position close enough to the road to allow her to speak more or less comfortably to any traveler passing by. Justin, Tayse, and the other soldiers deployed behind her, weapons out. Ellynor cloaked herself in darkness and pulled her mount so close that Senneth could feel the animal's body heat—though she couldn't see the Lirren girl at all.

With a lot of effort and a bit of luck, Senneth could turn herself invisible, too—but she had the uneasy feeling Halchon would not be fooled by her spell. For this maneuver, she wanted to take no chances.

Halchon Gisseltess and a small escort arrived precisely at the appointed time.

"That's near enough," Senneth called when he was fifty feet away. He lifted a hand and his riders came to a tidy halt.

"Senneth," he said, and his beautiful voice was warm with pleasure. "I am, as always, delighted at the chance to visit with you, though I must confess this venue is not entirely as civilized as I would like."

"Uncivilized men must make do with the opportunities afforded to them," she said.

He laughed softly. "Come, did you separate me from my army merely to insult me? Surely not. What offer do you have to make? Or what appeal?"

"The king is dead, you know," she said baldly. "But Amalie still lives. What bargain would you strike to end this here, now, before another death is recorded?"

"You know my terms," he said. "I want to be king. Amalie may abdicate in my favor."

"You would make a very bad king," Senneth said, shaking her head. "I fear you would destroy Gillengaria within a year of taking the throne. A man who uses violence to attain his ends will use violence to enforce his will."

"Richly ironic, coming from a woman who herself married a soldier."

"He fights to defend. You fight to acquire. Those are two very different things."

"Spare me the philosophy, Senneth. I want to be king. Hand me the crown and I will dismantle the armies."

"Surely there are other solutions," she said. She felt like a traitor even as she said it, but the next option had to be presented. "There might be a man of Gisseltess whom you would be glad to support as a suitor to the princess. A marriage between Ghosenhall and Gissel Plain would afford you some of the power you crave."

He appeared to reflect. "My oldest son is almost fourteen. Not a bad match for a nineteen-year-old girl, and a fine one in a few years' time."

She should have expected that, and she tried not to let her revulsion show. "I cannot broker a marriage on Amalie's behalf but I *can* promise that she will consider him, and will meet him with an honest and true heart."

Halchon's smile turned into a leer. "But here's a possibility that brings me even closer to the throne," he said. "My own wife is missing. *I'll* wed the princess and rule Gillengaria at her side."

She couldn't repress her gasp. "No! Amalie would rather die."

He laughed at her. "Just because *you* would rather die than come to my bed doesn't mean every woman feels the same way."

"Then *I* would rather see her dead or dispossessed than have to endure your touch for half an hour," she retorted. "There might be a chance you could put your son forward and have him considered as a candidate. But if *you* are the only suitor from Gisseltess, I can promise you no marriage will occur."

He was still intensely amused. "But I need a wife, Senneth, now that the bitch who bore my sons has run off—finding shelter with *your* brothers, if the gossip I hear is true. You owe me for that, I believe, for I know you were instrumental in her escape. I have made you this offer before. Become my wife. My son will marry Amalie. Together we will offer the young king and queen our seasoned counsel and our loving example. That would satisfy me, I think. That would cause me to lay down my arms."

Tayse hadn't said a word, and she doubted if his stony face had showed any change of expression, but she could feel the fury radiating from his coiled body. Forcing herself to speak calmly, she said, "I have a husband. And am not inclined to shed him for convenience's sake."

"But, Senneth," Halchon purred, "he could so easily be dead."

Behind the Riders, someone shouted. Suddenly there was the pound of hooves, the scrape of swords. "Behind us!" one of the royal soldiers cried out, and then there was a furious clash of weapons. Halchon raised his arm and drove his fist through the air, and the men with him charged toward the hill.

Wheeling her horse around, Senneth reached out a wild hand and felt Ellynor's fingers close around her wrist. She heard the cries of astonishment behind them, which meant she must have disappeared from view as completely as she'd hoped. Unseen, she and Ellynor swept up the hill and through the ranks of defenders. A line of enemy soldiers had crept up behind them while Halchon and Senneth engaged in insulting debate—just as Tayse had predicted.

"Leave them! Follow me!" Senneth cried, though, of course, none of the defenders could *see* her to follow. But they all managed one or two more devastating blows, then turned their horses and came thundering after Ellynor and Senneth. They had identified a low tumble of shrubbery as a meeting spot, and the two women reached it half a minute before the others. Ellynor released Senneth and muttered something that Senneth hoped meant an expansion of her magic. For a moment, they waited, strung with tension, holding their horses ready to gallop forward again. Their own soldiers plowed into the rendezvous point at a dead run, the attackers hard on their heels, and they all plunged forward again at a headlong pace. Only now their whole group was invisible.

Behind them, again, sounded more cries of confusion and fury. Senneth could hear Halchon's voice. "You fools! It's magic again! After them, after them!" There was the sound of tentative pursuit, but the hoofbeats were slower, the riders clearly mystified.

"Which way? Straight ahead?"

"What kind of magic is this? Fire and—and—vanishing? There's no sorcery like that in Arberharst."

"Quiet! Can you hear hoofbeats?"

"There—I think—something crashed through that line of bushes."

The attackers charged after them, but too late, too disorganized, too uncertain. Senneth and her escort drew away as rapidly as they could, flinging themselves toward the larger band of soldiers waiting on the other side of Ghosenhall.

The enemies could not see them, but inside Ellynor's protective circle, they could not see each other, either. They had not had much time to practice how they would ride close together at a very fast pace without treading all over each other. It was also difficult to see *out* of the dark haze Ellynor had summoned to hide them. Fortunately, the horses seemed less spooked than the humans. Maybe nothing was changed to them, Senneth thought. Maybe their eyes were so different that they were not blinded by magic.

She heard a big-boned animal edging ahead and, even before the rider spoke, guessed it was Tayse moving to the lead. "Answer quietly," he called in a low voice, "but everyone sound off."

"Justin" was the immediate first response.

"Senneth."

"Ellynor."

The other soldiers reeled off their names. Senneth spared a moment to wonder, almost hysterically, whether an enemy soldier had managed to infiltrate their ranks and was even now continuing along invisibly with them, clever enough to remain silent during this roll call. She could not imagine such a spy would long survive the dissipation of magic.

"Anyone injured?"

There was a chorus of no's.

"I think that went superbly!" Senneth exclaimed, allowing herself a moment of exuberance even while she was fleeing for her life. "We surprised them, we destroyed a few of their men, we confused them, and we escaped!"

"And we learned something else," Ellynor added. She sounded a little breathless. Senneth wondered how much energy she was expending to wrap twenty-five individuals in a cloak of darkness. And what kind of headache Ellynor might have when it was all done. Senneth's own skull was echoing with each hoofbeat, but on the whole she didn't feel as bad as she had at Danan Hall. She'd managed to keep her anger in check; that was always the key to enduring the most punishing spells. "Even Halchon Gisseltess cannot penetrate Lirren magic."

"I don't think I handled him very well, though," Senneth added. She sighed and tightened her hand on the reins. "I never do."

"I couldn't decide which of his offers was more attractive," Tayse said, his voice smooth but his anger palpable. "The one to marry Amalie or the one to marry you."

Senneth sighed again. "If I cannot bring myself to marry him to avert a war, I cannot ask her to marry one of his surely repulsive sons for the same reason. I think, 'Gods, the lives that could be saved!' And yet—and yet—"

"And yet Gillengaria would die a slow death under his reign," Tayse said firmly. "I absolutely believe it."

"Well, he would have killed all of us just now if he could have, even though he had agreed to parley in peace," Justin said practically. "That gives you some idea of the promises he would make and keep if he became king."

"He is not going to be king," Tayse said. "That is why we are going to war."

ELLYNOR had lifted her magic by the time they met up with Coeval and the others. Justin, Senneth was interested to see, had somehow managed to locate Ellynor despite the inconvenience of not being able to see her and was now riding beside her. He caught Senneth's eyes on him and grinned.

"All well here?" Tayse asked Coeval.

"Yes. You?"

"As planned. Let's break for a meal and ride out."

Senneth was glad she didn't have to rely solely on Riders for her conversation.

They were on their way again in fifteen minutes, traveling at a steady but somewhat less brutal pace. As always, Tayse rode ahead of the column to scout for trouble, and Justin dropped behind to watch their back trail. What was new was that Ellynor stayed with Justin. Senneth smiled to watch them until they abruptly winked from view. An even more effective rear guard, she thought—an invisible one. No chance any enemy would catch them unaware.

They rode late, camped for only long enough to give the horses a rest, then were on their way again before dawn. Senneth felt bleary-eyed and dull-minded, and her headache hadn't been helped much by the insufficient sleep. A few of the royal soldiers were yawning in their saddles, and Ellynor looked about as weary as Senneth felt. But none of the Riders appeared fatigued, and no one else dared complain.

Two more days of traveling, two more nights of uncomfortable and oh-so-brief repose. "Do Riders never sleep?" Senneth demanded of Tayse the next morning before he kicked his horse ahead of the rest.

He affected surprise. "Weren't you just sleeping? For at least three hours?"

"I will be too tired to make a fire, and then you'll regret your haste."

He smiled. "An army moves slowly, but it will be moving all the same," he said. "I want to join up with our own forces while there is time to prepare."

"We're a day ahead of Halchon by now, surely."

He shook his head. "Maybe. We can't count on more than twelve hours."

"Then let's ride."

But she cheered considerably a little before noon when two spring hawks spiraled down out of the sky and landed gracefully alongside the road. Senneth pulled her horse aside and waited as Kirra and Donnal materialized.

"Tayse pauses for no one, so tell me your news quickly so I can catch up," she greeted them. The rest of the soldiers had already moved past her, traveling at a steady clip.

Donnal grinned. "I don't have anything to tell, but Kirra wants to visit." In his breathtakingly rapid fashion, he transformed himself into a sleek black horse, complete with reins and saddle, and Kirra swung herself onto his back.

"*You* look bedraggled and cranky," she observed cheerfully as they jogged after the others. "Is that the result of hard travel or a failed mission?"

"Hard travel," Senneth answered sourly. "Please tell me we're close to Amalie, so I can lay down my head and die."

Kirra laughed. "Another hour away, perhaps. Cammon told us you were near, so Donnal and I came to greet you."

"And is our army deployed?"

Kirra nodded. "Acres and acres of soldiers. The Brassenthwaite troops found us yesterday, and Kiernan and Harris arrived straight from Danan Hall. Good news, though, you'll only have to deal with one of your brothers, since Kiernan is about to send Harris back to Brassen Court to assist Nate. Romar's got everyone very nicely organized—or so it seems to me, but you know battle strategy isn't my strong suit—and you'll like *this* a great deal. He's ordered Cammon to stay with Amalie at all times in some little pavilion they've set up at the back of camp. But, of course, the regent wants to be on the front line, and he wants to communicate with Amalie—and he wants to communicate with Kiernan, and the captain of the Kianlever guard—and how do you think he proposes to do that?"

"Magic," Senneth said.

"Magic, indeed! Romar has conscripted your old friend Jerril, who doesn't seem to quite know what's happened to him, and Jerril's parceled out the Carrebos mystics who are particularly strong readers. None of them is as good as Cammon, of course, but *he* can hear all of them, and they can hear *him*, so he has been practicing relaying complicated messages all across the battlefield. We'll see how well that holds in the stress of combat," she added, "but it does seem like an advantage Halchon won't have."

"He has plenty of others," Senneth said gloomily. "A few thousand Arberharst soldiers, for instance, who can ride right through my fires."

"But they couldn't see Ellynor, could they?"

Senneth brightened. "No."

"Then you'll like this news, too. This morning another couple hundred recruits showed up—from the Lirrens."

Senneth felt both excitement and dread at that news. "Really! That's wonderful—and terrible. If the Lirren men fall in a war that is not their own—"

"Donnal and I watched a few of them take an hour's combat practice," Kirra interrupted. "I can't imagine any of them falling. Donnal said they're not as good as Riders, but, Wild Mother watch me, they were pretty damn close."

"I wonder if Ellynor's brother is among them," Senneth said. "I met him—I liked him—but what a brash young man he is."

Kirra was grinning, and her blue eyes were alight with mischief. "Oh, her brother is here—two of her brothers—but what's even more significant is that her *cousin* has also ridden to war."

"Significant why?"

"Apparently Valri had something of a history with this young man before she crossed the Lireth Mountains and got herself named queen," Kirra drawled.

"*Really!* A broken romance in Valri's past! Well, it's almost worth going to war to see how this will play out."

Donnal tossed up his head till his mane flew, offering an equine laugh.

"Now all we have to do is hope Halchon dies in battle so that your brother Nate can marry Sabina Gisseltess, and everyone will be happy."

"Oh, I forgot to mention it. Halchon and I managed a brief exchange of civilities just before Ellynor made us all vanish and we went racing off to find you," Senneth said in a hard, bright voice.

"Did he renew his offer of marriage to you?"

"He did. Though when he thought about it, he decided it would put him closer to the throne to marry Amalie instead."

Kirra choked and then pantomimed gagging over Donnal's shoulder. "Someone really has to kill him," she said when she had recovered.

"If he ever gets close enough to Tayse, I think it'll happen," Senneth said.

"And Coralinda? Was she there?"

"I saw her at the head of the troops, but I didn't attempt any conversation," Senneth said. "I sometimes wonder how that would work, you know. Halchon wants to marry me, but his sister wants to kill me. Do you suppose I would be murdered on my wedding day?"

"Well, many women equate marriage and death," Kirra said blithely. "Why should you be different?"

That made Senneth laugh so hard that she almost gave up on conversation altogether.

Half an hour later, they came upon the royal armies of Gillengaria.

The sight was truly impressive, Senneth acknowledged, reining up to get a good look at the ranks of soldiers spread out over the rocky plains south of Brassenthwaite. Halchon might have assembled more men, but somehow these looked more beautiful to her—more earnest, more righteous, more passionate, more invincible. They were arranged by affiliation, grouped under their individual banners. The royal soldiers in their black-and-gold uniforms were deployed in the front. Behind them were the Brassenthwaite soldiers in dark blue, Merrenstow men with their black-and-white checkerboard sashes, Helven troops in their green and gold, Kianlever troops wearing sashes of plaited blue and green. Amid this welter of tents and banners, Senneth could not immediately pick out the royal pavilion, the cluster of Lirren warriors, the small blocks of mercenaries and individuals who always showed up for battles, offering their swords. She just saw the grand spectacle of an army preparing itself for war. It was the most awe-inspiring, the most heartbreaking display she had ever seen.

CHAPTER
34

AND then war came.

Spies had ridden in every hour to update the regent on the position of the enemy forces, but for days before they actually arrived Cammon had felt the march of thousands of feet. There were too many—he could not sort most of them into individuals—but a few broke through and made distinct patterns in his mind. Coralinda Gisseltess was as clear to him as if she stalked through the royal camp, her long black-and-silver braid streaming down her back. Twice he thought he actually saw her, standing amid the ranks of Riders, glancing around, counting up men. When he looked more closely, she was gone.

He did not have nearly as clear a picture of Halchon Gisseltess, but the force of the marlord's desire was so strong he projected an intense and smoldering hunger, and Cammon was always aware of him.

There were others—possibly Rayson Fortunalt, possibly some of the captains of the various armies, or maybe just particularly fervent soldiers who lived for battle. Except for tracking how close the army was coming, Cammon tried to shut them all out.

And then the soldiers arrived, and it was impossible to think, to feel, to know anything except violence and rage.

That first day was horrific. He and Amalie had promised Romar that they would stay far behind the line of combat, and so they loitered near the pavilion that had been set up to accommodate the princess. Amalie could not sit still. She paced through the sprays of new grass, she swung herself onto one of the horses that had been saddled for her—in case she needed to make a hasty escape—and tried to force her eyes to understand the ebb and flow on the battlefield.

"What's happening now?" she asked him every three minutes, jumping back to the ground.

He told her what he could piece together, but there was an onslaught in his head. Nightmare images chased each other through his mind—bloody swords, crashing bodies, horses trampling inert forms, whole lines of men giving way to a berserker wedge of attackers. He could not always be sure who was the enemy, who was the friend. He could not tell who was falling, who was fighting back. Battle lust settled like a red mist over both gathered armies; it was impossible to distinguish between them.

His responses were incomplete and halting. "Your uncle has successfully beaten back an attack. . . . Tayse is surrounded on all sides—no, Justin is there to aid him. . . . A troop of Brassenthwaite men is giving way to an assault from—I'm not sure—it must be the soldiers from Arberharst. . . ."

"But are we winning? Are we losing?" she demanded.

He shook his head. "I don't know. I can't tell."

Frequently he heard Jerril's voice in his head, strangely composed, conveying information from Romar to Amalie. Once he received an urgent but shaky message from the mystic assigned to Kiernan Brassenthwaite, sending an alarm about a flanking maneuver that was allowing enemy soldiers to breach a thin line of defense. Cammon didn't know how to respond, so he broadcast the cry for help to all the Riders. He felt Justin and Tayse charge through the clashing ranks of soldiers and instantly engage.

He got no more pleas from Kiernan Brassenthwaite.

"What's happening now?" Amalie asked a few minutes later.

"Riders have redeployed on the—the north side, I think. Holding the line there."

"Where's Senneth?"

He pointed. "There's another spout of fire."

Senneth's day had been as rough and disjointed as Cammon's. He could feel her frustration, her exhaustion, and her fury, all rolled into a hot ball of magic. She had known that her form of sorcery would only work intermittently on this particular foe, but he could tell she had hoped to have more success. Almost certainly in a move to thwart her, the Arberharst men had been strategically interwoven with the Gisseltess and Fortunalt forces; their imperviousness to magic had made it very hard for her mystic fires to take hold. Early in the battle, she had conjured up a line of flame right through the middle of the oncoming enemies, and that had caused turmoil for a short time. Yet somehow the Arberharst men were able to put the fire out, or hold the fire back—they created portals in the conflagration that allowed Gillengaria soldiers to pour through. So she let that fire die down, studied her ground, and flung up another one a half acre away.

Again, it was effective only briefly; again, the imported soldiers were able to beat it back just enough to open safe passage for native men.

She didn't give up, though. Circling dangerously close to the front lines, she continued to fling fire randomly into the ranks of soldiers. Twice she was able to locate supply wagons that held only domestic grains and rations, and these she sent burning to the ground. More than once she isolated pockets of Fortunalt men, or Storian soldiers, and surrounded them with walls of weaving fire; many went screaming to their deaths.

But the effort was immense, and Cammon could feel her losing energy and strength as the awful day progressed. She could sustain a single fire for hours, but she was not used to having to call up fresh flames over and over. Cammon almost thought that she felt every stamping foot, every suffocating hand, as the Arberharst soldiers doused her fires. For her, it was a battle as physical and draining as a duel with swords.

"Where's Donnal? Where's Kirra?" Amalie wanted to know.

"At the back of the enemy army. They're taking out men one by one. Kirra's a lioness. Donnal's a wolf. They've backed off a little, though—someone must have spotted them. That means someone's defending the rear of the army."

Both of them glanced at the raelynx, sitting at the edge of the pavilion in an alert position. Its narrow red face pointed straight toward the battle; its expressive tail slowly twitched from side to side.

"I'm afraid to let him loose," Amalie said softly. "I'm not sure he can tell who is protecting me and who is endangering me. And I can't direct him from this far away."

"I think your uncle would prefer that you keep him beside you," Cammon said. "In case any enemies break through and get close."

She nodded, but she looked haunted. If enemies drew that close, they had surely lost already.

"Where are the Lirren men? Can you tell?"

That made him smile. "No! But about half an hour ago, I felt this—this outpouring of terror and surprise from a troop of Fortunalt men. I think the Lirren contingent had crept around to one side of the attacking army and just began slaughtering soldiers. No one saw them coming." His smile faded, for emotions in that particular skirmish had been so strong that he had felt almost every blade and blow. "They killed a lot of men."

Amalie's face tightened. "Good." Then she turned away and swung herself back up into the mare's saddle.

There was no need to ask where Ellynor was. They had set up a hospital of sorts off to one side, and it was staffed by Ellynor, Valri, and a couple of the Carrebos mystics. Any wounded soldiers whole enough to move had staggered back there as the day wore on, and Ellynor had called upon her midnight goddess to help her heal them. Another few dozen, closer to dead, had been carried back by their bloodied comrades. Hundreds more still lay in the trampled fields, because no one could reach them, or because no one had time to drag them to shelter.

"I can't see anything," Amalie said impatiently, and slid out of the saddle. "What's happening now?"

That was how the entire day went.

THEY convened in Amalie's pavilion that night, when it was too dark to fight, when both armies had withdrawn to count their losses, see to their wounded, and revise their strategies. Cammon thought "pavilion" was a grand word for a rather large tent erected over a raised wooden floor. There was a low bed, a washstand, a brazier, a few tall stools, and a pile of rugs on the floor to blunt the chill from the ground. Still, on the battlefield, this space constituted civilization, and so here they gathered: Tayse, Justin, Senneth, Valri, Kiernan, Romar, and Romar's captain, Colton.

"Could have gone worse," was Kiernan's terse assessment.

"Could have gone better," Romar shot back. "We lost a platoon of men in that flanking maneuver!"

Kiernan shrugged. "Would have lost half the camp if we hadn't been able to communicate." He nodded in Cammon's direction. "Mark my words, that boy's going to keep us in this game no matter what the odds."

"What were our losses?" Amalie asked.

Colton reeled them off. Hundreds dead, more wounded. Cammon saw Amalie flinch at the totals.

"Brassenthwaite suffered the heaviest casualties," Romar said. "So tomorrow we redistribute the forces. I will put some Merrenstow soldiers under your command."

"Let's discuss strategy," Tayse said. "Can we expect a similar straightforward assault tomorrow as well, or do you think they'll try a different approach?"

"I'd guess they'll come at us straight on for another few days," Kiernan said coolly. "Wear us down first through sheer numbers. When we're weary and whittled down, then they'll try new tactics."

"I agree," Romar said. "I expect our approach tomorrow should be much as it was today. Form a line, hold fast, and disrupt them where we can."

Kiernan nodded at his sister. Senneth had taken a seat on the floor and leaned her head against the low mattress. Cammon could feel the pain in her skull as if it was inside his own. "Can you perform more of the same tricks tomorrow?" Kiernan asked her. "I don't know how many days in a row mystics can call on their magic."

"I can," Senneth said, her voice hollow. "But I am disappointed to have had so little effect."

"Well, you had a lot of effect as far as I could tell," Justin answered. "I just looked for your flames and then I led a charge in. The other soldiers were so confused by the fire that we were able to cut down a dozen with hardly a fight."

"What heartening news," Senneth said. Cammon could read the struggle going on in her head. *I am using my magic to kill men, something I never wanted to do. But how can I let Halchon Gisseltess usurp Amalie's throne?* Not as coherent as that.

"You might conserve your power," Tayse suggested in a grave voice. "We do not want you wan and wasted by pouring out all your magic in a single day."

"Can that happen?" Kiernan demanded. "You're one of our most potent weapons. We do not want you rendered useless in case we need you later."

"I'll strive to bear that in mind," she replied. "I will use flame only judiciously tomorrow."

Romar pointed at Tayse. "What about the Riders? Our other impressive weapons. What damages did you sustain?"

Tayse shook his head. "None."

Romar nodded. "Then the first day did not go so ill after all."

They talked awhile longer, but Kiernan and Romar had plenty of other business to occupy them, and they soon ducked out through the door flap of the tent, Colton behind them. Cammon, who had been sitting next to Amalie on one of the stools, rolled to the floor beside Senneth and peered up into her face. Her eyes were closed, and she was practically gray with exhaustion.

"Go somewhere and sleep," he told her. "You look ready to disintegrate."

"Head hurts too much to sleep," she mumbled. "And I need to eat something. Or I really won't be able to function tomorrow."

Tayse dropped to the floor on her other side and pulled her against him. "I'll work on your headache," he said. "Cammon, maybe you could see about getting us food?"

"It's been ordered," Amalie said. "I thought you would all come here so I—"

She hadn't finished the sentence when Kirra poked her head through the tent flap. "Is it safe to join you? All done talking strategy?"

"The regent's gone, if that's what you're asking," Cammon said.

She made a face at him, then came inside. She was carrying a tray of food, and Donnal, behind her, carried another. A cook came in bearing pitchers of water. Kirra glanced around, but there was no table large enough to hold everything, so she shrugged and laid her burden on the floor. The others followed suit.

"Eat," she said. "Justin, I've already had the cooks take a tray to Ellynor. She told me that whenever she performs a great deal of healing, she's absolutely starving."

He was biting off a huge chunk of bread, but he nodded. "I'll go to her as soon as we're done here and try to get her to sleep tonight," he said. "But my guess is she won't leave the wounded."

Kirra nodded. "Senneth, what should I do?" she asked. "Return to the battlefield and fight, or stay with Ellynor tomorrow and heal?"

Senneth was lax in Tayse's arms; her face was loose with relief. His hands had chased away at least most of the pain, Cammon thought. "Ask Valri," she said.

The dark queen stirred, though she had been so quiet during the earlier conference that it had almost been possible for Cammon to forget she was there. Almost. "There are more wounded than we can care for, Ellynor and I and those other mystics. We could use your magic."

Kirra nodded and glanced at Donnal. "Then if I'm not with you, you have to be particularly careful tomorrow."

He grinned at her, his teeth white through his dark beard. "Serra, I always am."

Cammon scooted across the rugs till he was beside Amalie's stool again. "Majesty, you must eat," he said.

She shook her head. "No, I—I think I'll throw up if I do." She glanced around the tent, her face apologetic, tears welling up. "I'm sorry. I know—I know it was much worse for all of you today. But I—these terrible things—and people *dying*—and more people dying tomorrow, and I—I feel so much at fault. People are dying for *me*. And with a few words, I could stop it, I could say, 'Very well, I give it all up. Here is the crown, I will sail for Karyndein tomorrow.' "

"And the armies who have gathered in your name will be leaderless and lost, and have no will to fight, and Halchon Gisseltess's men will swoop in and slaughter them all," Tayse said quietly, speaking over Senneth's shoulder. "Because marlord Halchon will never trust a Brassenthwaite man, or a Helven man, or a Kianlever man, and he will find it easier to dispose of them now than to let them disperse back to their Houses and plot against him once he's on the throne."

Valri nodded sorrowfully. "One of the reasons I left the Lirrens was because there was so much conflict between the clans," she said. "So many feuds between families—all of them pointless. But, Amalie, I believe there are times you must defend not only what is yours, but what you have been called upon to protect. Gillengaria has been put in trust for you—the land is your responsibility. You think you could save it by walking away, but instead you would betray it. And I know you could never bring yourself to do that."

Amalie sniffled and shook her head and looked around for a handkerchief. No one had one immediately handy, so she sniffled again. "No. I won't. I'll be strong. I just—I want to be strong in whichever way is *right*."

Kirra leaned over and handed her a square of lace and cotton, clearly manufactured on the spot. "Here. Blow your nose on that. And I'll calm your stomach so you can handle food. You need to eat, Majesty. We all do. We have another grueling day ahead of us tomorrow."

THEY dispersed quickly enough after the meal, some of them instantly seeking their beds. Cammon had hoped Amalie, too, would try to sleep for a while, but she said, "I want to go with Justin to see the wounded." Naturally, Cammon accompanied her, and Kirra came with them.

The hospital consisted of two tents, each about the size of Amalie's, and a few acres staked out by a fence of slow-burning torches. The light was poor, but this wasn't a sight that invited close inspection. The gravely wounded were housed in the tents, both of which glowed with their own interior firelight. Those who needed less care had been assigned pallets on the ground outside. There were hundreds of them.

Moving through the rows of injured men was almost as bad as watching the battle itself, Cammon thought. All of them, *all* of them, were wracked with pain, horrified by memories, nauseated, wretched, afraid. Some were thirsty, some were delirious, some were desperate—and even those who lay on their blankets mute and miserable seemed to be yelling and moaning in Cammon's ears. There was a clamor in his brain; he held his breath and tried to shut down, close them out, but they were still hammering at the edges of his mind.

"Sweet gods," Kirra muttered, and just sank to the ground beside one of the suffering soldiers. She put her hand on his forehead and spoke a few words. Cammon felt the shouting in his head grow quieter by a single voice.

Justin glanced around. "I thought we brought Ghosenhall doctors with us, as well as mystics."

"We did," Amalie said in a soft voice. "I expect they're in the tents with the men who are the worst off."

"Well, I'll go see if they need any help holding down someone who needs surgery," Justin said, and picked his way carefully through the bodies.

Amalie stood still for a moment, as if gathering her strength, and then stepped up purposefully to one of the wounded men. "What's your name, soldier?" she asked, bending over to see his face better in the bad light. A lock of her red-gold hair fell over her shoulder and brushed his cheek.

The soldier opened his eyes. He looked about Cammon's age, but beefier and rougher. His eyebrows were knitted together in pain, but when he saw the princess stooped over him, his expression cleared and he seemed touched by awe. "Majesty," he whispered. "You came to see us."

"I did. Tell me your name."

"Benton, Majesty."

"I'm proud of you, Benton. You fought well for me today. I am lucky to have soldiers like you in my army."

"Majesty, I was glad to fight."

The man was filthy, and streaks of blood still colored his face, but Amalie impulsively put her palm against his cheek. "Heal quickly," she said in her soft voice. "May your pain be gone."

As if he were that soldier lying on the ground, Cammon sensed the heat of her touch, experienced a jolt of magic along his bones, a golden sparkle, then darkness. Benton's voice was thick with wonder. "Thank you, Majesty."

She nodded, straightened up, and moved to the next bed. Again, she asked for the soldier's name; again, she laid her hand against his skin and offered a quiet benediction. Again, Cammon felt that flare of magic, felt the pain ease back, grow tamer, more bearable. This soldier turned his head and pressed his lips against her wrist. "Thank you, Majesty," he whispered.

At the third pallet, it was the same. At the fourth, Cammon caught her before she could speak to the soldier. "Amalie, what are you doing?" he murmured in her ear.

She turned toward him; the footing was so tricky that she practically had to lean against him to reply. "What do you mean?"

She didn't even *realize* it. "Your touch. It's acting like a narcotic. You're taking away the pain—and I think you're helping the healing begin. You're dusting them with magic and it's having a true effect."

She was pleased. "Really? Is that why my hands tingle?"

"How did you learn to do that?"

"I don't know. I saw Kirra lay her hands on a soldier's face, so I thought I would just try it. I didn't think it would do any good."

He was indecisive. "I don't want you to wear yourself down, using up magic you don't even know you have."

"Yes, but if I can give a few soldiers some comfort—after they have earned their wounds fighting for *me!*—I should do that, don't you think? For as many as I can?"

"Maybe for the ones who hurt the most."

She glanced around. "How can I tell that?"

He smiled a little grimly. "Oh, I can help you there." He thought a moment. "Give me your pendant."

Willingly, she reached up to unclasp it, but her expression was inquiring. "Why?"

"I have a strange kind of power," he said. "Sometimes I can feed it to others. Especially when I hold something that belongs to them. Well, it worked once with Kirra. Maybe it'll work with you."

"I bet it would if I had my moonstone necklace," she said, handing him the pendant.

His fingers closed around the braided circle of gold. "I bet it would, too."

Her eyes widened. "Oh! I felt that! What did you do?"

He smiled in the half-light. "Just—directed a little energy your way. I think if you use my magic in addition to yours, you won't be so exhausted by the end of this exercise."

She turned away from him. "All right. Tell me, then—who needs me the most?"

CHAPTER
35

AMALIE spent the next hour moving through the ranks of wounded men as Cammon directed her to those who were experiencing the most severe agony or the deepest hopelessness. Cammon felt a fresh charge against his skin every time Amalie put a hand to another man's cheek; he felt her draw upon the core of his own power. But it was peculiar, it was unexpected—the expenditure of magic did not seem to be draining her at all. In fact, every time she spread her glittering gift along another man's wound, she seemed to brighten a little, to expand. Her candle-flame hair held a richer color. Her pale hands seemed to be touched by stray moonlight.

It was the response of the soldiers, Cammon decided—their awe, their appreciation—these things were filling her up, making her glow. She basked in their adoration and grew stronger.

Amalie had visited the beds of maybe forty soldiers when Justin pushed his way out of one of the tents and joined them. "Majesty, if you have the strength, there's a man inside who I think would like to meet you. I saw him fight today, and he was unstoppable. Not particularly well trained, but he just wouldn't give up. Saved two of his companions when they were overmatched. But he's in bad shape now, and I'm just not sure—" He shook his head. "If he saw you, it might give him heart."

Amalie instantly turned toward the tent. "Of course. What's his name?"

Justin glanced at Cammon, grinning. "I don't want to tell you. I want to see if Cammon remembers him."

Cammon was surprised. "This is someone *I* know?"

"Well, you only met him once, but it was a memorable experience."

They stepped inside the tent. Instantly, the scents, sounds, and emotions of wounded men were intensified; Cammon had to pause a moment to fight for balance. A dozen men moaned and thrashed on low cots, or lay dangerously still. The air smelled of alcohol and wet linen and blood. Three branches of candles offered more than enough light to see by. Cammon wished he couldn't see—or hear—or hear with his inner ear.

Justin pointed toward one of the sickbeds, and Amalie went to her knees beside the cot, surveying the soldier. He was maybe twenty years old, with thick black hair matted with blood, a wide peasant's face, a full mouth crimped with pain. His eyes were shut tightly; his whole face was creased in an effort to hold on to consciousness.

Cammon stared at him, frowning. Familiar, and yet—

"I hear you fought very bravely today," Amalie said in a coaxing voice. "Won't you open your eyes and tell me your name?"

The young man's mouth moved, but no words came out. Cammon looked over his clothing to see if it held any clues to his identity. Not really. He wore a black-and-white checkerboard sash, so he'd ridden in with the Merrenstow contingent, but he had a black-and-gold scarf tied around his upper arm. An indication that he rode for the royal army, or a leftover dressing from rough battlefield medicine? His uniform bunched up under his arms to make room for the great swaddling of bandages that covered his lower torso. Gut wound—unlikely to live.

"I know you must hurt a great deal," Amalie said. "I'm not much of a healer, but perhaps my touch will bring you some peace." She leaned closer and spread her fingers gently over his bandage.

Cammon felt as if someone had kicked him in the stomach; he actually made a little *whoofing* noise as air punched out of him. He caught Justin's questioning look but didn't pause to explain. He was too absorbed in watching the patient's face as that infusion of magic raced through his body. First the lips pursed in surprise, then the clenched muscles of the jaw relaxed. Then slowly the soldier's eyes opened, and he looked straight up at Amalie, dazed and dazzled.

"Majesty," he whispered.

Now Cammon could sense Justin's intense curiosity, for the Rider had witnessed enough magic to realize when it was being worked in his presence. An even stronger emotion emanated from Amalie: fierce delight that her touch had eased this man's pain. But she kept her voice in a soothing register. "You fought valiantly on the field today," she said. "I want to thank you for riding to war on my behalf."

"Princess," the soldier said, still in a weak and thready voice. "I joined your father's army to make reparation."

She kept one hand on the bandage and used the other to smooth the dark hair back from his face. "And what were you atoning for?"

"I was stupid. I believed false promises. I—I joined the soldiers at Lumanen Convent because I believed the Daughters of the Pale Mother were good."

That was the instant Cammon recognized him. "Kelti! You were with the Lestra's soldiers the night Justin and I found you—" *Found you torturing a mystic.* "Found you near Neft," he finished lamely. "So you left the convent and became a king's man!"

"I told him to," Justin said, sounding pleased with himself, that he had given advice, and it had been accepted, and it had turned out so well—unless you considered getting a blade through the belly a bad thing. He came a step closer and bent over a little. "You fought well," he said to Kelti. "At least two others are alive today because of you."

Kelti looked straight back at him, trusting the other soldier to tell him a hard truth. "Am I going to die?"

"Might," Justin said. "It's a bad wound. But we have some mystic healers here who can bring a man back from death's doorstep."

"I don't mind dying," Kelti said. "If it's for something that matters."

"It is for the noblest cause imaginable," Amalie told him, stroking his cheek. She had not seemed so sure just an hour ago, but to reassure this young man, she had managed to summon true conviction. "To keep the kingdom safe and whole. To keep cruel men and women from gaining the power to kill and destroy at will."

"I never did anything that mattered before," Kelti said.

"And when you are recovered, will you still want to be a soldier in the royal army?" Amalie said. "Or have you seen enough of fighting?"

His dark eyes were shining with fervor—or possibly fever, Cammon wasn't sure. "As long as you have need of me, I will fight for you," he said.

"Then heal quickly, and come see me when you are whole again," Amalie said. "I have need of a few more Riders. I would invite you to be one of them."

Cammon heard Justin's quick intake of breath, but when he looked over, Justin was grinning. This must be how it was done; suddenly, the monarch just *knew*. And if that wasn't a kind of magic, Cammon had never seen a spell cast in his life.

"Majesty, I will be well in a few days. I'm sure of it."

She smiled and came to her feet. "Look for me then, Kelti. I'll be waiting."

It was late, and tomorrow would be another punishing day. "Amalie, you have to go back to your own tent now," Cammon said, leading her outside. She didn't even protest; she was too exhausted.

Justin followed them, still grinning. "Good to see that you're planning to quickly fill up the ranks of Riders again, Majesty," he said.

She gave him a searching look. "Did I choose wisely? Will you be willing to ride alongside him?"

"He proved his courage today. His fighting skills need some improvement, but training is something we can give him." Justin glanced at Cammon. "When we met him, he struck me as a man desperate to find a cause to give his whole heart to."

Cammon nodded. "I agree."

Justin continued, "And you've just offered him that cause. I believe he would be loyal to you to the death."

She sighed. "Which I hope does not come tomorrow."

Justin shook his head. "He won't even need magic now. Someone has faith in him. A boy like that, faith'll keep him alive for a long time."

"You speak from experience, of course," Cammon said in a polite voice.

Justin laughed. "I absolutely do."

Justin stayed behind to coax Ellynor to take a rest, but Cammon and Amalie returned to her pavilion. "You'll feel very tired when I give you back your pendant," he warned. "You've been pulling magic from me, and it's buoyed you up, but I think you're going to feel pretty bad when I hand it back. So promise me you'll just go to bed and worry about war again in the morning."

"I promise," she said, and held out her hand.

He laid the gold necklace in her palm, and she actually staggered. The glow that had seemed to sustain her flickered out. She dropped to the bed as if her legs suddenly could not support her.

"Ohhhh," she breathed, "I didn't think it would be quite so severe."

"Just take off your dress and your shoes," he said. "And I'll pull up the blanket. Go straight to sleep."

But she forced her eyes open. She hated anyone to think she might be weak. "What about you?" she asked.

He had slept in the tent with her since it was first erected. No one had commented on the arrangement. He actually thought Tayse might even be pleased about it—not because Tayse had any romantic notions about young love, but because Tayse considered Cammon a very good sort of weapon. "Yes, of course I will go to sleep, too," he said.

She shook her head. "No. If I've been stealing your magic, are you exhausted too?"

He sat beside her and began unlacing her shoes, since she seemed in-capable of performing that task for herself. "You haven't been stealing it. I've given it to you. A present."

"But has that gift left you drained and weak?"

He pushed her to her side so he could undo the buttons at the back of her dress. He figured it wouldn't be long before she was demanding to wear men's trousers, as Senneth did. A dress was clearly out of place on a battlefield. "No. I'm tired because this has been a dreadful day and I have not been able to shut out all the cries of pain and calls for help. But it didn't make me especially weary to share my magic with you."

He tugged the skirts of the dress up and had to half lift her to get it off over her head. "Why not?" she asked sleepily, lying back on the pillow.

He shrugged. "I don't know. Because I have a lot of power, I guess. I've never yet used it all up. Maybe that will happen someday—maybe it will happen during this war. But it didn't happen today."

"Good," she said, and closed her eyes. "I'll take some more of it tomorrow."

THE second day of war was much like the first one. Brutal, arduous, tense, and exhausting. As before, Cammon and Amalie stayed well to the back, Amalie fretful and Cammon struggling to sort out the noises and emotions besieging him. He managed a little better this day. He was able to focus, as Jerril had taught him, only on the voices he wanted to hear while he shut out all the others. The various leaders of the defending army were beginning to realize what an asset he was, and this day mes-sages came swiftly from the mystics attending Romar, Colton, Kiernan, and the captains of the other troops.

"We're able to shift forces to any line exactly when we need them," Romar said that night as they held another brief conference in Amalie's tent. "Our numbers are smaller, but we're able to deploy better. It's almost an even trade-off."

"I'd still like to see another thousand men ride up wearing Danalus-trous red," Kiernan said.

Senneth shook her head. "I don't think that will happen. Malcolm seemed very certain he would not join the war."

"Then we plan a strategy around the troops we have," Tayse an-swered.

No one said that there weren't enough troops, but Cammon could tell everyone was thinking it. They had lost more soldiers today; they were slowly being whittled down. Cammon saw Romar speculatively regarding his niece, and he could read the regent's thought: *How soon must we send her across the border to safety?* Not that there was certain to be any safety for Amalie, even in the Lirrenlands.

That night, again, Amalie spent an hour outside the infirmary tents, moving between fallen soldiers, offering thanks and encouragement. Cammon could see two shapes inside the pavilions, shadows moving against the low interior light. One he guessed was Ellynor. The other he knew to be Valri, for he had sensed her there the entire day, moving among the wounded and the dying. She moved with a grim purposefulness, almost all of her attention on the sober task before her, but a small part of her—a tiny, hopeful, selfish part—was engaged in a celebration of joy. Cammon smiled to feel it. The reunion with Ellynor's cousin must have proceeded rather well, he thought. He glanced around, in case he spotted the fellow lurking in the shadows, waiting for Valri to retire for the night.

There might have been a shape standing behind one of the tents, but it wasn't a Lirren man. Cammon stared harder, trying to make out details. It seemed to be a woman, dark-haired, stocky, dressed in black and silver. He shook his head and narrowed his eyes, but she was gone and he could pick up no sense of a lurking presence. Surely there had never been anyone there.

He bent his attention instead on someone who was in plain sight: Kirra, who had spent the day tending to fallen soldiers. She had been on the move the entire afternoon, but now she sat on a stool outside one of the tents, looking tired. Still, she had mustered enough energy to scowl at Cammon as she waved him over.

"You're doing something," she accused. "Amalie keeps looking back at you. You're pouring some of your power into her, aren't you?"

He opened his hand to show her Amalie's pendant. "Pretty easy to feed energy to a thief mystic."

Kirra pushed herself to her feet. "I want some. Give it to me."

He couldn't help laughing. "Well, that's gracious."

She hunted through her pockets until she found a small striated stone charm shaped like a lioness on the run. Kirra had found it last year in a deserted shrine set up to honor the Wild Mother, and she'd kept it as her personal token. "There are another five men in there who are so seriously wounded that they could die tonight," she said in an uncharacteristically grim voice. "I'm too tired to help them. But if you lend me a little magic—"

His other hand closed around the lioness. "Of course I will."

Kirra's eyes closed. For a moment she looked as if she was luxuriating in a scented bath. For such a wild creature, Kirra was really a hedonist at heart. "Ah. This almost feels like healing itself. I could just stand here and soak up your energy."

"Certainly. Do that. Don't think about those lives you wanted to save."

She opened her eyes and glared at him. "I never in all my days met a boy more irritating than you."

He let surprise come to his face. "Not even Justin?"

That made her laugh. "Very well, you're *both* irritating. But I must say, this is a very handy talent you have. I feel fresh as morning."

"You'll feel terrible once you've used up more magic and I give you back the lioness."

She nodded briskly and turned for the tent flap. "I know. But let me first do a little good."

Amalie had done a little good, too. Cammon could feel the soothing effects of her magic on a couple dozen of the wounded soldiers who had been suffering so mightily before she arrived. As before, the immediate impact on Amalie was both beneficial and powerful. Her hair owned a golden phosphorescence, and she glowed with a ghostly light as she picked her way through the pallets. But he still worried about the cumulative effects on her health, and he eventually insisted that she stop for the night and seek her bed.

"Kirra," he called. "We're leaving. I have to give you back your charm."

Amalie leaned against him, tiring already. "But Kirra has so much charm," she said sleepily. "How could you take it all away?"

A poor joke, but he laughed. "Well, I have special powers."

Kirra emerged from the tent with a bouncy step. "Keep it until I find Donnal," she said. "Because I know I'm going to collapse as soon as you return it to me."

He nodded, and they made their way through the camp toward Amalie's tent. Kirra and Donnal were billeted nearby—as were Senneth and Tayse, Justin and Ellynor. The other Riders were scattered strategically through the camp, and Romar and Kiernan slept near their men, but these six had chosen to stay near the princess and guard her even during their slumber.

Donnal had come looking for them, it turned out, and joined them before they were thirty paces from the hospital tents. "I just did one quick circuit over the enemy camp from the air," he said. "Everything looked quiet."

"Then put your arms around me and be prepared to help me back to my bedroll," Kirra said, holding out her hand to Cammon. "I'm about to collapse."

As soon as he placed the lioness in her palm, Kirra sagged against Donnal and seemed to shrink in size. Even her golden hair grew dull and a little lank. Donnal lifted her in his arms and carried her to their campsite.

"Time for all of us to go to bed," Cammon said. "Tomorrow will be just as terrible as today."

And it was.

CHAPTER
36

BAD news came late the next afternoon, dressed in Tilt livery. Justin found the man trying to sneak across the northern battle lines, and he escorted the messenger at knifepoint to Amalie's tent. Kirra was at the royal pavilion because she had come looking for Cammon, saying she needed an infusion of magic.

"Why, Justin, look what you've found," Kirra greeted the Rider. Of course she instantly recognized the aquamarine jewels on the man's vest, though Cammon was still struggling to identify the color. "I do believe he must be a courier from Tilt."

"He says he's got news from marlord Gregory," Justin said with a sneer.

Cammon could understand Justin's contempt. The man was small and scrawny, probably in his midfifties, and appeared to be shivering where he stood. Clearly he'd never seen much combat in his life and was terrified to be this close to it. Not the sort of brave messenger you'd entrust with a vital secret.

Amalie stood before him with her arms crossed. This morning, for the first time, she had dressed in trousers and a close-fitting jacket, and the ensemble added a certain sternness to her demeanor. "Well? What does marlord Gregory have to tell me? Is he finally going to commit troops to my cause, or is he too much of a coward to take sides, even so late?"

The courier looked around nervously. "I was told to deliver my message to the regent."

Amalie drew herself even taller. "I am the *princess*."

"Yes, but I—"

Justin stepped close enough to lay the edge of his dagger against the man's throat. "Tell the princess anything she asks," he said in a threatening voice.

The courier coughed and swallowed and bobbed his head. "Yes. I will. Majesty, marlord Gregory wants you to know that Arberharst soldiers have sailed to the northern seas and are disembarking even now. He thinks they number close to a thousand. They will be joining marlord Halchon and marlord Rayson as soon as they can mobilize."

Justin was so angry he almost lowered his blade. "Damnation!" he swore. "We're worn thin as it is—and the last thing we need is more foreigners prancing around, immune to our magic."

Amalie ignored him. "And why are these soldiers allowed access through Tilt waters and Tilt lands?" she demanded.

The messenger cut his eyes back toward Justin and licked his lips. "Majesty, the marlord is—he is loyal to you—but Halchon Gisseltess made certain threats, and the marlord was afraid. He agreed to allow the Arberharst men into Tilt harbors, but he instantly sent me to warn you."

Kirra struck her hands together in extreme frustration. "Oh, this is just *like* Gregory Tilton!" she exclaimed. "He finds a way to make each side believe he has played the ally!"

"Well, he has done us some good, if the news is true," Justin said practically. "It gives us time to prepare." He put away his knife and glanced at Cammon. "*Is* it true?"

Cammon nodded. "At least as far as *he* knows. He's not lying."

"I saw them," the courier said. "I saw the ships sail in, and I saw the men in their blue uniforms come to shore."

Justin swore again. "Then let's tell Romar and Kiernan and Tayse."

Amalie spoke softly. "Let them finish the day's fighting first." She pointed at the messenger. "You will stay with me until my commanders gather tonight, and you will repeat your news. Justin, thank you for bringing him to me. You may return to battle."

Justin hesitated. "Majesty—I cannot leave him here with you unguarded. He *says* he has brought news of a fresh invasion, but perhaps he has a secret mission, and that is to do harm to you."

"I didn't! No! I wouldn't!" the messenger cried, instantly alarmed.

"I don't think so," Cammon said.

Amalie just smiled and gestured toward the raelynx, who was sitting quietly nearby, its dark eyes fixed on the newcomer. "I'm not undefended," she said. "Cammon has a sword, and the raelynx is close by. I'm not afraid."

Kirra laughed and clapped Justin on the back. "Replaced by a mystic and a cat," she crowed. "A bad day for a Rider!"

Justin merely bowed, his fist against his shoulder. "Majesty," he said, "I return to fight where I will do the most good."

*   *   *

ROMAR and Kiernan read the situation much as Kirra had—a canny ploy by Gregory Tilton to prove his worth to both sides of the warring factions.

"I despise him, but I admire his strategy," Kiernan said calmly once the messenger had been dismissed. "This bit of information will keep us from dispossessing him as a traitor if we manage to beat back our enemies and win the war."

"Which seems even unlikelier, given this news," Senneth said. Cammon thought she looked even more exhausted tonight. She had managed to throw and sustain fire several times these past three days, effectively cutting off pockets of enemy troops, but Arberharst soldiers remained on the front lines and made it impossible for her to simply hold back the entire advancing army with a wall of flame.

"I had wondered why Rayson Fortunalt recruited so few foreigners," Tayse said in his serious way. He ignored Senneth's "So *few?*" and added, "He knew they would be most effective against us. He would have been justified in pouring all his resources into hiring those fighters. He was smart to hire another thousand men."

"Let's spend less time applauding Rayson's clever investment of gold and more time determining how we can block this new army," Kiernan said.

Tayse shrugged. "Unless we can spare forces to meet them somewhere north of Ghosenhall, I don't know that there is any plan we can make," he said. "And I don't think we have the soldiers to send."

"No," Romar said. He looked angry and trapped—not yet beaten, but staring straight at the possibility of defeat. *This is how the ending begins*, he was thinking. "Well, we thought they would start with a frontal assault, and then, once we were worn down, try a few tricks," he said. "I suppose that is what has started now."

"So then we must be on the alert for more maneuvers," Kiernan said.

Romar nodded wearily. "I suppose we must." He hauled himself to his feet. "Rest while we can. Make ourselves strong to fight another day."

It was a plan that Cammon heartily approved. He was not successful in keeping Amalie away from the wounded that night, but he did coax her back to the pavilion before she had used up all her strength. Even when they had blown out all the candles and curled up together in bed, he could see the faint luster of her hair.

"You're alight with magic," he observed, smoothing down the stray strands.

She laughed sleepily. "And prickly with it," she agreed. "My skin feels like it's crackling—like I'm standing too close to a fire."

"Do you like it now?" he asked. "Your magic? You were afraid of it before."

He felt the nod of her head against the pillow. "I like it so much! Because I can *do* things with it—things I want to do, good things."

"You haven't been singing the songs Ellynor taught you to honor the Silver Lady," he observed.

"I've been afraid to, with Coralinda Gisseltess so close," she confessed. "Maybe the Pale Mother will hear me but help her."

"I'm sure the Lestra is offering up plenty of prayers of her own," he said dryly.

"But I have prayed to her," Amalie said hesitantly. "At night. Silently. And when we've walked through the rows of wounded soldiers. I've asked for her blessing. I think she can hear me—at any rate, sometimes I feel as if *someone* is peering over my shoulder, smiling when I get something right. I don't know. Maybe it's my imagination." He heard the smile in her voice. "Maybe it's *you* that I feel."

"But maybe it's the goddess," he said. "I hope so. I hope she is watching over you. I hope she is watching over all of us."

Amalie fell asleep almost instantly. Cammon, who had trained himself to stay awake as long as she did, just in case she needed him, tumbled into sleep right after her. But even his dreams were not restful these days. It was harder to keep his mental shields up while he was sleeping, and so he was plagued by the unrelenting misery of the wounded men. Images of warfare clattered through his mind. He relived again and again the striking blow, the falling sword, the moment's inattention that had resulted in a blade through the leg, or the ribs, or the throat.

It was almost a relief to startle awake, still in the dead of night, and lift his head and wonder what cue had alerted him that something was wrong.

No sound broke the silence immediately outside the tent. All the souls that Cammon had a particular interest in lay quietly sleeping. He pushed his attention outward, searching for trouble, wondering what spike of violence or fear had ripped through his slumbering mind and jerked him awake.

There. A slow creeping movement, coming closer. A single soldier, dispatched on a dangerous mission, harboring a steady murderous intent in his heart. It was hard to judge distance, but Cammon thought the man had made it about halfway through the royal camp.

An assassin. Heading for Amalie.

Cammon gathered his energy to send an urgent summons to Tayse—but the message went unsent. He became aware of a second stealthy presence, just as intent, just as lethal, prowling through the sleeping rows of soldiers. It moved soundlessly and with a primitive joy, and it was stalking the intruder.

The raelynx.

Relaxing a little, Cammon covered Amalie's mouth and shook her awake. She immediately opened her eyes and rolled over to look at him. When he pulled back his hand she mouthed, *"What's wrong?"*

"Just wait," he whispered.

Another few moments they lay there, tense with listening, hearing nothing but silence and their own breathing. Then an unearthly scream split the night—an inhuman sound from a human mouth—and suddenly the whole camp was clattering with the sounds of soldiers jumping to arms.

"What was that?" Amalie demanded.

"Assassin. Raelynx," Cammon answered succinctly.

Amalie pushed herself upright. "Senneth will be here in a second."

"Tayse first."

"Then I'd better get dressed."

She had no time. That instant, Tayse ripped back the tent flap and bounded in. "Majesty? Cammon?" He was naked except for his trousers. In the faint moonlight, Cammon could just see the gleam of an upraised sword in his hand.

"I'm fine," Amalie answered. "Apparently the raelynx caught an intruder."

Senneth hurried into the tent, and all the candles instantly winked to life. Her hair was wild, but otherwise she appeared calm. Tayse looked like avenging death, but his expression was beginning to smooth back to normal. Outside the tent, Cammon could hear Justin shouting questions and commands.

He actually felt like laughing. Impossible for the princess to be any more well defended. What could harm her with safeguards like these in place?

"What happened?" Senneth asked. "Was that the raelynx?"

Cammon wanted to get out of bed, but he was completely nude and it seemed like a bad idea. Amalie, who was wearing a thin nightdress, merely wrapped the covers tightly around her body and assumed an expression of great dignity. Cammon tried for a similar look. "I woke up, felt someone sneaking through camp," he said. "I was just about to call for

Tayse when I felt the raelynx. I figured he could take care of whoever was coming."

Tayse still hadn't sheathed his sword. "Then all is clear? The assassin had no companions?"

Cammon shook his head. "I don't think so."

Senneth looked at Tayse. "Unless he brought Arberharst friends with him."

"I think the raelynx would have gone for them, too," Cammon said.

"We'll make a circuit of camp," Tayse said, and ducked back out the door.

Senneth surveyed them. It was the first time she had been confronted with direct evidence that Cammon was sharing Amalie's bed. "And now I suppose you'll tell me to be grateful that you've disregarded every warning I've given you to keep your reserve with the princess," she said. She didn't sound angry, but she didn't sound elated, either.

He risked a grin. "Well, actually, it was the raelynx that saved Amalie tonight, so I don't suppose I can even make that argument."

"Senneth, I want him with me," Amalie said. "I love him."

Senneth sighed heavily. "I suppose you do. I would kill him, but he's too valuable, at least for the moment."

Kirra poked her head through the tent flap. "Sen, Tayse wants you outside. Oh, look, Cammon and Amalie are sleeping together. What an interesting development." She wasn't surprised, either, Cammon could tell—but neither was she horrified. In fact, in typical Kirra fashion, she seemed to find the awkward situation delightful. "Nothing like keeping your bodyguards close at hand."

"Speak with more respect to the princess," Cammon said, trying to frown her down, but Amalie was smiling.

"He has continued to render me the most valuable services," Amalie said.

Kirra hooted with laughter and didn't even try to answer. "Sen. Outside," she repeated and then disappeared.

Senneth gave them both a darkling look and followed Kirra. The candle flames blew out as the flap fell shut.

"She didn't seem too angry," Amalie said.

"She's got other things to worry about," Cammon said. "At the moment. The conversation isn't over, I assure you."

Nor was the influx of people into the tent. "Is she all right? What was that scream?" came Valri's voice, and a moment later the queen ducked through the tent door. "Amalie? What happened?"

Cammon sighed, reached over, and again lit one of the candles as Valri felt her way across the floor. As soon as the light came up, she stopped, and regarded the two of them with disfavor. "The raelynx attacked an enemy creeping through camp," Cammon said. "Amalie's fine."

"I see that," Valri said in an icy voice. "But you—what are you *doing* in here? I thought you were sleeping with the Riders."

"Well," said Cammon. "No." He remembered their last conversation at Ghosenhall. "I thought you had decided you didn't mind if Amalie and I—" He waved a hand in lieu of completing the sentence.

Valri threw her hands in the air. "I didn't expect you to be so brazen! Now half the camp will be gossiping about your relationship." She sighed and rubbed a hand across her forehead. "I've been too lax. Ever since the attack at the palace—I haven't been as watchful as I should have been. Time for strict propriety again. Time for me to be sleeping here in Amalie's tent at night."

"Instead of at Arrol's campfire?" Amalie asked politely.

Valri's frown grew blacker. "I don't think—"

Amalie sat up straighter in the bed, letting the covers fall to her waist. "Valri, you have guarded me so long and so well. And now there is very little you can do for me. You cannot hide my magic anymore. You cannot keep me safe. You will always be my most treasured friend, but you can spend some attention on your own life now. I hope you *are* sleeping at Arrol's side tonight, but I was only guessing. *I* will be sleeping beside Cammon. Don't even try to talk to me about it. Just go back to bed."

Valri hesitated a moment, obviously unwilling to shirk her duty but unsure of what she might be able to accomplish in the middle of the night in the middle of a war. "You're still too young," was what she said, leaving them to guess at the rest. *Too young to fall in love. Too young to lose your father. Too young to face armies trying to steal your throne. Too young to make momentous decisions on your own.*

"I better not be," Amalie said. "For this is what my life holds now."

A few seconds longer Valri waited, then she sighed and spread her hands in a gesture of helplessness. "Then sleep now, and talk to me in the morning," she said, coming close enough to kiss Amalie on the cheek. She just looked at Cammon, then shook her head and quickly left the tent. But he thought she might have been wearing a faint smile.

"Do you think it's safe to put out the candle this time, or will someone else come barging in?" he asked.

"I can't think who. Blow it out," Amalie replied, and they snuggled together in the darkness. "Do you *really* think she's sleeping with Arrol right now?" she whispered against his chest.

"That's the name of Ellynor's cousin, right? Well, I can't be sure, but there's a part of her that seems almost blissful. So I think so."

Amalie drew closer. "Good. Valri has given up so much for me. I want her to do something that brings her happiness."

They were both silent for a while, thinking their different thoughts. "Amalie," Cammon said at last in a low voice. "You weren't controlling it, were you? The raelynx just attacked that man all on its own."

She didn't answer at first, and then she shook her head. "I think I would have slept through the whole event if you hadn't woken me up. Well, and if that man hadn't screamed."

"That's a little frightening."

She drew closer. "I find it reassuring."

CHAPTER
37

SENNETH was starting to hate the very feel of fire.

She had taken to keeping her hands down at her sides so that no one noticed the blisters on her palms. She imagined soot in her hair, cinders under her nails; the smell of ashes clung to her skin. At night she was haunted by images of flames. By day, her whole world was heat and color.

And frustration.

It had never been this hard to call fire, to bend it to her will, to make it leap and dance and bow and settle and flare up again. Once she had tried to burn down a house in the middle of a rainstorm, and the timbers refused to light and the soaked thatch of the roof stubbornly resisted every intrusive spark. She had spent a good hour forcing the flames to catch and then willing them to take hold in the water-soaked wood, and when she was finished she had been in such a bad temper that a migraine had dropped her where she stood.

Trying to cast a spell on the Arberharst armies was very much like trying to ignite a building in the middle of a downpour. Except it was an exercise that was lasting for days, it was more important, and she was having even less success.

And when she did succeed in finding a raw pocket of unmixed Gillengaria soldiers, and she was able to ring them with flame and cause their very uniforms to light, then she had to hear the terrified screams of soldiers who were burning to death. Because of the magic in her hands. Because of the conviction in her heart.

More than once during those opening days of battle, she wished she could not summon fire at all.

She tried, possibly a dozen times, to direct her smoldering weapon at the enemies she believed most deserved to die. It was hardly a surprise that she was unable to incinerate Halchon Gisseltess. He was inimical to her magic, and apparently his immunity extended even to his clothing and his horse.

Coralinda Gisseltess was covered in so many moonstones that Senneth's magic had no real effect on her, either. In fact, Senneth kept remembering what Cammon had said—that moonstones actually stole magic from mystics and fed it to whoever was wearing the gems. In which case, every time she tried to set Coralinda on fire, Coralinda merely grew stronger. Even if the theory wasn't true, it unnerved Senneth so much that she desisted after the second or third time she tried to make the Lestra's hair go up in flame.

She had hoped to have better luck with Rayson Fortunalt. Every morning she prowled through the battle lines, weaving past sword fights, trying to get a better look at the arrogant, disdainful marlord of Fortunalt. As soon as she spotted his puffy red face, she would fling her arms out and wish fire upon him, but it did no good. Oh, twice she caused his horse to go mad, rearing and biting as if to rid itself of hot sparks, and one day a curl of smoke drifted up from the front of his sash. But Rayson himself would not catch fire. She suspected he had dressed himself in Arberharst clothing, or anointed himself with oils imported from Karyndein—something that resisted Gillengaria magic, something she could not penetrate. Who knew, perhaps he had invested in a blessing from a foreign god, and her own goddess could not overcome it.

Even though her fires would not take hold in the places they would do the most damage, she could still use flame to cause some disruption in the enemy camp. So she continued wreaking havoc where she could, for three days, for five, for six. And she succeeded well enough to scorch her skin and please her brother and earn the praise of the regent—and feel grave despair about the uses to which she was putting her formidable talent. And she failed miserably enough to feel rage and disappointment and profound exhaustion. And fear. *We could so easily lose this war, and I am not able to help as I should.*

So, it was particularly disheartening, a week into the war, to have Donnal return one night from an aerial scouting mission to report that more troops were marching in from the south.

"Looked like a couple thousand men," he told Romar and Kiernan as they all gathered in Amalie's tent. Kirra, who usually tried to skip any conference that included the regent, had joined them this night to hear Donnal's news. "Some cavalry, most infantry. The lead men were carrying flags with what looked like a spray of grass on a brownish background."

Senneth looked straight at Kirra, whose blue eyes were wide with dismay. "Nocklyn!" Kirra exclaimed. "Oh, I knew it! Mayva's horrible husband is bringing his soldiers to war against us."

Kiernan shrugged. "It is hardly a surprise. We always counted Nock-lyn among our probable enemies. The only surprise is that they waited a week to join the rebels."

"Wanted to wear us out first," Romar said briefly. "We've suffered heavy losses, but we've held our ground. They wanted us complacent or hopeful before bringing in reinforcements."

"There appeared to be a second army traveling with the first," Donnal said.

Kirra slumped on her stool. "*Not* what we wanted to hear."

"What was the heraldry?" Romar asked.

"I didn't see a flag, but the soldiers were wearing maroon sashes."

Kirra sat up and Senneth felt the first wash of hope she'd felt in days. "Maroon?" Senneth repeated. "Rappengrass?"

Kiernan shook his head. "Ariane Rappengrass would hardly be riding against us in company with Nocklyn troops."

"Maybe Nocklyn's not against us after all," Senneth said.

"That's almost too much to hope for," Kiernan said.

"I have to agree," Kirra said. "When we talked to Mayva last year, don't you remember? Everything was 'Lowell says this' and 'Lowell thinks that.' And Lowell is Halchon Gisseltess's cousin. Our best hope was that Nocklyn would stay neutral. We can't expect it to ride for the crown."

"But Ariane," Senneth said. "She *wouldn't* betray us. Rappengrass is as loyal as Brassenthwaite."

Even Kiernan was nodding. "I agree."

"Well, I'll leave the wounded to Ellynor tomorrow and fly down there to meet with Ariane," Kirra offered.

Senneth took a deep breath. It meant submitting to Kirra's drastic magic again—but it meant a day's reprieve from internal and external infernos. "Change me," she said, "and bring me along."

ARIANE was standing with three of her captains, eating cold rations and clearly discussing a point of strategy, when Kirra swooped in for a landing. Senneth spared a moment to hope none of the Rappengrass soldiers thought that a hawk and a mouse looked like good bets for dinner before Kirra had a chance to restore them to their proper shapes. The transformation left her feeling dizzy and unsteady, but the Rappengrass folk staring at her looked even more off balance at her sudden appearance. She could not help but smile at their stunned faces.

"Ariane," she said as coolly as possible. "How good to see you on the road to Ghosenhall. Coming to Amalie's aid, I hope."

Ariane gave a sharp bark of laughter and strode closer to give Senneth a hard embrace. Ariane was big-boned and gray-haired, a plain-
faced, strong-willed, utterly indomitable force. "Senneth," she said in her
low voice. "I didn't know you'd added shape-shifting to your long list of
tricks."

"I haven't. Kirra brought me."

The explanation was unnecessary as, on the words, Kirra stood before
them, making a pretty curtsey. Senneth was slightly aggrieved to see that
Kirra appeared neither disoriented nor disheveled as a consequence of
transmogrification. "Ariane," Kirra said, giving the marlady a kiss on the
cheek. "We are *so* pleased to see you."

With a wave of her hand, Ariane dismissed her captains. "Tell me the
news," she said. "Baryn is truly dead? We heard the rumors, but any official couriers got turned back on the way."

"Murdered by hired soldiers who infiltrated the palace," Senneth confirmed. "Amalie currently keeps her title as princess. The regent stands
beside her. Forces from Fortunalt, Gisseltess, and Storian have marched
against the throne, augmented by hired blades from Arberharst—against
whom magic has no effect, much to the chagrin of mystics like me. We
have picked our battlefield and are currently contesting a plot of land
somewhere between Brassenthwaite and Kianlever. But we are overmatched."

"Yes—I knew it—but I had to put my own House in order before I
could come," Ariane said. Her full lips compressed in a frown; Senneth
wondered what measures she had had to take to quell any Thirteenth
House mutiny. "These are all the men I could spare."

"And we are grateful for every one of them," Kirra assured her. "But,
Ariane! You march with Nocklyn? All this time we have been expecting
Lowell to raise men for his cousin's army."

Ariane's plain, broad face brightened to a smile. "As did I. And I was
very worried about my position then, surrounded by enemies on all sides."
She shook her head. "Mayva has surprised us all."

Kirra's head whipped around so fast her hair went flying. "Mayva?
Is here?"

Ariane pointed. "Leading her own troops, though I can't imagine
she'll be any good on a battlefield."

Kirra's eyes grew huge. "What about Lowell? The flighty little serramarra I talked to last was no match for the cold Gisseltess man."

"It's an interesting tale—ask her yourself. But she's no longer a serramarra, more's the pity. Els died a week ago. She's marlady now."

"I *must* hear this story," Kirra declared. "But first, tell me, how is Lyrie? Still well, I hope?"

Ariane's smile came back. "Strong and lively and smart, smart, smart. My favorite of all my grandchildren, though I know I shouldn't say it. She speaks of you often, and the time you turned her into a dog to save her life. If she could figure out a way to make herself magic, she would do it. I think her greatest disappointment is that she is so ordinary."

Kirra laughed. "I didn't think she was ordinary at all."

"No," said Ariane, "and I don't, either."

"Let's go talk to Mayva," Senneth said. "I want to hear her story."

One of Ariane's captains returned. "Marlady," he said, casting a wide-eyed glance at her unconventional visitors. "We'd best be on the move again."

Ariane nodded. "Find my friends a couple of horses and let them ride with us awhile."

In a few moments, Senneth and Kirra were mounted, the whole army was on the march, and Ariane was leading them to the head of the column. Yes, there was the wheat-and-ochre flag that Donnal had described. Riding a few feet behind it was Mayva Nocklyn.

She looked very little like the shallow and impatient young woman Senneth had met several times before. Her face was still round and child-like, but the sulky expression was gone, replaced by a look of deep sadness. Instead of curling in ringlets around her face, her dark hair was pulled back and tied with a plain scarf. The full lips looked like they had not smiled in a very long time.

Kirra cantered up alongside her. "Mayva! What are you doing so far from home, riding in the company of soldiers?"

Mayva's face showed first astonishment and then real pleasure. "*Kirra?* How did you get here? I did not see you arrive! Oh—I suppose you flew in, like a butterfly or a bird or something like that."

Kirra laughed. "Something like that," she said. "Mayva, you remember Senneth Brassenthwaite, do you not? I brought her with me."

"Oh—serra—of course," Mayva said as Senneth rode up on the other side of Kirra. "Why have you come? Both of you?"

Senneth answered. "We heard rumors of a Nocklyn army on the move and we had to make sure it was coming to help us, not harm us."

Mayva's pretty face tightened. "If my husband were here, he would be leading Nocklyn troops to Ghosenhall to try to push the princess off the throne."

Kirra looked around as if in surprise. "Yes," she said. "Where is Lowell?"

Mayva's chin lifted. "In a common prison cell in Nocklyn Towers."

Kirra practically choked. "Mayva, what happened? You always seemed so—well—I thought you allowed Lowell to make many of the decisions in your House."

"He killed my father," Mayva said.

Kirra was horrified. "No! I thought—Els has been sick for a long time—"

"Poisoned," Mayva said in the bleakest voice imaginable. "I discovered it quite by accident. My father had gotten much worse, and I had brought a woman in to watch him during the nights. One evening I spent a few hours at his bedside, but he never woke up. The nurse said I looked sickly, too, and I said my head was aching. I said I would return to my room and take some powdered silwort. And she said, 'Oh, serra, that's no good for pain. That's only something you spread on a wound to fight infection.' "

"It is," Kirra said. "It works marvelously well, but if you swallow it—" She shuddered. "You'd need to take a lot to die from it, though."

Mayva nodded. "Indeed you would. A lot over a long period of time. Lowell had been feeding it to my father for months."

"But—surely—I mean, didn't you hire doctors?" Senneth asked. She was trying to keep an accusatory tone from her voice, but no one could have been that stupid. "I know Lowell would not have allowed a mystic healer in the House, but there are trained physicians—"

"There most certainly are," Mayva said in a flat voice. "We brought in the best. All the way from Gissel Plain. Nocklyn doctors weren't good enough for my father, Lowell said."

"Wild Mother watch me," Kirra murmured. "There's a cruel and cold-blooded man."

"So cruel," Mayva said. "So cold."

"What did you do?" Senneth asked.

"I did not want to let Lowell know that I suspected something was wrong. A troop of Gisseltess guards had been brought in recently, ostensibly to help keep order if there was any unrest among the vassals—as there has been so much unrest at other Houses. I did not want to accuse Lowell and have him call his soldiers against *me*. But I knew my father had always completely trusted the captain of his guards. I had never dealt with Worton much—I had never thought about swords and soldiers! Why should I? I left such things to my husband—but I sought him out that night once Lowell had gone to sleep." She laughed mirthlessly. "You will not be surprised to learn that he despised Lowell. He was happy to see

me there, eager to swear fealty. He picked five of his best men and followed me back to the rooms I shared with my husband. They kept Lowell under guard for the next few days while I rode to the homes of my
father's favorite vassals. None of them, as it turned out, cared much for
my husband. All of them were willing to organize their own house guards
and send a small army back with me to overcome the Gisseltess men
camped in my courtyard."

"Mayva—I'm astonished and humbled and proud," Kirra said, leaning over to squeeze the marlady's hand. "I don't know that I could have
been so clever or so fearless! How brave you were!"

"I didn't feel brave," Mayva said. "I felt afraid. I was sick to my stomach the whole time I was riding for help."

"I know that feeling well," Senneth said quietly. "But tell us the
rest of the story. Your father could not recover from the effects of the
poisoning?"

Mayva shook her head. She was trying very hard not to cry. "Of course
he received no more silwort! But his body was too weak. I thought—
if there had been a mystic nearby—perhaps magic would have saved
him. But all the mystics have been chased out of Nocklyn by Coralinda
Gisseltess—and my own husband. There was no one left to save my
father. And he died."

"Oh, Mayva, I am so sorry," Kirra murmured.

Mayva's chin came up. "So I am marlady now. And I must decide so
many things. It is very hard, and I honestly don't know that I can manage. But I knew I must support the princess in this war. If my husband
was in favor of it, it must be wrong." She shivered. "Besides, Coralinda
Gisseltess tried to murder my cousin's son."

"No!" Kirra exclaimed. "Tell me what happened!"

"He's just a little boy—but he's a mystic, you know. He was staying
with my aunt and uncle, and Coralinda sent her soldiers out to burn
down the house. It was a miracle that he escaped—a miracle that some
kind man found him on the road and took him to safety. My aunt and
uncle are dead, of course." She paused a moment to get her voice back
under control. "Lowell told me the story wasn't true—that my cousin
had made it up to try to discredit the Lestra. Houses burn down all the
time, he said, and it's nobody's fault. But I believe she did it. And if
my husband defends Coralinda Gisseltess—well, then, I want to destroy
her." Impatiently she brushed at her cheeks. "So I have come to fight for
Amalie."

Kirra squeezed her hand again. "Mayva, we are so glad to have you."

* * *

KIRRA flew back to carry the news to Amalie and her assembled advisors, but Senneth said she couldn't stomach another wild flight clutched in Kirra's talons. In truth, she wanted a break from violence and fire. "I'll ride with Ariane for the rest of day, then gallop on ahead of the army tomorrow morning," she told Kirra. "Look for me then."

She still traveled among soldiers and could not escape the constant clank and sparkle of weaponry, but, compared to being in the thick of the fighting, the journey was peaceful. When they camped that night, a few of Ariane's captains joined them for dinner, but Ariane dismissed them as soon as the meal was over.

"So who have you left behind at Rappen Manor to watch the House while you go to war?" Senneth asked. "Kiernan is leading the Brassenthwaite forces, but Nate and Harris are protecting the bloodlines by taking cover at Brassen Court."

Ariane smiled briefly. "I wanted all five of my children to stay behind, but Darryn insisted on coming. I should not be surprised, I suppose, since he has flouted me at every turn for the past six months."

Senneth tried not to laugh. "Well, he must be close to thirty by now. Naturally he will find himself disagreeing with his mother from time to time," she responded. "And yet he seems like such an easygoing young man. I can hardly imagine him flying into rages and stalking out of the manor."

Ariane gave a little snort. "No, he simply gives me his most pleasant smile, thanks me for my opinion, and goes off to do whatever he wants."

Senneth asked cautiously, "Does that include falling in love with Sosie?"

Ariane frowned. "You've met her?"

"I did. I liked her a great deal. But then, I have low taste in companions, as everyone knows. Have *you* met her?"

"I've refused that honor. Consequently, Darryn will not ride with me, or even speak to me, though he's traveling with the army."

"I can't actually say I blame Darryn."

"Senneth, you must think me an impossible snob, but he cannot marry her! Not now! I have four other children, and they have all married well, and so perhaps, at some other time I could say, 'Well, let him wed for love. The bloodlines will be carried on by Bella and the others.' But not *now*. He should have pressed his suit in Ghosenhall! He should have been betrothed to Amalie! There would be no better match for the princess than Rappengrass! But he wouldn't even try. He says he confessed to Amalie that he loves someone else! What woman of spirit would wed a man who told her such a thing? You know her. Would she be willing to overlook such a slight—if I could force him to abandon this unfortunate nameless girl?"

Senneth flung out a hand. "Ariane, Ariane! First, she's *not* nameless, she's Sosie. Second, I rather think you would like her. She's resourceful and loyal and unpretentious, and she truly loves your son. Third—it doesn't matter if you coerce Darryn into making an offer for Amalie. I'm not sure she'd have him now. I'm not sure she'd have anyone. For *she*, my dear marlady, has gone your son one better. She has fallen in love with a wretched boy who has *no* family connections, nothing whatsoever to recommend him, except his magic—which is considerable. If you think *you* are at a loss, imagine how *I* feel, trying to guide this rebellious girl away from a disastrous relationship! And *I* can't even point to myself as a good example! I have given up for now. We must win this war, or it doesn't matter who Amalie loves. Afterward—well, we shall see. But if I were you, I would forgive Darryn and welcome Sosie and abandon all hope of an alliance with the throne."

"Bright Mother burn me," Ariane swore, and then started laughing. "What are we coming to, this little kingdom of ours? The marlords engage in civil war—the Thirteenth House vassals mutiny against the marlords—and young nobles fling aside their heritage to marry serfs and soldiers and serving girls. Are we all to be brought down, leveled at once? I tell you now, Senneth, I will not give up Rappen Manor. Not for anyone. They will have to pull it down around me, stone by stone."

Senneth smiled with a little constraint. "I do think the world is changing," she said. "Baryn was reluctantly in favor of reducing the power and influence of the marlords—giving away lands to some of the lesser lords and hoping that would help keep the peace. I have a certain respect for Kiernan, and Malcolm, and Heffel, and you—strong individuals who run prosperous and well-regulated households. But you know I am no aristocrat. I am not entirely in favor of power being concentrated in a few hands. Maybe if there were several dozen Houses, there would be less unrest, there would be less ambition, and there would not be war. Maybe. I don't know. I do know that Brassenthwaite will never fall into my keeping—and I think that's good. I wouldn't know what to do with it if it were mine."

"Well, I know what to do with Rappengrass," Ariane grumbled, and then she sighed. "Perhaps you're right about Darryn. I keep thinking, what if we ride to war and Darryn falls? What if my last words to him were cruel?

What if *I* die, and for the rest of his life what he remembers is that I could not forgive him? Tomorrow morning I will meet this—this—"

"Sosie."

"This *Sosie*. I don't know that I will be able to welcome her, but at least I will not be unkind."

"Her nephew is a mystic," Senneth said in an innocent voice.

Ariane glared at her. "And I will *still* strive to be kind."

Senneth laughed. "Oh, Ariane, you have such force of will. I am sure you will manage."

I<small>T</small> was not long after dawn the next morning before the armies were once more on the move. At this rate, Senneth estimated the Nocklyn and Rappengrass forces should be joining the royal soldiers within a day. Romar and Kiernan, she assumed, were already planning how to utilize them to take maximum advantage of the added numbers.

She knew she should hurry back to the battlefield and add her own particular arsenal to the fight against Gisseltess and Fortunalt, but she lingered long enough to observe Ariane make her first overtures to her son. Darryn always wore such an amiable expression; it was hard to tell if he was truly moved by his mother's sudden concession, and yet Senneth had to assume he was. She watched as he introduced Sosie with every evidence of pride, watched as Sosie tried hard to hide her nervousness and make no clumsy mistakes. Ariane's expression remained a little stiff, her gestures formal, but Senneth was confident the thaw would soon be complete.

She told Sosie as much once Ariane had taken Darryn away to consult with her captains. "She can be frightening, and she can be fierce, but she would do anything for her children," Senneth said. "She'll come around. She can't stand to be estranged from Darryn."

"I don't think I breathed once the whole time she was talking to me," Sosie said. Indeed, she still sounded like she was gasping for air. "Darryn is so different from her!"

Senneth laughed. "Darryn is certainly less imposing, but Ariane is one of the people I trust most," Senneth said. "I would choose her over my brothers any day. Be good to Darryn and she will be good to you. And when someone like Ariane Rappengrass is on your side, well, life becomes a little easier."

Sosie looked doubtful and changed the subject. "Senneth, you remember I introduced you to a mystic named Lara when you were in Carrebos?"

"Yes. She was very strange."

"She *is* strange, but she's traveling with us, and I think you'll be glad. She has amazing healing powers, and I have to guess that many soldiers are being wounded in this war."

"Hundreds," Senneth said. "We will be profoundly grateful for her services. I'd be happy to have her ride with me, but I'm about to head out right now."

Sosie glanced around, smiled and shrugged. "I don't know where she is. She might already have ridden for your camp. But if I see her again, I'll tell her that you need her as soon as she can arrive."

Senneth nodded and swung back onto her borrowed mount. "Then I will look for her, and I will look for you as well. I know it is a war—but—try to stay safe."

Sosie waved good-bye as Senneth pulled the horse around. "You, too."

Senneth grinned. "And good luck with Ariane." She waved, clucked to the horse, and took off at a steady gallop.

The day was fair, a little chilly, but spring had definitely arrived in this rocky, undulating land that led straight toward the foothills of the Lireth Mountains. As if overnight, the brown winter grass had put on a green coat; the early bushes had already flowered and lost their petals, while the late ones were sprinkled with color. Patches of wildflowers waved their bright heads in the cool air, turning their faces toward the sun. Even the hard earth had softened up. Her horse's hooves scarcely jarred against the packed ground as they raced along. It was so easy to imagine the frenetic life unfolding just under the topsoil—the busy insects working through clumped dirt, the sleepy moles nosing through their clever tunnels, the clenched roots of trees and bushes uncurling and stretching toward water.

Senneth almost laughed at herself, for she was not in the habit of thinking in such poetic terms. She thought perhaps the mystic Lara had ridden this way just an hour or so before her, leaving a trail of spring magic in her wake. That would account for Senneth's strange fancies; that would explain her sudden and unjustifiable lift of hope.

She rode steadily, stopping once to water the horse and eat a quick meal. She estimated she could be back at the royal camp before nightfall—in plenty of time to spray a few sparks across the enemy lines, perhaps even disable a whole regiment. Just the thought caused her blisters to ache, made her hands tighten on the reins.

But fire was what she had to offer the princess, and fire was what she would deliver.

It was about an hour before sunset when she pulled close enough to pick up the muted roar of battle. The terrain was just hilly enough to prevent her from seeing the clash of opposing armies, but she could hear faint sounds of voices shouting and weapons ringing, catch a slight whiff of smoke. Dread settled back over her heart, and fear as well. What terrible events might she have missed in the day and a half that she had been gone? Nothing too awful, of course—Donnal or Kirra would have brought extraordinary news. But that left a whole range of ordinary terrors. . . .

The thought had barely passed through her mind when she saw a rider racing her way, dressed in Brassenthwaite blue. The feeling of dread intensified; she urged her horse to a gallop. The messenger was clearly looking for her. He pulled his horse up in a spray of loose dirt as they intersected.

"What? What is it?" she demanded.

"Serra Kirra," he panted.

Kirra? If Kirra had been injured, there was no way Donnal would have left her side to find Senneth. But why hadn't Cammon sent out a frantic cry? Sweet gods, could there be so many other things happening at the battlefront that Cammon didn't even *know*? She kicked her horse into a run and called over the hoofbeats, "What happened? How badly is she hurt?" It was inconceivable that Kirra could be dead.

The messenger, pounding along beside her, could scarcely get his breath. "She had—changed shape—lioness. Gisseltess man—got off a lucky shot. Brought her down."

Senneth's stomach cramped. "Where is she now?"

The Brassenthwaite man was having a hard time keeping up. Indeed, if she hadn't wanted the rest of his information, she would have left him behind. "That man of hers—"

"Donnal?"

The messenger nodded. "He was able to—bring her to safety. But her—her wounds are deep. She wasn't—conscious—"

More and more terrifying. Now Senneth's lungs were seizing up, while her stomach was still tightly clenched. "Is she with Ellynor?" *Has Lara arrived yet? Oh, Bright Mother, bring all the mystics to camp right now to save Kirra. . . .*

"I don't know—who's with her, serra." He gasped. "Your brother sent me after you."

Senneth nodded and leaned lower in the saddle, coaxing more speed from Ariane's horse. Senneth had a rough-and-ready sort of healing power herself, and it worked well on injuries. If she could get there in time—if she could lay her hands on Kirra's wound—oh, surely, surely, she could save that bright girl's precious life—

"This way," the Brassenthwaite man called as Senneth turned her horse toward the east, following the path that would take her around the worst of the fighting. "There was a skirmish there—this morning. I don't know—if enemy soldiers are still in place."

She let him take the lead on a more indirect route, though every nerve in her body was screaming to go faster, cut straight cross-country, never mind the obstacles. She had completely forgotten any fancies about hope and spring. All she could see now were barren hillocks, stripped trees, the unfriendly and stony terrain that lay between her and her goal.

They swept around one of those low hills to find a handful of men scattered across their path. *Scavengers*, Senneth thought first, for they wore no identifying colors from either army. And then, with even more contempt, *Traitors*. For one of them wheeled his horse right in front of her, pulling a sword to bar her passage. She saw a flash of topaz on his finger. A Storian man.

She lifted her hand to fling fire, to scorch her way through this roadblock, but just then the false Brassenthwaite man crashed his mount against hers, sending them careening off the road. Her horse bucked and skidded; the fight to stay on its back momentarily diverted her from magic. Before she could raise her hand again, one of the other riders swooped close enough to grab her left wrist and practically yank her from the saddle.

She felt all her nerves arc with shock and then go dead.

"Ah, Senneth," Halchon Gisseltess purred in her ear. "How careless of you to fall into my hands."

CHAPTER
38

THEY rode for perhaps an hour. Wherever he was taking her, it wasn't back to his army's camp. That was about the only coherent thought Senneth could form while Halchon Gisseltess carried her before him on his horse.

He had caught her. He was taking her somewhere. She was powerless against him. He was touching her, and he might well be planning to rape her, and she could do nothing to stop him; and she would rather be dead.

She tried to force herself to take in details, to guess which direction they were headed. West and a little south, she thought. She had a terrible suspicion they were on the way to Ghosenhall. He had always said he wanted to install her as his queen in the royal city. He had to know she would not consent to such a farce—that the minute he released her, she would turn on him with fury and fire. Perhaps he did not intend to release her until she had been well and truly immobilized. Perhaps, while they had been fighting at the tip of Brassenthwaite, a regiment of his soldiers had marched through Ghosenhall and occupied the palace. Perhaps he had already prepared a bed of moonstones to be her bower, had fitted a room for her with shackles and chains. Perhaps, after all, she was doomed to be his lover and his queen.

She had been afraid of him her whole life. From the day she had first met him, his touch had wiped her clean of power, had filled her soul with depression and her mind with utter bleakness. When she was seventeen, she had broken with her father in the most drastic fashion to avoid an arranged marriage with Halchon Gisseltess. She could not bear to think, after all her travels, all her adventures, her life had brought her back to the same desperate point.

One of the accompanying soldiers pressed nearer. "Marlord. The others are just ahead. Will we camp for the night or keep moving?"

Halchon spoke over her head. "Camp, but not just yet. I want to travel as far as we can even after the light fails."

"Do you expect a pursuit?"

Halchon laughed softly. "I do. But not until her distracted friends realize that she's missing. They won't know who's got her or where. We have some time, I think."

Speaking in a rather hesitant voice, the Gisseltess man said, "But aren't they mystics? Her friends?"

Halchon's own voice dripped with contempt. "*She's* a mystic, and *she* was quickly taken. Don't be afraid of magic, soldier. It is so easily overcome."

It's not, Senneth wanted to cry. *Only mine! Only by you!* But she did not even have the energy to speak.

In another five minutes they had come upon a group of soldiers stationed along the road. Senneth tried to count—maybe fifty of them—all in Gisseltess black and red. Her despair intensified. Perhaps, if she had been able to free herself from Halchon's hold, she would have been able to fight off the six or seven men who had helped him handle the ambush, but she could not outmaneuver this many. She had no idea how quickly her magic would return once Halchon released her. Instantly? In five minutes? In an hour? The way she felt now, she might never be able to call fire again.

And there was no guarantee Halchon would ever release her. . . .

After a brief conference, the two groups merged and continued on the westward journey, traveling much more slowly now that it was almost completely dark. There were no jokes between the men, no wasted excursions off the road. This must be the marlord's most elite and devoted guard, efficient and seasoned.

None of them were likely to be moved to pity by Senneth's situation.

No one would help her. She could not help herself. She could so easily die.

She would rather die, if the alternative was to take Halchon Gisseltess to her bed.

After about another hour of riding, the lead soldier came trotting back to where Halchon rode in the center of his men. "Marlord, up ahead about a hundred yards is a good place for camping. Under a natural overhang, with water not far. Defensible and out of the wind. Or did you want to keep riding?"

"No, that sounds good. Make it ready."

The soldier nodded and rode off. Halchon gave Senneth a little squeeze and murmured, "Did you hear that? I'm sure you're glad to hear we're about to make camp. You've had a long and tiring day and must be longing to lay your head down."

She did not answer. She wasn't sure she could. She tried not to shiver, she who was never cold, but a small shudder passed through her, and she was sure he could feel it.

He laughed. "Senneth, Senneth, Senneth. All these years we've been friends, and you're still afraid of me? I'm not going to take you on the cold ground surrounded by a few dozen of my men. I have waited too long to enjoy the pleasures of your body. We will be in Ghosenhall, perhaps, or Gissel Plain—or at least some fine inn with clean sheets and a decent brandy!—before I make you my lover." His arm tightened again. He leaned forward and brushed his lips against her cheek. She felt as if he had laid ice against her skin. "But that day will be very soon, I promise you. I have waited a very long time, and I am not in the mood to be patient much longer."

There was no need to reply, for they had arrived at the evening's campsite. *Now*, Senneth thought, trying to will her muscles to tense, her mind to plan for action. *Now, in the chaos of dismounting, in the confusion of many bodies. Break free of him. Set all his men on fire.*

But she couldn't do it.

He didn't release her, in any case. He freed himself from the stirrups and then leapt lightly to the ground, still holding her clutched against him. For a moment, her feet wouldn't support her and she swooned against him, feeling dizzy, feeling weak. But then his hold shifted. He kept one hand clamped tightly around her right wrist, but no longer had an arm passed around her waist. She could breathe again, and she took in great windy gusts of air. She almost felt steady, almost believed she could think.

Surreptitiously, she made a fist of her left hand, but her fingers were cold. There was no fire in her. Halchon still had hold of her, and all her magic was in abeyance.

"I need a moment of privacy," she said to him in a raw voice.

Someone had started a campfire, and so he had just enough light to peer into her face. "She speaks! And asks for impossible things."

She stared at him steadily, letting him see all her hatred, all her defiance. She didn't have to put her hopelessness on her face; that he had obviously discerned for himself. "Then I suppose I will wet myself here in the middle of your camp."

He seemed amused. "We might both attend to our bodily needs a few steps out of the firelight," he said. "Tricky, yes, but we are modest, resourceful people. We shall each endeavor to turn our eyes away and let the other attend to his or her business."

Revolting, embarrassing, but unavoidable. She followed him past the overhang, crouched when he did, accomplished her task with the minimum of grace, and followed him back into the firelight. Someone had already laid out a simple meal, and Halchon pulled her down next to him on a blanket before the fire.

"Are you hungry, my dear?" he asked her in a solicitous voice.

Not at all. She thought she might choke if she tried to swallow anything, but the gods alone knew what the next few hours, the next few days, held for her. She must try to keep up her strength. Who knew when an opportunity might present itself? "A little."

"Then here. Some bread, some dried meat. Plain fare, but tasty after a hard day's riding."

Both of them ate one-handed, for his fingers were still locked around her wrist. She was clumsy with her left hand, but that forced her to focus on using it, and that meant some of her attention was distracted from her fear and anger and revulsion. When would her friends realize she was missing? Had Cammon, perhaps, sensed her distress, or was Halchon's antithetical nature preventing the other mystic from picking up any signal from her at all? Tayse would have started worrying by now, particularly if Kirra had reported that Senneth planned to be back by nightfall.

Assuming Kirra herself had made it back.

She forced herself to look at Halchon. "So was it a lie then? About Kirra?"

"Oh, she's quite healthy, as far as I know," Halchon said. "Of course, I missed half of the day's battle, so any number of your friends could have fallen by now." He took a bite of meat. "Serramarra Kirra Danalustrous. Marlord Kiernan Brassenthwaite. Princess Amalie." He took another bite. "Your husband."

"All of them would gladly give their lives," she said quietly, "if it meant keeping you from the throne of Gillengaria."

"Well, once they realize I've got *you*, I think some of the fight might go out of them," he said.

"Do you think to ransom me? Use me to convince them to lay down their arms?" She shook her head. "The regent would never advise the princess to make such a disastrous trade. Neither would my brother. Not very sentimental men."

"No, and I quite applaud their hard-heartedness. But I think, when they see how easily I have captured *you*, they will reassess their chances of success against me. They will say, 'Ah, that clever Halchon. We cannot win against him. We will cut our losses—we will surrender while we can.'"

"I don't believe the loss of one mystic will weigh that heavily in their calculations." They were far enough away by now that it didn't matter what he knew. "Besides, there are reinforcements on the way even as we speak. Ariane Rappengrass has brought an army to fight for the princess."

He was unimpressed. "Yes, and I will counter with fresh soldiers of my own—Arberharst troops marching down through Tilt. You still do not have the numbers, Senneth. You cannot win."

"We have numbers we didn't count on," she said. "Nocklyn forces ride with Rappengrass."

She had the satisfaction of seeing his eyebrows twitch together in a frown. "Impossible. Nocklyn is—" He pressed his lips together.

She felt a moment's triumph, and it was sweet. "Nocklyn is under the control of marlady Mayva," she drawled. "Whose husband has been arrested for murder. Oh!" She put her free hand to her mouth. "Wasn't her husband a relation of yours?"

His eyes narrowed, but he offered her a cold smile. "So. Mayva surprises everyone, and my cousin most of all, no doubt. You may be pleased, and I may be disgruntled, but it makes no material difference. I still have superior forces—and I still have you. Next to Amalie, you are the most visible figure in the royal army. And you are in my power. That will shake the princess. That will shake her defenders. Mark my words, when the fight resumes in the morning, the royal camp will be in turmoil, and my allies will press their advantage."

That's not why you took me, she wanted to say—except she didn't want him to answer, didn't want him to speak of his plans for her. Instead she said coldly, "You will be surprised at how fiercely they will fight. Whether or not I am with them."

"Well, I might be, except I will not be there to see it," he said. One of his men took away their plates and Halchon stretched his legs out comfortably before him. "You and I, Senneth, are headed to Ghosenhall. I have a regiment stationed there, and I understand the residents of the city have become quite—ah—eager to accommodate my soldiers in all regards. I thought it an interesting move when you decided to abandon the city—strategically wise, perhaps, but symbolically disastrous! Ghosenhall is where the king resides—whoever resides in Ghosenhall is the king. Once we are installed in the palace, my dear, we will be hard to dislodge. And if, as seems to me very likely, your little princess is soon advised by her regent to flee for her life, well, then! She will be in Brassenthwaite or

Kianlever—but I will be sitting on the throne in Ghosenhall, with you at my side. It will be easy for me to call myself king, then, don't you think? It will only seem natural."

"It will never seem natural to think of *you* on the throne," she said.

He laughed. "Nonsense. You will quickly grow resigned to the notion, I think." Unexpectedly, he jerked her into his arms and laid his mouth heavily upon hers. It was like being kissed by death. Senneth felt as if she was suffocating, as if her body had been coated with ice. He held her tighter, and she lost all ability to breathe.

When he finally lifted his head, he smiled down at her, his own breathing harsh and his eyes lit by dark satisfaction. "I have waited so long to taste your mouth," he murmured. "And it is just as delicious as I had always hoped. Senneth, I live for the day I take you as my wife." He bent his head to kiss her again.

She struggled madly in his arms, trying to at least get one hand free. She was a swordswoman; she had trained with Riders. Surely, even if her magic had failed, her physical strength was still uncompromised. He shifted his hold, and her right arm slipped from his grasp. She balled her fist and swung her hand hard into his ribs.

Halchon grunted and loosened his grip, and she punched him again. Dimly she was aware of movement around them—his men, hearing their struggle, coming to his aid—but she paid them no attention. She struck him again and fought to her knees as his hands flailed and his fingers slipped and, just for a moment, he lost contact with her.

She kicked him hard in the groin and somersaulted backward, calling flame from both hands as she landed in a crouch. Shouts rang out from all around her; the campfire leapt skyward. Halchon would not burn, so she sprayed the rest of the soldiers with a fine fire, and they yelped and started running away from her. Could she hold them all at bay? She got one foot under her and tried to push herself to a standing position.

Someone struck her a hard blow from behind, flattening her to the ground, and then Halchon was sprawled across her, covering her body with his. Instantly, the flames at her fingertips went out. The campfire hissed and died away to coal. Instantly, she was wretched and dull and wracked with misery.

Halchon was breathing heavily in her ear. "So! Not quite as docile as you have pretended all afternoon! To tell you the truth, I was beginning to be a little bored, but this display of temper reassures me. Such a tumultuous life we will have together, Senneth! But I see I will never be able to relax my guard for a minute."

"I'll kill you when I get the chance," she panted.

He hauled himself to a sitting position, dragging her up with him. "But you'll never get the chance, my dear."

"Everyone is careless," she said. "Even you."

He patted her hair, as if she was a rebellious child of whom he was inordinately fond. "I think soon you will become so used to me that you'll lose all desire to murder me in my sleep," he said. "That, or you'll become so worn down that you'll be unable to summon the strength to fight. It will be interesting to see which."

She didn't answer him; indeed, she didn't speak to him again as the whole camp began to bed down for the night. Once she was under Halchon's control again, the soldiers returned, clearly unnerved by her display of power and sheepish about how quickly it had routed them. The marlord and one of his men discussed their route in the morning while the other soldiers divided the watches. Someone built the fire back up. The rest of them distributed themselves on the ground or took their stations to guard the perimeter.

Halchon pulled Senneth back to the blanket where they had sat for their meal. A second blanket had been unrolled on top of it, and Senneth silently allowed him to situate her beneath it and then lie down beside her. He slipped his arm over her waist and pressed his body to her back. Sweet gods, such a horrific mockery of the loving embrace she was used to sharing with Tayse every night.

Halchon kissed the back of her head. "Sleep well, Senneth, and recruit your strength. Today can't have been easy for you, and I'm afraid we have a long ride ahead of us tomorrow." His arm squeezed her closer and then relaxed a little. "I'm so glad you're here with me tonight."

She didn't reply. She wasn't sure if she should try to sleep, and thus be rested enough to make another try for freedom in the morning, or if she should stay awake so she could attempt to slip away from him while he slumbered. His touch was still poisonous, still nauseating, but a sense of fierce elation was helping her combat the helpless despair his very presence engendered.

As soon as she had escaped from him, she had been able to call fire. It bided in her blood, ready to be summoned at an instant's notice. All she needed was a second. All she had to do was get free.

DAWN arrived, overcast, cold, and grudging. It was barely light enough to see, but Senneth heard a few of the Gisseltess soldiers grumbling as they rolled out of their beds, stoked the fire, and quietly assembled a meal. Most everyone else, Halchon included, was still sleeping. His arm was still leaden across her waist. He had not moved an inch away from her all night.

Senneth had slept fitfully, jerking awake over and over again, convinced that she was drowning. But that was just Halchon's touch making it hard for her lungs to draw in air. Weariness had settled deep into her bones, right alongside fear—but determination was making a hard, cold shell around her heart.

Halchon would make a mistake. He would be careless. And she would make her move.

Not lifting her head from the blanket, Senneth sent her gaze around the camp, noting how many were stirring, how many were sleeping. It looked like five men were still on watch and three were preparing the breakfast. Two or three others were sitting up, checking weapons or digging through saddlebags. The rest appeared to still be lost to sleep. Her odds would never be better than this.

Just to be sure, she glanced around one more time, and she saw Tayse.

He put a finger to his lips and disappeared.

For a moment, astonishment left her rigid, and then her mind started to race. *Tayse was here!* Had crept into this camp entirely undetected and vanished apparently at will. So either fear and sleeplessness had combined to give her hallucinations, or he had been escorted to this place by Ellynor. And if Ellynor was here, Justin was here. And if Justin and Tayse were here, other Riders might be with them.

And if the Riders had come to rescue her, Senneth was as good as saved.

Now all she had to do was make it possible for them to save her.

She sat up hastily, pulling Halchon's arm with her. Almost, it was enough to break his hold, but even as he fought back sleep he snatched her wrist and prevented her from scrambling away. "I see a night of calm reflection has done nothing to reconcile you to your changed situation," he said through a yawn.

"There are not enough nights left in my life to accustom me to the thought of being your prisoner," she answered coolly.

He laughed softly. "I hope you are wrong about that, or you have a melancholy existence ahead of you."

What she had to do was separate Halchon from his men. "I need to relieve myself," she said baldly. "Pull yourself to your feet and take me to someplace that approximates privacy."

"Gladly, my dear," he said, rising and helping her stand beside him. "Then we shall eat, and then we shall be on our way."

He led her a short distance away from camp, though all his soldiers were still plainly in view. Keeping one hand on her wrist, he reached down with the other and began to fumble with his trousers.

Tayse materialized before them like a furious god, his sword upraised and gleaming. "Release her before I kill you," he growled.

Too swiftly for Senneth to anticipate, Halchon jerked her against him and drew a knife across her neck. "Come a step closer, and she dies," he hissed.

For a moment, the three of them were frozen, the Rider with his sword arm reared back to strike, the marlord with a dagger to his hostage's throat, and Senneth motionless between them. Behind them, there was a sudden outcry and the furious clash of weapons. Whoever else had accompanied Tayse had apparently just engaged the Gisseltess soldiers. But Senneth couldn't risk even a glance in that direction. She was focused on Tayse, watching his face, waiting for any signal that would let her know what to do next. Halchon was surely dead, but she might be, too, if she wasn't very, very careful.

"I have waited a long time to kill you," Tayse said in the iciest voice Senneth had ever heard.

Halchon almost laughed. "You will never do anything to jeopardize her life, and I swear to you I will take it this instant if you do not back away and let me ride to safety."

"There is no safety for a man such as yourself. You have commissioned regicide, and you are scheduled for execution at my hands. Even if you do not fall to me today, you are reviled throughout the kingdom, and any man who sees you may feel justified in cutting you down."

It was a masterfully delivered speech, but Senneth missed some of it when a small, cold, invisible hand took hold of hers where it dangled free just under the restraint of Halchon's arm. It was all she could do not to flinch and scream, but, of course, she instantly understood the message. Ellynor was there. Senneth should make herself ready.

Therefore, she was not surprised when Halchon's sneering reply was abruptly interrupted. "Any man who sees me may call me 'king' for I— *ufght!*" Halchon gasped as someone landed a body blow from behind. His hold loosened just enough for Senneth to spin away.

Only two revolutions to her pirouette, but when she planted her feet and gazed back at her erstwhile abductor, Halchon was already kneeling on the ground with a blade through his heart. Tayse stood above him, staring remorselessly down, his hands still on the hilt. "You deserve a cruel death than this," he said, and tore the blade downward with such force that Halchon's body practically split in two.

Senneth had to fight back a sob of horror and relief. Ellynor was suddenly standing beside her, concern on her face. "Are you hurt?" Ellynor asked.

Senneth shook her head wildly. "No—no—he didn't harm me. He just—his touch—I couldn't—"

Tayse wrenched his sword free and strode over to take Senneth in a hard embrace. Oh, how different the feel of *this* man's arms around her! Strength flowed from his body into hers; her soul ignited. "His touch will never trouble you again," Tayse said.

There was no time for a passionate reunion. Behind them, the sounds of conflict intensified. Senneth pulled free and forced herself to run toward the battle, calling, "How many did you bring? Halchon had about fifty men."

Tayse and Ellynor were racing along beside her. "We number twenty," Tayse called back. "But eight are Riders."

Senneth nodded and raised her arms above her head.

Gods, it felt so good to summon fire again, to feel it kindle in her veins and pour from her fingertips. This was close fighting, so she must be careful, throw her bolts at precise targets. There—a man in red and black. She twisted her wrist, and his uniform went up in flames. He dropped to the ground, shrieking. Beside him, two Gisseltess men were boring in on the Rider Wen, whose blade flashed exquisitely as she lunged and parried. Senneth clenched her fingers, then snapped her hands open, and both of Wen's attackers erupted into fire.

"To me! To me!" someone cried—another Gisseltess soldier shouting for reinforcements. Excellent; four of them bunched together, back-to-back, making a vigorous stand. Senneth turned them into a private conflagration. Their swords dropped and their screams of agony rent the air.

Around her, the Riders and their fellows were making short work of the rest of Halchon's forces—those who did not cut and run, galloping off in five directions to escape the slaughter. Senneth saw Justin swing his head around at the sound of hoofbeats, then he turned to Tayse and called, "Should we go after them?"

"No," Tayse replied. "Let them carry the tale to the rebel armies. Halchon Gisseltess is dead."

Justin was surveying the carnage around him, his bloodied sword still at the ready, but at that he looked over with a grin on his streaked and dirty face. "He *is*? Then this has been a damn successful day."

Tayse's eyes had sought out Senneth; he nodded at her gravely. "Indeed," he said, "it is a day to celebrate."

THEY took another half hour to comb the small camp for survivors, finding none. Senneth was a little surprised to find, among her rescuers, a handful of Lirren fighters.

"I know you," she said, approaching two compact, dark-haired men who stood with Ellynor. "You're Ellynor's brothers. Torrin and Hayden."

"We are kin," Torrin said immediately, for when they had met last fall, they had established their tenuous familial connection.

"Thank you for coming to my rescue."

Now Torrin showed the brash grin that reminded her so much of Justin. "We're kin," he repeated. "We can't let you languish in the hands of enemies. Though we do think it was careless of you to get caught."

"Torrin!" Ellynor exclaimed.

"It *was* careless," Senneth agreed. "And, although the entire experience was dreadful, I'd go through it again just to see Halchon Gisseltess slaughtered before my eyes."

Justin charged up and swept her into a hug that took her off her feet. "Someday I'll describe to you the look on Tayse's face when Cammon came running up to tell us that you'd been taken," he said before setting her back down. "It was clear at that point that Halchon would die at the end of Tayse's sword. But, Bright Mother burn me, I never want to be that afraid again. And all Cammon knew was that the marlord had grabbed you. He completely lost touch with you after that—and apparently he couldn't read Halchon Gisseltess at all."

"Then how did you find me?"

Justin nodded toward the Lirren men. "They tracked you. Never saw anyone able to move through the landscape like that, just reading every print and broken bit of bark. They helped sneak us into camp this morning, too. I thought Ellynor was good, but—"

Hayden looked scornful. "Women have their skills, but they are insignificant in battle."

Justin laughed outright. "I might not be saying that in front of Senneth. Or even your sister."

Torrin gave Senneth a sideways look. "But Senneth was captured," he said, clearly intending to provoke her. "How good can her skills be?"

"How did it happen?" Ellynor asked.

"A man wearing Brassenthwaite colors came riding up to tell me Kirra had been injured," she said and shrugged. "He described the arrow through the lioness's body. I believed it, and I followed him. But when I got to the place where she was supposed to have fallen, Gisseltess men were there instead."

"I might have been tricked, too," Justin admitted.

Tayse joined them at that moment, putting his arms around Senneth from behind. "Nothing here left to do," he said. "Are we ready to move on?"

She leaned against him, knowing it was a weakness to need his strength, but nonetheless reveling in his presence, his touch, his mere existence. She had not even dared to hope he would be able to find her. All because of Cammon—and Ellynor—and the Riders—and the Lirren men. So many had come together to save her. She felt a moment's regret. "All these swords were subtracted from the fight because you came after me," she said. "I hope that loss does not weigh heavily against Amalie's forces."

"We brought down as many enemies here as we would have in a day's pitched battle," Torrin said with a shrug.

"And Halchon Gisseltess is dead," Justin added. "I'd count it a good day's work."

"But more work ahead of us to do," Tayse said. "Let's ride out."

CHAPTER

39

CAMMON knew the exact instant Senneth broke free of Halchon for the second time. He had felt her first brief, thwarted bid for escape, and so at least he knew she was still alive—until suddenly magic shut her down again, and he could not sense her at all. Therefore, he was so elated he was almost giddy when Tayse's surge of profound relief woke him early that morning. Tayse had seen Senneth, and she was whole.

A few minutes later, Senneth herself burst back into Cammon's consciousness, blazing with fury. The swift, brutal fight twenty miles away was clearer to him than the one that had unfolded on the nearer battlefield yesterday afternoon, since he experienced it from Senneth's point of view, as well as Tayse's and Justin's.

He turned to Amalie, who was just sitting up in bed, willing herself to face another day of bloodshed. "Halchon Gisseltess is dead," he said.

Her eyes widened. "And Senneth?"

"Alive and safe, if a little bruised."

She threw her arms around his neck and kissed him on the mouth. "I have to go tell my uncle Romar!"

Indeed, the news flew around the camp within the hour, and more than one individual sought Cammon out for confirmation.

"Halchon Gisseltess is dead?" Kiernan Brassenthwaite demanded. "You're sure?"

"Positive."

"What of my sister?"

Cammon thought it was interesting that Kiernan had asked first after the marlord. "Weary but unharmed."

"This changes the very essence of the war," he said, and disappeared.

Indeed, it was a day when their fortunes seemed to shift altogether. By noon, the forces from Nocklyn and Rappengrass had arrived and flung their fresh bodies into the mix. The rebel armies were actually pushed backward for the first time since battle had been joined. Cammon could feel Romar Brendyn's fierce triumph—indeed, every soldier in the camp exuded a sense of rising optimism. They were all awash with hope.

It was harder to hold on to that hope when the day was spent among the wounded and dying soldiers. With Ellynor gone, healers were in short supply, and Amalie had gone straight to the hospital tents after she had told her uncle the good news. Despite the fact that she had only the most rudimentary powers of healing, her presence had a powerful effect on the hurt soldiers. Cammon could feel them struggling to mend themselves even faster just so they could risk their lives for her again.

"If no more soldiers would fall, I do believe we might be able to save those who have been hurt so far," Kirra said around noon that day, as she and Amalie and Cammon took a break to eat. "But, gods! This is hard work."

They were sitting outside a tent on three rather uncomfortable stools. Cammon glanced up to watch the progress of a hawk circling overhead and angling downward. "Donnal has news," he said.

Kirra gave him a glance of irritation. "It's annoying that you can tell it's Donnal even before I can."

More practically, Amalie said, "Good news or bad?"

Donnal landed a few feet away and shifted into his human shape so quickly they could not follow the changes. "Good, I think."

"Then this day continues to be the best one we've had so far," Amalie replied.

Donnal came closer, bowed to Amalie, and grinned at them all. "The regent asked me to go to Tilt and check on the progress of the Arberharst reinforcements," he said. "He wanted to know how close they were and if I could get a more accurate count."

"And?" Kirra demanded.

Donnal shook his head. "And they're gone."

"*Gone!*" the three of them cried in unison. Kirra added, "What do you mean, gone? Back on their ships? Eaten by wild animals? What?"

"Intercepted by Danalustrous forces and harried back toward the sea."

They all exclaimed at that, Kirra most vociferously demanding the rest of the story. Donnal dropped to the ground beside her and told his tale.

"I heard the sounds of battle before I was close enough to see anything. Eventually it was visible from the air—the soldiers of Danalustrous fighting the soldiers of Arberharst. I couldn't count precise numbers, but it was clear there were far more Danalustrous men. The fight was almost over by the time I got there. Looked like maybe six hundred foreigners broke and ran, heading north to where I'd guess their ships are anchored. Half of the Danalustrous army pursued them."

"This is wonderful news!" Amalie exclaimed. "But—so unexpected! Didn't your father say he wouldn't risk Danalustrous in this war?"

Kirra nodded. "Did you ask anyone for an explanation?" she said to Donnal.

"Not in so many words," he replied, grinning again. "I did take human shape and introduce myself to the captain as an emissary for the princess. I didn't recognize him, but he seemed to know my name, for he was very civil."

"Every Danalustrous man is civil," Kirra said automatically. "What did he say?"

"That Malcolm Danalustrous considered this invasion by Arberharst troops to be an assault on Danalustrous," Donnal replied. "I can't tell property boundaries from the air, but he swore that the Arberharst army had not moved through Tilt land, but instead had marched through unaligned territory between Tilt and Danalustrous. Too close for the marlord's comfort. So he was justified in—I can't remember how the captain put it—'patrolling his borders and discouraging any outsiders from crossing.' Something like that."

Kirra practically bounced on her stool. "Well! My father comes through, and most gloriously, I might add! And does us some real good without compromising his principles. Oh, this makes me fonder of him than I have been in a long time!"

Cammon felt Valri approaching and turned to beckon her closer. "Good news," he called.

She hurried over. "Are they back? Senneth and the others?"

"Even better news," Amalie said.

Valri's smile looked strained. "What could be more welcome than the sight of all our friends returned to us unscathed?"

She was worried about someone in the rescue party, Cammon realized. "They're safe," he assured her. "Everyone unharmed."

She was trying not to ask outright. "All of them?" she said. "Even Ellynor? For I know you generally can't read the emotions of Lirrenfolk."

"He'd certainly read Justin if something had happened to Ellynor," Donnal commented.

But, of course, Valri's concern was for someone else, and Cammon had finally realized who. "Did Lirren men ride with Tayse?" he said. Valri nodded dumbly, and he added, "No one in the rescue party was injured. I would know from the reactions of the others. They are riding back with all speed—in fact, they should be here within the hour."

"Thank the Great Mother," Valri whispered and seemed to slump a little.

Amalie jumped to her feet and put her arms around Valri's waist, murmuring comforting phrases. Cammon could see Kirra's face alight with interest, though she managed to keep from blurting out any questions. At least right at that moment. As soon as Donnal had disappeared to share his information with Romar, and Amalie and Valri had ducked back into one of the tents, Kirra turned on Cammon.

"Tell me, tell me, tell me," she demanded. "How is the queen's romance progressing with the Lirren man? Arrol, is that his name? Handsome enough, but a little too reserved for my taste."

He couldn't help but grin. "I would imagine *you* would be the last sort of woman a Lirren man would be able to tolerate," he said. "They like their girls meeker, I think."

"Valri's hardly meek," she retorted. "Though I would admit she's not quite as *animated* as I can be. But you didn't answer my question."

"You know I don't gossip about things like that."

She grabbed his throat and pretended she would choke the life out of him. "I will turn you into some kind of repulsive night-crawling creature if you don't answer me," she threatened.

"And I'll send images of Romar Brendyn into your mind every night," he countered. "I think I can do it, even if I'm a vole."

She released him. "Oh, now that was cruel! What an awful boy you turned out to be." She gave him one of her most radiant smiles, clearly designed to dazzle. "Come now, Cammon," she coaxed. "Just a little information. Nothing too revealing. Does she love him? Does he love her? Is she happy?"

"She's happy," he confirmed. "Or she will be when the whole party is back safely."

"And Halchon Gisseltess is dead," she said. "So Sabina Gisseltess can be happy, too."

"I don't think that's why Tayse killed him," Cammon replied. "I don't even think he did it to help win the war. He did it to protect Senneth."

"Yes," she said, "and that's the best reason yet."

CAMMON knew the others had returned when he felt them cross into camp. Everyone else knew they were back when fire exploded in the middle of the enemy army. Except for Ellynor, all of them charged straight back into battle—the Riders, the Lirrenfolk, and Senneth. Bent on making up for lost time. Bent on retaliating for the sting of Senneth's capture.

When the day was over and darkness abruptly descended, they had forced the rebels back another half mile.

The mood that night was one of tempered elation. So much accomplished, so much still to do. They all gathered in Amalie's tent and discussed how to capitalize on their many bits of good fortune.

"Halchon dead, Rappengrass and Nocklyn soldiers on hand, and Arberharst reinforcements turned back at the border," Romar enumerated. "The advantage is definitely ours."

"Our numbers are still no more than even," Kiernan warned. "And they still possess Arberharst fighters who are immune to our magic."

Cammon caught the droll look Senneth turned on Kirra. *Our magic.* As if he would claim it for his own.

"Do you think they have learned yet that Halchon is dead?" Romar asked.

Cammon spoke up. "I believe so. I caught a great sense of dismay emanating from their camp shortly after Senneth and the others arrived."

"That might break their spirit a great deal," Tayse commented. "He's the one who wanted the crown. Why keep fighting if the chief rebel is gone?"

"You're forgetting Rayson Fortunalt," Kirra said. She rarely attended these conferences or spoke up when she did, but tonight was a special occasion. Tonight, they all wanted to participate. "He supported Halchon in the bid for the throne, but he's ambitious, too. Surely he's saying to himself right now, 'I would make as good a king as any man from Gisseltess.'"

Romar glanced at Kiernan. "Do you agree?"

Kiernan nodded. "I don't see Rayson being turned aside by this setback. And some of the Gisseltess men might be energized by Halchon's death, willing to fight even harder to avenge him."

"The Arberharst men might lose some of their motivation, however," Senneth noted. "If he was paying them to fight and he's gone—" She shrugged.

"My guess is Rayson now controls their joint purse," Romar replied. "So it won't matter to them that Halchon Gisseltess is dead."

"What if Rayson Fortunalt were also to die?" Tayse asked.

There was a moment of silence in the tent. "Could that be accomplished?" Kiernan asked finally. "For I'm not above singling out a man and bringing him down if it means the end to war."

"He stays well to the back—hard to reach even for a skilled archer," Romar said. "Our attempts to infiltrate the camp in stealth have been so far unsuccessful."

"Maybe we could try magic," Justin said. His eyes were fixed on Kirra. "Send in a lone fighter shaped like a night creature. Change him to a man when he's past all the sentries."

"If it's as easy as all that, why didn't we kill off Halchon Gisseltess before battle was even joined?" Kiernan demanded.

"Because Halchon is—was—immune to magic," Senneth replied. "I don't believe I'm the only mystic who found her power useless around him. He could not have been assassinated in any way that depended on sorcery."

"And I'm not sure Rayson can be, either!" Kirra exclaimed. "It is true I could change Justin's shape and follow him to Rasyon's tent, and then change him to a man with a sword in his hand, but there is still some danger. Each transformation takes time. We might be interrupted by Fortunalt soldiers before I could safely change us both back to creatures that could fly away."

Donnal spoke up from the rear of the tent. Even more rarely than Kirra had he joined these councils, and Cammon could not remember a time he had ever offered an observation. "I have a simpler plan," he said.

"Then by all means, tell us," Romar invited.

"I go. I kill the marlord. I escape." He shrugged. "I can take any form, including that of a swordsman. And I can change so rapidly that even if soldiers burst into the tent while I battle with the marlord, I will be able to elude them. I am the best choice to send on such a mission."

There was a silence while they all considered his proposal, each of them in their own way testing it for flaws. Kirra didn't like it, Cammon could tell, and yet part of her was suffused with pride that he had the skills to accomplish such a bold mission.

"The idea has great merit," Kiernan said at last. "I can think of no objections."

"Nor I," said Romar.

Tayse and Senneth exchanged glances, and she shook her head. "Nor can we," Tayse said.

Amalie turned to hold her hand out to Donnal. He uncoiled from the floor and came forward to take it. "If you are willing, and if you believe you will survive it, I would ask you to do this thing for us—for me," she said steadily. "But I would not want you to lose your life in such a chancy venture. There are other things we can try."

He smiled down at her. "But I think this is a service I can perform," he said softly. "And I am happy to do so for my country and my queen."

"When can you go?" Romar asked. "Tomorrow night?"

Donnal dropped Amalie's hand and spun gracefully to address the regent. He said, "Why not now?"

In the end, Kirra went with him. They waited till most of the rebel camp was likely to be bedded down for the night, and then met with Tayse to receive last-minute instructions. Cammon left Amalie sleeping in the pavilion and went to see them off. He found Senneth and Justin also awake and seated on the ground before a small fire, listening to Tayse and trying to mask their uneasiness.

"We'll be fine," Kirra told Tayse at last. "I won't even take human shape. We'll be back in a couple of hours, and no doubt we'll have a gory tale to tell."

Donnal had already taken the form of a bat, adept at night travel. More slowly, Kirra transformed herself to a very similar creature, and they both took off without a backward glance. Cammon dropped beside Senneth. Tayse stood awhile, watching the night sky as if he could actually still see their winged shapes, and then he, too, took a seat before the fire.

"You can follow them, of course," Senneth said quietly.

Cammon nodded. "Of course."

"Let us know when anything happens," Tayse said.

The four of them were silent for the next fifteen minutes. Cammon's attention was focused so tightly on Donnal and Kirra that he could almost feel the lift and caress of wind as they darted through the air. Below them, he could see the dense pattern of sleeping armies, divided by a dark trench of muddy, torn-up ground. Occasional campfires sparkled on both sides of the demarcation line. From the air, in the dark, the world seemed peaceful; every sign of battle was erased.

Finally Senneth stirred. "I wonder how Donnal will bring himself to kill an unarmed man in his sleep," she said.

"I could do it," Justin said.

Tayse turned his head to appraise the younger Rider. "No, you couldn't."

Justin flashed his careless grin. "Maybe not. But I could wake him up and then kill him before he had time to say a word."

"They're at the camp," Cammon said abruptly. "Hovering above the tent they believe is Rayson's."

"How do they know?" Justin asked.

"Fortunalt flags. And there's—" Cammon tried to convey Kirra's sense of bewilderment. "Singing? Men outside the tent having some kind of celebration?"

"A wake for Halchon?" Senneth suggested. "Or maybe Rayson's actually glad that Halchon is dead. He wanted the throne all along."

"I don't know," Cammon said. "But Donnal is pleased. The singing will cover any sounds they make."

He fell silent for long enough to make Senneth impatient. "Well? What's happening?" she asked.

"Oh. They landed for a moment to change to smaller creatures. I can't tell what—moths or something." Donnal could alter shapes so quickly that he could transform himself in flight, but Kirra's shifting took too long for such midair maneuvers. "Now they're aloft again—and seeking a way inside the tent—and in."

He was silent again, unprepared for the swift backlash of emotions he was picking up from both Kirra and Donnal. Fury, disgust, hatred. He frowned.

"What?" Senneth demanded. "Why do you look like that?"

He shook his head. "They're—oh. They're witnessing Rayson—in bed with some girl—a very young girl, from what I can tell. . . ." His voice trailed off. Kirra's anger was so hot that he thought she might have tried to rip out Rayson's eyes herself if she had been some kind of predator.

Senneth said something, and Justin replied, but Cammon scarcely heard them. The scene before him was so clear it was as if he was standing in the tent, watching it unfold by candlelight. The girl in Rayson's bed couldn't have been much more than fifteen, dark-haired, terrified, shrieking. The heavy red-faced marlord was laboring over her, grunting with pleasure, pinning her arms back against the rough wool of the blankets. The men outside finished one drunken song and began another one.

Donnal had shifted smoothly into human shape—and beside him, Kirra, reckless Kirra, had assumed her own form as well. The girl caught sight of them and shrieked even more loudly.

With his left hand, Donnal jerked on the marlord's neck, causing him to cry out in alarm and roll off his victim. In his right hand, Donnal held a sword. The naked marlord scrambled to his feet, snatching up his own weapon, and they immediately began a furious battle. Kirra ignored them both. She had gone directly to the bed and began whispering something in the girl's ear while she wrapped the top blanket around her shivering body. Outside, the singing went on undisturbed.

Donnal shouted something—Cammon couldn't tell what—and Kirra reached up, knife in hand, to slash a hole in one side of the tent. Then she put her arms around the sobbing girl and both of them melted into much smaller shapes. Cammon could barely see them on the rumpled bed.

On the instant, Donnal shifted again, transformed himself into the deadliest of all creatures, a red raelynx. Now Rayson Fortunalt showed true horror, but not for long. Three swipes of those huge, ferocious paws, and the marlord was turned into strips of bloody flesh quivering on the floor.

Outside the tent, the singing had stopped. Maybe someone had seen Kirra's knife cutting an escape route through the canvas; maybe someone had heard Rayson's shrieks of agony. A voice called, "Marlord?" at the tent flap, and then the door was ripped open. Three men pushed through, blades drawn.

"Rayson!" one of them shouted, and they all surged forward.

Donnal had already blurred and reformed into the shape of a feathered owl. He swooped across the bed, snatched up the tiny creatures huddled there, and dove through the fresh rip in the side of the tent. In seconds he was free, winging his way silently back to camp, carrying a most precious cargo.

Cammon took a deep breath and felt the vision fall away from him. Abruptly, he was back before the campfire, aware of the tense regard of his three companions. "They're on their way back," he said, and realized those were the first words he'd spoken since Kirra and Donnal breached the tent.

"What happened? Is Rayson dead?" Senneth asked fearfully. "Are they safe?"

Cammon nodded. "He's dead, they're unharmed. But they're bringing a passenger."

That caught them all by surprise. "What does that mean?" Senneth said.

Cammon felt himself almost smile. "Kirra had to rescue the girl in the tent, of course. Justin, I think you'd better go wake Ellynor, for the girl is in pretty bad shape."

Justin was already on his feet. He said, "And that's how you bring yourself to kill an unarmed man."

CHAPTER
40

KIERNAN was hoping for a surrender flag, he told them at dawn, as their own troops were stirring and they prepared themselves for the day. They were all in Amalie's tent, both exhausted and elated, having listened to Kirra's somewhat edited account of the night's slaughter and trying to guess how it changed the fortunes of war. Even Ariane Rappengrass and Mayva Nocklyn had been invited in to hear the news. Cammon was yawning through the meeting, since he had returned to bed quite late. He had woken Amalie to tell her the story, but the others hadn't learned it till now.

Romar said, "I don't know if we can count on surrender, but at the very least I would expect some of the foot soldiers to run. Rayson and Halchon dead! They will be thinking about what they have given up to fight for their marlords. They will be thinking about their families back home, undefended now. They will desert in droves if they believe the war cannot be won."

"I would let those common men go," Amalie said in her soft voice.

"Amalie, they're traitors to the throne," her uncle said. "Not to be trusted."

She shook her head. "Conscripted by their lords. Ambitious, maybe, and hopeful of reward, but peaceful enough men in the general run of things. Let them escape under cover of night. We won't chase them down."

Kiernan shrugged. "But any Thirteenth House noble who threw in his lot with the traitors deserves either a quick death on the battlefield or imprisonment in Ghosenhall," he said. "You want the common men to go free—very well. I disagree, but I will back you. But the nobles should be punished. They could have more easily supported you than betrayed you."

"And there will be the matter of Gisseltess and Fortunalt," Ariane said. "How shall we keep their heirs in check? Shall we assign advisors to Halchon's sons and Rayson's daughter?"

"Don't savor your victory before the enemy has laid down his arms," Tayse warned.

Kiernan turned his gaze on the Rider. "There is no one left to urge them to fight," he said somewhat impatiently. "Nothing left to fight for."

Senneth spoke up. "The foreign mercenaries are still being paid," she pointed out. "But as for our homegrown rebels, don't forget that some of these soldiers rode to war with no hope of political gain or riches."

Tayse nodded at her. "Men will fight for faith sometimes harder than they will fight for a king."

Senneth was watching Amalie. "And who knows what stories have started to circulate about the princess?" she said. "If any of our own soldiers were spies and have run back to tell tales—well, clearly Amalie has some odd powers. Coralinda could have capitalized on that. 'Look, your princess has a strange kind of magic! This woman will sit on the throne unless you fight her to the death!' A fanatic is always more dangerous than a mercenary."

"Then let's go slipping into the camp tonight and slit Coralinda's throat," Ariane said. She sounded serious. "Anything to be done with this!"

"Magic won't serve us this time," Senneth said regretfully. "I don't think even Donnal could get close to her undetected. Too many moonstones."

"Well, I have some archers who are very good," Ariane said. "I will have them train their arrows on her."

"In any case, we still have a fight on our hands," Kiernan said.

That, unfortunately, proved to be true.

Cammon could sense a renewed sense of purpose emanating from the upstart Gillengaria men during the day's long and ferocious fighting. Coralinda must have whipped the soldiers to a frenzy that morning as she sent them off to war. *Another of your marlords felled by magic! Are you not afraid of a princess who commands power like that?*

Cammon shivered a little. Perhaps it was even more frightening. Perhaps she didn't even need words. Perhaps her own magic was so powerful she could inspire men to fight, *force* them to fight, enflame them with a battle lust they could neither resist nor comprehend.

If so, they were in for a long and grueling war.

"This has been our deadliest day so far," Kiernan said heavily that night as they all convened in Amalie's tent. "Coralinda is proving to be a better general than her brother, even—or at least a more reckless one, with more power to sway her troops."

"And yet, as far as I know, she does not want the throne," Romar said thoughtfully. "Maybe there is something else we can offer her. Would she be open to a parley, do you think?"

Cammon almost laughed when "No" came from so many people all at once—Senneth, Tayse, Kirra, and Ariane. He suspected that if Ellynor had been in the tent, she would have repeated the negative in an even more heartfelt voice. Coralinda was not the kind of woman who negotiated. She was used to having everything her own way—and she had no qualms about destroying anyone who opposed her.

"Then what do we do?" the regent demanded.

Kiernan stood up, resettling his weapons belt around his waist. "We fight again tomorrow."

As it turned out, Romar Brendyn had not been so far off in his suggestion. For the very next day, Coralinda *did* come to the royal camp, looking for a way to end the war.

It was mid-afternoon. Cammon had escorted Amalie to the hospital tents, where wounded men were being brought in by the dozens, so fierce was the day's fighting. Valri, Ellynor, and Kirra traveled slowly between the pallets, kneeling beside each fallen soldier, laying their hands on the flushed cheeks, the gouged rib cages. Four of the Carrebos mystics could also be glimpsed moving inside the tents or kneeling beside the hurt soldiers.

Another woman, a stranger, paced between the beds and paused at each one to bend down, touch her fingers to a man's face, and move on without speaking.

"Who's that?" Amalie asked. "She hasn't been here before."

Ellynor, who was close enough to hear, stepped over to answer. Her dark hair was plaited into a long braid down her back; the bright dye of the clan pattern showed through in random snatches. "I don't know her," Ellynor replied, "but she was here this morning when I arrived. I think she was here all night."

"Is she a mystic?" Amalie asked.

Ellynor nodded. "Oh, yes. But she has a kind of skill I've never seen before—very different from mine and Kirra's. It's like she places her hand on a man's body and his cuts instantly start to heal over. They brought a man here this morning—his head was practically severed, and I know they just brought him here to die. She put both her hands around his throat and it was like the flesh just knit itself back together. We were all gaping. A few hours later, he was sitting up and drinking water."

"What's her name?" Amalie asked.

"I asked. She didn't answer."

But Cammon knew. He was watching the placid, thick-limbed, brown-haired woman make her way slowly down the avenues of fallen soldiers, her face so expressionless as to seem entirely indifferent. "Lara," he said.

Amalie glanced at him quickly. "You know her?"

"Met her once last year. She has a strange kind of magic, all right— very powerful. It's not like anything I've ever seen before, either."

Amalie gathered up her skirts. "Well, then, I'm glad she's here tend- ing *our* soldiers. I'm going to thank her."

"I don't know if she'll actually hear you," Ellynor warned. "She seemed very distant. Almost not present."

"I understand," Amalie said. "I will thank her anyway. It would be rude not to."

Soon enough, Amalie and Ellynor were back among the soldiers. Cammon loitered nearby uncertainly, ready to run errands if necessary, ready to relay information if any came. Sensing the grimness in both Tayse and Justin, he could tell this day's battle was not going well. Once again, the rebels were flinging themselves into combat with zeal and abandon.

Cammon glanced at the sky. The half moon was already out, more proof that the days were rushing by. They had been engaged in war a week and a half already; how much longer would they have to endure?

He turned his eyes back toward the battlefield, as if from this distance he could actually see the swipe and clash of blades, and instead he saw Coralinda Gisseltess.

She was standing a few yards away from him, a short, stocky figure dressed in black and silver. Her form was insubstantial enough that Cam- mon knew it wasn't her true body. He had never heard of someone send- ing her spirit walking through the world, but obviously such a thing was possible—and Coralinda had mastered the trick. He could see the solid shapes of tent poles and supply wagons through the shimmering outline of her body. She was not strictly corporeal, but she was definitely there.

On her square face she wore a frown. She swept her gaze around her, seeming to dismiss everything she encountered, and pivoted slowly on her heel. She lifted one hand and tapped a finger to her mouth, as if con- sidering.

Cammon glanced back at the tents, but Amalie and Kirra were out of sight. No one else was close enough to call.

He pressed his lips together, then strode over to the apparition, which had already moved a few paces on.

Cammon planted himself in her path. "Looking for somebody?" he asked.

By the way she jerked upright to stare at him, he could tell she was startled. Her face showed no alarm, however, merely narrowed to a look of calculation. "You can see me?" she replied.

He nodded. "I'm probably the only one who can."

She sneered. "A boy with mystical ability, no doubt."

He almost laughed at her. "You have mystical powers of your own, it seems."

"No," she said sharply. "The Pale Mother has lavished gifts upon me, but they are not magic. Magic is an abomination."

"All magic flows from the gods, even yours," he replied. "It is all sacred."

Her face showed revulsion, and she waved a hand as if to brush away his words. "The Pale Mother reviles creatures such as you," she declared. "You and all your sorcerous friends."

"And is that what you have come here for," he asked, "to look for mystics?"

"Do you know who I am?" she demanded.

"Coralinda Gisseltess. You call yourself the Lestra of Lumanen Convent."

"I have come here to offer a bargain."

A chance for a parley, after all? "I can summon Romar Brendyn," he offered.

"No," was the instant reply. "He means nothing to me. The goddess disregards him."

"You want Senneth," he said slowly.

Majestically, Coralinda nodded her translucent head. "Senneth Brassenthwaite," she repeated. "Yes. She's the one to whom I would make my offer."

Sen. I need you, he sent the message out at that instant. Blessedly, she was not far, having left the battlefield for a brief respite. He knew she would receive nothing more than a vague but powerful sense of urgency that would nonetheless send her instantly running in his direction. But it took only a few seconds to send a second summons, distinctly worded in language that would be understood.

Amalie. Get Kirra. Come find me. I'm near the tents on the north side of camp.

Casually, as if he had not just called for reinforcements, he said, "And what offer would you make to her?"

She studied him, seeming to debate whether or not he was worthy of hearing her confidences. "A way to end this war quickly and decisively, taking on a single opponent."

"You'll have to be more specific."

There was no sound, but he could feel Amalie and Kirra hurrying up behind him. From Kirra, he felt only bewilderment, but Amalie registered a sense of shock. So she, too, could perceive the spectral visitor. *Don't come any closer,* he told her. *I don't want her to see you.*

"A duel of sorts," the Lestra replied. "Between Senneth—and me."

He reared back at her words. "How would that work? She would try to scald you with flame while you tried to keep from catching on fire?"

"Simpler than that," Coralinda Gisseltess said. "We would merely try to destroy each other."

He heard running footsteps and knew that Senneth was almost upon them. "I don't understand."

Coralinda turned her head; apparently she had heard Senneth's rapid approach as well. "Tell her I will meet her tomorrow at moonrise," she said, and disappeared.

Cammon heard Amalie's cry of wonder, Kirra's quick questions, and the sound of Senneth's voice, all coming at once. They had enveloped him in a small feminine circle before he could even turn around to seek them out.

"Cammon!" Amalie exclaimed. "How did she get here? What did she want?"

"Who? What? What in silver hell is going on?" Kirra exploded. "Senneth, why are you here?"

Senneth was still breathless from her race through camp. "Cammon called me. I don't know why. Amalie's not in danger?"

"I'm fine," Amalie said. "Coralinda Gisseltess was here."

That caused all sorts of commotion, and Cammon had to raise both hands to silence the others. "It wasn't really her," he explained. "It was her ghost or something. I think her body was back in her own camp, and she was just here looking around."

"I couldn't see her," Senneth said.

"No, neither could I," Kirra replied. "But Amalie could."

Amalie nodded. "Very distinctly."

"That's not entirely surprising," Senneth said, "if Amalie has the same kind of magic as Coralinda."

"I'll have to try to learn such a skill," Amalie remarked. "It seems most useful."

"She says she doesn't have magic," Cammon said.

Senneth smiled grimly. "Let her call it what she will, it's magic. I'm just surprised she hasn't used this particular talent before."

"She has," Cammon said. "I've seen her here a few times before. Just glimpses. Never to talk to."

He saw the look Kirra exchanged with Senneth, but Senneth didn't take time to laugh. "What did she want?" Senneth said. "This time?"

"To duel with you."

There was a moment's silence.

"And what does *that* mean?" Kirra said.

"I don't know! She said she would make a bargain with Senneth. They would try to destroy each other. I asked if that meant Senneth would try to burn her up, and she would resist, but she said it was simpler than that. I have no idea what she was talking about."

He looked at Senneth hopefully, but Senneth seemed mystified. "So—what? I'm supposed to throw my power at her without using fire? How will that work?"

"I think that's probably exactly what it is," Kirra said slowly. "It's like the first time I tried to change someone other than myself. It was like I was shoving the magic outside of my body. I knew where it was going, but I was using it in a different way. I could almost feel it leaving my fingertips."

"But I've never done anything like that!" Senneth exclaimed.

"She said she'd be back tomorrow," Cammon said helpfully.

Senneth sent him a wrathful look, as scorching as true fire. "And then what? We wave our hands in the air and try to knock each other over simply by intention? I'm going to feel like an idiot!"

"Try it," Kirra suggested, pointing at one of the empty supply wagons nearby. "See if you can demolish something without setting it on fire."

Senneth made a huffing sound and threw her hands in the air. "This is ridiculous!"

"She said it could end the war," Cammon said.

"I suppose if I kill her, all the fanatics might lose heart and surrender, but I don't think I *can*! This doesn't make sense to me!"

"Try it," Kirra urged, taking Senneth's shoulders and turning her toward the wagon. "Call up your power, but just hold the flame at bay. See what you can do."

Senneth made a strangled sound but stood there a moment, scowling at the cart. Her white-blond hair was tangled and streaked with dirt; she was spattered with mud and drops of blood. She didn't look remotely ridiculous.

Slowly she lifted both hands, fingers spread, palms flat to an invisible wind. Her scowl deepened; her gray eyes darkened. She suddenly clenched her fingers and then flicked them open hard.

The supply wagon shattered as if it had been smashed by a gigantic invisible boulder.

Cammon and Kirra yelled and applauded. Senneth stood for a moment, staring at the backs of her hands.

"That was strange," she said at last.

"Could you feel it? What was it like?" Kirra demanded.

"It was a lot like flinging fire. Without the fire."

"See? I told you."

Senneth put a hand on Kirra's cheek, and Kirra exclaimed aloud. Senneth said, "My hands are cold. It feels so odd."

Kirra stepped back, and Senneth's hand fell. "Do it again," Kirra said.

Senneth glanced around. "What else should I destroy? I should pick my target fairly carefully, don't you think?"

"Amalie's pavilion," Kirra suggested.

"Kiernan's tent instead, perhaps?" Senneth replied.

"Maybe something less useful," Cammon said. "There's a tree stump right behind that tent. See if you can crush it to splinters."

"Cammon, Cammon," Kirra said. "Always the voice of reason."

But Senneth had shifted just enough to align herself with the stump. Again, she concentrated a moment before attempting any destruction.

Again, the object in her way was pulverized by her magic.

"Oh, that was too easy," Senneth said. "I need something bigger to see what I'm really capable of. A boulder. Maybe even a mountain."

"Behind the camp about half a mile," Kirra said. "The ground gets pretty rocky. Let's go practice."

"Not too long," Cammon said. "You don't want to wear yourself out."

"When did she say she'd be back?" Senneth asked. "Tomorrow, but when?"

"Moonrise."

Kirra glanced at the sky, where the waxing gibbous moon was faint against the blue. "Daytime," she said. "Now why? Isn't she stronger at night?"

"So the troops are all engaged," Senneth guessed. "If I fall, my allies falter, and her troops move in rapidly for the kill. If she falls—same thing, only we're victorious. A quick ending for certain."

"Then we have a little time to get you ready."

"I don't like it," Amalie said.

It was the first time she had spoken since Cammon had recounted Coralinda's offer. As usual, her voice was so soft that it could have been hard to hear her, but there was so much intensity in her tone that it was impossible to ignore her.

"What don't you like?" Cammon said.

Amalie was shaking her head, and the red-gold hair went flying. "Why today? Why now? If Coralinda Gisseltess wanted to destroy you with magic, why didn't she do it before? Why even give you notice? Why not just bring you down while you were on the battlefield?"

They were silent a moment. "All very good questions," Kirra acknowledged.

"She knows something about this duel that you don't," Amalie said. "She has a weapon that she hasn't shown."

Senneth nodded. "Maybe. But you must admit the offer is attractive. If I destroy her, the war is over. The fanatics lose their will to fight, and the mercenaries lose their employer. Battle ended."

"And if she destroys you?" Amalie said.

Senneth shrugged. "The rest of you continue fighting."

"Tayse won't like it," Amalie said.

"Tayse would take the same offer if she sent forth a champion swordsman," Senneth replied. "Even if the man was half-mystic and imbued with magical powers."

"You're stronger than she is, aren't you?" Kirra asked. "You're stronger than anybody."

Senneth shrugged again. "Who knows? Until recently we didn't even know she had magic. I can't guess how deep it runs in her. But it's true I've never come across anyone else who was as strong as I am. I don't see how she can defeat me."

"I still don't like it," Amalie said.

Senneth smiled at her. "You don't like the thought of anyone risking death for you," she said. "But sometimes it's the only risk worth taking."

SENNETH and Kirra moved off to find fresh targets for Senneth to obliterate. Cammon and Amalie returned to the infirmary tents, but

Amalie found it hard to concentrate. She smiled and spoke to the wounded soldiers, but Cammon could tell her thoughts were elsewhere. Lara's presence was so powerful that he reasoned Amalie's was not as necessary as it had been before, and so he convinced her to return to her pavilion before the sounds of battle had ceased for the day.

Amalie had been correct in surmising that Tayse would not like the offered deal, which Senneth explained as succinctly as possible that night in Amalie's tent. The others were all heartily in favor of the encounter—as much as they could understand it, of course, though it was clear the concept of a magical duel was impossible for them to fully grasp. They did not, however, consider themselves bound to abide by an unfavorable outcome.

"If you die, we will not surrender," Romar said.

"I don't think she expects you to," Senneth replied.

"Then she doesn't expect to die," Tayse said.

Senneth looked at him. They were sitting across the tent from each other, a half dozen others between them. Yet, Cammon thought, they were as connected to each other as if they stood wrapped in the closest embrace that their bodies would allow.

"You're right," Senneth said. "I don't think she does."

"Then she will not behave fairly or honorably," he said. "Expect treachery."

Senneth nodded. "I do."

Even though Tayse was uneasy, Cammon realized, it wouldn't even occur to him to ask Senneth not to accept the challenge. "I'll stand with you tomorrow as you battle the Lestra," Tayse said. "In case a sword will accomplish what magic will not."

"There must be a way to take advantage of Coralinda's absence from the field," Kiernan said. "Ariane. Perhaps if we moved your troops around to the southern edge, and sent Brassenthwaite troops deep into the line—"

Talk of strategy went on much longer than Cammon had the stomach for. Indeed, he was sure that Kiernan and Romar and the others continued their discussions for some time after the conference ended. Tayse and Senneth had long since disappeared, no doubt conscious of the fact that this might be their last night together and unwilling to spend it brangling over military matters. The thought gave Cammon a peculiar feeling. Impossible to imagine a world without Senneth in it. Impossible to think a few vengeful sprays of magic from Coralinda Gisseltess could have the power to extinguish Senneth's extraordinary warmth and light. But this was clearly the Lestra's intent, so no matter how unlikely such an eventuality seemed to him, Coralinda Gisseltess must cherish real hopes of achieving it.

"Senneth might die tomorrow," Amalie whispered to him late that night, as both of them lay awake long past midnight.

"No," he said. "It simply can't happen."

But he knew it could. He wrapped his arms even more tightly around Amalie, but somehow, fear managed to squeeze between them anyway.

CHAPTER

41

CAMMON was hardly surprised by the group that assembled in front of Amalie's pavilion the next afternoon to accompany Senneth to her meeting with Coralinda Gisseltess. Tayse, of course, and where Tayse went, Justin was sure to follow. Kirra would not be left out of such an adventure, and Donnal naturally accompanied Kirra. Senneth argued that Amalie should stay behind, somewhere that danger was less likely to strike, but the princess was adamant that she witness the event. Cammon would have gone with Senneth in any case, just from a vague sense that if magic was necessary for this encounter, many mystics should be on hand, but it made his choice simpler that Amalie would also be present.

The raelynx sat on the ground at Amalie's feet, its red tail curled around its paws, clearly ready to join them on any foray.

Ellynor and Valri had also elected to join their group, and Cammon had to admit he *was* surprised by their presence. Ellynor, he knew, had useful skills in any battle. But Valri?

"I am here to disguise the princess," Valri said when Cammon sidled over to question her. "I don't know what kind of weapons Coralinda Gisseltess intends to deploy. Perhaps this talk of a mystical duel is all nonsense and she is bringing in an elite troop to murder all comers. I do not want her to realize that Amalie is present. And Ellynor has agreed to help me spirit her away if necessary."

Cammon glanced at the sky, where the lopsided moon was just making an appearance. "Then we are ready."

He wondered how long they would have to wait for the Lestra's summons, but two minutes later, Coralinda Gisseltess's image wavered into view. Cammon felt his stomach tighten, and behind him he heard Amalie's faint gasp, but no one else seemed aware of the Lestra's presence.

"And these are all the companions Senneth Brassenthwaite has gathered to assist her in the greatest battle of her life?" Coralinda asked in a mocking voice.

Cammon moved in front of her, to remind her that he could see her even if no one else could. "If it is to be simply a duel between the two of you, she should need no assistance at all."

"Witnesses, then," the Lestra replied.

"And where are yours?"

Her ghostly shape gestured toward the south. "Assembled a mile from here, where my true body waits. Gather your friends and bid them follow me."

He turned to alert the others and found them all staring at him. All except the raelynx. Its eyes were fixed on Coralinda Gisseltess; its tail lashed back and forth, whipping across Amalie's legs.

Cammon waved at his companions. "Southward about a mile away," he said. "She'll take us there."

Coralinda set a good pace, since she wasn't actually treading on ground, and the rest of them had to hustle to keep up. Tayse and Justin pushed to the lead, swords at the ready. Cammon told them, "Just go straight, at least for a while," and dropped back to join Senneth, Donnal, and Kirra.

He pointed at Senneth. "Take off your moonstone bracelet."

She glanced down at her arm, as if surprised to find the jewelry still there. "Probably a good idea," she said. But when she unfastened it and held it out, Cammon laughed.

"*I* can't touch it!"

"Don't look at me," Kirra said, and Donnal smiled and shook his head.

"You can't give it to Ellynor, either," Cammon said.

"Well, I'm not just throwing it down in some passing field," Senneth said. "Tayse! Take this!"

Tayse turned back willingly at the sound of his name, but only with some reluctance pocketed the moonstones. "I am sure somehow she can turn these against you," he said.

"Not if they're not touching my skin," Senneth replied. She flexed her fingers. "So curious. Usually I'm not even aware of having the bracelet on, but once I take it off, I feel like fresh fire is running through my blood."

"Good," Tayse said. "The more energy you have, the better." He lengthened his stride to catch up with Justin.

"She can't realize just how powerful you are," Kirra said. But she sounded nervous.

"Or she knows that *I* don't realize how powerful *she* is," Senneth replied.

"We'll find out soon enough," Cammon said.

Indeed, within a few minutes, they had arrived at what was obviously the site of combat. Coralinda's ghostly double had disappeared, but there was no need for her guidance anymore. They were in a shallow valley, the Lirreth Mountains rising up behind them and low foothills making a near circle around them. The ground was pink and green with spring flowers and new grass; sunlight sparkled through the air like tangible delight. The soil was coarse and rocky, but a species of low, dark shrubbery seemed to flourish in it, and so the whole valley ran with haphazard lines of its bushy olive-colored branches.

Across the way from them, a small group of people had gathered. Justin and Tayse had come to a hard stop and were clearly assessing the opponents.

"I make out more than a dozen men," Tayse said. He glanced at Cammon. "Can you tell the precise numbers?"

"Give me a minute," Cammon answered, but Donnal was already shifting and had lifted himself into the air to reconnoiter.

"How long do we stand here and wait?" Senneth said. "And what are we waiting for?"

She had barely finished speaking when a single shape detached itself from the group amassed across the valley. Short, confident, dressed in black and silver. The Lestra. "*Senneth!*" Her voice carried easily across the space dividing them. "Come submit your magic to the judgment of my goddess!"

"Time to fight," Senneth said. She touched Tayse on the shoulder, kissed him on the mouth, and strode a dozen paces into the festive spring arena of the valley.

"I'm here, serra," Senneth called back. She lifted her arms, graceful as a dancer. Sunlight busied itself in her white-blond hair and polished it to a halo shine. "Kill me if you can."

Cammon heard Tayse catch his breath at that invitation, but there wasn't much time for anyone else to react. Senneth clenched her fists and thrust her hands outward, and a great ball of light seemed to arc through the air. It landed on Coralinda Gisseltess with a flash so bright that everyone in her camp, everyone in Amalie's, stepped backward a pace. A dozen voices cried out in fear and astonishment.

But the light dissipated, and Coralinda was still standing, pulsing with a dark fever of her own. She lifted her arms and snapped her fingers wide. It was as if lightning sizzled from her body, arrow-straight across the valley. It struck Senneth in the chest, and she went down.

Kirra screamed. Tayse was beside her in an instant, but Senneth was pushing herself up, to her knees, to her feet. She was shaking her head as if to clear it. "I'm all right," Cammon heard her say to Tayse. "I'm all right. That was more than I expected."

Just then a hawk circled down from overhead and came to land by Justin. Seconds later, Donnal appeared. "In her camp, she has twenty soldiers wearing the black-and-silver of Lumanen Convent," he reported. "But a half mile away are another thirty men, waiting."

Justin did a quick pivot as if to reassess their own small troops, but it didn't take much analysis. "We need more swords," he said. "Cammon? Can you call any Riders?"

Cammon's attention was almost wholly on Senneth. She was on her feet but shaky, Tayse's hand under her elbow. How could Justin think of anything else? "Uh—I don't know. I can try—but I don't know if I can give them directions here—"

"I'll go fetch some," Donnal offered. He was almost instantly a bird shape again, and just as quickly in the air.

"Step away from me," Cammon heard Senneth warn Tayse. The Rider backed off a few paces, and Senneth moved forward. Cammon could sense her focus and her determination; so much heat rose off her body it warmed him from a couple yards away.

She tilted her head back and flung her arms in the air, and for a moment stood as though frozen by shock or magic. Cammon could feel the energy build inside her; his skin prickled with the charge. Then she flexed her fingers, and power poured from her in one long, continuous, undulating river of light.

Again, cries went up from both camps, but nothing broke the concentration of the two combatants. Again, Senneth's assault reached Coralinda, bathed her in bright color, and left her unharmed. Indeed, the Lestra seemed suffused with Senneth's light, engorged with it; her black hair sparkled and her skin seemed to glow. Her own arms lifted languidly, and almost as if she was batting away a troublesome insect, she pushed Senneth's power aside. Pushed it *back*. Seemed to alchemize it into something darker, more sinister, laced with poisonous glitter, and redirected it toward its source.

Cammon saw that black stream of energy forcing its way against the ongoing current of Senneth's attack. Senneth saw it, too, for he felt her redouble her efforts, brighten her own magic, pour even more of her power into the attack. At the halfway point between them, Coralinda's shadowy river was halted, shoved back in her direction, and finally forced to disperse into the sunny air.

But only briefly. Cammon saw the gleaming blackness coalesce, gain force, gain substance, and slowly inch its way forward along that pathway of light, straight for Senneth.

He couldn't move. He couldn't breathe. Around him, he felt everyone straining forward, terrified and bewildered, and he realized that none of them—with the possible exception of Amalie—could view the battle as he did. Perhaps they saw streaks of light and darkness; perhaps not even that, just two women, widely separated, waving their hands and waiting.

Yet all of them could sense a grim and momentous struggle playing out just beyond the reach of their senses, and all of them were afraid.

The black light crept nearer, past the halfway mark again. Senneth dug up reserves of power and forced it back toward its creator. Again, the malevolent mass seemed to partially dissipate, then re-cohere, gather its strength, and ram itself hard against the implacable onslaught of light. At either end of that shimmering rainbow of light and dark, the two women stood, so rigid with power that they seemed to be statues of black granite and white marble, representations of night and day.

Overhead, simultaneously visible in the sky, the sun dropped and the moon climbed.

For a moment—a few seconds only—Cammon's vision blurred. It was as if, instead of Senneth and Coralinda, he saw two goddesses battling, women taller than the Lireth Mountains. One was dressed in moonlight, silver and creamy; the other wore sunlight, yellow and ragged. Their faces were set, their movements stately, but they flung bolts of power at each other like stones, like arrows. And every missile hit its mark, and each goddess cringed and staggered every time she was struck.

Even as he stared, openmouthed, the image faded. He was again in the middle of a newly green field, surrounded by silent onlookers, watching as Coralinda's black magic sliced its deadly way through Senneth's pure band of energy—past the three-quarter mark—half the distance remaining—closer—closer—almost at her heart—

With a cry, Amalie pitched herself past Cammon and knocked Senneth to the ground. The place where Senneth had been standing erupted into muddy red flame and oily black smoke. The air was suddenly heavy with a bitter odor.

The rest of them rushed over to crowd around Senneth and Amalie. Senneth was trembling; her gray eyes were wide and pale. Amalie was bending over, both her hands on Senneth's left arm, and was shaking her with impatience.

"Don't you see? Don't you see?" Amalie cried. "It's a trick! She's using your magic against you!"

Senneth looked dazed and unsteady as she climbed to her feet, but she was trying hard to focus. "No—I don't understand. I can't believe how much power she has. I don't know—I'm not sure—it might be more than mine."

Amalie shook her arm again. "No—it *is* yours. She's stealing yours and turning it against you! She doesn't have any power of her own at all."

They all fell silent and gaped at her, but Cammon understood it first. "Thief magic," he said in disgust. "She invites you to a duel, then she takes your magic and turns it back on you. The more you give her, the more she has."

Senneth took a long, shuddering breath. "Then I—how can I defeat her?"

"You can't," Tayse said. "*You* are her weapon. You have to lay down your arms to render her powerless."

Senneth pressed a hand to her eyes. Her fingers were shaking. "I want so much to strike her down."

"You can't do it," Tayse said.

"But I can."

It was Amalie's voice. All of them turned to stare at her in astonishment—except Valri, who wore a look of horror. "No. Majesty, no," the queen said in an urgent voice. "If she can steal Senneth's magic, she can certainly steal any small power you might have to offer."

But Amalie, as always, looked serene and confident—aware of dangers but not particularly afraid of them. "I would not send my own power against her," she said in her quiet voice. "I would take Senneth's—and Cammon's—and Kirra's. Anything they were willing to give me. And their reflected light is what I would use to battle Coralinda's darkness."

"But—Majesty—how can you do such a thing?" Kirra asked in a puzzled voice. "I would gladly give you any power I have, but—" She shrugged.

Amalie held her hand out to Tayse. "Give me Senneth's bracelet."

Mystified as the rest of them, Tayse dug it out of his pocket and laid it in Amalie's palm. Instantly, Cammon felt that primitive spurt of dread as some of his energy was siphoned away. Kirra actually gasped, and Senneth's eyes widened as if someone had just pinched her hard.

"*Oh*," said Kirra.

"I can feel it, too," Ellynor said. "But will it be enough? Or will she turn all of our combined power back on Amalie? For that would be unacceptable."

"She will not be able to steal it from me because it is not actually mine," Amalie explained patiently. "It has already been borrowed."

"It doesn't matter! The cost is too great!" Valri cried. "Amalie, you are the one we are all battling for! If you are lost to some—some—trick of magic, the whole fight is in vain! You are the one who must be saved, not the one who should be risked!"

"But I am the only one who can take the risk," Amalie said. "And it *is* my fight. And I am glad to make it instead of asking others to lay their lives down for mine."

A hawk circled above them and made a smooth landing, transforming itself into Donnal. "Riders are on the way," he said briefly. "What's wrong here?"

Kirra instantly poured the story into his ears, while Valri continued arguing with Amalie. Tayse had put his arms around Senneth from behind and she leaned against him, literally seeming to draw strength from his body. She put one hand up to the gold charm she wore at her neck, the pendant he had given her upon their marriage. She closed her eyes, but some of the color began to return to her face.

Cammon felt as if he had been slapped by certain knowledge. "Senneth!" he exclaimed. "Give it to me!"

Senneth opened her eyes and stared at him. "What?"

He had his hand out to her but he was looking around at the others. "And Kirra—give me your lioness charm. Ellynor, what do you have? One of those black opals you Lirren girls wear? Let me have it. Donnal, do you carry anything you can give me?"

Kirra understood first. "Oh, this is like the time you helped me change Justin!" she exclaimed, rooting through her pockets for the small stone lioness she always carried. "You're going to feed our power to Amalie."

"I'm going to try," he said.

Senneth had already stripped off her wedding gift. She lifted it to her lips, gave Tayse a smile from over her shoulder, and passed it over. "If it melts in your hands, I swear I'll never forgive you," she said.

Ellynor offered him a gold bracelet set with black opals, but Donnal shook his head, smiling. "I don't carry anything like that," he said.

Kirra took his hand. "*I'll* be his charm," she said. "You can pull his magic through me."

"I don't understand," Valri said.

"Cammon is an amplifier," Senneth said. "He can take someone else's magic and boost it with his own." She shook her head. "Impossible to explain. Impossible to understand. But he seems to think he can feed all of *our* power through his own, and give it to Amalie, and make her even stronger."

Cammon slipped Senneth's pendant over his neck, fastened Ellynor's bracelet around his wrist, and cupped Kirra's lioness in his hand. He felt prickles of magic dance along his skin; his blood was bubbling in his veins. It was hard to stand still. "I think I can," he said.

"Please don't," Valri whispered. "Amalie, please don't do this."

Amalie kissed her stepmother on the forehead. "Valri, I must."

From across the field came Coralinda's voice, raised in mockery. "Senneth! Have you failed so quickly? Have you spent all your power on one attempt to destroy me? Or do you finally see how my goddess protects me from all such abominations as your magic?"

Without another look at Valri, at any of them, Amalie turned to face the Lestra and took a few steps deeper into the valley. "I will duel with you on Senneth's behalf," she called, and quiet though her voice was, it carried across the field that separated them. "Coralinda Gisseltess, I will strike you down."

Amalie did not throw her hands in the air or take a melodramatic pose. She merely folded her fingers before her, and bowed her head, and *thought* about Coralinda Gisseltess. Cammon could almost see her mind building a bridge across the valley, a tumbling, haphazard structure that nonetheless raced across the grass and flowers with an implacable speed. And across this insubstantial structure her curious soul went questing, and crowding behind her came the blinding energy of a half dozen mystics.

It was as if she had opened a tunnel for an invading army, and Cammon felt himself standing on the threshold of the tunnel door. They stampeded across him—Senneth blazing in the lead, Kirra and Donnal bounding after her, Ellynor and even Valri stealing behind the others, armed with dark and mysterious weapons. They were across the pathway—they were descending upon Coralinda—they were laying about them with blade and claw and sorcery.

A shriek of pure rage went up from across the valley, and it was so forceful it seemed to rock them all backward. Amalie stumbled, and

Cammon briefly lost his footing. A silver onslaught had set all their own soldiers in retreat—Coralinda's mirror magic turning their own weapons on them, forcing their armies back across the bridge.

But only briefly. Cammon felt Senneth's surge of renewed determination, racing through him with an actual heat, pouring into Amalie and back across that bridge. The others, too, pressed closer, offered him more, filled him with wild and kaleidoscopic impressions. Senneth raged in orange and gold; Ellynor and Valri brooded in saturated blue. Kirra and Donnal danced between them, shifting and uncontainable. Cammon had the strangest thought that he was a prism in reverse, collecting the whole spectrum of color, feeding it into an indescribably delicate piece of crystal, and compressing it into a single beam of pure unadulterated light.

That light broke against the blackness that was Coralinda Gisseltess, and was absorbed, and reformed into something still and dark and insatiable. She ate their light, she negated their color; they drove themselves against her, and she did not waver at all.

He felt Senneth's body burn higher; he was flushed with fever. Hotter. Impossible that anyone could sustain such a temperature. *Hotter.* She staggered a few steps toward him, cried out in a hoarse voice, and fell to the ground.

Instantly, there was chaos. Amalie faltered; Kirra dropped to her knees beside Senneth. Coralinda's black-and-silver counterassault came charging across the bridge, straight for the princess.

"*Kirra!*" Cammon shrieked, frantically summoning some of his own buried power, feeding to Amalie any of the fuel left in his own magic. Coralinda's dark force was halted at about the three-quarter mark. "Leave her! I need you!"

Tayse was on the ground beside Senneth, and Kirra leapt to her feet again, pouring a furious stream of energy directly into Cammon's head. It wasn't enough. Coralinda was regrouping. In seconds, she would begin battering against their greatly weakened defenses.

Cammon sent an impassioned plea a mile away, across the battlefield. *Jerril! Areel! Help me!* he cried. He felt Jerril's attention jerk his way, felt Jerril's power immediately and completely accessible to him. More slowly, he sensed Areel scan the battlefield, comprehend the plea, and unlock the closed treasure chest of his mind.

Power poured through him like rainwater through a parched riverbed.

But there were other mystics on the battlefield this day.

He sent his mind skipping across the royal camp, seeking out those Carrebos recruits, begging for assistance. One by one, startled or frightened or pleased or confused, they responded to him, turning from their ordinary tasks to wage an extraordinary war against a common enemy. Their power rolled to him in a bewildering array of strengths and colors, but he bundled it all up, coiled it into a weapon, and thrust that weapon into Amalie's hand.

Coralinda's army was halted, but he was not sure it could be defeated. For a long moment they all stood frozen, tense, suffused with magic, perfectly balanced and perfectly opposed forces that could move neither forward nor back.

A single plaintive yowl split the silence. Cammon was startled to feel a warm weight suddenly push against his thigh, and he stared down into the savage face of the raelynx. It made that piteous noise again, and again batted its paw against his leg.

Sweet gods. This lawless creature was offering him its own wild power.

Cautiously, Cammon opened his mind to the raelynx, but even so he was not prepared for what boiled into his body. A rush of violent red, a fever-bright fury, a thoughtless and primitive instinct for carnage. He took the raelynx's rage and magnified it and fed it straight into Amalie's veins.

From across the valley, Coralinda choked and stumbled, and Amalie's forces pushed her back to the halfway point of the bridge.

But only halfway. They were locked again in symmetrical combat— too strong to yield to the Lestra, too weak to destroy her. All the mystics in all of Gillengaria could not defeat Coralinda Gisseltess.

Behind him, small noises—a whispered word, the rustle of clothing. *Help me stand,* said a voice, very faint. There was the sound of a boot striking a rock.

Senneth was on her feet.

He felt her presence in his mind first as a gentle glow, the faint gleam of candlelight in a room at dusk. But quickly the fire gained strength, gained brightness, began to consume everything in its vicinity. Soon it was a blaze, then a bonfire, then a roaring inferno of uncontainable rage. From ten feet away, Cammon felt the heat radiating off her body, intense enough to make him perspire. He turned his head just enough to glimpse her from the corner of his eye. Her eyes were closed, her arms were raised above her head. As he watched, her whole figure erupted into fire.

As if he were connected to her by a powdered fuse, Cammon saw a spark race toward him across the grass, and he was enveloped in flame. He was a coruscating wick, a walking conflagration. He cried out, more in wonder than in pain, and lifted his hands to watch himself gesture with fire. His breath rasped in and out of his seared lungs; his skin burned like kindling. Cinders stung his eyes and skittered across his skin. He thrust his hand through the air and sent the blaze straight for Amalie.

She did not burst into fire but she seemed to bloom with light. She was suddenly wrapped in so much radiance that she appeared to be twice her size, and she was too bright to look at. Within that fierce halo, he saw her arms move—he almost thought he heard her speak. She pointed her right hand toward Coralinda Gisseltess, and a white fireball exploded across the valley and incinerated the Lestra where she stood.

Cammon was deafened by the noises that followed.

Surely everyone heard that cannonball crack of thunder. Surely the others should have been knocked off their feet by those percussive repeating booms. Cammon covered his ears and went rolling to the ground, trying to drown out the elemental cacophony of a deity falling to her knees, but no one else seemed to hear a thing. Amalie was beside him, her face worried, her lips moving, but it was as if she whispered, as if she made no noise at all. Ellynor had knelt beside Amalie, and her cool hands tugged at his hot ones, pulling them away from his ears. She said something to Amalie, but he had no idea what. The world was empty, erased of all sound.

Something jerked Amalie's head around, and he saw her staring out at the field, with her hand pressed against her mouth. He struggled to sit up, for if he could not hear, he could still see. He experienced a moment's horror at the sight of Coralinda's black-and-silver soldiers tearing across the valley straight for their small party. But then he became aware of a contingent of their own soldiers sweeping out to meet the enemy, and he realized that reinforcements had arrived while the mystics were battling. There—that was Wen, that was Coeval. A dozen other Riders raced out shoulder to shoulder with Justin to meet the Lumanen soldiers in the middle of the field and plunge into furious combat.

Tayse was not among them.

Scrabbling on his hands and knees, Cammon swung around to locate the other Rider. Tayse was sitting in the grass, Senneth across his lap, rocking her gently against his chest. Cammon felt a spasm of fear so intense he might almost have been facing the Lestra again. He had been burned so clean by magic that he could not even tell if his own talents were still intact. He could not, at this moment, sense Senneth—sense Amalie—sense any of them at all.

It was not possible that Senneth could be dead.

Kirra was on her knees beside Tayse, and she had wrapped both of her hands around one of Senneth's. Kirra's face was white and exhausted; her lips moved as if she was praying. Tayse didn't even look at her. He didn't glance at the battlefield. All his attention was on the woman in his arms.

Terrified, Cammon grabbed Amalie's hand. He couldn't speak; he couldn't hear her if she answered. *Is she alive? Is Senneth alive?* he demanded silently.

Amalie put her hand to his cheek and brought all his attention back to her. Her pale skin was flushed; her dark eyes seemed, in a day, to have acquired some impossibly ancient knowledge. She looked unutterably weary, as if she had not slept for days, and peaceful, as if that didn't matter.

Senneth is unconscious, but alive, she replied, and her voice reached him as clearly as if she had spoken and he could hear. *And Coralinda Gisseltess is dead.*

He stared up at her, consumed by too many emotions to sort them out—relief, hope, wonder, exhaustion, and bewilderment. *I saw them, Amalie—I saw the goddesses sparring,* he told her. *The Bright Mother and the Pale Mother, using our power to battle each other. But if—but if—if the Lestra fell, is the Pale Mother gone, too? Destroyed on this field before our eyes?*

Amalie took his hand and spread it against her heart. Her smile was utterly tranquil. *The world changes and the world stays the same,* she told him, still in those utterly clear syllables that sounded only in his head. *The old moon sets. New moon rises.*

CHAPTER

42

SENNETH missed the immediate aftermath of war.

When she regained consciousness, everything had been settled, everything had been tidied up. Romar Brendyn and her brother Kiernan had accepted the surrender of the rebel army. The Arberharst forces had fled to the various ports where their ships lay waiting, chased halfway across Gillengaria by royal soldiers. Troops had been sent to secure the major cities of Fortunalt, Storian, Gisseltess, and Tilt. The mystic Lara had healed every last wounded soldier—from both armies—then walked the length and breadth of the battlefield, repairing the damaged earth and coaxing shy blades of new grass to poke through the churned and bloodied soil.

It seemed Senneth had slept for almost three days.

It had not exactly been sleeping. It had not been a peaceful, restorative sort of slumber. She had been lost in chaotic darkness, falling through tunnels of emptiness, buffeted by exotic and sourceless winds. And she had been so *cold*. Shivering and frightened and falling and lost.

But not alone. Always, throughout that whole strange, terrifying journey, she had been conscious of a shadow at her back, a protector at her side. When she cried out, he comforted her. When she shivered, he warmed her body with his own. When her lungs seized up, he put his mouth against hers and breathed.

When she clawed her way back to sentience, he was there. Lying beside her on some bed she did not remember, gazing at her, guarding her sleep.

"Tayse," she whispered.

The expression on his face—hope, relief, joy, and love—was so raw it was almost painful to see. "Senneth," he answered. "Are you with me again?"

Strangely, a smile came to her face. She wouldn't have said she remembered how to smile, hadn't remembered what a smile was. She lifted a shaky hand and touched his stubbled cheek. "My love, I am always with you," she said.

He leaned in and kissed her gently on the mouth. "And now I am returned to the world," he said.

They lay there a moment in silence, his arms around her, her head against his chest, content for the moment just to exist. But she couldn't escape the consciousness of time passed and important events going forward without her.

And she felt like red and silver and black and opal hell.

After a moment, she stirred in his arms. "Feed me something," she said. "Bring me water. Tell me what's happened."

Carefully he helped her sit up, though the movement made her dizzy. She seemed to be in a sizable tent, maybe Amalie's; she couldn't bring herself to care enough to try to identify the furnishings. Tayse held water to her mouth and, sweet gods, nothing had ever tasted so good. After that, he offered her juice, and then broth, but only a little. She was ravenous and hollow with the certainty that no amount of food would fill her up.

"How long have I been lying here?" she demanded when he finally let her eat a piece of bread. "What happened to me? What happened to everyone?"

He didn't get a chance to answer. The canvas door flapped back and Kirra pushed inside.

"You *are* awake!" she squealed. "Cammon said you were! And lucid? Sane? Oh, but you look absolutely dreadful."

Automatically, Senneth's hand went to her hair, and found it filthy, matted, and crisp with soot. Oh, yes, the last thing she remembered, she had been standing in a circle of her own flame, intent on setting the entire world on fire. She must look even worse than she felt, though it was hard to imagine.

"I think I'm lucid, but I couldn't swear to sane," she replied cautiously. "So what happened? Is Coralinda dead?"

"Dead and her army dispersed," Kirra said. She emptied half a pitcher of water into a small towel, perched on the side of the bed, and began to wipe Senneth's face. Tayse grinned and moved over to allow her room. "You've been out for three days. Romar and your brother left for Ghosenhall yesterday to prepare the palace for Amalie's return, and the rest of us are hoping to leave soon—whenever you are able to move. Everything is in utter turmoil, but nobody seems to mind. We are victorious, Amalie is secure on the throne, and you are not actually dead."

Senneth tried a smile again. "Did you think I was?"

Kirra scrubbed a little harder at what must have been a particularly stubborn streak of ash. "Let's just say it was the thing everyone was most afraid of. *I* couldn't do anything for you. Ellynor couldn't. That strange woman—Lara—she came by but said you had to heal yourself. She did do something to take away your pain, though."

Senneth remembered pain, but only dimly. "I had one of my headaches?"

"Well, your hands were clutched around your head and you kept moaning, so that's what I assumed. But once Lara left, you seemed to relax a little, although you still didn't wake up." She glanced at Tayse. "Your husband never left your side."

"I know he didn't," Senneth said quietly. "I felt him here the whole time."

"I wanted to be here," he said, "in case you needed me."

She reached for his hand, and his fingers instantly closed over hers. She felt her throat closing up, but it was stupid to cry now. "What of everyone else? Amalie—she's safe? All our friends?"

"The princess suffered surprisingly few ill effects from her mortal combat with the personification of evil," Kirra said. She had laid aside the towel and now she was pulling a comb very gently through Senneth's tangled hair. "She was tired, of course, but eerily serene. Which was good, since around her there was complete and utter mayhem. On top of everything else, she had just made it indisputably clear that she is a mystic of no uncommon power, and anyone who hadn't figured that out already was left stunned and nervous. So far there has been no fresh mutiny, but I feel certain there will be a reckoning of sorts when the news is carried to the four corners of the kingdom."

"And everyone else?"

"The Riders bore some losses, but all of our friends survived," Kirra said.

Senneth cut her eyes Tayse's way. The death of any Rider would strike him hard. "Who?" she asked.

"Coeval. Brindle. Moxer," he replied. "Janni was severely injured, but she's been healed. Justin was badly hurt in the fight against Coralinda Gisseltess, but Ellynor was instantly beside him, and he is mending quickly."

"Cammon was deaf for a full day," Kirra continued. "It was strange, because he found it hard to talk while he couldn't hear, and so he didn't say anything, and you know Cammon never *shuts up*. But just as I was beginning to think I could get used to a Cammon who never says a word, his ears started working again, and now he's our same happy street urchin again."

That made Senneth smile. "So what's the plan? Return to Ghosenhall as soon as we're all well enough to travel?"

Kirra nodded. "Tomorrow, I would think. Everyone is eager to get back and assess the damage there."

The tent door fluttered and Amalie's voice sifted through. "Is she awake? Can I come in?"

"And me?" Cammon asked right after her.

Senneth gaped in horror. "Not while I look like this," she said to Kirra. "Will they let me bathe first?"

Kirra and Tayse were laughing. "I'll hold them off," Tayse said, rising and crossing to the door.

"I'll fetch bathwater," Kirra said. "But you won't be able to keep them out for long, you know. Everyone has been worried about you."

Senneth smiled faintly. "The way I feel, everyone was right to be worried."

"Back in a few minutes," Kirra said, and disappeared behind Tayse.

Alone for the moment, Senneth tested her strength. Her hands were too weak to clench. Her legs moved when she kicked them against the bed, but even that small effort was exhausting. Her back was sore and her vision did not feel particularly reliable. She'd only been awake fifteen minutes and she was ready to sleep again.

She held her right hand out before her, palm-up, and studied its lines and calluses. The other hand she placed over her heart, seeking out the eternal heat at the core of her body. But her fingers were chilled and there was no great combustion rumbling inside her chest.

She balled up her fingers, and splayed them wide, but no fire danced from the tips of her hand.

She remembered those last desperate moments of the battle against Coralinda Gisseltess. As if the Bright Mother had been watching, as if the goddess would take such a sacrifice, Senneth had offered herself. *Burn me. Burn my body. Turn me into your elemental fuel.* She had not, actually, expected to survive the encounter.

And it seemed she had not survived it whole.

Kirra returned quickly, lugging a small metal washtub, and then made a half dozen trips between the tub and the tent door to fetch buckets of water. Steam rose from the surface of the tub; the water must have been close to boiling.

So Kirra knew.

"Come on, come on," Kirra said, motioning Senneth over. "I have a nice big towel, almost clean, and a sliver of soap. This water won't stay hot forever."

Senneth sat on the bed unmoving. "I've lost my magic," she said.

Kirra nodded. "I know. Come on. Wash up."

Senneth stood, a little shakily, and discarded items of clothing as she crossed the small space. "How did you know?"

"Your skin was so cold. *You* were so cold. In you go."

The tub was so small Senneth practically had to crouch inside it, but the hot water felt unspeakably good against her skin. "Will I ever get it back?"

"I can't even begin to guess," Kirra said. "Here, bend your head down and I'll pour some water over your hair."

Kirra's matter-of-fact acceptance of this dreadful truth was making it easier for Senneth to keep talking about it; but it was such a huge thing, so impossible to assess, that she was sure she hadn't absorbed it completely yet. "Does Tayse know?"

"Maybe. He lay beside you for three days, keeping you warm with his own body. He doesn't know much about mystics, but he knows a lot about you."

Senneth shook her head. It was hard to tell whether those were tears on her cheeks, or stray rivulets from the water Kirra was pouring over her. "There have been so many times I cursed my magic and what it had made me," she said, trying not to sniffle. "But the thought—of having it leave me—of being completely ordinary, completely ignored by the gods—Kirra, it feels so strange. I don't know that I will still be *me*."

Kirra was briskly rubbing soap in her hair, and Senneth could feel the silky lather bubbling up against her ears. "I hardly think the gods are done with you so soon," she said. "You have proved too useful so far. If indeed your magic is gone, they will find some other way to employ you." She paused long enough to pour another bucket of water over Senneth's head. "Certainly Amalie will want your services, whether or not you can burn down Ghosenhall."

Senneth sniffled again. "Maybe I can become a Rider. I suppose now there are even more openings in their ranks."

"Maybe you can become a teacher. I bet Jerril could use you to train all those wild Carrebos mystics, even if you don't have magic of your own."

"But I want magic of my own," Senneth said softly, and started crying in earnest.

Kirra instantly threw her arms around her, heedless of splashing water and Senneth's wet skin. "I know you do, Sen. And maybe someday you'll get it back. But for now I don't care. Tayse doesn't care. Nobody cares. We thought you might be dead, and you're not dead, and *all* of us would have given up our magic if it meant you wouldn't die. So we know the gods still care about you, or they would have let you go."

SENNETH was able to compose herself enough to face the others when, twenty minutes later, her hair was combed and she was dressed in clean clothes. They burst into the tent as quickly as the small flap would allow—Justin, Donnal, Cammon, Amalie, Ellynor, Valri, Tayse again— each of them hugging her with an unrestrained delight. They permitted her to eat more food and vied for her attention to tell, and retell, their own individual parts in that last spectacular battle. She listened, exclaimed, teased Cammon about his deafness, examined Justin's latest wound, commended Ellynor on her healing skills, and generally warmed herself at the fire of their affection.

But their presence was exhausting, and Tayse chased them out before an hour was up. "We want her to be well enough to travel in the morning," he said. Not until he lifted the tent flap to encourage them to leave did Senneth realize that it was nighttime again. Excellent. Time to go back to sleep.

But she was still sitting upright on the bed when Tayse sat beside her, taking both of her hands in his. It was so odd to feel his body warming hers, instead of the other way around.

"How are you feeling?" he asked.

"My magic is gone," she said bluntly.

"I don't love you for your magic," he replied.

That made her smile, just a little. She moved over to lean against him, and he wrapped an arm around her shoulder. "Then why do you love me, Tayse, Queen's Rider?" she asked. "If not because I have bespelled you?"

"Because you own my soul."

She lifted one hand and laid it against his cheek. His skin was rough; he still had not bothered to shave. "Ah, that was magic," she said. "I beguiled you and I stole your heart."

He turned his head to kiss her palm. "You didn't steal it," he said. "I had already tucked it inside your hand. Not my fault you didn't realize it was already yours, so you had to waste your time with sorcery and theft."

That made her laugh. As always, his body against hers was feeding her power. She absorbed him, the way others might absorb sunlight, and she felt restless energy kick through her tired bones. She shifted in his arms, locked her hands around his neck, and kissed him on the mouth. "Whose tent is this anyway?" she whispered. "Amalie's? Would it be an affront to the throne if two lesser mortals made love inside the queen's private quarters?"

"You are barely returned from death," he said against her mouth. "You can't possibly have the strength for such a thing."

"It would give me strength," she said, kissing him more insistently, feeling her skin flush with a different kind of heat. "You would pour yours into me."

He laughed softly. "Well, I've never heard it described quite that way—"

She tugged him down onto the bed beside her, still covering his face with kisses. "Love me," she whispered. "Or I think I truly will die."

And so he did.

CHAPTER
43

DURING the journey back to Ghosenhall—which took four days and was exceedingly tedious—Senneth recovered rapidly, though not to what she considered her full strength. She was well enough to ride, hungry enough to eat, tired enough to sleep dreamlessly, and not required to do anything else. At odd moments during the day, surreptitiously, she would curl and uncurl her fingers and check the tips for flame. But there was no fire in her. Her body was healing, but her magic was still broken.

She couldn't bear to think about it. She would wait until the rest of the world was settled, and then she would grieve.

Their march down the streets of Ghosenhall was hardly a triumphal victory parade. The town itself had been largely spared by the rebel army, but random buildings had been destroyed, particularly those nearest the palace, and many residents had flown the city, which was still half empty. A few ragged crowds gathered on the street corners to cheer Amalie's appearance, but among the applauding merchants Senneth could spot a few glowering individuals with their hands clenched on their moonstone pendants. The princess was a mystic, that had been pretty well established. Clearly many people were unhappy about the idea of a sorceress taking the throne.

Cammon rode close beside Amalie, turning his head this way and that, scanning the crowd for dangers. Six Riders ringed her to prevent any malcontents from drawing too close. But Amalie peered around these protectors, and smiled, and waved, and even the scowling men, the frowning women, smiled at her and waved back.

Senneth thought, *Amalie will have to address this concern about mystics, and soon. How will we respond if we have another rebellion on our hands?*

THEY had been back three days before it became apparent that there was another crisis brewing inside the palace, of a smaller and more intimate nature, to be sure, but one that could rock the kingdom just as surely as magic.

During those three days, a great deal of effort had been spent trying to restore some normalcy to the city's routines. Shop owners and residents were flooding back into Ghosenhall; every day, dozens of nobles and merchants requested an audience with the princess. A flurry of messages arrived, from Danalustrous, from Helven, from Coravann. Couriers rode out with stern summonses for the heirs of Fortunalt and Gisseltess and Storian. Senneth didn't have the knowledge to steer Amalie through these political tangles. She allowed Valri and Romar and Kiernan—even Ariane Rappengrass, who had stayed behind—to offer advice and hammer out strategies. She stayed mostly in her own cottage and mended.

Until Kiernan came to her door one night, fuming. "You must talk some sense into that young woman," he said. "I have come to admire her greatly through this ordeal, but she is behaving like a silly schoolgirl now, and we can't have her jeopardizing the future of the whole kingdom."

Senneth opened her eyes wide. Kiernan was always an impressive figure, but when he was in a rage, he could be overpowering. It was hard to imagine that Amalie hadn't instantly acceded to anything he had promoted while in such a mood. Casually Tayse came to sit beside Senneth on the sofa, but she wasn't fooled. She knew he did it to protect her in case Kiernan became violent, and the thought made her grin. "What's Amalie done now?" she asked. "Decided to show off her magic in some public venue?"

"She's already done that, I think, and rather spectacularly," Kiernan replied. "No! She won't listen to reason! Her uncle and I believe that the sooner she marries, the better, but she says—she says—" He was so furious he couldn't get the words out.

Senneth rather enjoyed the thought of Kiernan being balked by a nineteen-year-old girl, but she happened to agree with him on this particular issue. "Amalie met a number of young lords before the war interrupted everything," she said. "I don't believe any of them caught her eye—but there were a few I thought she would be willing to consider. Did she turn down your best candidate? Who did you have in mind?"

"I had thought Ryne Coravann, though I mislike the fact that his father held back from the war," Kiernan replied. "Alternatively, we could salve some wounds by marrying her to a Fortunalt man, or a Gisseltess man. Even Storian! Though not Rafe's eldest son, he's unreliable and stupid."

"So far I agree with you," Senneth said, somewhat regretfully. "What's the problem?"

"She says she won't marry any of them! It's that—that—mystic boy of yours or no one, she says!"

"Cammon?" Senneth said faintly. Beside her, Tayse was laughing.

"It's not funny," Kiernan snapped.

"I apologize, marlord," Tayse said. But he was still smiling.

"I thought she understood—I thought *Cammon* understood—I mean, they've been very close these past few weeks," Senneth said, floundering through the words. "But—she always knew, *he* always knew, that she would have to marry nobility."

"She seems to think otherwise," Kiernan said. "So you must talk to her."

Senneth glanced at Tayse and bit her lip. "I am not, perhaps, the best example of marrying to oblige one's family."

"Well, she trusts you," Kiernan said. "And I believe that, whatever your faults, you have the well-being of the kingdom at heart. So talk to her tomorrow. Take care of this. We are dealing with too many other problems to add this absolutely unnecessary one to the mix." He nodded curtly and let himself out of the house without another word.

Senneth looked at Tayse again. "You see why I didn't talk to my brother for seventeen years."

"What will you tell Amalie?" he asked.

Senneth sighed. "That if she's going to rule the kingdom, she must first rule her heart."

"Will she listen to you?"

"She's an intelligent girl, our young princess. I think she will."

SENNETH brought Kirra with her the next day to the rose-and-cream parlor that Amalie had apparently made her headquarters. Baryn had always done most of his work in a very masculine-looking study, so for a moment Senneth was disconcerted by the sheer frilly *girlishness* of the room. Life would be very different when Amalie wore the crown. But maybe that would not be such a bad thing.

Valri met them at the door, looking stormy. "I wash my hands of this matter," she said. "She will not listen to *me*. See what the two of you can accomplish." And she shut the door behind her with rather more force than was necessary.

"Well! You're putting *all* your friends in a frenzy," Kirra said in her cheerful way, advancing deeper into the salon. "What a pretty room this is! Oh, can we sit in those chairs in the sunlight?"

"That's my favorite spot," Amalie said, leading the way. She perched rather primly on the seat she selected, and Senneth sat very upright on her own, but Kirra frankly lounged in her chair.

"I suppose you know why we're here," Senneth said.

Amalie nodded, and a faint smile crossed her pretty features. "To dissuade me from marrying Cammon."

That caused Kirra to scramble to a more or less upright position. "You can't *marry* Cammon, even if you keep him around," she said. "I thought we were here to persuade you to marry someone else."

"Well, I won't," Amalie said in a very pleasant voice. "Shall I have Milo bring us some refreshments?"

"If you want," Senneth said impatiently. "Amalie. You do understand, don't you? You must marry a nobleman. You will be the queen and your children will be crowned after you. This war was fought to prove that you have the right to be on the throne. You cannot throw away all the sacrifices made by everyone who fought for you by marrying a man who isn't fit to be the king."

"Cammon will be a splendid king," Amalie said calmly. "He's wise. He's honest. He's incapable of being unfair. He supports me completely, and I trust him utterly. Even if I didn't love him, I would want him at my side."

"Certainly, and he *can* be at your side," Senneth said. "Many monarchs have trusted advisors with whom they can talk over the most serious problems—men and women with no official titles but a great deal of power and respect. Cammon can be such a man for you."

Kirra added, "And many kings and queens have married for the sake of allies but kept lovers on the side." She ignored Senneth's hiss of reproof and said, "Your husband might have his own arrangement. It is not necessary that you love the man you wed. Cammon need not be absent from your life just because he isn't beside you on the throne."

"But I want him beside me on the throne," Amalie said. "I will be queen. I should be able to marry whomever I want."

"Unfortunately," Senneth began, but Amalie interrupted her.

"Both of *you* should have married nobles, and both of *you* married commoners."

"I had renounced my heritage, however, and you have not," Senneth replied.

"I haven't married anybody," Kirra said blithely.

Amalie folded her arms. "And I might not, either."

Senneth took a deep breath and slowly released it. "Well. Perhaps you might not—right away. Perhaps in a year or so you will think differently. Perhaps it would be better to let the dust of battle settle. Then we can all make a wiser choice about who should be named king."

Amalie leaned forward a little. The sun caught that red-gold hair and burnished it to a high gleam. She looked perfectly composed, Senneth thought—and completely intractable. "You don't understand," she said. "I will marry Cammon, or I will marry no one. Ever. I won't change my mind in a year. I won't change my mind no matter who rages at me or tells me I'm a foolish girl. I'm not a foolish girl. I'm a very serious woman. I've always been serious. And I tell you now that Cammon will be my king, or no one will be my king. And you can either find a way to make that decision palatable to your brother or you can continue to argue with me, but in the end nothing will change. I will be queen, and I will marry Cammon."

There was a long, long silence. Senneth stared at Amalie and Amalie stared back, while Kirra sat absolutely motionless. Amalie raised her eyebrows. "*Now* should I have Milo bring us some refreshments?" she asked and leaned over to tug on the bellpull.

Senneth turned to gaze at Kirra, the only possible ally in such a situation. "How," she murmured, "*how* can we make this acceptable to the marlords of Gillengaria?"

Kirra was already thinking, tapping a slim finger against her perfect nose. "We make him one of us," she said. "Someone's lost son."

Senneth snorted. "Too convenient! No one will believe it."

"Perhaps not, but they won't be sure. There might be whispers, but there wouldn't be proof."

"Whose?" Senneth demanded. "I tell you now I don't believe Kiernan would go along with such a charade, even to save the kingdom. Would your father?"

Kirra thought about it. "Lay claim to a bastard son? I doubt that would trouble him—and he likes Cammon—oh, but I simply can't! Pretend Cammon is my brother? It's offensive on so many levels."

She shuddered delicately, but Senneth ignored Kirra at her worst. "I didn't mean for him to be your father's son. Surely we can step down a few rungs in the hierarchy. Enlist one of your father's vassals, perhaps. Would they be willing to pretend Cammon was a child set adrift some dark night? He's got magic in his blood—surely it wouldn't be too great of a disgrace to admit they had abandoned him for that reason? And now. Well! The kingdom embraces mystics again, and they're ready to atone!"

"That might work," Kirra said. "But I wonder if Danalustrous is the place to be looking for Cammon's mythical parents. Everyone knows my father is loyal to the crown. They would suspect a lie."

"Then what other House?" Senneth said. She tilted her head to one side. "Rappengrass?"

Kirra considered the name and liked it. "Oh, yes, Ariane might be just the marlady to back us in this," she said. "And remember, she owes a debt to Cammon! He helped me last summer when I saved her granddaughter's life. I think she would be most willing to find some hapless vassal to claim Cammon as his son."

"Good, then we have solved this problem," Amalie said.

"Not quite so fast," Senneth said. "We still must ask her! And she must agree! And then we must fabricate some story and—"

"If not Ariane, then Eloise Kianlever," Amalie said. The door opened, and she waved Milo inside. "Or Mayva Nocklyn. Someone will be willing to earn my lifelong gratitude by telling a simple lie. I'm very glad the two of you came to me this morning. I knew you would solve this problem, and you have, very neatly."

For a moment, Senneth stared, for that had not been her intention when she entered the room this morning—far from it. Beside her, Kirra started laughing helplessly, both delighted and appalled. Senneth spread her hands because she couldn't think of an answer. In the end, all that was left was to laugh along.

S ENNETH and Kirra tracked Ariane down in the sculpture garden. The day was exceedingly fine, and the marlady and her youngest child sat in the sun on one of the marble benches, deep in earnest conversation.

"I'm so glad to see there has been a rapprochement between mother and son," Senneth greeted them.

Darryn smiled and came to his feet. "We're still finalizing the terms of our accord."

"I hope they're favorable to all parties," Senneth said.

Kirra put her hand on Darryn's shoulder and gave him a little push. "Go away. We need to talk to your mother about Amalie's matrimonial prospects."

Darryn's pleasant face darkened. "Then I think I'd better stay."

"Trust me, you're not the one we're going to try to marry her off to," Senneth said. "You're perfectly safe to go."

He left, though with some reluctance, and Ariane sighed. "Much as I'd like to see him beside Amalie on the throne, I have to admit I've come to like his little Sosie very much," she said. "I have no other unmarried sons, so how can I help you?"

"Amalie has her heart set on marrying Cammon, the young mystic boy you met last summer," Senneth said bluntly, seating herself next to Ariane. Kirra settled on Ariane's other side. "She swears she will accept no other bridegroom, and I have come to believe her. Kirra and I hoped you could help us fashion a pedigree for him—find some Rappengrass nobles who are willing to claim him as their son, cast off long ago. These would have to be vassals you trusted absolutely, of course, for the only thing worse than foisting off such a lie on the people of Gillengaria would be having that lie discovered."

Like Malcolm Danalustrous, Ariane Rappengrass was rarely shocked, and Senneth watched the marlady as she analyzed the situation. "How old is Cammon?"

"Twenty."

"So this couple would have to be in their forties or fifties. And why did they abandon him?"

"He's a mystic," Senneth said dryly. "It was the fashion twenty years ago for nobles to rid themselves of such inconvenient encumbrances."

"Still, if he was only a baby—"

"Perhaps they kept him until he was three or four, when his powers began to manifest," Kirra suggested.

Ariane pursed her lips. "Or perhaps they did not give him up at all. Was Coralinda Gisseltess actively persecuting mystics so long ago? Perhaps she stole him from his parents, and they have spent all this time grieving."

Senneth laughed. "By all means, tailor the story however you wish! All we need is someone willing to embrace it—and withstand a certain inevitable scrutiny."

Ariane had folded her hands together and rested her fingers under her chin. "But who . . ." she said in a ruminative voice. "My daughter Bella is too young, of course . . . and my friend Amanda would be willing, though she does not lie well. . . ."

"Oh, a talent for prevarication is essential in this case," Kirra said.

"But if we changed the story . . ." Ariane said, and then fell silent. Senneth watched the older woman's face as her eyes narrowed and her thoughts settled on a new possibility. The marlady meditated for a few moments, and then gave a decisive nod. "Why not me?"

Senneth peered around Ariane to give Kirra one quick look of surprise. "You?" she repeated.

"Well, I'm not *that* old," Ariane said with some asperity. "I'd have been forty-three when Cammon was born. That's not unheard-of."

"Yes, but wasn't your husband dead by that time?" Kirra said. "We don't want to ruin *your* reputation! If you claim Cammon as your son—"

Ariane nodded. "Easy enough to explain away. An indiscretion. My husband had been dead a couple of years, and I was lonely. I began seeing an unsuitable man. Everyone was quite shocked and pressured me to give him up, so I did. But it was too late by then, and I was already pregnant." Ariane unfolded her hands and tapped her fingers together lightly. "Yes, I think that will serve."

Senneth felt Kirra's eyes on her face and knew Kirra was thinking exactly what she was: *This actually happened.* Kirra said softly, "What's the rest of the tale?"

Ariane gave her a quick sideways glance. "For the purposes of this story, I made it known that I was ill, and I retired to a secluded house where I could make an unobserved recovery. There I delivered the child—a boy. I planned to keep him with me, pretending he was my maid's son, but my advisors spirited him away in the night. I never knew what happened to him after that. But then—last summer when you brought him to my house—I felt a strange affection for this complete stranger. I began to make inquiries, and I learned he was the son I had given up so many years ago. Naturally, I was overjoyed."

Senneth laid a hand on Ariane's arm. "What happened to your baby?"

Ariane didn't reply at first, as if unwilling to admit the tale was true. "He arrived two months early and stillborn," she said at last. "I didn't believe them when they told me he was dead. I had to see for myself. But it was true." She shook off a spell of melancholy and said more briskly, "Enough people know part of the story to be able to confirm that I indeed took a lover and bore his child. Very few people were present at his death, and all of them would tell any lie I asked. The dates are not exact, for my son would only be eighteen now, but no one will remember that."

"Ariane—" Senneth said, and then stopped, not sure of what to say. "I hate to take advantage of your personal tragedies in such a way."

Ariane gave her a somewhat painful smile. "You have lost a child yourself, Senneth, though the story is not generally known. And I believe you would exploit your own sad history if you thought it would help Amalie in any way. Permit me to do the same thing. I will be happy to claim Cammon as my own. I have always longed for that sixth child, the one I lost so long ago." Her smile widened. "And, of course, I am not at all reluctant to have Ghosenhall indebted to Rappen Manor."

"No, indeed, there are benefits all around," Kirra agreed.

"There's just one more thing," Ariane said. "Before we buried him, I had him branded with a housemark. Anyone who knows me realizes I would never have given up my child without stamping him as my own."

"That will be tricky," Senneth said. "We can give him a Rappengrass housemark, of course, but it won't look twenty years old."

Ariane stood. "I'm sure you can find a way around the difficulty. Bring me my son, identified with my emblem, and I will give your princess her husband."

CHAPTER
44

CAMMON was wholly bewildered by the sudden changes in his fortune that unfolded after their return to the royal city. He had never, not in any scenario he'd been able to devise, imagined that he would be allowed to marry Amalie. All his energy had gone to trying to figure out a way to stay at the palace, a way to serve her—a way, even, to be her lover, if she was willing, if her powerful protectors did not find it preferable to separate them completely. Of course, he was profoundly relieved that the war was over and all his friends had survived it whole, but it had always been clear to him that the cessation of hostilities would signal the end of his idyll with Amalie. What was allowed on the battlefield during tumultuous times could not be permitted in ordinary life. Now that she had won the right to take the throne, Amalie must prove herself a worthy ruler. And her first act must be to choose her husband wisely, with an eye to placating the marlords.

But she loved him. He knew she loved him. And the minute they had five minutes of privacy, he promised he would stay in Ghosenhall as long as she needed him.

"In any capacity," he added. They were alone for the first time since their return to Ghosenhall, as Amalie awaited the arrival of yet another visiting lord, come to swear fealty. "I will work in the kitchens if that is the only job open to me. I will stay on as a footman. As long as you want me here, I will stay."

She was almost crying, and he risked taking her in his arms, though he was supposed to be standing impassively behind her throne, scanning the emotions of petitioners. "But that's not fair to you," she said against his chest. "To make you live a life in shadows! Just waiting for the few minutes I have free! I wouldn't be able to do it! If you were king, and I was some serving girl they wouldn't allow you to marry? I'd run away. I would! I'd marry the first handsome soldier who marched through the city, or the first merchant who brought me a bunch of ribbons for my hair."

He laughed helplessly and stroked that hair, just now free of ribbons, though a small silver tiara kept its radiance somewhat in check. "Well, I've never been good at running away," he said. "Whenever anyone has loved me, what I've always wanted is to stay nearby. As long as you love me, I think, I won't be able to leave you."

He was prepared for it to be hard. He was prepared for it to be heart-breaking. But he was not prepared for his life to be lived without Amalie in it.

Two days after that declaration, she called him to the rose-and-cream parlor where, for a wonder, she was completely alone. Naturally, he did not lose an opportunity to kiss her right away. She was bubbling with happiness, but he could not sift through her thoughts and tell what had elated her.

"I have good news," she said, standing still with her arms twined around his neck.

"You will be alone in your bedroom tonight and you want me to come to you there," he guessed.

She kissed him. "Better."

"Your uncle has decided you don't have to marry anyone for another whole year. And no one will be watching you closely that whole time."

"Better."

He laughed and shook his head. "You never have to marry, and I can have free run of the palace."

"They're going to let me marry you."

"*What?*" he whispered.

"It's very complicated. You have to pretend you're Ariane's son. And you have to get a housemark, which will be quite painful, and I'm sorry about that. But then everyone will think you're long-lost nobility, a bastard from the Twelve Houses, and good enough to marry me. I think we should have the wedding right away, and then we can have the coronation next year for both of us."

Cammon usually considered himself fairly quick-witted, but it took her another ten minutes and repeated explanations to make him truly understand what she was saying. Abruptly, he sank to a seat in one of her favorite chairs, and stared at her in bewilderment when she sat in the chair beside him.

"But I can't be king," he said at last.

"You'll be a charming king," she said.

"But I—what do I know about—kingdoms and governing and—and—money—and strategy—and whatever it is kings know?"

"You've traveled halfway around the world and all through Gillengaria!" Amalie replied. "You know so much! And you learn so quickly! I think you'll be a marvelous king."

"Amalie," he said, shaking his head, "I want to marry you. I could never dream of anything I would want more. But I'm afraid to be king."

For a moment, she rested her head against the back of her chair, thinking. "All right," she said in her usual fashion, her voice seeming so soft but really so decisive. "I'll be crowned first. And you'll be my—my prince-consort or some such title. And every few years I'll ask you again if you want to be king. And if you do, we'll have a nice coronation for you. And if you don't, well, you'll just be my consort forever." She lifted his hand and carried it to her mouth. "But you'll be my husband before the month is out."

RECEIVING the housemark was the most agonizing physical experience Cammon had ever endured. He yelped as the brand was laid against his skin just below the hollow of his throat, and the smell of burnt flesh nearly made him gag.

"And you do this to *babies?*" he demanded of Kirra, who had wielded the instrument of torture.

"Well, *I* don't," she replied. "But all the nobles do. Yes. When they're too small to stop us." She patted him on the head. "You were very brave. And you lay completely still! I was sure you'd be thrashing all over the place."

"I wanted to kick you. It really *hurts.*"

"Don't whine so much," Justin said. "I've had way worse wounds and never even bothered to mention them."

"An example of stoicism that inspires us all," Kirra said.

Ellynor stepped over. "Let me see what I can do," she said. "I ought to be able to heal it so thoroughly that no one will be able to tell how fresh a wound it is."

Her fingers were cool and gentle against his newly scarred skin, and her mere touch filled him with a sense of extraordinary well-being. He wondered if, while she was there healing the burn, she had just decided to rummage around in his body and chase off any incipient ailments that might have been loitering in the blood. No wonder Justin looked so offensively healthy these days. With Ellynor at his side, he need never suffer a minute's illness for the rest of his life.

When she was done, they all crowded around him and exclaimed in pleasure. "Look at that," Kirra said, pulling down the neckline of her dress to show off her own tasteful housemark, a small representation of the letter D. "It looks no different from mine. Well, the *style* is different, of course. But otherwise just the same."

Cammon squinted down at his chest, where he could just make out the diamond-shaped scar, appearing as faded and scuffed as if he'd sported it since birth. "Look at that," he repeated. "I'm Cammon Rappengrass."

NOT until the housemark had been applied was he brought into the presence of his new family. "I'd be more intimidated at the notion of having Ariane Rappengrass for a mother than at being crowned king," Kirra told him as she escorted him through the palace to the rooms Ariane occupied.

Strangely, perhaps, Cammon did not find Ariane frightening at all. He had met her under extraordinary circumstances almost a year ago, when her granddaughter was dying and Ariane would have made any bargain to keep the girl alive. What he had thought at the time was how much he wished someone had loved *him* enough to go to such lengths to save him. He had been impressed, not so much by her ferocity, but how that ferocity had alchemized to love.

"Don't let her make you nervous," Kirra said. "Ariane always orders everyone about. It's simpler just to do what she says." She knocked on the door and then smiled in her wicked way. "I'm not staying. Best for you to learn how to handle Ariane on your own."

But when he took a deep breath and stepped inside the room, he was hopeful, he was excited. And right away, as he faced that strong-willed, broad-faced woman, he knew that she was just as hopeful as he was.

"Cammon," she said, holding out her hands. "You can't know how many years I have waited to see my son again."

She took him in a powerful embrace, this indomitable woman whose force of personality was legendary. And all Cammon could think was how her generosity had reshaped his life, and how easy it would be to love her.

THEY had been back in Ghosenhall a week when Amalie insisted on leading a procession through the city. Everyone protested, of course—the Riders, the regent, her stepmother—but Amalie was adamant.

"I have been shut up in this palace my whole life," she said in the gentle voice that covered such determination. "I will not cower inside these walls while I am queen. I will go among my people so that they know me and I know them."

Since it was clear that she would walk out the gates with or without an entourage, Tayse and Romar and Senneth hastily arranged an escort of soldiers and sorcerers. Cammon, in his new role as her betrothed, was allowed to walk beside her through the streets, holding her left hand in his—and seeking through the crowd for anyone filled with ill intent. Six Riders ringed her round; Donnal and Kirra circled overhead. Senneth, who had no fire to summon if fire was called for, strode at the head of the column, waving the royal flag.

The raelynx pranced along on Amalie's right, gazing about with undisguised interest. No amount of protest had been able to convince her that he should be left behind. Indeed, he had become her official mascot. The Riders wore their new sashes sporting the traditional gold lion interspersed with the raelynx rampant. The flag that Senneth carried contained lions in two quadrants, raelynxes in the opposite corners.

Cammon thought it actually would be a good thing if the raelynx were to accompany Amalie on all her public appearances. The creature had offered ample proof that it would fight to protect her, and certainly its presence would cause any would-be attacker to think twice about getting too close. As long as it didn't eat any innocent spectators, Cammon thought, he was happy to have the beast along. So far, it was proving very well behaved.

Unlike the day they had returned from battle, the streets were crowded with well-wishers, waving and cheering. So many flowers had been ripped from the gardens and flung to the cobblestones before Amalie's feet that Cammon had to think there wasn't a single blossom left in any garden. The day was gorgeous, sunny and warm, and beneath that perfect sky, Amalie seemed to glow and shimmer. Or maybe, thought Cammon, it was the affection pouring out from the gathered crowds that brightened her hair, turned her pale skin lustrous. Certainly she seemed to grow more beautiful every time a young woman tossed lilacs at her feet, every time a little girl blew her an untidy kiss.

But here and there, Cammon could sense darker pockets of hostility and unease. He wasn't sure if the words were being spoken aloud or if he merely heard them in his head. *Mystic. Sorceress. Not to be trusted . . .*

They had been following a slow route for almost an hour before true trouble cropped up. Cammon sensed it first, a surge of discontent emanating from a group of young noblemen gathered on the street corner, and he silently directed Tayse's attention toward them. Cammon didn't recognize them, but their colors gave them away. One wore the pearl-encrusted vest of Fortunalt; another had the Storian topaz pinned to his hat. Two others wore sashes embroidered with a black hawk clutching a red flower. Men of Gisseltess.

From all four, Cammon picked up grief and bewilderment as much as anger and fear. They had probably believed passionately in their mar-lords, had accepted without question the doctrine of the Pale Mother. Now their idols had been overturned. Who were they to believe now? How could anyone know the right path to follow?

One of the Gisseltess men stepped into the street, partly blocking Senneth's progress. She had her free hand on her sword, but she didn't draw it. "And you're to be queen now?" the young lord called out to Amalie, his voice hoarse. "You're to rule over us all?"

Amalie came to a halt and peered past the Riders to see him. "Yes. I will take the throne early next year."

His three friends crowded behind him. Cammon felt Tayse's impulse to force them away with outright violence, but from Amalie he was picking up a desire for colloquy. *Just wait. Hear them out,* he thought in Tayse's direction, and the Rider pulled out his sword but made no move to attack. Beside Amalie, the raelynx fixed its eerie eyes on the speaker and waited.

"Mystic," the young man said, spitting out the word. Beside him, his friends echoed the word. *"Mystic,"* he said again. "And we're to have *you* as our queen?"

Now the rest of the crowd began a troubled muttering. Cammon sensed both confusion and uncertainty from the onlookers. Some of them had no particular dislike for mystics, though the thought of one on the throne did make them uneasy. Many, he thought, were anxious to have Amalie explain away her power—or at least give them reasons they should not fear it.

He squeezed her hand and dropped it. *Talk to them,* he told her.

She nodded and stepped forward, brushing past Senneth, though the raelynx stayed firmly at her side. "I *am* a mystic," she said calmly, address-ing the malcontents but raising her voice enough so it could be heard by everyone in the vicinity. "I have the power to draw strength from those around me when I need it most. I believe it is a gift from the Pale Mother herself. I believe *all* magic flows from the gods—and I believe there are many gods and goddesses that the people of Gillengaria have long forgotten."

That caused a murmur to ripple through the crowd, full of surprise, dissent—and speculation.

Amalie made a half-turn, spreading her arms as if to envelop every onlooker. "Not only that, I believe all of us have been touched by the gods to some degree," she said. "Some of you have feared mystics your whole lives, without realizing that you, too, possess a kind of magic." She pointed at an old woman wrapped in a shawl despite the day's warmth. "You. What is your special skill? Can you make flowers grow in the hardest ground? Can you ease a child who is coughing in the night? A goddess has blessed you with her own magic."

She pivoted and pointed at a young man who looked clever and dexterous—street thief, Cammon guessed, though Justin would probably know better than he would. "You. What is your particular talent? Can you steal behind a stranger in utter silence? Can you convince anyone of your sincerity? Can you sing? Can you fight? If you can do any of those things, you have been touched by one of the gods."

She spun back to face the frowning young lords, still standing on the corner and starting to gape at her. "You—from your clothing I see you are from some of the great Houses of Gillengaria. You've witnessed the marlords as they've watched and worried over their properties. Have you ever seen a marlord pause for a moment—stop and listen—and seem to be *hearing* the land speak to him? Don't you realize that is a kind of magic? Don't you know that every marlord, every marlady, is a mystic under the protection of a powerful god?"

Now the muttering of the crowd was louder but not, Cammon thought, unfriendly. It was just that the idea was new, yet so universal. Every single person who could hear the princess's words was starting to review his own peculiar skills, her own useful range of talents, heretofore taken entirely for granted. Could it be true? Could these be divine blessings?

Amalie turned again, spreading her arms even wider. "We are all mystics," she said. "We must honor our gifts, not despise them. Yes, I'm a mystic. I will lead the way for all of my people."

AFTER that, even Romar had to admit that it wasn't such a bad idea to let Amalie go out in public from time to time, connecting in a most personal way with her subjects.

"And take the damn cat with you when you go, if you like," the regent said. "Until he eats the first small child, he's a most excellent bodyguard and should see you safely wherever you travel."

Romar had stopped in Amalie's parlor to say good-bye, at least for a time. His wife had been taken to bed with labor pains, and he was off to Merrenstow in the morning. Cammon could tell that he was both excited and a little frightened at the notion of becoming a father. "But I'll be back as soon as I can," he promised. "You and I have much work to do."

Amalie kissed him on the cheek. "Give Belinda my love."

The regent was only one of many who were poised to leave Ghosenhall now that, for a time at least, the realm was peaceful. Kirra and Donnal had barely bothered to make farewells before taking off on the very evening of Amalie's grand procession.

"I am so restless I almost can't stand my own skin," Kirra had said frankly. "We must be gone by sundown or I swear I'll descend into madness."

"If you hear a wolf howling at the moon tonight, that will be me," Donnal said.

"Better if we're gone."

And so they left.

Three of the Riders also departed after taking formal leave of Amalie. They praised her father, expressed pleasure that they had been able to serve her briefly, but claimed that they could no longer endure the burdens and responsibilities of their calling. Amalie thanked them extravagantly, pressed significant sums of money on each of them, and sighed to see them go.

A fourth Rider departed without any ceremony at all. Wen strolled into the city one afternoon after taking her shift on duty, and never bothered returning to the palace. She left a note for Janni that stated merely, *Don't worry about me. I've decided to leave and I don't want to be talked out of it. Serve the princess as best you can. Think of me as you guard her coronation.*

All the remaining Riders were shaken up by her abrupt disappearance, and half of them gathered outside of Tayse's cottage once the letter had been discovered. Sensing distress, Cammon had hurried in that direction in time to hear Janni read the note. "What happened? Why did she go?" was the general tone of the baffled questions.

Janni seemed as perplexed as the rest of them, but Tayse had an inkling. "She was fighting side by side with my father when he and the king went down," Tayse said. "She might have thought she betrayed them both by living. A king should never die unless every Rider beside him has already been murdered."

"But no one would have been able to save Baryn that day!" Janni exclaimed.

Justin and Tayse exchanged glances. "Tir died," Justin said quietly. "I think both Tayse and I would have been dead that day, and our bodies found alongside Baryn's. Wen feels she failed as a Rider. And she is not willing to fail Amalie. So she left."

Tayse's eyes sought Cammon. "Where is she?" Tayse asked. "Close enough for us to go after her?"

If he concentrated, Cammon could sense Wen, a small, sad, and sturdy shape even now drawing farther from the city. He shook his head. "She wants to go," he said. "I can't help you change her choice."

Justin growled and punched him hard in the shoulder. "You show your scruples at the most inconvenient times," he said.

Cammon shrugged helplessly. "You wouldn't want to be kept against your will. It's not fair to fetch her back."

Tayse nodded. "So. Another position to fill among the Queen's Riders. All of you be on the lookout for candidates to present."

So those were losses, and Cammon hated each of them, but the hardest one came a week later. Milo had chased him from Amalie's parlor to discuss meaningless topics like a royal wardrobe, and Cammon had wandered down to the walled garden where the raelynx still stayed when Amalie had no attention to spare. The difference was that the wrought-iron door, though it remained closed, was no longer locked. Cammon could not rid himself of the suspicion that the raelynx came and went pretty much as it chose.

Valri was standing just outside the garden, as he had found her one time before. Her hands were wrapped around the bars, and her gaze was fixed on the giant cat sleeping inside the enclosure. She turned her head as she heard him approach and gave him a smile that seemed a little sad.

"I always thought I would be taking him back with me to the Lirrenlands one day," she said without preamble. "I always thought he should not stay here, this wild creature, penned up in such a small space. And yet he has come to belong in this palace more surely than I ever did. It would be cruel to remove him now. Amalie loves him—and I believe, in his unfathomable way, he loves her."

Cammon came to stand beside her, resting one hand on the rough stone of the wall. "And you're not going back to the Lirrenlands," he said.

"But I am," she replied.

He knew his dismay was written plainly on his face. "But you can't! Amalie needs you! It's months till the coronation—and all these stupid marlords are coming in every day—and—and, there's so much to learn about running the kingdom—"

"I never really knew that much about politics," Valri said with a shrug. "All I knew was how to keep her safe. How to prevent anyone from guessing she was a mystic." She shrugged again. "And now everyone knows, and there is nothing I can do for her anymore."

"She needs you!"

"She needs advisors, and she has plenty of those," Valri said. "Romar will be back in a few weeks, and I don't see Tayse and Senneth riding off any time soon. And Kiernan Brassenthwaite seems to have forgotten he *has* another home to go to. Amalie doesn't need me."

"But she loves you," he said.

Valri gave him her dark smile. "She loves *you*," she corrected. "And you have won the right to stay beside her." She shook her head. "I don't know that I would have been able to leave her behind with any other husband. I knew she had to marry, but I didn't believe there was a noble I could give her to with a whole heart. I am glad you have found a way to trick the marlords into accepting you. You love her, and I am free to go."

"It's not enough to have one person who loves you," Cammon objected. "You need as many as you can find."

That made Valri laugh out loud. "Yes, I suppose that *is* how you live your life, isn't it, Cammon?" she said. "You and Amalie both. You seem to enrich yourselves on love, and the more of it there is, the happier you are."

"Isn't that true for everyone?" he said, bewildered.

"Not for me. Love takes so much energy, and I don't know how to parcel it out. So I reserve it for a very few."

Cammon glanced around, as if, in the shadows, he would spot a dreamy-eyed Lirren man. "Is it Arrol? Are you going back to the Lirrenlands to be with him?"

Valri nodded. "And to see my family. And to decide if I can live among the clans, as *bahta-lo*, though I have abandoned them once, and they have all but forgotten me."

"That won't be easy," Cammon said.

She gave him that dark smile again. "I cannot remember part of my life that *has* been easy. This at least should not be as hard as the past few years."

"Will you be back? Sometimes? Now and then? Amalie will miss you, of course, and I—" He did not know how to complete the sentence.

"I expect I will," she said. "Not often. It is hard for anyone to live between two worlds, I think, and harder for me than most. I tend to commit myself completely or walk away. But I think I will need to see Amalie from time to time—to know she is well, safe, and happy. And I will want her to know the same things about me."

"I'll know," he said.

That earned him a sharp look from her extraordinary eyes. "What will you know?"

"If you're well. If you're sad. If you're joyful. I'll know how you are."

Valri was silent a moment. "That might fade in time," she said. "That connection you have with me."

"I don't think so."

"Even when I am across the mountains and married to another man?"

"Even then."

She made a slight gesture with her hands. Her pale cheeks were washed with the faintest color. "Then think of me kindly, Cammon, when you think of me, and know that I will remember you with the utmost fondness."

She did not lay her hand on his arm or touch him on the cheek. She was not a woman for casual expressions of affection. But her face was still warm as, without another word, she turned and paced away. Cammon stayed behind feeling both bereft and strangely peaceful, and with his mind followed her all the way back to the palace doors.

Amalie was crying when he found her an hour later, and she flung herself into his arms. "Valri's leaving," she sobbed into his shirt. "I knew she would—but I thought—I hoped—and she says she doesn't know when she'll be back—"

Cammon held her close and stroked her head, murmuring into her hair. Amalie so rarely needed comfort that he almost enjoyed the chance to soothe her. "And *Kirra's* gone, and *Donnal's* gone," she added with a hiccup. "And Uncle Romar is gone. And I know I'm supposed to be princess, and I know I'm supposed to be strong, but I miss them. I miss everybody."

"Shhh," he said, resting his cheek on her hair. "I miss them, too. But they'll all be back. And more friends will arrive. No need to be lonely, not ever again."

She sniffled, rubbed her nose against his shirt, and raised her head to kiss him. "And you're not leaving," she said. "Promise me."

It was as if she had asked him to promise to keep breathing, to notice sunshine, to permit the spinning of the earth. What choice did he have? Even if he left her, she would be camped in his heart, an insistent and willful presence. She would match her strides to his on any journey he ever took; she would lie beside him on any bed.

"Amalie," he said, "that's the easiest promise I've ever had to make."

CHAPTER
45

ELLYNOR was teaching Senneth how to cook.

Like anyone who spent much time camping, Senneth could throw together a meal of dried rations and fresh game, but she was baffled by the intricacies of spices and marinades. Truth to tell, she wasn't even that interested in learning her way around a kitchen—but she liked working at the stove and oven. She enjoyed the close communion with fire, even when she couldn't control it.

She was also enjoying the chance to spend time with Ellynor, who was still something of a mystery to her. Kirra's abrupt departure a month ago had left Senneth unexpectedly lonely for female companionship. She was friendly with Janni and the other women Riders, but with them, she didn't have that powerful connection she shared with Kirra. She didn't have it with Ellynor, either, but she was hopeful. It was impossible to dislike Ellynor; that should make it easy to learn to love her.

"Now, strictly speaking, salt bread should only be offered on feast days, but Justin loves it so much that I've been making it fairly often," Ellynor confessed. "Have you ever made bread? No? I think you'll like it. It requires both energy and attention, but it always rewards you."

At that Senneth laughed out loud. "And you think that is the kind of activity that appeals to me? I suppose you're right."

"Well, you seem to be the kind of woman who doesn't mind hard work, as long as it results in something worthwhile," Ellynor said with a smile. The Lirren girl had tied her long hair back in a rather sloppy braid, and a smear of flour decorated her face. She looked about seventeen, Senneth thought—but a much more contented seventeen than Senneth had ever been.

"I might say the same thing about you," Senneth retorted. "Although, you know, I'm not used to thinking of us as having much in common."

Ellynor's smile widened. "Except that we both have difficult and domineering brothers that we've gone to some trouble to escape."

Senneth laughed again. "True. I suppose that shapes a woman more than she'd like to admit."

"Family always shapes you," Ellynor said. "For good or for ill. You strive to become what your family wants you to become, or you fight to become exactly the opposite. I've done a little of both." She measured out some kind of aromatic spice that was already making Senneth hungry. "You would say you've only fought to be free, but I think you'd be wrong about that."

Senneth leaned against the stove, soaking up the heat through her trousers. "I refuse to admit that I've done anything to please Kiernan and Nate," she said. "But I have to say that I have never entirely been able to shake off my pride in what Brassenthwaite stands for, and I have to confess that I believe Kiernan represents Brassenthwaite admirably. Whether or not I do—" Senneth shrugged. "Not so clear."

"Brassenthwaite serves the crown. That's what Justin says," Ellynor replied. "And so do you."

"I do indeed," Senneth said. "So perhaps after all I am a splendid example of my House."

Ellynor began slowly and methodically kneading the ingredients together. "What now?" she asked. "With the realm more or less at peace? Will you stay in Ghosenhall? Justin says you have toyed with the idea of petitioning to become a Rider."

"I don't know that I'm serious about that, but both Tayse and I feel an obligation to stay at the palace with Amalie. The kingdom is no longer under the threat of war, that's true, but there is still some turmoil among the Houses! I think she needs us, and so we must stay. Though I am a little restless, I must admit. I cannot remember the last time my life was placid. I'm not sure I will know how to get through days that are not marked with strife and trouble."

Ellynor gave her a swift look from her midnight blue eyes. "You could have a baby," she said. "That would enliven your days considerably. Have you and Tayse ever discussed that?"

"No," Senneth said blankly.

"Do you think he would want a child?"

Senneth crossed her arms on her chest and thought about it. "I don't know," she said at last. "He never had any deep bond with anyone in his own family. He admired his father, of course, but it was difficult to feel close to Tir. And although he's always been kind to his mother and his sisters, it's not like he—well, it's not like he really *thinks* about them. So I have no idea how he would feel about a child of his own."

"He loves *you*," Ellynor said. "And it would be *your* child. I think he would find himself head over heels in love."

Senneth wasn't sure. "Maybe." And then, since it seemed the reciprocal question should be asked, she inquired, "Do you think Justin would ever want children?"

All of Ellynor's attention was on the dough taking shape beneath her hands. "I hope so," she said softly.

Senneth jerked upright. "What? You're pregnant?"

Ellynor nodded.

Senneth threw her arms around the Lirren girl. "That's wonderful! When is the baby due? Does Justin know?"

"I'm only a few weeks along. No, I haven't told him yet. But I think— I'm pretty sure—he has said things that make me think—well, his own family was so dreadful. He would do anything in his power to create a better life for any child of his own." She looked up, and her pretty face wore a smile, though there were tears in her eyes. "I think he'll be both the gentlest and the fiercest father you ever saw."

Senneth wouldn't have expected to be so delighted, but the news filled her with elation. Justin a father! Having never given such an eventuality a moment's thought before, she now found the picture irresistible. "You're quite right! May the gods protect anyone who offers harm to any child of Justin's. But he'll be absolutely struck dumb with love. Oh, this is wonderful. You have to tell him right away, so I can tell Tayse."

"That's why I'm making the salt bread," Ellynor said. "For celebration."

After that they talked about names and clan connections and how important it would be for a half-Lirren child to spend at least some time across the Lireth Mountains. By the time the cooking lesson was over, Senneth not only knew how to make salt bread and spiced pork roast, she found herself feeling closer to Ellynor than she ever had.

Tayse was amused to learn that she had prepared the evening meal and careful to seem appreciative. Although he rarely had much interest in food outside of its usefulness as fuel, he praised every dish extravagantly.

"Thank you," she said, once the meal was over and the dishes were washed. "But I don't know that I'm going to spend much more of my time in the kitchen. I think I like it much better when someone else cooks for *me*."

She settled down on a plush rug laid on the hearth, and Tayse built up the fire. No need for it, of course, on this early summer day, but Senneth never felt quite right unless there was a fire somewhere in her vicinity.

Tayse carefully laid another log on the blaze, then moved back beside her. Drawing her against his chest, he extended his legs on either side of her body. She leaned against him, folded her hands over his forearms as they crossed over her waist, and experienced a moment of utter satisfaction.

"But if I'm not going to cook, and I'm not going to fight, I need to find some other activity to keep me occupied," she continued after a moment's silence.

"You've worked harder than anybody," he replied. "I think you might have earned the right to a year or two of complete slothfulness."

"I don't think I'm the kind of woman who can sit idle for more than a day," she said. "Maybe I'll take up blacksmithing again. I always enjoyed that. Maybe I'll forge a sword for you."

"A dagger, perhaps," he said. "To start with."

She laughed at him over her shoulder. "What? You doubt the quality of my workmanship?"

He was grinning. "It's just that it's really important that a sword be of the highest caliber."

She settled back against him. "I'll forge a sword for *myself* and challenge you to a duel. Then you'll see how good I am at smithing."

He kissed the top of her head. "But I would appreciate a dagger that you crafted with your own hands. You can set a Brassenthwaite sapphire in the hilt and etch a raelynx along the blade. That would be a knife worth carrying."

She liked the idea. There was a blacksmith on the palace grounds, of course, a wiry middle-aged man who won every arm-wrestling challenge, even against Riders. "I'll look into it tomorrow."

They were quiet a moment, relaxed, at peace. It might not be so bad after all, Senneth thought, to share an uneventful life with Tayse, puttering around the cottage, helping Amalie when requested, setting off on occasional visits to Danalustrous or Brassenthwaite or Rappengrass. Playing with Justin's baby. *Babies, perhaps, and soon,* she corrected herself. The thought made her smile.

The heat of Tayse's body soaked through her clothes to warm her back. Her face and hands prickled from the nearness of the fire. It had been weeks since her skin felt flushed with fever, since her body had run at a dangerously high temperature. But now all the forces of the day seemed to combine and combust inside her—happiness for Ellynor, contentment with Tayse, serenity, security, a sense that her life had been graced by so many gifts that they spilled around her with abandon. Who could want more than this? Why had she been given so much?

The top log shifted and collapsed with a shower of sparks. Senneth held her hand out as if to catch any fiery splinters that might fall so far from the grate. None did, yet she kept her hand extended, palm turned upward, feeling a line of heat track across her skin. She cupped her hand and felt the bones kindle. A tiny flame danced in the center of her palm, eager yellow, intemperate red. Only a moment, then the fire disappeared. The scent of smoke was fragrant in the air.

"Very pretty," Tayse said.

Laughing, she turned in his arms to kiss him on the mouth. The hand that had summoned fire she laid against his cheek; her other hand she slipped beneath his shirt. Desire raced through her with a leaping grace, and she welcomed it, this parallel manifestation of fire. Tayse had long ago proved he was not afraid of conflagration, and he kissed her with a passion to match her own. Soon enough it was impossible to tell where flesh ended and flame began, or maybe the whole world was ablaze. If she could call no other fire for the rest of her life, Senneth thought, she would be content with this one, a fire that melted her bones and turned her skin opalescent and lit her heart so brightly from within.